Syl Cheney-Coker was bor̶ and educated at the Universi̶ in the USA. He has held univers̶ appointments and was a visiting Writing Programme at the University of Iowa in 1988. The author of three volumes of poems, *The Last Harmattan of Alusine Dunbar* is his first novel.

SYL CHENEY-COKER

THE LAST HARMATTAN OF ALUSINE DUNBAR

HEINEMANN

Heinemann International
a division of Heinemann Educational Books Ltd
Halley Court, Jordan Hill, Oxford OX2 8EJ

Heinemann Educational Books Inc
361 Hanover St, Portsmouth, New Hampshire, 03801, USA

Heinemann Educational Books (Nigeria) Ltd
PMB 5205, Ibadan
Heinemann Kenya Ltd
Kijabe Street, PO Box 45314, Nairobi
Heinemann Educational Boleswa
PO Box 10103, Village Post Office, Gaborone, Botswana
Heinemann Publishers (Caribbean) Ltd
175 Mountain View Avenue, Kingston 6, Jamaica

LONDON   EDINBURGH   MELBOURNE   SYDNEY
AUCKLAND   SINGAPORE   HARARE
MADRID   ATHENS   BOLOGNA

British Library Cataloguing in Publication Data
Cheney-Coker, Syl
The last harmattan of Alusine Dunbar.
I. Title   II. Series
823 [F]

ISBN 0–435–90572–4

Photoset by Wilmaset, Birkenhead, Wirral
Printed and bound in Great Britain by
Cox and Wyman Ltd, Reading, Berkshire

90 91 92 93 94 10 9 8 7 6 5 4 3 2 1

CONTENTS

*To the memory of my mother,
who died the month I started
writing this book, but who
told me the fantastic story
about the goldsmith who came
back from the dead, married,
had children and lived
happily until some friends
from his previous life
'rediscovered' him.*

PROLOGUE

Two nights after his failed coup, General Tamba Masimiara sat on a cold slab in his island prison cell and thought about the series of events that had led to his moving against the corrupt government in Malagueta. Earlier, they had brought him blindfolded, handcuffed and partially naked; a captive leopard gleaming in the semi-darkness of the night, with his polish of amber and good health. When his captors had gone, he scrutinised his new home – a grim colonial dungeon where, in centuries past, the blood of his countrymen and -women had mixed with their own excreta and vomit, before they were transported across the treacherous sea to die in the swampy bleakness of another world. Outside, the roaring Atlantic lashed against the rocks, creating the same deafening noise that had frightened the Portuguese pirates of the fifteenth century, who had named the place. Later, in order to placate the djinns of that most barbarous of oceans, they had built the fort and spent seven days and nights offering sacrifices to the Black Madonna for a safe passage through that hellhole, and for deliverance from the teeth of its infamous cannibals.

Now, as he sat on his slab, tired, unshaven and bruised, battered by the harmattan of his misfortune, General Masimiara began to reflect on the future of his country, which was in the hands of the worst bunch of cutthroats that had ever ruled the place, and where members of the aristocracy spent countless hours conjuring the magic of their illusions about the power of God to change the place.

'They sure believe in that,' he murmured, but was checked in the drifting sands of his thought by the certainty that they were mere caretakers of time, condemned to rot in their beds of impotence. Five years earlier, he had given up on them, convinced that the brightest among them were obsessed with a sickening greed for the fleshpots of wealth, and for which they were prepared to prostitute their daughters and sell their own mothers. He was not a politician, nor did he have any intellectual pretensions about how to solve all the problems of Malagueta. But in twenty-five years as a soldier, the last five as army commander during the reign of a despicable government that had embarrassed him by jailing its critics and hanging some of its opponents, General Masimiara had wondered at the docility of the people, and at their ability to receive the endless instruments of pain. So now that he was alone, with the rats beginning to emerge from their holes, he shuddered with the realisation that it was for these people that the legendary warrior Thomas Bookerman had attacked the British garrison in the nineteenth century, when they had arrived, uninvited, to threaten the peaceful town that a group of black people had established not too far from where the general had staged his coup.

In the cloister of his cell, the labyrinthine darkness of his age gripped the general. But he was glad of the precious minutes of thought, to see what life was all about. Like some apocalypse of God, he saw that life was an avalanche of revolt which was born out of hunger. Fuelled by the hurricane of desperate people rising against their leaders, it had produced the sweltering rage like a wound more putrid than the open belly of a pig, and for which, among other reasons, he had moved against the government.

Strengthened by that assessment, General Tamba Masimiara felt a wave of anger beginning to rise in him. It flooded through his blood vessels, going to his heart with an uncontrollable sensation that made him want to move from that slab and smash the door. Suddenly it left his body, circling him in that vertiginous instant when his room looked like an unruly garden which gave his anger its own power and force. Then, as unexpected as it had come, his rage moved across the room, out through the window and scaled the prison height. Then, in a mood contemptuous of those Portuguese who had laboured to build the fort, it climbed over the stone wall and, like a prodigal wave returning to the ocean, left the general numbed. A moment after, thinking that he had to be awake when they came for him that day, the next or in two weeks' time, he fell asleep.

Several hours later, General Masimiara woke up with a stir and walked across his tiny cell. Like a man measuring the movement of the earth, he came to the only window in the place, and looked at the sea. He had slept badly, his ankles ached, his mouth tasted of raw eggs and he felt an urgent desire to piss, though he could not think of where to ease himself. When they had brought him there, he had not noticed how small and dilapidated the cell was, and how the sea had over the centuries eaten it away – the place had not been used since that memorable morning of expiation, when the slave traders had sent the last slaves away, washed their names off the wall and thrown their chains into the sea. The clear signs of bird droppings were there in that cell whose size and gloom were in sharp contrast to the warmth and beauty of his former house, with its luxuriant bougainvillæa garden cascading over a wall of white concrete down a slope of ancient black and white stones. No doubt they had brought him to that cell to break him down bit by bit before the rigmarole of a trial, after which he was sure they would hang him. Because as the sea returns to the shore he was convinced they were going to kill him. He had a pact with death. This certainty that life in Malagueta would go on after his death, that they would display his body in front of the prison walls as they had done with that revolutionary journalist who dared to oppose the president, did little to prepare the general for the day he had to face God, held, as he was for the moment, in the dark confinement of his cell, the second step into the cold density of a grave. The first had been when they surrounded his house, beat up his wife and brought him to the island to feel how their power like the sea was vast and crude. That sea which in some unexplained way had tormented him since he was a child and which, belatedly, he had come to believe held the key to the terrible wound and pain that was his country's history.

He looked at the large expanse of water and felt a deep sense of awe for the Portuguese pirate Pedro da Cintra who had defined honour by challenging the greatness of the sea on his way to plunder the gold and spice treasuries of other nations. 'The sea has a place for all of us,' he thought. 'We just have to find it and stop being bastards and cowards.' He stood for what seemed like an eternity, then walked back to the slab, sat down and removed his boots. He looked at his wrist to see what time it was, but he no longer had a watch as they had removed it soon after his arrest; in a way, he felt happy and his calm returned. The joy of a total absence of time, of age, being in his small cell and possessed of a feeling so vast was the most pure and expansive of sensations.

In that frame of mind, General Masimiara recalled a dream his wife Augusta had two weeks before the coup; a dream whose symbolism more than any other reason had convinced him the time was ripe to move against the corrupt government.

He pieced the threads of her dream together, sewed them into a fine patchwork of colours like one of those skilled lacemakers whose work he had marvelled at in Soviet Central Asia many years ago, conscious that a dream like a patchwork has a hundred layers of meaning. Augusta's dream, he recalled, went like this: she dreamed she had gone into her kitchen, switched on the light and had been held speechless by the hissing noise coming from one of the pots left on the stove with its lid on. She couldn't recall leaving anything to cook on the stove before going to bed, and furthermore the stove was unlit. She walked like a cat about to pounce on a mouse, opened the pot and was seized by a great horror seeing the contents. Swimming in a sea of boiling water were lizards: fat lizards, thin lizards, blue lizards, black lizards and lizards the colour of her nail polish. Recalling a time when as a child a mouse had crawled out of a hole on to her toes and she had screamed, she let out a shriek loud enough to wake up the dead and then fainted.

'It's the sign of a ghost trying to warn us about a disaster in this country. There will be lots of blood but he can't say when,' was the analysis of Amina, Augusta's mother.

Later, she revived her daughter with a soup of onion leaves, alligator peppers and cloves and then put her to sleep, but not before she had chalked the letter X on all the windows to drive out the demon of Augusta's dream.

General Masimiara saw in his wife's dream the sign he had been waiting for. Before that revelation he had been convinced for a long time that something had to be done to rid his country of the plague of cutthroats and mercenaries who formed the government. It wasn't a question of honour or of history; generals did not make history. They were merely agents drawn by the winds of revolt to try to change the tide and the pace of events, to add a little page to the terrible book of the struggle of ordinary people, and the conquest of their own fear and exploitation. No, it wasn't power either, because no one could accuse him of wanting power: that detestable ambition of the little generalissimos the continent had a way of turning out, or the lawyers and other professionals, who, once they had power, became brigand politicians. If he had any claim to history, it was that five years earlier he had personally handed over the reins of the government to the president after the victorious young soldiers had overthrown a unpopular regime. But the president had turned the country into a joke, plundered it and shared the loot with his friends. When he wasn't doing that, he was inviting the Lebanese smugglers and others to 'come here and dump your miseries, there is room for all of you'. Now, the postal stamps and monetary bills, the ones with the head of the president, the ones that no one wanted to buy but had to buy, were infested with the stench of the garbage that the country had become. Everywhere you looked, you could see the dogshit and dead dogs where once there had been beds of violets and fountains in gardens with clear alabaster statues. The general felt something had to be done. Garbage has a way of producing more garbage.

He consulted a fortune teller who told him: 'Look at the country. It is experiencing a plague worse than the one that happened thirty years ago, when the crippled soldiers came home from the British campaign in Burma.' They came back to their women who, tired of waiting, had gone off and slept in the beds of other men. But they were forgiving soldiers who wanted their women back. Men who, after all, before the war, drank raw liquor and could paralyse constrictors just by looking at them. When they had gathered the remnants of their marriages, in the dim light of the mudhouses, the women baked a bread of flour and cornmeal and cooked crocodile meat to bring back the fires into their men: soldiers who had fathered children, who were themselves not afraid of the skinny creatures in white flannels and bowler hats who had presumed to rule the country. If those brave men had sacrificed their homes just so that their lives would improve, then the present rulers had to be got rid of.

General Masimiara shook with rage recalling the humiliation he had suffered when, on a visit to the United States to inspect some military hardware the government was buying to protect itself against the people, he had been shown the infamous headline: 'US company to dump nuclear waste off African coast'. It was his country, all right, there was no doubt about it. He read how for the sum of twenty-five million dollars the president had agreed to have the toxic waste dumped in the waters of his country, and kill off all the children.

'The son-of-a-bitch has gone too far,' he raged.

Later that night, while the American general who was his host toasted the health of the African president, who was a good ally and a disciple of the commonsense policy of free-marketeering, unlike those Marxists whose people were starving and had to rely on American rice, General Masimiara could barely conceal his rage. On the plane back home he barely heard the lovely blonde stewardess who told him, 'Fasten your seatbelt, General, we are about to take off.' He had planned his coup.

When the coup failed, the president went on national radio and television and made an exasperatingly comical speech. He referred to himself as 'your humble servant, the father of the nation'. He told how 'Yesterday some disgruntled elements within the army, backed by street hooligans and ungrateful university students, fed at government's expense' had attempted to overthrow his government. But how, because of the vigilance and loyalty of the people, they had failed. The men who had moved against the government were dwarfs and chameleons who thought 'they could take on the load of an elephant on their heads, because, let me tell you, the government had the weight of that enormous beast and only select people like myself can undertake the task. We have reasons to believe that the lackeys had received some help from foreign governments and from foreigners living in the country, whom we shall be expelling soon.' To those who had looted and plundered the shops of Lebanese and Indian merchants, 'lawful taxpayers and diamond dealers', he promised the severest punishment, and assured the people that the ringleaders would be dealt with ruthlessly: their guilt was established and there would be no need of a trial. God bless the people and good night to them.

The man who put down the coup was a colonel with the unforgettable name of Lookdown Akongo. He had the habit of always looking down when talking to people, giving the impression that he was shy and inadequate in some area of his private life, but who was in reality an expert in counter-intelligence and a secret confidante of the president. Unlike General Masimiara, he was not a career soldier but had started life in the other frontier of adolescence as a construction engineer where, it was rumoured, his hands and his heart had been toughened so that when he was drafted into the army to build bridges he earned the reputation of being able to bend iron bars with his bare hands. Born into a family of court-messengers and cabinet-makers, he had been twelve when the trade unions had risen against the colonial government, and the police had shot and killed twelve workers who had been uprooting railway tracks and pulling down lampposts in the general strike of 1951. The horror of witnessing that massacre – the terrified look of the rioters as they fled the deadly bullets – and the aftermath when a disdainful government resolved the grievances over workers' pay by simply jailing the ringleaders and threatening to send other rebels to the infamous cocoa plantation on the mosquito-ridden island of Fernando Po, was to accompany the boy for much of his early life. Most nights, he had bad dreams about men who came to him, looking for water for their parched throats. But in the endless catalogue of images that said a lot about his own status in life, there was one that he could never forget.

Everyday, as he walked home from school, he saw the big yellow house on Circular Road, where women in gaudy bandeaux drank cheap rum and listened to the calypsos of Calendar the Left-Handed. Although no one told him, Akongo could guess that the women spent much of their time waiting for the American sailors, who came and left, sometimes doing up their buttons in view of everyone.

Try as he might he could not escape the coils of the class serpent that was the rage of his society. Modes of behaviour long abandoned in the factories and gutters of England were still being copied with diligence by the despicable lot who made up the middle and upper classes. They were men and women whose other passion was to drink tea in the afternoon in the ovens of their drawing rooms and parlours modelled on the antediluvian style of pre-abolition America while worrying about the cost of taking holidays in England. Whereas visitors put their strangeness down to a case of bad blood, they lived in such a shocking state of unreality that they considered the cultural images of the other people in the rest of Malagueta as contemptible and crude. And Akongo, not being part of that spurious class of human beings whom he hated but secretly wished to emulate, had wept bitterly when his application to attend the school by the sea, named after some drunken English prince who had a passion for other men's wives, had been turned down on the grounds that his father was a cabinet-maker, and a suspected brewer of illicit gin at that. Accordingly, the boy who was to grow up and put down a coup twenty years later in the chilly harmattan of General Tamba Masimiara's life had been forced to enrol in a school on the hill, especially reserved for boys whose horizons were more limited.

The first oath he took when he was drafted into the army, after the Burma disaster, when all he could hope for was an advancement to captain, was not the usual one about the defence of king and country. That day, while the white major dreamed his dream of a native-trainer, his dream of a big-game hunter, young Akongo swore unswerving hatred under his breath for the upper classes. How could he be a man and a soldier at that if he could not reorder his world in his own image? Becoming a clairvoyant with the power to leap into the future that day, he saw a world where they would anticipate his wishes, because he would not have to give the command if he wanted a monument to some worm in history pulled down. He would merely have to dream about it for his men to act. They would be happy because he was doing it for them, plastering those cows with their own dung; those sons-of-bitches aristocrats who ought to be suffocated in their beds – their wives and children too.

Colonel Akongo still dreamed about this world; he dreamed about a landscape with houses of gilded bedrooms, of gargoyles created by master stone-cutters, of marble terraces and ornate bedrooms – with such a violence that he would wake up perspiring in spite of the fan in his room, and go to his sideboard for a drink. Although he had ulcers, which his doctors had told him could kill him, he still indulged in bloody marys and had a passion for women. When he made love – especially to the wives of the nouveau riche who, now that he was the chairman of the rice distribution board, cooed between orgasms, 'Don't forget our allocations, sweetheart, you don't know how mean our husbands are, Black Label whisky is messing up their brains, the bastards, they don't even look after their own children, what beasts' – he saw in those voluptuous breasts, those outlandishly coiffed heads, those bird of paradise necks, those legs that entwined him like snakes, how afraid they were, because their history was coming to an end.

The night before he moved against General Masimiara, Colonel Akongo went to see his mother. Except for a toothless cleaning woman who came in three times a week, she lived alone in a respectable wooden house on a street where the British had once garrisoned the West Indian and Bambara soldiers on their way to die in Burma and India. She never tired of telling people, 'This was the route to death, such innocent boys.' She was small and sprightly, and although she was past seventy she wore her years well, like a tortoise, and did her own cooking, waking up at six every morning to brew her tea which came from the country across the Senegalese river. It was to this house that she had retired with her young son after her husband had gone back to the provinces when his carpentry business failed, pushed out by the competition of the new class of importers. Battling the rain and the pervasive slur of urbanised women who took a dim view of her trying to break into the fabric retailing business, she had brought up Akongo on money saved over the years of self-deprivation and biblical austerity. Thus his rise to the number two position in the army was a source of great pride to her.

He came when it was getting dark. She was putting the white lace over the radiogram and covering the mirrors with less expensive fabrics as she had done for fifty years to 'keep the bad eyes out'. The sound of his heavy boots frightened her a bit because he had never come this late before. Something about the way he looked told her that his visit was not a family one; not about sorcerer's help to rid his drawers of djinns in bottles left there by enemies. He had about him the look of a hawk, or a constrictor mesmerising its prey, and in the deep furrows of his brow, the hard metallic glow of his eyes, she saw him take everything in as if he was seeing them for the first time. For once in his life, he did not go into the kitchen to see what she had cooked but stood in the middle of the parlour, facing a window through which he had a clear view of a monument to a great footballer erected by the colonial government.

Colonel Akongo felt he too had to lead a team, score goals and build monuments. He needed only to have his mother's blessing before acting. Sensing that he wanted to talk, she led him into her bedroom, locked the door and asked him what it was.

When she heard what it was she reacted with a mother's instinct and clasped his hands. She listened as if in a dream, and she saw a young man many years earlier coming home as a captain after training in England, handsome and smart in his bright khaki. She recalled the expostulation of her diviner: 'Watch him, he will go places.' The tightness she felt in her throat, when he had gone away through the jungles against the smugglers and hoarders, came back in the way that only mothers re-enacting the terrible moments of delivery remember. She had not admitted it in the past but somewhere, in that unspeakable anguish she had suffered to bring him up, she had wanted not so much for him to succeed as a soldier but to be a man among dwarfs, to do justice to his father who had been crushed by the obsequious acceptance of his own station in life.

She tapped her belly twice; 'Do it for your mother, son. This is your chance! Do it for your father who was a good man, God grant him peace where he is. He did not listen to me, but got mixed up with them. Show them that you came from my belly, let them know you sucked my breasts for twelve months, yes, twelve months at these breasts! That I did not put some of my milk in your nostrils to turn you into a fool! Show them you are a man, yes, especially their women. Good God! The way they walk, you would think someone else wipes their arses! But first, before you act, kill a young bull and anoint yourself with the splendour of its blood, then dry its hide and wear it under your tunic so that you will be protected against the voracious worms of envy.'

When he left his mother's house, Colonel Akongo decided to drive to the coast to clear his mind of all doubts about the justice of his decision, and to feed on the contempt that he felt for the ruling class. He laughed when he recalled that incongruously with their three-piece woollen suits and the Sunday charade of going to church, they were the biggest practitioners of sorcery, lost in the chimerical illusion of history that blinded them to the fact that their chickens were coming home to roost. He wanted to be there at the breaking point of that link, corrupted by social upheavals whose banality fuelled with past debts and insults occupied an idelibly stained page of the country's history. He wasn't a born leader and did not have mountains to climb or rivers to ford. But in that world of corrupt people he knew which way the dice were loaded, who held the cards; and he was determined to dispose of his enemies as ruthlessly as they had once condemned him and others to the quarters of the underdog. But Colonel Akongo knew that in order to do this, he had to get rid of the general who had married into that class of upstarts and sometimes assumed their airs, although no one could accuse him of being corrupt. The general had gone up with them in the early days of his career and Colonel Akongo knew he had to be careful. He even felt a deep respect for the general who had helped him through the jungle-house of the army. As a lieutenant, Akongo had polished the older man's boots with his saliva to bring out the shine, ran errands for him, fetched his children from school and lied to his wife for him. Now, however, the general stood in his way, blocked his road to glory, and was putting black pebbles in his rice.

So when the general nailed his own coffin by confiding in him, the colonel had sworn loyalty to him, but had then made counter plans to be the man at centre stage. He was going to rewrite that terrible history begun in 1787 but stamped more cruelly into his brain when all those years ago he had listened to the distant echoes of his own voice drifting on a bleak mountain when he wanted so much to swim in the reserved swimming pool of a princely grammar school.

'I arrested him myself,' the colonel boasted when they brought his former boss to the fort. But when he saw the contempt and scorn for him in the prisoner's eyes, Colonel Akongo quickly walked away, convinced that General Masimiara would soon be part of history. The days passed, and two weeks after his arrest they had still not gone for General Masimiara. He had been denied visitors and knew it would be useless to demand to see a lawyer. They had offered him the services of a priest if he wanted to talk, and had sent him prison rations which they passed through the iron grilles to him, but he did not need a priest in this or the next world. He felt he could talk to God without assistance, especially if his meeting with the Creator was at the sound of the bullet. He wanted them to come for him and get it over with before he stopped believing in himself. He had never believed in redemption because there was no such thing as redemption when the clergy couldn't make up their minds about whether to serve the poor or the rich in this kingdom. Worse, they prayed for the president every Sunday.

The general felt an insouciance and calm in spite of the cold, desolate walls of his prison, and thought he had never felt better. As the first cold winds of the Atlantic blasted through his cell, he knew he was ready for anything. He would order the formation of stones, of birds, of winds to bear witness to the formation of a firing squad, which he knew had no power over him because he was already seeing things past the present time, where birth gave way to death and death to life; where no one was judged or condemned. Everything met at the confluence of ideas and creation and if only they would get on with this farce, this little headache of a trial, he would feel better. He stretched out on his cold slab and imagined he saw reflected on the ceiling the face of his mistress. Would Sadatu understand? She was so much a part of her history, with a clinical respect for the wardrobe secrecy of relationship and order, even order in bed. She had not been informed about the plans for the coup even though the general sometimes confided in her. Whereas she was secretive, his wife was good-natured and exuberant. But would she understand, although she shared his contempt for the crooks who formed the government? Suddenly he felt lonely and shivered from the cold. They had not given him a blanket nor returned his clothes, and at that moment he experienced a revelation that arranged and rearranged all the cards. A great calm engulfed him, and General Masimiara knew that he had come full circle to where it had started in that cold grotto of awakening where man had learned how to make fire. Man, General Masimiara concluded, was born cold in a dark cave, the fruit of an action without too much meaning, and which was sometimes brutal and quick, chained to the feet of Adam. Seizing for an instant the spark of his imagination, he cut the chain of his banishment, and created a greater fire of exploration out of that cave. If he had missed the way in his search for the purity of ideas and the independence of his identity, he had at least tried, and for that he felt happy, and General Tamba Masimiara went to sleep.

BOOK ONE

1 The Magic Lantern

She had been prophesied in the looking-glass of the Nubian, Sulaiman of Khartoum, a hundred years before. On that May morning as she stood on the deck of the *Belmont* anchored in the English harbour, Jeanette Cromantine seemed like a woman with an esoteric past. Although the air was dry and cool, she opened her parasol, more out of habit than of necessity, and stared at the distant water, as if in its bluish-grey reflection the secrets of her past were written. At twenty, her life was only just beginning, but Jeanette Cromantine had the aspect of a woman who had been the mistress of a man accustomed to the sybaritic pleasures of the East Indies then fashionable and greatly copied by young English planters. Many of them had gone out to the West Indies to trade in coffee, sugar and spices, and once they had made enough money they bought large estates, hired overseers and retired back to England, or the East, to live off their profits.

Jeanette Cromantine was an octoroon but was very proud of the dilution of black blood that gave her an emanation of *fleur-de-lis*, which, with her smile of sea corals, made her the most desirable woman for any redblooded man. Her mother had been a beautiful mulatto cook on a plantation in Georgia, and one evening, after she had retired to her room at the back of the kitchen in the big house where she cooked for an old planter and his family of two, she heard three faint sounds on the door, and then saw the big blond white man as he pushed it and walked in.

'Is anything you be wantin, Master Willie?' she asked.

He had been away at school in New England, and came home only once every year because the slave business did not interest him. Although the woman had been bought when he was merely a boy, he had never known how to respond to her, even though their lives had been shaped not so much by their individual fates but by what he considered the inscrutably calm presence of the woman. Her name was Sophie Mahogany. Despite the social standing that separated them, he had come to regard her as part of a historical trick in the ambiguities of young manhood that was tormenting him, and for which he had to cross the river that divided them and find peace. When he had been growing up, he had watched her as she served him his meals, took the plates away and went to her room where she sang in a warm pinewood voice which surprised him because of her position in life. Knowing that he could not have her except in that degrading and matter-of-fact way that he had come to associate with slavery which he found so detestable, Willie Blackburn had fled to school in the east coast of the country. There, he threw himself at his studies with a resoluteness that belied his torment. He plunged with a nightly fevour into the philosophical essays of Locke, which gave him neither clarity nor the peace of mind that he had hoped to find in Boston. She would turn up in the most unlikely of places: in the shape of the sculptures of Diana the huntress that some rich planter had donated to the school as a sop for his conscience, and in Titian's painting of love that he kept in his room. One day, he went to see a visiting French company that had come with the girls who had performed for the Empress Catherine. When the curtains went up, Willie Blackburn was suddenly hit by a desire to weep. There, transformed into one of the actresses, was Sophie Mahogany. She had the same dark look which hinted at faraway islands, the mouth of a woman of great passion and voluptuousness that put her at a certain distance from those insipid virgins that Willie Blackburn saw every day in Boston. At the end of the play he caught the attention of the woman, and Willie Blackburn saw in her eyes the bittersweet forlornness of all trapped women in the world – the actress, like the slave girl, was at the mercy of men. He felt an urgent desire to get away from those eyes, to run to the end of the world where he could dream of other things; away from the fire that was beginning to engulf him in a terrible anguish.

A month later he came home, determined to confront Sophie Mahogany, to put her out of his mind in that house of bondage. After he had closed the door behind him he looked round the room, noticing its cleanliness and her few possessions. They were mostly hand-me-downs that had come from the mistress of the house: the torn blue rug with the picture of the fountain of Rome, the ceramic face bowl, the four-poster bed with its patchwork of bright colours, and the cheap sailor's trunk on which she had arranged the imitation silver earrings and necklaces that she was allowed to wear on her day off. But now that he had come into the room, Willie Blackburn felt temporised by the presence of the woman, although it was he who held the power of possession over her. He found it hard to speak and, when he eventually did, it was with difficulty.

'I came to see how you are, Sophie.'

'Fine, Master Willie,' she replied.

'I wish you would not call me that, Sophie; after all, it is not as if I own you, and you know how I feel about this situation.'

She quivered a little as he sat on the bed beside her. But she was determined not to lose her calm because she did not want to reveal how she felt for this man who had shown her nothing but kindness, unlike his mother who treated her like dirt. He was different from his father who, although he was generous by nature, believed implicitly in the dubious notion of his own superiority over the dark men and women whom he felt Providence had placed in his care and control.

'You de master, and ah ain't nothing but a slave girl.'

'That's what my mother says, but what about you, are you not a woman first?'

He could not tell her about his studies, of his evenings at the play or of the time he had eaten a bowl of chestnuts and had nearly choked on them thinking about her. Fate had brought them under the same roof and crossed their lives on an undecipherable chart from which he could be released only if he possessed her. But he knew that he would be forever marked by the dark creatures of her eyes once he had done what was expected of him. He tried to think of how to accomplish what was less painful for him, but felt like a man who had to travel on two separate roads neither of which led to honour. And he was shocked that she could induce honour in him when all around life was marked by a bestiality against her kind, committed by even the best of men who went home to their wives, trailed by the smoke of their dark women.

He tried to get up and leave, but some invincible hand kept him firmly planted on the bed. A powerful sensation whirled in his head and tightened his entrails. Suddenly he felt a deep need to be loved as he had never been loved before, and because his torment had the face of an orphan he did not see the hand of the orphan sitting close to him as it came up to his face which was shaking like a plant in a storm. 'Little master, little master,' the woman said, as she covered his pale cold body with the dark flames of her own body so that his blood was warmed and fired by a beauty which made him groan, and Willie Blackburn did not

3

know that what he was about to receive was an act of tenderness and love that his own mother had not given his father, her mind crippled by an arbitrary fear of the marital bed where she had conceived him without love.

When she discovered she was pregnant, Sophie Mahogany began to feign a relish for foods she had hitherto not eaten. By taking them to her room, where she kept them until she could give them to the dogs late at night without being seen, she was able to persuade the mistress of the house that she had been eating too much, and that was why she was fat. She ate ginger first thing in the morning which controlled the involuntary vomiting and she tied a double waist band round her belly which restricted the expansion of her pregnancy.

Soon after she was born, Jeanette Cromantine's mother took her away. Not too far from where she worked lived an old black preacher. He was a free man who, because of a heart ailment, had earned the chance to pass his remaining years in his pursuit of the meaning of the curse of Ham and the dispersal of his sons upon seas and in deserts. After years of exploring the curse, he came up one morning with a startling revelation: 'Dey bin a walkin for three thousand years, but de good Lawd done hear their tears and he gon bring 'em home soon, yes sir.' He was convinced that the second coming of the Messiah was just around the corner, and that they were the last of a strong breed of men who had to undergo the trial by fire in that land before they went out to repopulate the world with the seeds of their accumulated wisdom.

It was he who raised the unnamed child, vowing to save her from the fate that had been her mother's. It was not an easy task because he knew very little about children, not having any himself – his wife died when she was young, kicked by a mule in the field. But he did not lack support because, upholding a tradition traced back to Africa, the black women who came to his ministrations took turns nursing the baby. Whenever she could, her mother came to see her child, making sure that no one in the big house knew of her double life. She kept silent about the night the blond young master came to her room, tormented by his mother's inability to love him; and, deprived of the chance to nurse her own child, she trained her eyes to turn away from other people's children. When she felt the need to nurse she would put big, wet towels on her breasts, and to take her mind off her predicament she experimented with new recipes and discovered that the entrails of pigs tasted better when garnished with parsley than the best sirloin then available on the plantation. For someone who had always been afraid of funerals and who thought death was a reminder of what men owe themselves, she developed a morbid interest in how people died. She found some excuse to be present at lynchings, to be in a room when an old slave was preparing to meet his maker. Sophie Mahogany was afraid of death, because she wanted her child to live. When she could not control the bad dreams she had about an evil woman who was trying to kill the child, Sophie Mahogany induced such a spate of irrational bunions that they made it impossible for her to walk.

Summoned to have a look at her, the doctor of the white family in the big house was emphatic in his diagnosis:

'It's pig fever,' he said. 'An infection brought about by a prolonged association with the animal, which as you all know is the agent of the devil. This is a punishment by God to those who try to deceive him. Nothing escapes God,' he concluded.

Sophie Mahogany had no quarrel with God, especially as he was new to her in the form presented by her captors. But his closeness was more a matter of supposition than of any deeply felt need to believe in the abstract nature of that existence. If God existed in the old form told her by her grandmother she could have offered a red chicken, and stood naked on the stones of the nearby river, and God would have saved her child. The fact that she had given the child away was proof that she rejected the impartiality of the alien God, because whereas she was owned by the father of the man who had given her a child, she did not own her child. That state of affairs left a bitter taste in her mouth which not even the pastor's consecrated water could wash off.

Over the years luck, the kindness of other black women and the sheer determination of the pastor helped turn Jeanette Mahogany into a vivacious young woman. She was loved by the pastor whom she called father. While he was raising her, he prayed to God that she might be spared the clutches of slave-breeders and would one day find a nice black man to marry.

As well as his fascination with Christianity, the pastor had a deep knowledge of herbal lores which he used to cure the wounds of the black men from the surrounding plantations. He tried to hide the brutality of life from Jeanette Mahogany but the young woman found a way to go beyond the illusory mirrors of her time. What the preacher thought she had been spared occurred with such regularity that she could not fail to notice it. Thus she came to learn that 'sawdust' was another name for a black man who worked with the most unyielding variety of tobacco plants and that 'cow udders' were the black women who nursed the

5

children of the plantation owners. In that angry and painful awakening of her conscience, the black men and women seemed to be tied to the stakes of their impotence.

She felt a deep compassion for those men who, bloodied by their repeated but ineffective bouts of rebellion that were cruelly put down by their masters, seemed to have gone to some cave to die.

But she did not then know of the rivers that were raging in those hearts, nor did she know of the cutlasses that were unsheathed in the dark moments when the moon was not visible. But no one was to tell her why the black women did not seem to be having too many children, until that morning when she eavesdropped on a conversation between the preacher and one of his female converts. She heard the sacred oath taken by the black women to drink a bitter potion to abort all children forced upon them by their owners until they were called by 'the loas' of the swamp to bring forth strong children who would grow to wield cutlasses and cut the throats of their masters. Jeanette Mahogany was moved.

For once in her life, she was making contact with real people, whose smell was animal, whose life was brutal. The cotton fields came alive with their voices, as they praised God with their parched lips, convinced that his coming was only a matter of time. The tongue of the sun sometimes flickered and licked the backs of the men, which became brown and dusty with time. In the evenings, when they went home to their wives, who were only partially theirs, their hands were rough on the quivering bodies of the women.

In due course, Jeanette Mahogany came to regard the years spent in the minister's house as a fraud, camouflaged to look like happiness. In the blood brimming in her heart, she felt she had been denied pages of real knowledge. But whether it was the denial of the psychology of suffering or raptures of liberation among those dusty men and women in the field, Jeanette Mahogany did not know. Later, she was carried away by an instance of hate and, shocked at what she had seen in the liquid eyes of the cotton men, exclaimed:

'One day, the white men will know that the world has two faces, and that they only have power over one.'

Jeanette Mahogany wanted to serve the cotton men. Effulgence of light would sometimes shine on her face thinking of another world, where they could walk together. She was that kind of woman, wanting to cross frontiers to save those men. But they were already dead men, some of them, and when the sun left her face she dreamed about them lying in the marshes, holding their heads like waifs.

Their hands were big and calloused but they had the patience of resilience, a gift learned in childhood that not even the whips could kill. She began to love those men and, when she thought she was ready, she left the clerical confines of the pastor's house, and rejecting the possibility of the anger of the Lord surrendered her restless body to a big black man.

His name was Sebastian Cromantine, a semi-free man whose owner was a rheumatic old woman who had promised to let him go before she died. He looked forward to that moment every day, and now that God had given him a woman he could care for, he wanted to do everything to hasten the prospect of freedom. But that was before the events on the other side of the world changed everything, and he had decided to fight alongside the English.

When the rebellious citizens took up arms against the British, the men who kept slaves did not find it easy to sleep at night. They kept their guns loaded at all times because they thought their slaves would revolt, rape their wives and daughters and cut their throats. Out of a fear of being poisoned by their cooks, they took to preparing their own meals. It was not an easy task: men who had never been inside a kitchen before almost succeeded in setting fire to their homes when they tried to cook on open wood-burning stoves. The cooks for their part never felt better. Suddenly finding themselves with so much time on their hands, they stayed at home and cooked large meals for their families with ingredients saved from their toil in the big kitchens, and they prayed that the pending war would last for a long time so that they would not have to go back to work.

Faced with the inevitability of having to fight, the plantation owners met one evening and decided to fight to the last man against the colonial army, blaming their loss of domestic bliss and privilege on the Quakers who had been calling on their slaves to revolt and had even written to London for support.

'It's dem liberal Yankee bastards come to mess up our nigras,' one planter complained, when two of his slaves escaped to join the colonial army.

The war itself was fought away from the county where Sebastian Cromantine and Jeanette Mahogany had been. News would come from several battlefronts about how the war was progressing. On those plantations where cultivation had ceased, wives bade goodbye to their husbands who left their slaves in the care of over-zealous overseers. Many of the soldiers did not return to their plantations, and some of

7

those who came back were crippled and became extremely cruel not only to their slaves but to their wives.

Following his decision to join the forces of the colonial army, Sebastian Cromantine fought like a man obsessed. On the battlefield in Richmond he had begun as a water carrier, but after a particularly nasty battle when he had saved a colonial officer from death he had been allowed to carry arms. That was how he came to see that there were other men like himself who were afraid of being taken prisoner, and held in bondage. For the first time in his life he saw black men being embraced by white men, and for the first time in his life he was invited to share a meal by white men who were fighting for a cause that meant little to him other than the fact that he was now a free man and was prepared to die for his liberty. During the turbulence of the war he sometimes found time to go and see Jeanette, who was living with other women in one of the camps of the colonial army.

In the few hours that they spent together, they made love with a feverish passion that made his going back to the battle always difficult.

'Promise you gon come back to me,' she would say to him, clinging to his shirt collar when it was time for him to go.

Although freedom made him happy, Sebastian Cromantine was nevertheless aware of the difficulty that lay ahead for men like himself. Going back to the battlefield, he felt a mixture of anxiety and concern about what would happen to himself and his woman once the war was over. Until then he had not thought much about his life, regulated as it was by the vagaries of his old mistress's demands. At thirty, he was a big man, solitary and withdrawn. Before he had gone to join the colonial army, his life had been a set pattern of looking after his mistress and tending her cows and his own two goats. During the insufferable summer months he farmed a small plot of land and, after coming from the big house, went to his cabin to eat a solitary meal of corn cooked with spinach and pig's entrails. He had been content to go on living like that, to go on waiting for his mistress to give him his freedom, until the night snakes started taking shelter in his cabin from the heat.

Staying up throughout the night, he killed the first two snakes and managed to drive the other two back into the yard, but try as he might he could not forget the incident after that.

He started hearing voices in his head and kept his lamp burning all night, not so much because he was afraid of snakes but because he felt other things would come, and he would not be prepared for them. One night he had a terrible dream. He saw a beautiful black woman riding a

8

white horse deep inside some woods. The horse came to a house and lowered itself so that the woman would alight. When she opened the door of the house, she saw that there was another door at the back of the house. She went across the room and saw that beyond the house was the most beautiful valley she had seen in her life.

Sebastian Cromantine awoke from his dream and shook like a leaf. He was not a dreamer and the fact that he had dreamed soon after the incident with the snakes made him feel all the more restless. He did not realise then that the meaning of his dream had more to do with what a magical looking-glass had predicted a long time ago in a place far removed from where he was living.

Soon he was mixing things up: he confused the medicine bottles with the soup tureen of his mistress; he saw eggs in parts of the kitchen when in fact they were potatoes; and the old woman, who a long time ago had given up the habit of feeding the cat first to see whether what Sebastian cooked was poisonous, woke up from the amnesia of old age one evening and said, 'Sebastian, your brain is full of water.'

Then, as if he was being regulated by some unknown hand, he not only lost his appetite, but found it impossible to go to sleep. One night, when he had stayed awake for hours trying to expel the terrible winds of his unhappiness, someone called him three times.

It was a voice that he remembered from another time, deep and lonely. It had the faraway gravity of a rootless man burdened by his inability to find a resting place. When the voice called him for the third time, Sebastian Cromantine got up from his bed and went to open the door to see who was there.

No one was there so he went back to his room and tried to sleep, but he knew he could not forget that voice. He tried to remember where he had heard it before, in what chain gang, on what wilderness of hopelessness, anger or rage, on what plantation, what humiliation and secrecy sworn by pricking the blood bound him to that voice? Weighed down by such confusion, Sebastian Cromantine was happy for the demijohn in his room, and when he had taken a swig of rum he tried to push the voice out of his mind.

'It's a trick, he trying to mess up ma mind, if ah ain't careful!' he said.

He stayed awake all night, listening to the distant noises of the ferocious mountain lions that had been attacking the cattle of the farmers throughout the county, who became more cruel to their slaves, threatening to whip them if they did not do something about the predatory animals. Weak and exhausted from lack of sleep, Sebastian went about his chores next morning and returned later in the evening to collapse on his wooden bed. It was when he was getting up to get a cup of water from the earthen jug that he saw it move, and heard the voice again. He went closer and saw three small bones at the bottom of the jug. He threw the cup to the floor and started screaming:

'You don't frighten me, you don't frighten me!'

He ran back to his bed, threw the blanket over his face and broke out in a terrible sweat. But in that instant when he thought he was to be attacked by the bones, Sebastian Cromantine felt someone touch him on his shoulder and call his name three times in a voice that was friendly and reassuring. Tense, he knew that it was the same voice that had called him that former time.

Although the hand disappeared as miraculously as it had appeared, Sebastian Cromantine was left with the conviction about the ownership of that hand and how far its possessor had come to wake him from his intolerable burden. It was the hand of a dead man who had walked over innumerable swamps dragging the metallic evidence of his chain and the implacable look of his misery. Sebastian left his room and started running, afraid to turn back; he ran over the crops, over the poison ivy, the sharp-toothed traps for the wolves, with the steps of the dead man on his trail. In that quick journey, between the pounding of his heart and the quixotic attempts to ward off the dead man with his hands, the mirror of the organic meaning of his relationship to the dead man shone on him; and the futility of his flight merely served to lessen his steps. It was his father who had looked at him in those bones, who had touched him with his hands of a spiritual navigator, with his horns of a diviner, with his eyes of an overworked bull and with the dull steps of his lugubrious presence behind him.

Sebastian Cromantine suddenly understood the unmistakable continuity of an ancient rite that had given meaning and force to the mortification of all earthly and transient powers, in that frightening revelation of the possession of his soul by his father who had died ten years earlier. Poisoned by his own hands, the dead man was obeying the call from another world to which he had returned, where the first man and woman had mated without disturbance, in the enchanting garden of primordial love.

Hastening his steps, Sebastian barely had time to understand the meaning of the divine purpose in life before he collapsed on the preacher's steps where he had come so often to listen to sermons. When he woke up, the beautiful woman who hovered above him in the dark was applying a cold towel to his brow to break the fever that had raged like a fire in him during the day.

'How long ah been here?' the black man asked.

'Sshh, sshh, don't talk,' she replied. 'Pa is getting some herbs.'

Sebastian tried to raise himself up from the canebed. He felt his bones creak and somehow he suffered from a momentary loss of power in his hands though he could move his legs. He looked round the room and noticed that instead of one there were three candles burning, though the effect was not one of unnecessary brightness but, in the rich birch of the cabin, a brilliant and warm glow. The woman sat on the edge of the bed and continued to apply the towel to his head. Her nearness unnerved him, but after his recent bout of exorcism and his prolonged melancholy he wanted nothing better than to be near her, to be enveloped in her soft aura of being, to touch that delicate skin of golden cinnamon and, even beyond that, to feel those braids of moss hanging loosely down her shoulders, if only to calm that intolerable turmoil that was beginning to eat away at his entrails. Then he remembered who he was, his invincible chains came back and he felt the heavy yoke of his slavery in a way he had never felt before.

'Gotta get back to ma cabin, Missy will be missing me,' he said.

'She already know you here, and you not to worry; stop talking and drink de soup,' the woman protested. Sebastian Cromantine noticed the dark shadows. He thought he was seeing the images of his parents, of bounty hunters, the skeletons of his dead cows rotting down a well. It was hard to tell one from the other. Forgetting those shadows, he heard the dogs barking in the distance and the wheels of coaches rumbling by, bringing back some white men from secret meetings about the war. Suddenly, Sebastian Cromantine was jolted out of his reverie by the surgical confirmation of the seriousness of the war. What if it was true that the colonial army and the rebels were murdering each other, the streets strewn with legs, disjointed heads and wailing women beating their breasts? Like a flash out of the dark, an idea possessed him, and its urgency had the miraculous power to heal him and unshackle him from that bed. Why had he not seen the hands of the clock moving before now? Everything turns twice, he thought, even the earth. Suddenly he dismissed his mistress and decided he was going to join the colonial army. Looking at the woman, he wondered whether he would have been able to make that decision if she had not entered his life.

Jeanette Mahogany looked at the big black man whose arms were so powerful she was convinced he could wrestle a bear. He was a good-looking man, and his attractiveness lay in the combination of a kind, strong face and a bittersweet smile, especially when he lay asleep. But even when asleep, something about him hinted at an unbridled energy whose consummate power filled the room. Moreover, she found him unsettling in a way she could not explain. She had had no experience of men, except for those lost souls she served coffee to who came to the pastor's ministration: men wearing their forlorn hope heavily on their shoulders; men who had lost their maleness serving other men. She had pitied them and in the quiet of her room at night, terrified by her own desires, she would take her clothes off and look at her breasts, wanting to give herself to a man she could love.

Sebastian Cromantine was different. When he had come in the past he had merely been one of the congregation who listened to the pastor talk about the three thousand years that black men and women had been condemned to suffer in the desert and on the plantations.

'Pray, pray, ma people, so de Lawd gon bring us out of dis sinful worl,' the pastor would intone.

Now, the presence of the big black man lying in that room filled Jeanette Mahogany with dreams of a life she could have. Beginning that morning, she found an excuse for being in that room, to bring him some fruits from the garden in the back and to read him some of the stories that the pastor had recently taught her how to read.

When Sebastian Cromantine confessed that he could not read too well, Jeanette told him not to worry.

'One of dese days ah gon teach you how to read real well,' she said.

He found the prospect of being taught by such an enticing woman exhilarating. For that reason, Sebastian Cromantine began to think of ways of prolonging his stay in bed. But the prospect of doing so seemed not too bright, especially as his mistress had already been to the pastor's house to complain about having to make her own meals.

Things would have gone on like that, but one day, realising that she could not live without him, Jeanette Mahogany had confessed her love for him. He seized her in his big arms, kissed her face and thanked God for giving him such a woman. There, on the floor of the preacher's house, he stretched the woman out and they made love for the first time. They left that same night when it was dark and, keeping to the densely wooded paths, they managed to reach one of the camps of the colonial army where they were welcomed.

When the war ended, Sebastian and Jeanette Cromantine, who had been married by another black pastor, found themselves in England. But the rigours of the English weather, the miserable poverty of many people both black and white, upset them.

'Dey sure is poor here,' Sebastian Cromantine said one night, when they were coming to the end of the ration given to them by the army captain who had brought them across the ocean.

So when the offer of sailing to a new land had been made, the Cromantines had been the first to join. They waited for four months before they set sail, but when they eventually did, they did not look back on the period of bad luck that had bedevilled their stay in London. The people on the boat had about them an air of expectancy mixed with trepidation, which made them a not too enterprising lot to establish a new settlement. When they had been abandoned in London, they had not imagined being on ships again, hugging the sea to their breasts, sailing to an uncertain destiny. But by some miraculous luck some of the men had succeeded in bringing their wives and children with them. The women were a beautiful lot: tall, ranging from dark coffee brown to light-skinned mulattresses. Unlike their men, who seemed to have drunk too much rum to prepare themselves for the voyage, they had made a small list of things to bring, and, hidden in those secret places which only women know how to find, they had supplies of okra, aubergines, onions, radish and lettuce seed, which they hoped to plant before the rains. Oblivious of their parents' preparations, the children went on a wild exploration of the ships and ended up turning them into large playgrounds. In that atmosphere of wild excitement, the children sucked on the bonbons and other sweets their mothers had baked in London before the departure.

Sebastian Cromantine stood by his wife's side. He was a long way from his snakes, a long way from the nightmares of those battlefields which, despite the frantic efforts of his wife to calm him down, seemed to recur at regular intervals. He looked at the sea, closed his eyes and imagined what the land would look like.

'What you think we gon do when we get there?'

'Well, ah suppose we can plant dem seeds that we brung after we done some clearing of de land dey gon give us,' said Jeanette Cromantine, who had all along anticipated her husband's question. This beautiful woman, remarkable for her belief in a dream whose origins had

13

shattered the mirror of Sulaiman the Nubian a hundred years earlier, raised in the cloistered fanaticism of her time, was preparing for the future with a meticulousness that surprised her husband. She had, in addition to the seeds, saved from the abandoned camp of the departing colonial soldiers a few cups, pots and the hand-me-down clothes of the officers which she mended with care, washed and put inside a trunk for Sebastian.

'And how much land you think dey gon give each of us?' she wanted to know.

'Don't know,' said her husband, 'but ah hear de place is open, big enough for all of us four hundred men, women and chillum to grow our own food,' adding, as it started to rain, 'build log cabins and raise families.'

'And de people, dey bad? You scairt of 'em?'

'Ain't scairt of no one no more. We free now and goin to de place where our faders come from, and ah got dat skull, and we gon be happy.'

'Skull, what kinda skull?' the woman asked.

She experienced a momentary terror.

'Pa's skull,' the man replied. 'Came to me one evening, rattling dem bones like dey hanging him and he ringing a bell to tell me to wake up, and his throat hoarse, and he crippled by insomnia, 'cause he ain't sleep for a long time 'cause he be wandering like Moses, so ah digs up de skull during de war.'

Jeanette Cromantine was aghast. 'And what you gon do wid it?'

Sebastian Cromantine did not answer right away. Never having thought about the power of ghosts to appear and disappear at will or of the great burden that his father had imposed upon him, he suddenly felt oppressed by an immense solitude as he tried to imagine the untried chasm of supposition that he had to cross to understand the world of his father. But because he had come so far after the war, and the land was near, he knew that he was no longer afraid of the things that had hurt him, of the time when he had gone out, chased by the relentless force of his father. Now, he could evoke a lineage that was not defined by time, but by the spirit, by the force of all eternities and the running music of ancestral water that coursed through his blood. He believed he would be lucky because he had come from a death more prolonged than the one suffered by the carpenter's son who had not wanted to break his chains, as he had broken his chains.

He felt like a conqueror and if he did not have a gun he had his bloody history to remind him of what he had to do. And he could hope, buoyed by the potency of the black man's sperm that had begun to explode and generate its force in the universal womb of woman. No door was closed to him now, and he was determined that never again would any be closed because he knew the magic words, Open Sesame, and he would discover the soul of his own Adam which, when he thought about it, was already growing in the vegetable bed of his soul. So when a tumultuous wave broke his thoughts, he answered his wife with the sincerity of a man who had come ashore from the last tidal wave of death.

'Am gon use it, cause it's de Magic Lantern.'

2 The Spotted Navel of the Scorpion-Woman

Two days before they reached the coast of Kasila country, tragedy struck on the *Belmont*. Up till then they had passed a peaceful time, with the men, now that they were nearing the coast, urging their women to be wary of soldiers, to check that all their children were on board, and that their supply of food was still there. It was a moonlit night and Sebastian Cromantine was just beginning to light his pipe when he heard the voice of his wife calling him as if she had seen the face of the dead. She had. Isabel Smith, the oldest woman on board, who hated the name that circumstances had forced upon her and who insisted on being called Fatmatta and was known as the Bird, died after exerting a promise from the captain that she would be buried on land. Unknown to the captain, she had also got her fellow travellers to swear that they would kill him if he reneged on his promise.

'You won't let him feed me to de crocodiles, will you?'

They promised that they would not let him do that because they themselves looked forward to touching the soil of their heritage with the spades that they had brought along. Some had also brought the bones of their dead ones which they were hiding under their bunks so that the crew would not find them. During the periodic storms at sea, the rattling of the bones in the bags helped to reassure their owners that they would make it to the shore. At eighty-five, Fatmatta the Bird-Woman was clearly the oldest passenger on the ship. They called her the bird-woman because of her habit of singing in a rich contralto voice that touched even the saddest members of the blacks. No one knew how she had come to London and, except for Jeanette Cromantine's account, very little was known about her life in America. The purity of her voice would break out on the languid afternoons of despair, on the tempestuous evenings at sea when the sharks came close to the ship, and in the smoke-filled kitchens below deck where the travellers would sometimes gather to share the anxieties that accompanied them on the trip. During the long wait before they started sailing, it was she who had consoled them with 'Don't be sad, ma chillum; life ain't no mirror, but ah sees we gon get outta dis trouble worl.'

She died peacefully that night in her bed, with Jeanette Cromantine holding her head. During the last days of Fatmatta's life, when getting out of bed had been a difficult task for her, it was the younger woman who had fetched her soup, lighted her pipe and pulled up her cashmere stockings. In gratitude, Fatmatta had blessed Jeanette Cromantine, prayed to God that Sebastian Cromantine would be a good husband to her and that they would be blessed with children.

When news of her death spread through the ranks of the travellers a deep gloom descended upon them, but Jeanette Cromantine, in keeping with the wishes of the dead woman, told them there was to be no crying.

'Fatmatta don't want no crying 'cause she done live her life full, full. She is seeing de Lawd now. He done come down from his chariot and lifted her up and she is happy. Ah sees de sister face when she gon meet him and she looked real fine, real fine.'

The next night, they organised a wake for her. The captain and the crew members, unaccustomed to the riotous way in which the mourners kept their wake, put their loud singing down to the practice of people who worshipped their dead. The knowledge that they were soon going to reach land consoled the captain, who could not wait to get rid of the noisy travellers.

Jeanette Cromantine told the members of the expedition about Fatmatta the Bird-Woman during the wake. She had been born in what had been a busy town on the banks of a great river where 'dey git so much gold nobody be wantin dem'. Shaped like a diamond, noisy on a Saturday market day, the town – which was called Kasila after the river – had started life as a trading post along a caravan route where marauding bandits exchanged their goods. Its proximity to the sea and its supply of fresh water and salt had gradually turned the itinerant men into settlers. Over the years they had gone back to the towns across the river and the desert, loaded their camels with their belongings and brought their wives. By the time Fatmatta the Bird-Woman was born, the town was enjoying such an unheard-of prosperity that once every year the people of the town would close it at both ends, barring all strangers from entering while they indulged in a week of licentious living.

When she was growing up, Fatmatta the Bird-Woman had been the subject of much gossip. The man that she had assumed was her father but who was only her mother's husband had been a caravan dealer in gold. He had carried on a prosperous business, going away for months on end until the alchemy of a desert magician confused his brain. Among the people he met during his wandering across the desert were women who were so beautiful that only one day was reserved for men to look at them so that they would not go blind from a prolonged exposure to such an overpowering beauty. He got so carried away with his tales that he did not pay too much attention to his young wife who, fearing that he was losing interest in women in his pursuit of money, deserted him soon after he left for the desert town of Orphir.

She was a ravishingly beautiful woman, bright as a desert rose and with the body of a weasel. Before her marriage to the caravan merchant, men had gone out of their heads when she rejected them. Now that she was free, she quickly found herself a lover and proceeded to spend her husband's money.

Because of a mix-up in the route through the desert, the unpredictability of the wind and the unreliability of guides, N'jai the caravan merchant did not get to Orphir. Instead, he found himself in a town not known to even the most seasoned traveller on those routes. Nothing was heard of his whereabouts for over a year and the now uncaring Mariamu, who had developed a voracity for making love with her lover under a baobab tree at night, dismissed her husband as a bad dream. When a group of travellers arrived one day from Ouagadougou hawking leather goods, alligator pepper and ostrich feathers with news that they had seen him in the country of a famous king who was going to die soon, she dismissed out of hand the possibility of his return.

'If he ever comes back, he would be in a golden casket,' she said.

She did not realise how close to the truth she was in that prediction.

Rain did not come early to Kasila that year. The lush green plains and valleys looked bare for miles and miles on end, and for the first time in living memory the horde of itinerant Moorish traders did not appear with their goatskins selling herbal remedies compressed in small bottles which they tried to pass off as the prescriptions of the Jews of Morocco.

In place of the Moorish traders, Kasila was invaded by a group of female beggars who camped in the central market and refused to move even when threatened. They were not like other beggars. They had the aristocratic bearing of women who had known better days but had been forced to leave their towns because of some planetary upheaval. During the day the older women would send the young ones to beg from the men, and when they did not get anything the fiercely independent girls would wrap their legs round the unfortunate men until they parted with some valuable they were carrying. Without asking anyone, the beggars soon cordoned off sections of the market, chased out the touts and built themselves rudimentary rooms shielded from the rain by palm fronds. While they continued to live off begging, the oldest among them soon set themselves up as practitioners of the art of tattooing feet and hands. Mariamu went to have her feet tattooed one day. The old woman was half-way into her delicate art when the deep lines of Mariamu's hand made her stop. 'Someone is coming who is going to change your life. I see another man who was once your husband, but don't worry about him. He is waiting with others like himself for the gold king to die so that they can immerse his body in alchemy and try to retrieve the gold from his body.' Without understanding what the old woman had said, Mariamu went home to her lover and pressed her shivering body to him.

Unexpectedly, the caravan merchant did reappear one day! It had been years since he had gone out into the day of the sun, chasing the mirage on the desert. During that time he had been lost in the labyrinths of schemes and speculations, pushed by an unbearable thirst to search for the gold king whose history had tormented him all his life. Now he was back, looking like a bedraggled eagle. He had lost some of his hair and his clothes were covered in the red sand of the desert. Whatever had happened to him, though a matter of conjecture, was tremendous because he seemed less agitated than before and had the look of a convert to some mysterious religion. Of the three horsemen who had originally accompanied him, only one came back, because he had given the other two all the money he had and sent them away. That evening, he barely touched the feast of the prodigal that his other wife had prepared for him, because his stomach had shrunk somewhere in the desert, in that frightening hour of death he had witnessed in the mortified afternoon when the gold king, laid out in ermine and gold in the alabaster solitude of his palace, had decomposed before they could bury him. Next morning, they took him out into the desert for the vultures to feast.

On the day that he returned, N'jai the gold merchant refrained from talking about his journey, except to announce that a man who was going to 'read the life of Kasila in a mirror' was coming to town.

'He will be here this evening, so prepare the best room for him,' he said to his startled wife.

Sulaiman the Nubian, also known as Alusine Dunbar, arrived that evening, accompanied by a young, ragged-looking man with restless but dull eyes. He had been rescued from some Arabs only a week before by the Nubian not so much because he wanted a disciple, but because he could not bear the thought that another person, however different, should be made to suffer in another country at the hands of human pirates.

The Nubian was old but his ageing was of a kind that had escaped the ravages of time and chronological oblivion. Although his body had the leathery patches of an aged land turtle, and his face was lined with the parchments of men of the desert, his eyes were clear and kind like a great marabout's. When he looked at you, he had the power to mesmerise as if he knew all the legends of his and other ages, which he was getting tired of reciting, but who because of the recalcitrant nature of man had not given up the art of divination. He was a long way from the occult wisdom of Abboud of Omdurman, whose writings and those of Hassan of Basra he professed to teach. No sooner was he settled in the big room the gold merchant had turned over to him than he made his first prediction.

'This place has the devil of a name,' he said. 'One day a great disaster will take place here, and many years after that, black people from across the sea, who will be speaking a barbarous language, will come here with their wayward manners.' He told them that although Almoravid diviners had come to Kasila before him and had blessed the place and driven out all the djinns, there was nothing to save it from the plague of those people. But the citizens of Kasila were not to worry, because although the foreigners would control the place for one hundred and seventy-five years, and would establish a most spurious society with laughable manners, and would for a while live under the impression of being in control of their destinies, they would in the end be pushed aside by the 'tumultuous onslaught of the soapstone people'. Two hundred years later they would have become pieces in a museum, he concluded.

The declamation of Sulaiman the Nubian came as a shock to N'jai the caravan merchant who, until his young wife ran off, had never been outsmarted by anyone, not even by the dubious virgins they had sent to his bed who had rubbed chicken blood on the marital quilt, because he had slept for ten months in his mother's belly. Now, in that soporific spell of the Nubian, he found himself responding with the disbelief of the initiate. He tried to maintain his objectivity and calm, to remain faithful to that world in which he had grown, but he was also open to the wisdom of the Nubian sage.

'Men,' said Sulaiman the Nubian, 'have moved centuries from the age of the stone, but they are still centuries away from the age of "the great book of the age" where everything is written and preserved.'

N'jai did not allow him to continue. 'But man has moved a step ahead of the camel. He has learned how to walk with two legs.'

'So you think that because man has learned how to walk upright he has moved a step ahead of the chameleon, that he has mastered the lores of his age?' He raised himself upright, licked a large quantity of honey from a bowl to 'lighten the burden of recollection and interpretation'. 'Try to imagine what modifications the growth of knowledge has made. In the hundred books of the learned sheikh, only the first three alphabets of universal wisdom and teaching are covered, and that to satisfy the vanity of kings; but the remaining twenty-three would require a thousand books more. Such is the road that man has travelled.

'Let me tell you,' he said, producing a looking-glass and a calabash from his bag, 'that without the discovery of the looking-glass which is the same as the water in the calabash, we would still be riding each other's backs instead of camels.'

He was back in Omdurman, among the sultans in the city of the ten domes, where his preaching had first been heard and where he had earned the accolade of the teacher of the age. Now, he spoke of a time when men had to scourge themselves to allow enough blood to flow to warm themselves in the endless cold of time 'before they had discovered fire'. Trapped in the great divide between knowledge and conquest, man made the deduction that in the time alloted him in this universe he could accumulate enough wisdom to grant him a place among the immortals. 'But I have seen men come and go,' easing himself carefully on the mat, relaxing his legs to drive away the cramps, 'and I know about kings and emperors and the little men who ride on fine horses and plunder and take slaves and hostages.'

That evening, listening to the Nubian, the caravan merchant was left in no doubt about the paucity of ideas in his own age. He had journeyed to the other side of the great unknown in search of gold, but here it was without the putrefaction and greed of fancy. Somewhere men were rattling sabres, manifested in the fury with which the glass in the

20

calabash moved, creating fragments of interpretative shadows which in the steaming twilight and humming melancholia of that place presented an unmistakable feeling of lunar vibrations. Thus it was that Sulaiman divined and told his host that the Moors, smarting from their defeat at the hands of the Christian armies that had reconquered Spain in the fourteenth century, were preparing to launch another attack on the peninsula. Much later, when the looking-glass of the Nubian was on the world, he saw across the vast solitude of the desert the dwarf princes of Kanem, whose cavalries were busy sacking the kingdom of the great lake, taking large numbers of prisoners and harems.

'Soon they won't have a cattle shed left to fight over,' he thundered. He could predict the future because he had mixed all the conflicting elements of time in some hourglass of knowledge where natural phenomena became more a matter of his invention than of any logical result of cosmic movement on the earth. In that way plagues, famine, droughts and hurricanes required only a tap on the looking-glass for their dates to be known. 'I can see into the future, and there is confusion at the bottom of the river which one day will respond to a stimulus other than Kasila's, and will experience a terrible urge to go beyond the bounds of human knowledge.'

Trapped in that spell of magic and revelation, the caravan merchant began to show his confusion and doubts. In his wanderings across the desert, he had come across men with pythonic powers but none had the effect of unsettling him, making his memory redundant in the same numbing way as this man whose exegesis had the undisputable stamp of an oracle, so much so that the merchant wanted to know more and to learn how the discovery of the looking-glass presupposed an alteration of the fixed formula of Balla Faseka the Griot.

Sulaiman did not spare the merchant the limits of his knowledge. 'So you need proof of what will happen to kings in the future? I have perceived their torments and their stupefaction at finding themselves pushed aside by their misue of power. In the nineteenth century will be born an emperor with a spurious claim to the lineage of the Queen of Sheba, who will feed meat to his lions, and he will be followed by a chimerical king who will be remembered for his cruelty to children and for cutting off the hands of thieves.'

A pool of perspiration began to form on the head of the merchant. Although he had been cured of his wanderlust and fascination with the gold king of the desert, he still had a profound respect for the pantheon of kings, and he could not imagine a future without them, and so protested; but Sulaiman merely said:

'Men would have lost their fear of gravity and will then attack kings.'

'And their fear of God?' asked the merchant.

'Yes, their fear of God, for God would have grown tired of sitting in judgement. And now, let's be done with them, I have to sleep.'

◇

The news that her husband had returned with a man who could stop rivers, talk to mirrors and unearth genii was, as to be expected, greeted with interest by the runaway Mariamu. She had abandoned her husband when he seemed to be going mad over the miracle of the gold king and not over her body. She was a beautiful woman with the passionate desire and elegant neck of the Mandingo, and eyes that would have done justice to a gazelle. But although nature had endowed her with all those attributes, it seemed to have denied her the one thing she desired most, a child. Throughout her marriage to the merchant, she had had to endure the slight of her mother-in-law who had wondered whether it was a cock that her son had married, and often advised him to get rid of his young wife. It was also rumoured that Mariamu was an androgynous creature, the result of a tryst her mother had kept with a spirit.

In the circumstances, her flight to the bed of a lover at the insistence of an old woman who had given her a potion to 'prepare your womb for new man' was not only a desperate attempt to find happiness somewhere else, but a daughter-in-law's answer to a difficult situation. But after living with her lover, Mariamu's hunger for love still remained unfulfilled, although her fervour for the excesses of lovemaking was not diminished. Time, pain, disappointment and frustration did not alter the elaborate preparations she made to arouse her lover's hunger. Every evening, before welcoming him to her bed she would paint her lips with henna, smear her breasts with honey, put myrrh to burn inside a silver urn and sprinkle lavender water on the bed. Her lover grew accustomed to hear her talk of the child that she had been promised by a dark man, but who was always escaping her charm although, as she put it one evening, 'I thought that it was you.' When he reproached her for believing too much in the incantatory powers of old women, he was met with such violent tears that he swore to go to the ends of the world in search of the herbs to unlock her womb, and to keep on performing his manly duty every night until she became pregnant. They lived together in that manner; he was a passionate man in his own way with a kind heart and delicate hands, who owned a shop where he sold Moroccan slippers and Malian damasks which he bought from the travelling Arabs. His name was Modibo Kamara, and because he had found such an enchanting woman to love him, he was content in his own way and untroubled by even the occasional fear that her husband might come to kill him. He was however much disturbed by her tendency to brood over her lack of success as a woman.

Mariamu for her part feared that although she had been with two men, the consequence of her mother's rumoured relationship with a djinn had condemned her to a state of permanent barrenness. She would have gone on, haunted by that supposition, but for the coming of the Nubian whose magic began to water the desert of her despair.

When she eventually returned to her husband's house, she was shocked at how dishevelled he looked. Rather than being offended at what she had done, she discovered that he had gone beyond the realm of ordinary husbands who took offence at wives who disappeared and returned at their whim, and that he was not anxious to know where she had been. Asked how his own journey across the desert had been, he replied, 'I didn't know what I was missing until I met him.'

Locked inside the circumscribed wonder of Sulaiman's world, seduced by his alchemy, the merchant's desire for women that in the past had made him a master of the concupiscent art had receded into a corner of his heart which was now dead to the temptations of women. He was immune to that world where Mariamu, like other women he had known, was faded and lost in the shadows of past desires. But it was not to his bed that she was returning, and they soon established a mode of co-existence which left each of them preoccupied with their respective obsession.

One week later, protected by an eager and fascinated crowd which, drawn by the mysterious air of the Nubian, was trailing him everywhere, Mariamu watched him perform his magic. Using a small hoe, Sulaiman dug several holes at random in front of some huts, and while the crowd watched he unearthed parrots' feathers, monkey heads and medieval bracelets which the first pirates had traded for gold and salt.

'Men are still burying their heads in sorcery,' he said. Next, he demonstrated by the most unbelievable experiment, unknown to even the most renowned practitioner of the occult wisdom of the Dogons, that animals were subjected to a most startling change of organism; that creation was more in the line of an orderly transformation worked out long ago in the last murmur of a man and woman who had been joined together in a forbidden love. Holding a drake by its neck, he rubbed hot ashes all over its body, spat on its head and threw it to the ground, after which it became dizzy and stretched out like a praying mantis. Then, facing the curious crowd, Sulaiman put a large calabash over its prostrate form. Working his mouth in some intricate pattern which made him more distant and awesome in that remote harmattan morning, he started chanting in an alien language and the spell was felt in the rhythmic movement of the calabash which, as if responding to its own involuntary force, rose from the ground to reveal to the startled crowd an armadillo which in that part of the world had disappeared and been confined to the remotest corner of existence.

Transported to that world of the Nubian, Mariamu forgot that it was cold and that it was November in that lachrymose and trembling crowd. She forgot the frightful balls of thunder in that inclement season of disaster and death because she was aware of a sensation as powerful as the rumbling in the sky, which seemed to have taken hold of her womb, and whose effect she wanted to expel, transfixed in that place by the crustaceous evidence. Suddenly she felt a desire to run to that man and hold his hand, to touch the lips that had induced the miracle, but was stopped in her reverie because at that moment Sulaiman was about to reveal the utter limitlessness of his power.

'It is all in the nature of the divine teaching because life is a two-faced mirror, which can prove that you can kill a snake by whipping its tail with a cassava stalk and that pregnant women are immune to its bite.'

A ravishingly beautiful woman in an advanced state of pregnancy came forward, urged on by the excited crowd. She let herself be led by Sulaiman and did not show the slightest hesitation or fear as the Nubian released a cobra from a basket which began to crawl towards her in that breathless afternoon of suspense and expectant disaster, which however did not come because the snake stopped near the woman, breathing in heavy spasms. Sulaiman handed the woman the stalk of the cassava plant and when she started whipping the serpent on the tail, the bewildered crowd heard the terrifying explosion that accompanied the dislocation of muscles breaking a taut mass of flesh that left the snake paralysed by the protean effect of Sulaiman's powers.

Mariamu visited him later that night. She found him reposed and serene, sitting on an expensive rug in a room lit by a small lamp fuelled by shark's oil. His face was so soft and peaceful in the dark that she had difficulty recognising the man who earlier had mesmerised the snake and made the pregnant woman safe. It was this image of the woman that filled Mariamu's head as she settled down on the floor, determined to seduce him now that she was convinced he had the power to ignite the damp hay that was her womb and release the trapped roots of her infertility. As a young woman listening to the gossip of abandoned wives, she had heard of holy men who though wifeless had nevertheless possessed the trembling bodies of women desirous of the children their husbands had not been able to give them, and considered it a miracle when they became pregnant.

Deep in meditation, Sulaiman did not let himself be distracted by the presence of the woman. He had been in Kasila long enough to know what the men and women desired, how they survived their turbulent history, and it seemed natural to him that burdened with the premonition of the coming of the strange black men and women who would be speaking a barbarous language, the people of the town would want to prepare themselves, and would use every means at their disposal to get near him and experiment with what they perceived as his wisdom. Everything was mirrored in the looking-glass: the octoroon woman who would bring the potato plague, the albino who would marry the most beautiful woman in the world, the man who would be afraid of snakes and would use the skull of his father as a guiding light, and the one-eyed man who would lead a great mission in the atmospheric darkness of the forest tracing the first strangers who would be wiped out because of the potato plague. So the coming of the woman was not unexpected; he had known at what time she would come, and how she would smell of the lingering odour of her failed loves which would accompany her for much of her life, until she finally found a man to love her, because she couldn't live without love.

He raised his head from tracing the hearts of desires on the mirror and looked at Mariamu. Although the idea of flight momentarily possessed her, she did not move from the spot. When she eventually managed to say something it was a stammer that showed the deep level of her anxiety.

'I hope . . . I am . . . not disturbing you,' she said.

'Get rid of your torment; one should not be ashamed of one's heart,' said Sulaiman.

She had rehearsed what she would say to him, how she would tell him about her husband who had neglected her, how her lover had been not much of an improvement, and how she had placed flowers in vain on the graves of her aunt who had three children for men younger than herself, and had had the pleasure of dying in the arms of one of them when she was over seventy, just so that the older woman could reveal the secret of her success with men. But her will deserted her. She lost her tongue in Sulaiman's presence, and began to shake with a terrible lightness until the diviner rescued her from a further loss of certitude.

'Sit down,' he said, 'and tell me about your problems.'

Mariamu sat on the rich carpet and only then did she take a closer look at the room, which in some evanescent way seemed to have come alive with a beautiful animation. Hanging above the door, encased in a golden frame, was a Moroccan painting of that primeval couple, Adam and Eve, in that faraway paradise where they had lost all notion of shame between them. The serpent, coiled on the tree of damnation, was proffering the woman the apple of her revelation; on the wall above the Nubian's head, as if to advance his power, someone had reproduced the galloping phenomenon of turbaned men from a remote and warlike past, mounted on thoroughbred horses and glaring at young nubile women they seemed determined to capture. Mariamu had never been inside this room before. In the years of her marriage to the merchant, he had insisted on his privacy and had kept this room as a place where he could pass away the solitary hours of the harmattan while he waited to go off on another trip into the desert. He had always gone to his women in their own rooms, so that Mariamu was seeing this room through the eyes of the magic man, excited by its newness.

The Nubian rose from his bed but did not advance towards the woman on the floor. He seemed younger in the twilight than when he had mesmerised the snake, but the aura of greatness that hung about him was no less evident than when he was sitting down. He was undecided about what to do with the woman whom he could have sent away, but that was not in the nature of his life because he had learnt that the more he prevented people from hoping for the improbable elements, the more he had to convince them that their fascination with his world precluded a clearer understanding of their own ability and gifts. Moreover, he felt compelled to listen to Mariamu, so he sat down near her, prepared to soothe her.

Mariamu found her tongue; she felt that he could not fail her because in some mysterious way his power and his manhood combined were the reward for the indeterminate wait and hunger she had suffered when the caravan merchant had abandoned her to the caprices of her own body and dreams. In a voice barely audible she was conscious of another woman in her who spoke the calm, sensuous words that were meant to close the great chasm between her and the diviner.

'I want you to give me a child,' she said.

Sulaiman looked into the night, past the artificial wall of his room into the vast imponderable of what the woman had suggested. Although he was a master of incantatory verses and could invoke from the most profound memory images of Hasan of Basra on pride and merit, when it came to the business of pleasing women he had always thought himself a not too passionate man though he lived with the sensation and satisfaction that the power of his clairvoyance presupposed a certain mastery of the pleasures of the flesh. He had never married but his memory was alive with the images of women in veils, perfumed with the spices of Arabia, who had offered their bodies in appreciation for some changes he had brought into their lives: curing their sons of stammer, of polio; getting their husbands back from mistresses who had paid practitioners of the occult to turn them against their wives; or for bringing back the potency to their husbands. In those dimly lit rooms of the desert, in those tents smelling of couscous and goatmilk, protected by all those women who had flocked to him, Sulaiman the Nubian was certain that his seeds had sprung up and become sons and daughters who had been given to unsuspecting husbands happy that their wives had produced 'the spit of my father'. The woman who was now offering to make him a father was upholding the oldest secret of women whereby a child knew its mother but had to be shown its father by its mother.

Mariamu felt the presence of the Nubian beside her, enthralled in his smoke of wild flowers and the incense of the exotic peoples of the Nile. It was to that world of the Moors who had left their seeds in Spain that she was carried that evening in his embrace, when his face did not look old, and his esotericism was dissolved in the hot molten fires of his loins. She gasped in the drowning abyss of her surrender to the Nubian in that cataclysmic moment of their coming together, heightened by its own supposition of conception. She felt that her marriage and the dalliance with her lover were juvenile rehearsals for this outpouring of moans and happiness, expressed by her calcarated fingers that dug deep into the dark mystery of the Nubian's body, as they were watched by the man and woman clad only with the leaves of their innocence in that paradise lost where they had come together and created the first sibling.

The conclusion that Mariamu had been the mistress of the Nubian was not reached until many years later when her daughter began to display the same sense of clairvoyance. It was then easy for people to see that the girl with the fine exquisite features was the daughter of the Nubian who had cast such a spell over the people of Kasila. Meanwhile, a phenomenon as unexpected as it was hard to explain happened. One morning the people of the town woke up and discovered that all the dogs, which had kept the town safe from bandits and frightened away evil spirits that came to milk the goats and cows at night, had died. Because of the mass slaughter, they concluded that it was not the work of man but that of a spirit. She was believed to have twenty suckers, the body of a bitch and the legs of a centipede. An old Tuareg who had given up the habit of wandering all over the desert and was versed in the nature of the existence of djinns was asked to help. He asked for the heart of an eagle which he could nail to the tree where the spirit was believed to live, so that when she came out at night she would see the inside of the most beautiful and handsome bird-man in the world and die of shame. But that precaution taken in the panic following a cruel night did not prevent the inescapable feeling of disaster that was taking hold of the place. Because soon after the dogs had been buried, the streets swept and people had begun to forget about the spirit of the vengeful mosquito, the hens got off their eggs and wandered off into the river where they drowned in their thousands. No sooner were the people over this new tragedy than the monkeys, on which they relied for early warnings about invasions and which used to dance on their heads for sweets, stopped coming and moved to a part of the forest unknown to man. As no one could remember such a strange aberration on the part of the world they turned to Sulaiman.

'Let's hope we will be alive to hear what the mirror says,' he said.

That night, when he talked to the mirror, he was met with such a shattering reply that the confusing evidence of the omen of the previous week, and of the disaster that he himself had foreseen, shocked him. He read in the mirror that the exactness of the date of the storm of evil had escaped him in the first instance of his divination. Now, however, it was clear in the hardness of the face of the earth, in the smell of things that were getting ready to die, in the laughter of women galloping on winged horses at night, that the hand of destruction was upon the town. It was then that Sulaiman remembered that it was July, but that it had not rained that year. Suddenly he understood that such an unnatural phenomenon in the planet was a prelude to the swansong of a glorious period in the history of that part of the world, which had been foreseen before his time by the magician whom Sogolon the Buffalo-Woman had consulted in that fabulous land of the Dogons, to teach her seven-year-

28

old son how to walk. He delved deeper into the fires of the mirror and recognised the face of Sundiata Keita the legendary King of Mali who was about to unleash a storm because Kasila had been enjoying a period of laxity before Sulaiman arrived, and he concluded that only those who remembered the story of how Sundiata's father had finally overpowered the Buffalo-Woman stood a chance of escaping the storm.

A deluge of hurricane proportions unleashed itself on the town, tore the bamboo roofs off the beams, unhinged the windows, blasted the market off the face of the earth and felled the giant trees, some of which crashed on the fine stallions of the men who had travelled to the ends of the world to purchase them. Crouching under the beds of their now useless houses, cringing with fear, the people of the town heard the shrill voice of the hurricane. They saw the heads of their now bloated cattle as if in supplication, borne by the muddy river of penance. Some were inconsolable in their grief not so much because they feared death or the loss of their properties, but because they had been in strange beds, trapped without ablution, so their death was swift and they woke up on the other side of the globe sucking their thumbs, thirsting for water, even though they had died of the fury of water. If they had hoped for salvation they searched in their hearts for words to turn back the repugnance of their own making but they had lost the innocence of spirit and the magic formulae of words.

Then, as unexpected as the omen had been, the rain stopped. Sulaiman, who had spent the time of the hurricane in a state of relaxation, was sitting in a position of meditation when he heard the first sounds of the birds of the forest that had escaped death. The sun was out, and he saw that many people had survived the disaster, though some of them came out of their ruined houses slowly, trembling like thieves who had been caught stealing the stones in the belly of the crocodile that told how old the world was, after the terrible period of the planet's movement.

'It's as it was revealed to me; Kasila has eaten itself,' Sulaiman said.

It had not only eaten itself, but, emerging from the chaos of the terrible rage and the quivering destruction felt in their souls and their bodies nourished by that once great town, the oldest men and women cried with the discovery that the spell of bad omen which henceforth they would refer to as 'the season of the shark' had stripped them of everything. They picked their way through the terrifying and lacerating evidence using pickaxes and shovels, and saw with the aluminium horror of their eyes the corpses in the streets: there were corpses of men, of women, of children, of dogs, of camels, of goats, of cattle, of horses, of cats, of dogs, in such a high state of putridity that the river which had grown to three times its size stank for six months.

Because his apotheosis had begun, Sulaiman who had predicted the disaster became more apocalyptical and lucid. He revealed through the trembling looking-glass at what time the scourge of the wandering Arabs would come, with their coral beads and Babylonian salt with which they would hypnotise the town and transmogrify the people. He announced with the incisiveness of a sabre that the town would grow lethargic again, and waking up would find the Arabs from the Shouf mountains, with their smell of garlic, their belch of onions, their parasitic breeding and pugnacious competitiveness, in charge of the town; because despite the sanctimonious public display of piety by the black people who would come from America before the Arabs, despite the regulated formula of their baptism in the name of the father, the son and the Holy Ghost, as God was his witness, despite the farcical re-enactment of the beating of Judas Iscariot on Good Friday, those bastards would hate one other in their parsimonious hearts; what would you expect of the children of those men who would never never lose their tricks of a monkey with black hands, and would be prepared to sell all they had built because they were used to selling and being sold for a hundred pieces of silver, for a yard of cloth, for gunpowder, for gold and – worse – for liquor? People who would spit on their God, if you would pardon his language, so much so that it was enough to make a holy man like himself puke.

He could not bear the look of moroseness and desperation he saw on the faces of those people after the storm, and Sulaiman decided to cure them of their present unhappiness by the simple formula of taking them upriver and washing away their putrefaction. It was an old ritual, going back to when men were first learning how to shape tools on the banks of the Nile, and wanted to thank their gods. From there, they emerged light as newt, and concluded that Sulaiman's apotheosis had transcended the occult possibility of his age. That night they did not bother to turn the faces of their mirrors to the wall, freed of their anxiety.

Sulaiman was now an old man who seldom left his room, and what little he needed was brought to him by his young acolyte Ahmed the Elephant who, in the more conducive atmosphere of Kasila before the storm, had lost his tense look of a caged animal that life among the Arabs of Zanzibar had stamped on him. Weighed down by the immensity of his knowledge, fearing that he had carried the burdens of that power too long with the attendant danger that he would pass into the great divide without transferring some of it, Sulaiman summoned Ahmed to his room one night, told the people not to disturb him, and set about instructing the young man in the wisdom of the teachers of the age.

◇

Mariamu introduced her daughter to the extended family in the compound seven days after she was born. In keeping with tradition, she did not leave her room until a diviner came to see her, washed the child in a bath of the juice of lemon and avocado leaves, put some goat fat on the navel and rubbed a powder of burnt ore and the beak of an owl on her brow to keep witches away from her. The baby was golden in colour, and had long limbs and a mole over her right eye. Her head seemed unusually small though that was overshadowed by the evidence that she would have a rich and healthy crop of hair and that she already had eyes that were glassy and magnetic. She did not cry and, when left for a long time, she tried to put the big toe of her right foot in her mouth, which the diviner put down to her amazing power of strength and domination in the future.

'You will have to watch this one,' said the diviner. 'She will have the power of three women.'

By some alchemy which was possible only between married people who had lived together for such a long time that they had ceased to be surprised by one another, and did not bother with any transgression that one of them might commit, Mariamu had secured the complicity of her husband in trying to pass her daughter, whose name was Fatmatta, as his own. Since that day when he had come under the spell of the Nubian, the gold merchant had retreated into a solitary and mystifying world. He forbade all contacts with him, lived on goatmilk and chanted incantations at all hours of the day, which gave him the aspect of one possessed by a djinn. Thus he was immune to the tempestuous jealousy of wounded husbands, and placed little store on the vanity of ownership which in his previous boisterous life included the hereditary ownership of women by men. To go along with his philandering wife, since it was inconceivable for her to have a child by another man while still living under his roof, he considered accepting the child as his a little price to pay for the preservation of his mind and his dedication to seances.

But greater than that, he was generous because he was an important man tied to a great heritage, and on the morning when Mariamu brought her child out, she made him put on his ceremonial gown, his golden Moroccan slippers, his sword of a warrior of the desert and his skullcap. She saw to it that his wallet was stuffed full, and she made him carry the child in his arms of a forgiving husband, and smile down at it with his eyes of a proud father, and announce to the crowd, 'She is a true flower, and anyone thinking of marrying her should start saving up to buy a hundred cows!'

Taking her child from her husband's hands, Mariamu acknowledged the greetings of the other women in the compound. They shared a common destiny: the same cycle of child-bearing, of waiting for husbands who went away for long periods, and of being discarded after they passed childbearing usefulness. They knew about Mariamu's long wait to have a child, of her tryst with her lover, though they then barely suspected her affair with the Nubian. Summoned by the confirmation that God had answered her prayers, they wanted to celebrate with her. Someone began to toss gold coins at Mariamu, and when the kora player struck a chord on his harp Mariamu handed the child back to her husband and began to dance. She swayed to the music of distant lineage, of dark swamps and virgin weddings, of incantations to the divine power, voiced by the cacophony of drums which rose above the harp and the harmony of voices praising the father of the child. N'jai let himself be carried away by the tremulous assertion of that dance which protected himself and Mariamu from scandal in the synchronised instance of hands clapping, of feet stamping in that celebration heightened by the exuberant rhythm of Mariamu's breasts, bouncing in the pavane of woman and spirit.

◇

Soon after she cut her first tooth, borne by the wind of her imagination Fatmatta began to talk. She pointed to a conclave with those eyes which were not the eyes of an infant, where women were sucking the blood of children. She talked about strange men, humped, deprived and urgent, 'who did it to donkeys' so that they could become rich. Saying 'they are everywhere', she pointed one evening to a vague object when Mariamu was shelling peanuts, attesting to her powers which had been fuelled by the prodigious tributaries of the Nile, from where the art of Sulaiman had come. Confused by the undecipherable object of her daughter's talk, Mariamu felt she had given birth to a witch because that night she saw a scorpion with the predatory claws of ill-omen and the colour of golden cobra in her daughter's eyes. Terrified, she sent for Rasheeda, the old woman who had advised her to dump her husband and seek happiness in another man's bed. She was a small woman with the ancestral wisdom of the Dogons of Mali, who had come to Kasila fleeing from a plague of locusts in the desert; first making a living by sharpening teeth and restoring the sanity of men who had been associating with female devils. She had herself had nine children; seven shepherds of the desert whom she had not seen in years, and two girls who had gone into the harem of a wealthy cattle owner. She was convinced that each woman was born with her own genie, and bore a relationship to him that was circumscribed by the sexual happiness she gave him in return for the eternal fires of her youth. Thus, in that scheme of things, she feared that Fatmatta's talk was the sign of her precociousness, which meant that 'she had eyes' which could see into other people's lives before they realised it.

'Things could happen with that girl around,' she said. 'It was like that with one of my daughters until I had her eyes darkened.'

Using the same skills with which she had restored the manhood and sanity of those men who had been possessed by she-devils, Rasheeda set about trying to cure Fatmatta of her early relationship with her genie. First, she made three small marks on each side of her cheeks, and she was surprised that the child did not move; then she rubbed a black ointment made of honey, melon seeds and goat fat mixed with the crushed tongue of an iguana, passed some smoking guava leaves over the child's head and predicted that in a week Fatmatta would stop seeing objects. After the period was over, she not only continued to see objects but she went on to an even higher form of magic where she could open doors merely by looking at them, and change the colour of water by touching it, so that no one was left with any doubt that fate had played a terrible joke on Mariamu by giving her a child in whose body the mysterious forces had been lodged; that her clairvoyance was merely the sign that she was a child apart from others, with an inviolate protection in the whirlpool of events then and in the future where she was immune to the powers and evil of humans.

Over the years, Mariamu felt uneasy about her daughter, especially as she was unable to reach her, to be a mother as she had dreamed. When she had discovered that she was pregnant, she had been overwhelmed not so much by the discovery that barrenness was a fate that she had overcome, but with the sensations that made her past sufferings understandable and the future bright. She had dreamed of a child in a nursery surrounded by the soft colours of evergreen plants, of

evenings when they would be serenaded by the violins of the trouba-
dours who knew the genealogy of the town. When the child was a baby
she would come and pick her up, silently, when she was asleep, just to be
sure she was alive and thirsting for her breasts. The purity of her milk
gave life to what she and Sulaiman had created. She wanted joy but it
was not to be. If she had any happiness, it was of the memory of
Sulaiman who had gone away and did not come back until a month
before he disappeared for ever. Many times she would imagine him in
another form, coming back, riding a large black horse with a golden
bridle, galloping across a vast universe of thirsty desert, hurrying to get
to her so that she could once again be swept up in his embrace. But the
reality of her life, the loneliness of her world was one that she could share
with no one, and once the disappointment of having a daughter who did
not belong to her had sunk in, Mariamu found herself lost in a sphere of
anxiety and nightmares, once again hungry for love and understanding.

One day, believing that she had seen the unmistakable signs of
mockery and contempt in Fatmatta's eyes, she was seized by a terrible
urge to strangle her. In a voice that did not sound like hers, Mariamu
raised the drama of her unhappiness to the pathetic level of a
competition between two women, and lashed out at her daughter.

'Get away, you witch,' she said. 'We are not concubines in the same
harem.'

They went their separate ways, and no one remembered who started
the wicked rumour that Mariamu and her daughter were not speaking
to one another, or that the younger woman had threatened to expose her
mother. At sixteen she was still bathing naked like a child in the river,
causing everyone to wonder whether she was a hermaphrodite because
they had never seen the like of it before. She could talk to birds and
monkeys, put her cat to sleep by simply looking at it, and she had the
clear and melodic voice of a nightingale which rang out through the
house, like the first signs of the return of the orioles after the dampness
and mildew of the rainy season. Mariamu gave up waiting for Sulaiman
but she did not lose her hunger for love, though the idea of going back to
her husband's bed after so many years was something that she could not
contemplate. In the hermetic world in which N'jai had sealed himself,
dabbling in seances, he did not give the impression of wanting a woman,
and the estrangement between the two women seemed to go unnoticed
by him. It was not until the man with the face of another arrived,
frightening the flamboyant pheasants, to marry Fatmatta that the gold

merchant relaxed his austere composure to join in the celebration that went on for a week.

◇

On a day no one was to forget for a long time, Sulaiman the Nubian appeared again. His jawbones had slackened, his teeth had yellowed and he ate only what little he felt was needed to keep him awake during the long solitary nights of meditation and occult practice. The first indication that an epoch was coming to an end and that the lucidity of that sage who had dazzled the town with his wisdom and power would soon become a thing of the past came one night when the owls began to hoot in such a manner that they had to be chased away by the dogs, and because of the hysteria of the creatures in all the streams in the town. Something seemed to have happened to those bottomless creations where the Nubian had gone so many times to bring the wonders of the seven worlds to the once sleepy town. If he was dying, the nature of that death was in keeping with the sensation with which the people recalled how he had come to their town, a strange man offering to show them the wonders of the Sultan of Omdurman. Not surprisingly, on that last day he was alone, and after he had arranged the treatise on learning which Ahmed the Elephant would find after Sulaiman had gone, the sage drew a circle on his mirror, which he had placed between his legs, squatting on a mat. He commanded the mirror to show him the pages of the learned fakirs, the chronicles of the seeker by Mahmud Kati of Timbuctoo; that city where the progression towards the future had been stopped since the time of Sundiata Keita who was buried in a spot from where he came out every night to embrace his people, because he knew their names even though he had died before the time of memory. Many years earlier, the good teachers of science and philosophy had kept his counsel every night before they went out to teach among the beggars who sat by the great stone wall of the gate that led to the forbidden city. Now, because the time of his disappearance was near, Sulaiman looked into the river which was reflected in the mirror. He was startled at what he saw.

'The world is a turtle head,' he exclaimed.

He saw the proverbial golden comb of a mermaid, which was not a comb but the tongue of a scorpion licking the head of a beautiful young woman at the bottom of that dark abyss of knowing. Then he could not help hearing the strange, beautiful woman talking about one surreptitious night that Sulaiman had forgotton about. It was thus he understood that in the kingdom of God, the fate of all men had been written many years ago before his time, by the trembling hand whose hiero-glyph did not conform to any arbitrary division of present and past, of man and woman. He realised that the enchanting music to which the woman had begun to sway was not the melody of the bowharps that the villagers had played for him when he had come to that part of the world, but the clash of cowries which was the music of a sorceress of indeterminate age and inconceivable beauty. He shook with the realisation that the half-woman was his own daughter whose face he had banished from memory as if her coming were a thing of no consequence, thus creating a new visage which was greater than the problem of dying from so much wisdom which was his fate. To overcome his torment, he looked at the river of his mirror one more time, with the tell-tale signs of his dwindling wisdom and his eyes of former times as when he had seen the great destruction of the stones of Zimbabwe, before going into Zanzibar where the chimerical Arabs were hawking incense, parrots, cloves and that melancholy boy whom he had bought so he could instruct him in the obscurities of Iskander of Balkh, and how to recognise the leader of the epoch. In that depth containing the codex of all eternities, Sulaiman saw the world as it was before the flood.

'While I have been wasting my time here,' he exclaimed, 'knowledge has progressed a thousand years in other parts of the world.'

He discovered that although it was easy to change swans into snakes, cure men of impotence and epilepsy and women of barrenness, he had not mastered the elemental laws of the transference of wisdom, which had its own bizarre logic and consequentiality, and thus did not conform to any laid-down interpretations. That was why the woman in the river who was a mermaid, who was his own daughter from that period of his interlude and woman confusion had a gold ring on her middle left finger while he still had his own. That was why the flames of her illumination found their way to the surface which was a bridge of pines between their separate powers. A great ball of fire surrounded her as she combed her hair of dense and unruly curls which were brilliant in that luminous night so that her aura seemed magnified in the threshing crinoids of the wind, which whistled like the beginnings of a miracle between the palm trees. It was then that Sulaiman had a transparent vision.

He trembled with the realisation that Fatmatta who had the look of a scorpion had reached a greater stage of clairvoyance than he, because his was a race destined to show its power in the farflung corners of the world. And because Fatmatta would leave one day, but would return through the labyrinths of the centuries-old abracadabra that would protect her against the putrefaction of human exploitation, the image of a possessed woman that she had in that river was merely a prelude to the creation of her legend, which not even Sulaiman could avert. For that reason he had to give way to her, to her terrible odyssey which told more of her protean sorcery than of the consanguinity that bound them together, but which at that moment was threatening to drown him in the deepest waters of oblivion.

Slowly he began to lose consciousness and was barely able to hear the heavy thumping of feet approaching his house. The thunder of those feet turned the thistle into trampled grass, and shook the ground like an earthquake. He dreamed that he was leaving Omdurman for the first time and that the beautiful Nubian girl whom he had been offered as a young man, and whose breasts were straining against her dress like a bitch on a leash trying to break loose, cried that morning as he followed the course of the Nile down to Rwanda where, in the service of the King of the Watutsis, he first discovered that he had the power to make men impotent by touching their gowns. Not wanting the sedentary life of a palace magician, he had wandered among the soporific Nilotic people who drank blood and ate raw meat; among the reptile smugglers who could mimic the sound of frogs to bait their prey; the elephant tusk thieves; the smokers of opium in the Arab cafés of Mombasa; the fire-eating women of Karamojo who waited for the rain in the treacherous and windswept desert, until he had met the peripatetic gold merchant who had induced him to come to the mosquito-infested corner of the world, where Divine Providence had given him that daughter with the eyes of the scorpion. After living in Malagueta for a while, they had taken to calling him Alusine the Magician of the House of Dunbar, the water spirit. Now, as he lay in that semi-consciousness in a world whose images were fast disappearing from his memory, borne down by the weight of his knowledge, Sulaiman did not hear the feet that were almost near his house nor the shrieks and grunts that accompanied them. A great herd of baboons emerged from the trees and, as if prearranged, made for the house. They demolished it in no time, going through the rooms, pissing on the expensive Moroccan rug where Mariamu had conceived Fatmatta. They tore the paintings off the walls, banishing for the second time the primeval Adam and Eve so that their solitude was dense and inexplicable. From some vague outline of a strange country that he could barely recognise, Sulaiman the Nubian saw them come into his room; he smiled like a man who had been expecting them, and he did not resist as they picked him up like a bag of dates. Making the loudest noise possible, they went through the debris of baked mud and thatched palms with the last Moor who was to wander in that part of the world with his tales of the teachers of the age, out of that chaos where he had prolonged the lugubrious time of existence following his ennobling epoch. It was a brilliant night as they went through the haughty and giant trees of another age, past the stupefied gaze of the creatures of the night, after which they started to sing. A great flash of lightning ripped through the sky as they disappeared with the limpid form of the old man into a nameless terrifying darkness under a torrent of rain that began to cool the fire which blazed from the thunder of their feet.

◇

The unfortunate incident that would change Ahmed the Elephant's life happened five years later. At that time he was a young man of twenty, with a forehead that hinted at the keen intelligence of an eagle. He was quiet and withdrawn, unlike the Nubian, the result of the rupture that had happened in his heart after his kidnapping by the Arabs. When he discovered the mess left behind in Sulaiman's house, he assumed that a great disaster had happened or that Sulaiman had smashed the place himself during a misreading of the uncertainties of the mirror. He felt a deep and wayward emptiness which was unlike the monkish devotion that he had given to the study of the teachers, to the elaborate admonitions to the disciples, and to the protection of the master's secrets. Being a young man who saw in everything that happened the possibility of good coming out of all adversities, he did not let the state of ennui continue for long. He had put behind him the memory of the two men who had come calling in his village in Pemba, and he was determined to fill the emptiness that Sulaiman's disappearance had created with something purposeful. His long immersion in the teaching of the sage, the determination to go beyond what he had been allowed to discern by the Nubian, moved him away from any prolonged anxiety.

But his paramount interest lay in Fatmatta. He had watched her grow during the fortuitous years of his orphanage, marvelled at her ability to talk to birds, though her penchant for worms left him breathless and uneasy. Expressing himself did not come easily to him and he had scrupulously avoided all contacts with her, convinced that his status as a sorcerer's apprentice made him low in the eyes of Mariamu who seemed to have lost her appetite for everything since Sulaiman left and was always arguing with her daughter. He tried to devise a way of getting to know Fatmatta, having overcome his shyness; he thought of various ways of approaching her: going up to her while she was on her way to the river for her evening's bath, helping her to pick the wild mushrooms that she seemed fond of or simply kidnapping her and running from that place. That seemed such a mad proposition that he put it out of his mind and tried to come up with something more acceptable for what he was sure was the beginning of a love he felt for the haughty woman.

'Don't confuse the legend of the past with love, and above all watch out for a handsome stranger with the face of a pheasant,' Sulaiman had warned him many years earlier. Ahmed had not thought about that injunction before now. Life was not a cobweb for him, with its struggle to break out, look for fresh air to breathe. If he had to become a man he had to start now, not when he was sixty-four. He waited for Fatmatta one evening on her way to the river.

'May I come with you?' he began.

She walked on. If she had heard him she showed no response.

'You shouldn't be going out so late alone,' he continued. 'What will people say – the gold merchant's daughter is out every evening?'

'What I do is none of your business, and for that matter is no one else's,' she snapped back.

'I was only trying to be friendly . . . well, to get to know you better, because after Sulaiman left you have become remote, and I too am lost because he was like a father to me.'

At the mention of Sulaiman's name Fatmatta's eyes became liquid. She was vulnerable where that name was concerned because although her mother kept her true origin hidden from her, she had not been deaf to the repeated assertions by those around her that she was the daughter of the Nubian. For that reason she secretly admired her mother for having the good sense to leave a doddering husband for the bed of the man whose blood made Fatmatta very proud and arrogant. Not wanting Ahmed the Elephant to see her tears, she turned her face away and pretended she had not heard what he had said.

Ahmed the Elephant was inspired. Though he was not privy to the intimate details about the link between Fatmatta and Sulaiman, he had sometimes guessed at it. Fate had not been good to him. He had lost a sister and a brother when he was captured but he had a good heart and he was one of those people who placed a high premium on love. He took his chance.

'If you want me to, I can accompany you every evening when you are going to the river, and wait for you at a distance.'

'It's all right, just don't expect me to be good company.'

Given the chance to walk beside her, he did not hesitate and did not let her earlier whimsical behaviour put him off from his objective which was to win Fatmatta away from her obsession with herself. Moreover, he reasoned that now that he was an orphan, he needed the support of someone receptive to his love, to ensure his happiness in Kasila. He had no clear idea of what he was going to do, whether he would stay, but he felt content to live for the moment, to be soaked in his fascination with Fatmatta. They walked in silence for a while, and although it was beginning to get dark, the sun was still bearing down on the land. Because it was March, the orchards were full of mangoes and oranges while the giant branches with their green and yellow leaves offered some shade from the heat. Somewhere in the distance, the buzzing of flies could be heard as they feasted on mangoes. Fatmatta sat under one of the trees but it was getting late. In that shadow of slowly descending evening, her neatly coiffeured hair ornamented with blue and white beads gave her the aspect of a woman much older and wiser than she really was. Her steely exterior held her emotions in check. As he searched for a way to get to her, Ahmed could not help noticing that her skin had the golden-brown colour of the peoples of the desert, that her hands were much longer and thinner than those of the people of Kasila, that in some peculiar way she was holding her head so that he could tell from her profile that she was showing her lineage to see what kind of effect that would have on him.

He reacted foolishly. 'Fatmatta,' he whispered. 'You are Sulaiman's daughter. I want to marry you!'

She rejected him outright. 'Poor Ahmed, you are too serious to be a lover. Why don't you become a celibate like my father – I mean N'jai?'

He did not sleep that night. For the first time since Sulaiman the Nubian had brought him to that part of the world, he wanted to run away. Not so much from the place but from the disaster that he had become in the mocking eyes of the woman. He felt like a drowner reaching out to someone to save him from the relentless waves of desire, but he saw in her eyes that she was going to let him drown, because she herself was trying to reach a shore as treacherous as his. Suddenly, he realised that his suffering was made unbearable by the boils that were beginning to break out in his armpits, while the serpent of his discontent threatened to drown him in the deepest desolation. Shaken by the labyrinthine dislocation of his own confidence, shocked at the swift and brutal way Fatmatta had rejected him, Ahmed sought the only consolation he could think of, the face of Sulaiman. The disciple had not embarked upon the divine process and the manipulation of the magical looking-glass since the Nubian disappeared, because he wanted to avoid all comparisons with the sage. He had limited himself to the elliptical interpretation of some phenomena and premonitions which usually left those who came to see him more confused and bewildered than before they had sought his help. Now, however, he had a great desire to touch the mirror and to hear the rattle of the glass beads at the bottom of the river where Sulaiman used to see the other side of the world. He took the protective covering off the mirror, dusted it and placed it in such a position that the sun's rays were reflected on it. Then he drew a few lines which looked like stalactites on it with a chalk, rapped his knuckles a few times on the mirror, recited a verse and waited.

Sulaiman the Nubian came through the door of the mirror from another country where, from his looks, it seemed he had been living a life of lavish indulgence. He sat in a large cane chair that had a high back shaped like the wings of an eagle, and he wore a gown of rich brocade and gold rings on all ten fingers. To complete his expensive look, he had put on shoes that were made from leopard skin and his feet rested on a tamed civet cat with a gold chain around its neck, its skin of luminous black, yellow and white contrasting with the Afghan rug that covered the floor. Sulaiman looked like a man who had been on a long holiday. He had the unmistakable air of contentment, of a man whose calm and happiness could not be shaken by even an earthquake, and Ahmed was not surprised that just as in former times when Sulaiman had enthralled Mariamu, the Nubian now had two women with the dazzling beauty of Somali shepherdesses standing on either side behind him and smiling down at him.

At first, Sulaiman did not recognise his former disciple. He had gone away for a long time, oblivious to the problems of the people of his former life, living in the tranquil world of the primates. While he was there, he had shed sixty years from his age, and now had the appearance of a youth of twenty though he had not lost the immense dignity and authority of his person. That was why he did not recognise the man who had summoned him until he saw the same forlornness of the boy whom he had rescued from the Arabs in Zanzibar.

Sulaiman expressed shocked surprise at his dishevelled state.

'What happened to you, my son?' he asked. 'You look like scorched earth!'

'It's the woman. She has driven me mad.'

Sulaiman laughed a bittersweet laugh. He had not forgotten how he had been confused by the protean power of Fatmatta's eyes. He felt a deep feeling of fatherly comradeship for the young man who had fallen under her spell, especially as he had predicted it, ever since that time when Ahmed, unknown to himself, had begun to talk in his sleep of going back to Zanzibar, taking Fatmatta as his wife.

'She is a child of the sea, an albatross that has to fly and must not be caged,' the Nubian said.

Ahmed had not thought of her as a bird; with her fiery eyes, her smooth skin, her provocative mouth and her ability to paralyse him in the instant of his looking at her, he had thought of her as a leopardess, cunning and waiting for a man that she could possess, but also wanting to be possessed by the man. And it was that power of possession that he sought from Sulaiman.

'You must tell me what to do, because I feel I am sinking into the bottom of a great pit.'

'Put some lime under your pillow when you sleep at night, and you will forget her. And consult the divine teaching of Nasrudin which you haven't looked at since I left,' the Nubian replied.

Sulaiman went back to his world amidst a cloud of smoke, engulfed by the mirror which began to shake in Ahmed's hands. The sensation was so powerful that he almost dropped it. Stunned, he felt that the chairs in the room were moving, and that the windows of the house were suddenly open although he had closed them before his consultation with the magical mirror. Suddenly, he saw the figure of a woman go by. She was of an indiscriminate colour and her face was long and angular but beautiful. He felt pinioned by a set of invincible hands so that he was unable to move as the eyes of the woman were riveted on him, putting him to sleep still holding the precious mirror, with the bitter taste of aloes in his mouth. It was Fatmatta. She had witnessed the second coming of her father. That night, Ahmed dreamed that Fatmatta had put on wings and was carrying him in her beak like a chick, but he had been dropped suddenly in the middle of a desert where only waifs live because a great storm was blowing, and that he had walked back for days before finding his house. He woke up, aghast at his weightlessness and at the idea that in his dream he had been reminded of the fragility of his own body and of the uncertainty of his journey in life. Taking Sulaiman's advice, he dusted up the treatise of learning that the old sage had left behind and, in the legend of Nasrudin, he came to a page where he read about the story of the unfortunate lover who was like himself, written as if by himself. He recalled that he was like the legendary orphan of the plains, left there to tend cattle and that one day the Sultan's daughter passed by. Seeing how handsome he was, she took him into her service as a page. A girl who was also in the service of the princess, and whom he had rejected, paid a travelling fakir to circumcise him, but she asked the diviner to make him impotent for years. Later, aroused by the dusty beauty of the young man, the princess, feeling that he could please her better than the doddering neighbouring king she had been forced to marry, summoned him to her secret chamber, where he had disgraced himself in front of the naked princess. That was why he had been sold to the Arabs of Zanzibar, that was why although his manhood later came back, he could not possess a woman because Fatmatta was a reincarnation of the young girl he had rejected.

While he had been reading, Ahmed had not been aware of the terrible heat, or that the buzz of flies, the symphony of the cicadas, the persistence of the mosquitoes or the incense in the urn had made his room uncomfortable. He felt a little hot in his groin, and suddenly and miraculously his testicles began to expand and sway, having a noticeable effect on his penis. Like that, he reached a high state of saturation, and realised that what he longed for bore no relation to the apocalyptical meaning of the writings of that book, but was to be found in the compulsive sirens which rang every night in his head and whose origins he had to find. He got up from the chair and went outside, unsure of where he was going. A dog barked in the night and the strong and penetrating smell of tamarind pap caught his nostrils. He walked towards the source of that smell like a sleepwalker. Something greater than desire took hold of him, laundered his brain, and as he hastened his steps he heard the clear and hauntingly beautiful voice of a woman singing. Because it was dark and quiet, the voice filled the night with the deep riches of a praise singer's, melodic and divine. He walked on, more like a man propelled than like one possessed. His steps did not conform to any set pattern and he was not conscious of the fact that it was towards an area of the village forbidden to men at that time of the year that he was heading to, urged on by the swelling in his groin. He pushed on and as he drew near to the source of the voice he did not see the waterline of the river which was the source of his entrapment. Instead, he had the unusual feeling of having discovered the magic that would unlock the prison of his manhood by listening to that voice, because he had been waiting for it to summon him to this rendezvous.

He felt he was losing time so he began to run. Because he had blocked out all notion of the existence of other beings and the consequentiality of what could happen to him because of where he was, Ahmed did not hear the other voices singing in a chorus. He headed straight for the river where he saw an unexpected image. Fatmatta stood on the edge of the river. She was naked except for the string of beads she wore round her waist. Her back was turned to Ahmed but in that twilight of white and yellow flowers, he saw a body of rich brown golden nudity; he saw the delicate and provocative curves of the hips and the elegant and beautiful hands of a desirable woman with her smell of an aroused animal, of fermented ginger. In that rush of desire he felt the rise and the blood-pounding power of his manhood, which had lain dormant like a volcano, against the metallic clamour of his loins. He went forward, freed of all trepidation, but his movements were fast and careless so that Fatmatta turned but she did not protect herself, and Ahmed saw the deep and treacherous valley of a temptress, straddled by shimmering breasts with their dark berry nipples. He had almost reached the woman when he saw in her eyes the scorpion, with the look which he did not know would produce a menacing rupture of the embryonic tissues of his youth. Suddenly, the hot and urgent fever pitch of his blood began to dry and he felt the solid evidence of his manhood turning into flabby flesh, drained of its liquid, like an udder. An immense pain gripped him, and he experienced the sharp needles of thorns growing in his heart, and he did not see the smile of a killjoy on Fatmatta's face as he collapsed, jettisoned by his quivering desire, into the slough of degradation.

◇

Antonio the Mulatto was just opening his shop when the black woman with the lustrous eyes of a gazelle walked in. The shop was a mud-brick structure with a cast-iron door which had come from a disused mine, built on a plot of land near where the sea was noisy and treacherous. By assiduously working day and night, he had built a prosperous trade in rum, tobacco, smoked herrings, cod fish and cheap Indian cotton which he bought wholesale from the pirates who frequented the Man-of-Wharf Bay on the unruly and rocky coast. Behind the shop was an old stone house of red laterite, thatched with palm fronds and protected by a fence of liana and guava stalks. No one knew where he had come from but he had about him the warm and inviting air of trust, the piercing concentration of an honest man, and was allowed to stay among the people of the town. He was dark and quiet, solitary like a crab and about forty. On the bridge of a slightly crooked nose he had a small mark which he said was the result of having been bitten by a shark while swimming in Portugal, and when he walked there was a pronounced limp which, with the touch of grey on his temple, made him a rather distinguished figure. When he came to the village he had left behind him the byways of the past: the veneration of the Black Virgin of Saragossa; the women in perennial black; the hot dusty roads where the men walked beside their donkeys laden with fruits; the village taverns in the small Portuguese town where his drunken father had returned to die, bitter from his experience in Lourenco Marques where he had failed as a coffee planter, bringing up the son whom he had forced upon the beautiful Mozambican woman who had died in childbirth.

It was to escape the mindless desolation and psychological post-mortem by his father that had made Antonio come to that part of the world; to escape his childhood in a house without laughter, where the clocks had been stopped, and where strange women in black came sometimes to see his father. They would talk about the Blessed Virgin, and how his wife, although an African woman, was being cared for by angels. When they could not arouse Antonio's father's interest in things other than the spiritual, they would sometimes look at Antonio with desire, touch him where it tickled when his father was drunk, and left the boy trembling, trying to understand the sensation those fingers created in him. Such abstract reference to religious subjects and symbols was to fill his life for most of his boyhood, even up to when he became a young man and had to watch his father become a mere shadow of the planter that he had been in Africa. After a while, he felt he could no longer understand the conflicting transcendental paganism and catholicism of his people, and went to bars and taverns to listen to the sailors talk about the enchanting and mysterious islands of Seychelles and Fernando Po; about endless Saturdays of merriment when they could forget the perils of the sea, the priests who admonished them for staying away too long and coming back to their wives with strange habits and licentiousness picked up from 'heathen' women whose only business was to corrupt good Christian men.

Life had not been good to him in Portugal where he had maintained a form of celibacy, not because women were unavailable but because he felt that trying to persuade them to take off their perennial black dresses was more than he could endure. At first, he sought solace in the novels of Miguel de Cervantes, in the ascetic writings of Eusebius Hieronymus and the ornate poetry of Luis Gongora y Argote. But his mind was not in those books, and because he was also terrified of the increasing violence

45

of his father, who when he got drunk would smash all the relics of the saints that the black-robed women brought to the house, Antonio escaped one night, joined a fishing expedition and came to the coast of Kasila.

He watched the woman come in, uncertain why she was coming so early in the morning. Among the women of the region, he had sometimes found secret, delicate passages of pleasure, taking considerable precaution to be discreet. He would lure those who came to his shop to buy, to his room where, in exchange for their bodies that smelled of molasses, he offered them the delicacies of the stomach that he bought from sailors. But he had not slept with this woman although she had been to his shop a few times, torturing him with her eyes and always leaving him breathless, yearning for her.

He could barely control himself when he saw the large portmanteau she was carrying, which she put down laboriously on the floor.

'Sardines?' he asked, shaking like a branch in a storm.

'I don't want anything, I just want to rest for a while and I thought I could do it here, that is if you don't mind.'

'You can stay for as long as you like,' he said. 'Here, let me take your portmanteau and give you something to drink.'

He offered her pitanga juice and watched her drink it with relish, savouring each gulp, quiet and meditative. He did not say anything, feeling that when she was prepared to talk, she would unburden herself, because he was convinced she had come for a special reason, that this visit went beyond the transience of a stopover on some other journey. If she was running away from someone, she seemed not to be in any hurry, and when after an hour she had not left and he offered to put the portmanteau behind the counter, she did not protest.

Mariamu was running away from the drabness of her new life that had been aggravated by the bad blood between her and her daughter. Having given up ever being able to reach the unpredictable girl, she had accepted it as her lot that she was living proof of what women before her time used to say about not being able to digest the food that they had relished eating. She who had desired a child so much, who had been in the beds of three men just so that she could have the child, had, because of her troubled relationship with her daughter, concluded that indeed the leaf that the goat desires most produces in the end the worst form of indigestion. She had, in eighteen years, been to as many diviners as possible, to get them to 'turn the girl around', to 'get her to know that she came from my womb'. Nothing had worked, so she was left with the

46

residue of a pain in her heart that nothing could cure. What had she achieved in life? she often asked herself. From the cloister of a Koranic and polygamous father's house, a man who had as many women as camels, she had been forced into an early marriage to a husband for whom the world was a vast desert; a man who explored all the regions of the globe in search of a king; a man who came and went like the storms of the desert without any regard for his women. When she thought of how many times her body had been hungry for love, of how many times she had waited for the other men who might come after Sulaiman, for the men who strayed into her dreams but were gone in the morning, Mariamu concluded that love was a terror, not only because it imposed the greatest form of suffering on those who loved, but also because she felt that the whole idea of love was a trap invented by men to keep women in chains. If her husband and Sulaiman had kept her for a while and then discarded her, if her own daughter – whom she had nursed at her breasts, whose bottom and nostrils she had cleaned, whose chicken-pox, measles and malaria had kept her awake at night – could talk to her as if they shared the same men, she was finished with love. Henceforth, she would look for a man who could care for her without the dubious talk of love; she was still an exotic woman, with breasts that were shaped like melons and she had noticed how the mulatto had eyed her several times in his shop. Now she was going away, turning her back on a man who had buried his head first in the sand of a king who was nothing better than a centaur, then in the magic of a travelling fakir for whom she had a child. Raised with the idea of pleasing men, Mariamu had not hoped for much in a loveless marriage, but when she had Sulaiman's child the dawn of motherhood had initially brought some happiness to her. So that if it had turned out to be different, it was not her fault. She wanted to be free of society, free of tyrannical men and tradition, free of that parsimonious society that had taken away from her the one relationship that had aroused her to the limits of her desires. She wanted to forget the young men who looked at her with lust but who, out of respect for her husband permanently shut up in his room, tracing the lost steps of Sulaiman, were afraid to go beyond mere glances. When she had left her house that morning she did so not with any idea of coming direct to the house of the mulatto to be his mistress, but more to get away from the bad spell of luck she had been having. He had always struck her as someone like herself who had been lost on the road to discovering the true meaning of life, who had walked in the rain in search of someone to whom he could confess all that he had not been able to say to his mother

47

who must have died when he was a child. With the intuition of an experienced woman, she had read the deep lines of anguish in the parchment of his face as a sign that he had been tormented throughout his life by the uncertainties and ambiguities of his own manhood, and the ability to open his heart to a woman. She was going to make him care for her, to make him become a man, so that he, unlike the other men, would never leave her.

The sun was going to sleep in its blue-grey bed of clouds over the vast blue sea; the music of the cicadas in the oleander and mimosa garden could be heard that evening as Antonio began to close his shop. After two hours he had concluded that the woman was going to stay, that something different was going to happen to him. If fate had sent this woman to him, it was enough that he let himself be guided by his good angel, by the one that had protected him from those women in black who had touched him in the right place, but at the wrong time! That night, he thought of his mother; about whether this was how she had gone to his father when it was dark in the other side of the mysterious region. He wondered whether his father had been gentle to his mother; whether she had been someone other than a woman who brought him only temporary pleasure in the wild desert of physical contact. He did not light the candle because the moon came out and shone through the windows. Instead, he went into a small room perfumed with the fragrance of the Madeiras, with Mariamu following him. While she unpacked and made herself comfortable in the strange house, Antonio the Mulatto cooked a complete meal for the first time in months. The smell of the mushrooms and garlic filled the house with an earthy sweetness which was still there the next morning when the sun reappeared and revealed, through the shutters, the dark, coffee body of the woman with her pendulous breasts, sleeping peacefully in the arms of the hairy mulatto, rescued from drowning in the vast loveless sea by each other.

They lived like that for many years. Antonio would write letters to his agents in Portugal and Spain for supplies to replenish his stock. Love, happiness and a restoration of his youth replaced a frugality that had marked his shopkeeping before Mariamu arrived. Whereas he had been meticulous in recording every minute detail about who bought what, about who owned him this and that amount, he suddenly found book-keeping a drudgery.

'Let's open the shop to everyone,' he said to Mariamu one morning.

'We can give credit to our neighbours and trust in Providence that they pay.'

But the more he gave out in credit, the more he received from Spain so that the shop was always full and Antonio found himself spending more time there than where he really wanted to be, which was in bed with the vivacious lover whom God had sent him.

When they had been living together for about a year, Mariamu began to show signs that she was regaining her passion for life. When she had been married to the gold merchant she had not succeeded in implanting some kind of domestic bliss into their lives because he was always gone on his desert trips. But Antonio was a different man: he liked the small details about shopping for bric-a-brac in the large market; he smiled when she told him how she had not known how to cook before she married her husband, but now enjoyed cooking for Antonio. Life had never been more peaceful and the bittersweet memory of Sulaiman was fast becoming blurred in her subconscious. Soon, their lives assumed a routine and they settled down to a kind of marital bliss although Mariamu vowed never again to get married or to fall in love. Many years later, long after they had died, Thomas Bookerman discovered a diary in her house, which Mariamu had kept so that one day someone would know how happy she had been in her final years.

◇

Five days after he saw the scorpion crawling in Fatmatta's eyes, Ahmed was sweating out his fever in his room where a large coalpot was blazing. Someone had put guava leaves on the coals and the pungent smell filled the room, but the medicinal effect was to be seen in the way the sick man was turning in his bed. While he had been sick, two women whom he did not know had kept his company, nursed him, force-fed him and got him to drink his medicine.

'You have to fight the fever, or it won't break,' one of them said on the third day when he came out of his delirium. He had travelled for an indeterminate period in his feverish condition. It was like an odyssey with the same obstacles appearing over and over because the same image kept coming to haunt him and he had to undergo a form of cleansing to overcome his uselessness. Whereas mirrors had fascinated Sulaiman, salt fascinated Ahmed. It was salt that was put in wounds, salt to garnish food, salt to preserve food and if he was not worth his salt in a country of salt he did not have much to show for himself. Trying to break out of the fever, he felt like a man who had been born in another

49

century. He had difficulty remembering the place, the sense of time, of belonging. In his eyes everything looked new, challenging and waiting to be named. He saw for the first time the possibility of leaving nothing behind, no remembrance or claim to the earth. From what could his name be redeemed or for what reason preserve it if unlike Sulaiman he had died and left nothing behind? Life was a challenge that had to be met with ideas, with great deeds, with conquest or creations, and he had not even begun to live yet. The more he thought about it, the more his anguish became pronounced on his brow.

'Don't think too much, it's bad for you,' the other woman cautioned.

It was then that it dawned on Ahmed that while he had been lying there, dying from his rejection by Fatmatta, men all over the world were doing things: trade was going on, wars were being fought, men were on the march, not too far from where he was, to change the face of another country. For the first time since he had woken up he looked at the two women: one was about thirty-eight, still beautiful even though by the way she sat with her hands folded in her lap he could tell that her life had not been easy. She had about her the calm assurance of a mother watching over her son who had given way to foolishness, and he felt like calling her mother, of making her the mother he had not seen since that day when he was dragged screaming and kicking by the Arabs in Zanzibar. The other woman was much younger, about nineteen, and Ahmed concluded by the similarity of their looks that she was the daughter. She too was beautiful but seemed more relaxed than her mother. It was they who had rescued him from his own vomit when Fatmatta had come from the river and announced:

'There is a man lying by the river who looks sick.'

They were Fulani women from the Futa Djallon mountains and he understood from their peaceful presence there that he had come through a long and terrifying struggle which they had witnessed and that the danger of his dying was past. He wondered if they knew about the fumarole of his anguish, the instance of his collapse and the unbearable loneliness that he felt in his life. He sought for a kind of reassurance in those gentle and kind faces. Their kindness was like a fountain from which he could drink a pristine quality of love which did not immobilise him but gave hope to him as he lay recovering his strength and his health, though the look of a scorpion with which Fatmatta had terrified him still shook his body. But he would not let himself think about that woman as the prospect of meeting her again filled him with a new terror. Trying to put as much distance between her and the promise of life without pain, he turned his attention to the women in the room, sought their eyes for an acknowledgement that he was still a man.

'I am all right now,' he said. 'I think I can manage on my own and thank you.'

The older woman looked at him for a while before she answered. Her look was neither one of pity nor one of concern but rather one that suggested men were a complicated lot and that they needed to be looked after all their lives by women, by their mothers and their daughters.

'You are not well enough to do anything, and you had better get any foolish ideas out of your head about leaving that bed.' she said.

Ahmed felt his loneliness return, but the feeling was temporary. New ideas filled his head like flashlights and he thought of what he would do when he was allowed to leave his bed, leave that forlornness that had gripped him in the past. He wanted to go away but could not think of where. The space waiting to be filled was out there but his equilibrium had been shattered, and he was losing his clarity. In their place was a loveliness which was a terror, and he felt he was trapped in schemes that were mere façades of reality.

He had experienced all that and more but now he wanted to be rid of that man who had existed in parts. Henceforth, he was going to live like an armadillo, protected by his shell held together by an invisible glue. And because he was sure the hurt and shame he felt over the abortive affair with Fatmatta was going to pass, he started fighting the ague with a determination to be up and out of bed as soon as he could persuade the older woman. There was also the matter of her daughter whose silent but haunting beauty left Ahmed confused like a man deciding which of two journeys he should embark on, both promising to open new vistas in his life.

Around that time, Fatmatta was adjusting to the idea that her mother was living with Antonio the Mulatto. She did not know of that other time when, tired of waiting for her husband to return with the gold of the fabulous king, Mariamu had gone off to live with another man. She did not reproach her mother because she could not feel any closeness to that woman whom she viewed as merely the vehicle through which she had passed from the stage of conception to birth. Why was birth so important if she could not feel any pain about the woman who had carried her through that difficult journey, who had given her life? Perhaps it was because Fatmatta was not of this world, and had a father more powerful and demanding than her putative father. What had been left to her by Sulaiman was a feeling of heritage: something more universal and challenging. She felt she had to go beyond the bonds of clan and country, that a new comet bearing her name had to be explored before she could allow herself to be stamped by someone's narrowness and demand. On the way to that planetary exploration everything that stood in her way had to be demolished: the business of the unfortunate Ahmed, the demands of a mother. If they bored her, it was because they belonged to the terrifying stagnation of the past, of the present. She longed for the future, to be seduced by the unknown and the violent, and she daydreamed about the comet, of a world of mirages and glass, though she did not know how soon her life was to change, how near to her doorstep the footprints of transition were, with their dried mud and disaster.

It was the peacocks that first raised the tempo. These birds, kept for their supposed pride of plumage, for their courtship dances, suffered a terrible case of fright on a glorious day. Clusters of yellow, bright green, red and orange feathers danced in the air as the normally peaceful birds took flight, headed for the branches of the tamarind trees where they continued to flap their wings, breathless and uneasy. On the main road leading to the town the dry choking dust of the season rose in a blinding cloud, and made it impossible for anyone in the town to see who was approaching. Someone was coming, and though he was still a good way from the centre of the town, his arrival was already beginning to arouse unusual interest among the townspeople. He arrived at the height of the feverish climate of preparation for the feast of the betrothal. This was the time when the age-old practice of letting men fight it out among themselves for the girl of their choice was held. Two rivals confronted each other like ancient wrestlers. Round them, a circle made up of their families and the girl's family urged them on and the two boys smeared with okra and palm oil fought it out. The loser not only did not get the girl but spent twelve months working on the farm of the winner's father, while the victor got the girl but in turn spent twelve months working on his prospective father-in-law's farm before consummating the marriage.

So when he came to the village the stranger thought that it was to welcome him that the crowd had gathered. His face was of a different race, alien to those men and women who were accustomed to the different races of the area, to the stock of men who had ridden on camel and mule backs in search of gold and been lost in the evaporating forests. His head was round and unusually large, but he was handsome in the way barbarian gods were handsome. He had a face that was smooth like ripe pomegranate, and a neck that had rings that looked like

52

expensive jewellery. His face was nectarine, and he was black and golden at the same time, tall with elegant hands that he kept moving; his eyes were so brilliant that he gave the impression of someone who had strayed into that world of dense magic searching for the lost queen of his fancy. When he smiled he revealed a set of gold teeth that were so beautifully set that everyone thought he was the lost king of Orphir for whom N'jai had spent two years lost in the treacherous pathways of the desert before succumbing to the magic of Sulaiman the Nubian. Because he had arrived at the time of the harvesting of the cocoa crop it was felt his coming was a sign that the year's yield would be good after a succession of bad harvests.

'Things are going to change now, you will see,' said the elder Fulani woman who had nursed Ahmed back to life, but who was now ready to abandon him to serve this newcomer, who because of his good looks and obvious wealth she secretly hoped would marry her daughter.

Fatmatta was not in the crowd watching the wrestling. Because she was unquestionably the most beautiful woman in that part of the world she was not a woman who required a contest, but knew that at the right time the most brilliant star in the constellation would appear to let her know that the time had come for her to be married. She spent the afternoon cooking mushrooms, couscous and goatmeat for supper, and was just sitting down to eat when she heard the wild ecstasy in the voices of the women running towards the entrance of the town. She heard the awe and fascination expressed in those voices about the arrival of the most handsome man that the town had seen; about the elegance of his robes, and the magnificent breed of his horse. Unable to eat her meal, she went to her window and saw that the light of the most luminous star was bearing down from the heavens and that the whole town had been enraptured by the unbelievable evidence of the glow. She left her room and went out, carried by the train of the commotion which was winding its way round the market place, past the spot where Sulaiman had first proclaimed the town destined for disaster, past where the ubiquitous beggars had been cleared away, down the esplanade where a great horse was making its way through the largest crowd that Fatmatta had ever seen. There, on the back of the great beast was the most attractive man that she had ever set eyes on. When their eyes met, Fatmatta felt a most shattering disorder in her entrails, and she had to dig her toes deep in the ground to prevent her from losing her equilibrium. She let the moment pass but the vertiginous air that had encircled her and frightened away the pheasants was something that was beyond the limitations of her knowledge. Then, she was forced to recall that other time when she had been encircled by the whirlpool of her power in the depths of the river where Sulaiman had been overcome by the unbearable notes of her tessitura. Now, it was this stranger who was unmasking her, with the eyes of his own scorpion which she felt powerless to resist, because she knew that to fight against the rupture in her heart was useless now that the orbit into that summitry of the other world that she had dreamed of was about to begin.

When the stranger asked N'jai for the hands of his daughter two days later he replied, 'I give her to you, and I hope you have more happiness with her than I had with her mother.'

They were married a week later under a canopy that a dozen men had worked feverishly to build. On the morning of the wedding, Fatmatta and her husband, who called himself Camara, a dealer in horses and carpets, walked from the compound of the bride's father on the dirt road to the esplanade where the best acrobats were putting on such a display that for years anything they did was measured against that performance. On the way to the wedding they had to pass through the young women who had lined the route to sprinkle the most exotic perfumes on the couple, and then spread their expensive gowns on the ground in the hope that Fatmatta would walk over them, and by so doing pass on some of the magic with which she had captured such a handsome man.

The night before, Fatmatta's hair had been braided with a hundred blue and white glass beads. She mascaraed her eyes and painted her heels with a reddish dye. On the wedding day itself, she wore a gown of expensive white lace, gold earrings shaped like eagles and sandals made by the best shoemaker from the skin of the rare python. Told by an old woman about how to behave when her husband came into the bedroom on the night after the wedding, she replied that she did not need any advice because there was nothing to it, only the surrender of what she had been tired of carrying around like a badge of childhood when she was no longer a child. So on that morning, while the decrepit priest chanted the rites of marriage and shook the censer, while the asthmatic chronicler recited the verses of the oral poet, Djeli Momoudo Kouyate, and the harpist invoked the blessing of the ancestors, Fatmatta could think only of the pleasure that awaited her after she and her husband had been offered the purified water blessed by the priest, which when they had drank it made them man and wife.

Shaken out of his nostalgia and solitude, N'jai the gold merchant put on his gown with the golden embroidery, and attached his sword of a warrior of the desert to see his daughter wed. During the ceremony, he secretly wept for the youth that he had banished from the monastic book of his heart, for trying to recall how he had married Mariamu and danced all night long to the music of the itinerant Tuaregs. Later that night, he felt a cold sweat in his groin as he watched Fatmatta who, unable to suppress the antlers of desire that were pricking her sides, pressed herself close to her husband and rode away into the night.

Stung by the way he had been rejected, Ahmed the Elephant at first contemplated death in the fire of unrequited love. He felt a deep pain in his heart as if he had been kicked by a wildebeest, and thought that he was going insane. That night, while the riotous celebrations continued after the newlyweds had left, he went to his room and banged his head against a wall and prayed that he would bleed to death and not wake up the next morning. His prayer was not granted and he only ended up hurting himself. He went into a deep sleep and became delirious. He was a great ostrich and was dancing at the wedding. Everyone was laughing and although he was trying to escape the mocking eyes of the crowd, the people kept coming closer and closer, surrounding him. He was just about to start growing feathers to fly away when someone cut off his long neck, and offered it to Fatmatta.

When he came out of his delirium, he deduced from the death image a most apocalyptical and horrible end to the marriage. Suppressing the desire of the rejected suitor for such an end to happen, he sneaked out amidst the uproar of drums and the exotic masquerades and followed the couple. He trailed them into the night of his unhappiness, sustained by the quivering effect of his concern for the girl who had hurt him, through the impenetrable forest where Sulaiman the Nubian had last been seen in the company of the primates. He was suffering from an indigestion that churned the blood in his heart; he hastened his steps so as not to lose the tracks of the horse, which formed and disappeared in the dry patch of the soil.

After more than two hours, he spotted them. He had been running like a wild animal of the jungle to keep up with them and as he neared them, trying not to be seen, he saw a most startling and unexpected object: there in the middle of that wilderness of a forgotten age was a small house overgrown with the century of iridescent plants that had flourished in that humid region. It was a yellow dusty house and as evidence of its decrepit state were its windows that were coming off their hinges, and the musical birds that flew in and out of the rooms, and the feeling that no one had lived there since the time of the flood, because at any time its roof of a lush garden of moss and lichen could collapse.

Fatmatta went up the steps leaning on the arms of her husband. She did not see the diaphanous skulls on the veranda which were used as plant pots, ossified by neglect, but felt a cold shiver run through her as if she were entering the deserted house of the lemures. When her husband pushed open the door, she saw a room that was lit by a fire whose flames were fuelled by an invincible blower. A large divan draped with animal skins took up an entire wall, and she saw her movements reflected in the large mirrors that lined the rest of the walls, and realised without being startled that the room was bare except for a collection of weapons and the stuffed corpses of wild animals. He led her towards the divan and Fatmatta felt her feet move through the thick carpet of a bewitching night which thankfully hid the boils that were beginning to break out on her face.

He began to undress her with meticulous care; first, he removed her long white gown embroidered with gold, the silk undershirt and the pearl necklace. When her shoulders were bare, he let his hands glide down their delicate texture the way a blind man feels a work of art. It was as if he was admiring the work of a genius that was of the utmost beauty, with her warm and supple flesh quivering at his touch. Suddenly, with a movement that was so abrupt that Fatmatta felt as if a whirlwind had lifted her, he impaled her on the bed, pinioned her so that her wings were clipped and she saw the look of an unspeakable anguish spread through the landscape of his face, as a blood-charged pole forced its way between her legs. The cicadas drummed their wings in a gesture of awe, and the wise chimpanzees experienced the first signs of dehydration in the humidity, as she passed out, smeared by her own blood that spattered like a boil, breaking the soft film of her hymen.

Unknown to Fatmatta, the man she had married had come from a country without a name to marry her, because it had been foreseen by Sulaiman during a night of lucid divination that a man with the face of another would possess the power to strip her of her innocence. When he arrived to claim her hand no one had been able to unmask him, not even Ahmed, because he was incapable then of clairvoyance. The gold merchant had not demanded the bride price that was customary, nor insisted that he perform the rite of the man-to-be-wed.

Lost in the enchanting dance of the pheasants during the time of the captivating nostalgia of how the town was before the rains when the men galloped on horseback and women played bowharps, they had turned the wedding into the investiture of a prince and princess. So he had escaped the haranguing over his origins. Now, lying next to his wife, he was tormented by an illness that he had kept a secret from everyone, which would have prevented the marriage. The fever that gripped him there had its origins when his mother had gone out one night when she was pregnant with him. That night, she saw the fearsome masquerade of a sect so secret that only old men were allowed to become members. No woman had seen it before, and in that stupefying horror, mesmerised by an object that wound its way skyward with the head of a goat and the body of a man, she had caught the infamy that was to plague her son throughout his short life. Soon after he was born, she discovered that he was different: he had the yellow skin and light brown eyes of an albino, the brown unruly hair of a camel, and the smell of radish. Running away with him, his mother had done her best to cure him of the terrible stammer that plagued him, until she had heard of an old man who knew the secrets of herbal lores. Every Saturday, which the old man said was a good day for chasing out the spectre of the devil, he made the unfortunate boy drink the blood of puff adders, drink water out of a bell, and eat with chickens that were allowed to peck his rice. He got his mother to squat over a dog and pee on it in an attempt to restore her son's pigmentation. Nothing worked; so he had gone through life shunned by the town and confined to the mysterious forest as in the time when they threw twins away because they were supposed to be bringers of evil. Nothing was ever heard of him again, and everyone forgot the story of the unfortunate woman and her son, until they had both disappeared, caught in the trap of his pleurisy. Now he was there in that mysterious house shedding the face of another, and he was in pain, the pain suffered by those who had journeyed across the forbidden pathways of life to assume the life of another.

Like all albinos he hated the sun, but when he had heard through the grapevine of the albinos about the beautiful woman who could talk to birds and had the power of a scorpion, he borrowed the body of the most handsome man to die of love, bought a bottle of lotion that the marabouts swore would restore his colour, and went off to marry her. He tried to move, to get to a small bag lying on the floor, for the lotion, but he had lost it in the schism of events for his wedding, and quickly, he began to disintegrate. He felt his skin turning yellow again and his soft hair becoming coarse. A cold shiver wrapped him, making him shudder in spite of the fire in the room. It was then that his childhood came back to him with its roads of bitter lamentation and the hated cups of snake-intestines brew that he had been made to drink. Bitterly, he realised that he had not been able to cheat fate. As his beauty began to fade quickly, his face contorted into a terrible scowl, he knew he was dying a second time without the power of regeneration. His second death was lonely and not assured of the forty days of mourning once received by those who died. As dramatically as he had appeared on that day heralded by the flamboyant birds, he crashed with a thud on the floor, foaming at the mouth, beside his wife.

Ahmed the Elephant found them like that, locked in the illusion of love. Although he had had a premonition about the evil behind that marriage, he was not prepared for the spectacle of an albino embracing the woman that he loved. He experienced an instant terror the more because the man lying there was old and looked like a faun. He perceived that in the moment of their coming together, the mortality of the woman and the ephemeralness of the man had found common meaning in the farthermost depths of a great river where they had struggled with the tumultuous thrashing of a predestined but profaned love and miracle, which were so inscrutable that not even the river had the power to show them the way out of their tragedy. And because it had its origins in an ancient sect that had baffled men for a long time, the nature of the cure suddenly became clear to him. It was in the opposite meanings of luck and disaster that such things were possible. Accordingly, he was left in no doubt that the reason why men kept pigeons was not only because those intelligent birds would warn them of the first signs of disaster, but also because all men were afraid to die without tidying up their affairs; afraid of banishment and loneliness in a world regulated and menaced by tradition and by the invincible spiders of their own anxieties. Rather than hate the man who had taken Fatmatta, he came to the conclusion that what he had been looking for in another life was understanding, and some love. He buried the albino the next morning just as the vultures were beginning to land on the ancient roof, and took Fatmatta back to town.

It was a moonless night when he arrived with the still shaken woman. Somewhere in the distance a lone hyena howled, the dogs berated the prowling spirits and scampered about for what remained of the great wedding feast. After the exhaustion of seeing his daughter married off, the gold merchant was fast asleep until Ahmed woke him up. He had great difficulty recognising the bedraggled-looking woman as his daughter who had ridden off only the day before in a glittering gown.

'What happened?' he asked, unable to compose himself.

58

'Get hold of yourself,' Ahmed said. 'This woman has been seduced by an albino.'

'You are going to keep it quiet, aren't you?' replied the gold merchant.

'These things cannot be hushed just like that. They are like a pregnancy that cannot be hidden, even at night.'

The gold merchant looked at his daughter, but it was as if he had not seen her. He was unable to speak, struck by the unbelievable evidence of the tragedy. He wondered what he had done to deserve this infamy. He had grown to love the daughter who had been forced upon him by Mariamu, and the memory of that morning when he had danced at her presentation was even more poignant than the poetry of her wedding. His eyes, filled with tears, were those of a man who was about to lose the only reason he was alive, now that his obsession with the teachings of Sulaiman was, like Mariamu, a thing of the past.

'I can't tell you what this means to me,' he said to Ahmed. 'How the shame will kill me, send me to my grave before my time.'

Ahmed the Elephant thought of the birds. He thought of them flying in a cycle and singing a rapturous song: blue and violet birds, malachite birds that sang of lakes teeming with fish, lilac-crested rollers that were lifting him up in anticipation of some miraculous discovery, the way he had not been able to fly when he dreamed he was an ostrich. They flew with him though he did not know how far they were going. Held between two birds, he had a lucid thought after the web of confusion that had formed in his mind. Transformed from an inadequate man, he was on his way to a great period of being sagacious. Thus he could see as he flew over the disastrous house that Fatmatta would drown herself if the curse of the albino were not removed from her. The thought of her suicide brought him back to earth, and he stated with an emphatic resolve:

'I shall cure her.'

'Do that, Ahmed, and you will have anything you want,' the gold merchant replied.

'But on one condition. The woman must marry me.'

The second time round, Fatmatta did not reject Ahmed the Elephant. After her experience with the albino, she was past caring or feeling and, for that moment at least, the fire that had emblazened her eyes had burned itself out into liquefied ashes. It was a Saturday, and while everyone busied themselves with household chores, with shopping and with clearing up the mess from the excesses of her wedding, she preoccupied herself with the forming of a plausible reason for her coming back so soon, to give to the women whose daughters had been shunned by the albino. Failing to come up with a reasonable answer, she decided that it did not matter what they thought because she had never really been part of the town, had always been aloof, and viewed with an unshakable inevitability the prospect of leaving Kasila for ever. So that accepting the proposal of Ahmed the Elephant bore no relationship to what she was thinking. She would endure him because she had left her heart in the blazing desert of a man who was less than a chameleon of an albino. This realisation that she could be tricked, that a terrible joke had been played at her expense, did not produce in her the slightest feeling of endearment for the patient man whose clairvoyance had saved her from certain death.

A week later, when she was completely recovered, she let Ahmed the Elephant take her as he had dreamed of on that night by the river before he was struck by the potent force of her eyes. But instead of the tender moments that he had imagined upon those tormented seas where he had always dreamed of loving the haughty girl in the past he found himself making love to a woman whose body was like a dead fish, foreign and unresponsive. He pressed on, laboured on an ocean without waves, on a moon without crescent, drained of his sap so that at the end of his journey the only pleasure he derived was the dull sense of an ejaculation that confirmed his manhood and nothing more.

It soon dawned on Ahmed the Elephant that he had married a woman whose mind had been affected by her disastrous encounter with the albino, in spite of his efforts to make her forget. He tried to be good-natured and loving in the face of what was her impenetrable silence.

'Get rid of your sadness. Love me and you will see that we have only just begun,' he said, trying to reach her.

But in the few times that she spoke, it was in reply to a request of his. 'Your soup is ready, will you have your millet porridge on the porch today?' or to ask questions about his pleasures such as, 'Are you going hunting today?' or 'Are you going for a walk tonight?' He had taken to going out most evenings to avoid falling into a state of unrelieved torment because of his wife's refusal to communicate beyond the essentials she had established. On such walks he would recall what Sulaiman had told him about how not to confuse the incantatory mirror with the love of mortals, but he found the prospect of living without love a most distressing one, and clung to the tenuous hope that one day the cobwebs of distress that had grown in Fatmatta's heart would disappear, and he could bring back some measure of happiness in her life, now that he was convinced that the look of a scorpion that had flattened him was something of the past. Although he had not succeeded in arousing in her a desire for him, he was content with the momentary triumph of having that woman who only a few months ago had seemed like the most unavailable woman in the world. He was therefore not prepared for the sudden turn in his fortune. One day, Fatmatta disappeared without warning. She had taken nothing with her, and the house which she had always kept clean and tidy did not bear the sign of a hasty departure. No one had seen her leave, and after a week, Ahmed the Elephant was resigned to the truth that she had gone for ever.

It was the beginning of the harvest. Men, woman and children scythed the crop and stored it in their barns. They thanked God that it had been a bumper crop and prayed that the communal good luck would last.

But the joy of others served only to aggravate his wound. Life had been unkind to him and he felt a bitter rancour against the world, against all men and especially women. He lost all interest in the teachings of Sulaiman, and in a fit of despair burned the legend of Nasrudin because its emphasis on life being like a tree that had nourishment in its roots, to give a delicious sap, no longer interested him. He was a rootless tree. As the book of the learned master went up in flames, Ahmed the Elephant walked to the river where he had been struck by the fatalism of his love. Because the birds did not sing in the trees, he felt a great lump in his throat, and tried to recall the moments in his life when he had been happy, and decided that they had been few. Suddenly, he felt like an old man weighed down by the grief of all orphans, but he did not want to go on living with that load. The unhappiness that life had become started to overwhelm him and he wept for the inability of salt to cure his wound, to make him a full member of the human race, to make him loved. 'I've suffered so much in life,' he said to himself. 'Suffered because I was born when there was a half moon.' Someone had told him that he was born during an invasion of locusts which was a sign of bad luck. The pests had plundered the place and departed the next day. That was why he himself had become a wanderer, and that was why those he had loved, Sulaiman the Nubian and Fatmatta, had disappeared like the locusts. It was his turn to disappear; like a man possessed, he walked into the dark silent river, and nothing was ever heard of him again.

The next day, a trail of blood streaming from under his door caught the attention of the villagers to the fact that something had happened to the gold merchant. They forced down the door and saw N'jai lying flat on his back with his throat slit, attracting the flies to his coagulated blood.

◇

If her conception, marriages and disappearance had been fortuitous, Fatmatta nevertheless was destined to destroy the men who came after the albino; men who, drawn by the invincible letters at the bottom of the whirlpool of her being, dared to come in contact with her. When she disappeared, she carried with her the tormented nature of a scorpion woman, possessed of powers that had their origins in the ancient art of manipulating mirrors perfected by the Nubians in the wide expanse of the Sudanese desert. Thus it was that Sulaiman, past the chronological span of his life, had come to the mosquito-infested town and had a daughter whose eyes could stop men in their tracks; and it was that power that she regained when they tried to turn her into a rabbit that bred other rabbits.

The man who had captured her did not suffer the ignominy of being emasculated by the scorpion in her eyes. Like all piratical dogs plundering the Kasila coast, he was motivated more by what the kidnapping of the citizens represented in terms of its commerce than in the enjoyment value of the women. He was an old dog with the smell of turpentine, a mercenary who plundered and killed without the slightest pang of conscience, and he had the scar-faced countenance of a hyena that was the result of some of the treacherous battles he had fought trying to capture fellow humans. He had come upon Fatmatta as she bathed in an isolated stream, hidden by the bullrushes, and though she kicked and kneed him in his groin, brute force had overpowered her. The last thing she remembered as she passed out was the rancid smell of stale oil on his skin which induced an involuntary vomit in her. For the second time in six months, she woke up in a strange room, a prisoner of fate, with her torn clothes revealing her fine thighs and with a splitting headache. The bandit kept her alive on dried cabin biscuits and cod fish, and when the ship arrived in Virginia he sold her to a young planter for one hundred dollars. The planter took one look at Fatmatta and decided she had the body to breed a dozen plantation slaves fathered by himself. The three-hour ride from the market to his large plantation was the fastest that Andrew McKinley could remember. It was a fine summer day with a thick blanket of maple leaves covering the dirt road. He hurried over the rough patches without the slightest concern for his horses. He pushed them into a mad gallop, wanting to be home earlier than in former times when he had bought other slaves. He had never bought anyone like this woman who uncannily set his blood vessels on fire and made him think of her as human, 'You sure are a fine wench,' he said to the terrified woman, 'and a man could lose his head over you if he ain't careful, despite the fact you a nigra.'

The lecherousness in his voice, the lust in his eyes, told Fatmatta what the alien language did not. Lying there on the floor of the wagon, she was nonetheless able to see the man urging his horses on, to see how nervous his hands were, how pale he looked in spite of the sun, how wide the dirt road was, unlike the roads in Kasila. Everything smelled so different that for a while she forgot about her condition, about her debasement – she who had been born in a beautiful world, had been brought up by a doting father and who, although she had married that albino, nonetheless commanded respect as the wild love of Ahmed had shown.

Andrew McKinley turned into his plantation and unshackled his horses. In the past, when he had come home with a new female slave, Bessie the big cook would be summoned to take over the latest addition to the plantation, teach her how to address the master and his missy, how to behave to their children, and tell her she was owned by the white man who had bought her, who could come at any time in the night to have her.

He went straight to the cabin that he had built as a place of relaxation away from the big house, where he had taken many slave women before. He loved the routine and the taste of conquest but had never considered sleeping with black women anything remotely connected with the pursuit of happiness, merely a release of a biological need. Some had struggled to defend their honour, kicked him in his balls, but a slap or two, the whip or the menace in his voice had always brought them to their senses, and he had performed his motions and had done with them. This time, however, he could conceive of the possibility of breeding this woman, so he was surprised and pleased that she did not resist as he tore off the rags she had worn since she had come off the slave ship. He took her unwillingness to defend herself as a sign that Providence had sent him the right slave woman who would apreciate being owned by him, and having his mulatto children now that his wife had sealed herself in her bedroom with the pictures of St Patrick and Mary of the Absolute, after giving him two sons who had turned out to be layabouts and interested only in horses and women. When she was naked, McKinley saw the most beautiful woman that he had ever seen standing before him. He had the impression that he was looking at someone who was not from the same stock as the other slaves on his plantation. The earlier decision to consider her slightly more human than the others was now adjusted to make her almost as good as one of his own kind. She had that way about her, serene and dignified, and the sight of that naked black body produced a great fire in him and he was propelled by such a great urge to penetrate her that he pushed his animal deep inside her, oblivious of the thin row of glass beads held neatly by a brown cord which hung on the woman's waist and which when his penis rubbed against them sealed his fate.

Andrew McKinley's family had not owned a plantation for long. Like all newcomers to a degree of wealth, they lacked the social graces. His father had shipped out to New England before the great potato plague because 'I had seen it coming', and for many years tried to make a living running a grocery store. In those days they were poor, and their clothes and skins showed it. To keep warm in the bitter cold and dejection in New England, Clive McKinley would collect all the discarded rags and pieces of wood to put in their fireplace, which also served as a stove, and in front of which they took their baths. Bitter at the fate that had thrown him into a situation without hope, unknown and scorned by the fortunate and frightened, Ireland seemed preferable to New England where they had not yet shaken off the yoke of the English in spite of the revolution. There was already one class of men and women who, as if they had not heard of the Boston rebellion, were organising their own sessions: a despicable oligarchy that wanted to confine him and others to the same servitude that he had left behind. Being a man who valued his freedom, Clive McKinley moved south with his family where his intention was to own his own land which he would farm and to put as much distance between the bubonic plague of his former life and the promise of good times ahead. First, he worked with other fortune seekers on the railway that was being built; later in lumber yards. When he had acquired some land he started to plant cotton and coffee. If he had the seeds of human tragedy in him, they did not manifest themselves until later when he and his son began to exploit others for their own prosperity, the way they had hated being exploited. Clive McKinley razored through the hard granite stone of his early life in the south with an implacable determination to succeed. He pounded on the doors of the rich that were hermetically sealed until they were opened, and his desperate expectation was rewarded with an undreamed-of prosperity. His wife, being a deeply religious woman, prayed to the saints, to St Patrick to St Christopher, and venerated the Madonna, lighting twelve candles every night for two years before going to bed.

'We were so poor,' he told some of his fellow planters when he had built a large plantation and acquired one hundred slaves, 'that we used to eat the peels of potatoes, just like pigs.'

Twenty years later he died, leaving his son a wealthy man, and a legacy stamped with the indelible marks of his cruelty and meanness. Like all men who had prospered savaging the lives of others, his death had been painful. Thrown off his horse while trying to recapture a runaway slave, he had been paralysed from his waist down and spent his last five years confined to a rocking chair in which the remorselessness of time had eaten deep into his heart, and his memory was eroded by the infantilism and senility of old age. On the day before he died he asked to be shown a picture of his wife as she had been on the day of their wedding. Told that she had died two years previously, he exclaimed:

'Godammit, I saw her only yesterday milking the cow!'

It was his old servant mulatto cook Bessie he was referring to. Infirmity and dotage had produced a dubious recognition of the importance of a woman who had washed his clothes, fed him and nursed him for ten years, though it did not in any way minimise the brutality that had reigned in his plantation which his son was to continue.

When Andrew McKinley returned to the cabin later that day bringing food for Fatmatta, she was waiting for him. She accepted the strange food with good grace, but was scarcely aware of the deep current of desire that flowed in the veins of the man. He had been drinking and moved heavily; whereas when he had brought her there in the morning he had rushed into possessing her, he tried to calm himself by sitting down next to her on the wooden bed and making some small conversation.

'It ain't bad here,' he said. 'You will soon see, 'cause ah intend to treat you real fine, not like any onnery nigger.'

Fatmatta did not respond. The idea of being a prisoner of this man had slowly sunk into her head since the trip from the slave market but she was resolved not to be brutalised by him. Although he was near her, he was as strange as the country, ridiculous and banal, and his presence filled her with a revulsion that not even Ahmed the Elephant in their pre-marital days had provoked. Convinced of her inviolability, even if he tried to possess her again, she maintained a posture that was at variance with the tension suggested by his person. When she did not respond, McKinley threw off his superficial calm and grabbed her wrist. Moved not so much by his desire but by the need to punish her, to let her know that there was no exit, no redemption from the damnation that her colour and captivity had imposed upon her, Andrew McKinley pushed her down on the bed; but when he tried to take her he discovered that the power of the arousal that only that morning had been his manhood had been calmed by a prodigiously cold wind that seemed to be blowing in his own belly, which left him trembling and awed by the velocity of its force. He fell back on the bed, and he did not know that what he was responding to was some incomprehensible movements of planetary commotion when Venus had moved in opposition to Mars, and that the woman had entered into a complex orbit of her two halves where she could drown him at the bottom of a billowing river in which his name and wealth were unrecognised. He saw a scorpion crawling in her eyes, where there were no signs of fear, and he thought with shame of the contempt that the woman, that bundle of black flesh he owned, must regard him with; suppressing a murderous rage to strike her, he stormed out and rushed to the big house, working his mouth like a man suffering from a bad case of dyspepsia.

Over the next ten years, Fatmatta became something of an enigma. The belief that she was a creature not of this world but of one where men would be tormented by the scorpion in her eyes and be tainted for ever by the curse of impotence once they had forced themselves upon her did not become widespread until after she had passed through a dozen plantations in two years. McKinley, having failed to turn her into a cheap concubine, hurriedly sold her off. He was bitten by the moths of his lassitude over his inability to triumph and he cursed the day he had gone to the slave market and seen the woman he now regarded as the true sister of evil. Other men could have her, he was relieved. The men who wanted to breed her, the men who wanted to cross rivers and savage blood frontiers with her, convinced of their power and superiority over her, were trapped in that perilous and humiliating vortex. 'In the old days we would have burnt you,' one exasperated and assured man told her, 'but shucks, I paid good money for you and you gonna work in the field.' Several masters put her out to work in fields picking cotton, where they were convinced she could do no harm. Sometimes, in order to punish her, they made her strip in front of their young sons who looked at her fine breasts, at her pubic hair and her round bottom, with the unmistakable lust of boys who were in a hurry to grow up, but were sure that she was a witch. Fatmatta bore her ordeal with a stoicism that was so effortless and contemptous of her tormentors that it reinforced the conviction she was an animal of the jungle.

The truth was Fatmatta had a spotted navel. Thirty years earlier when she was born of that union between the Sudanic magician and Mariamu, she had been marked by that spot, like a testimony to the divine certitude of the power of the man which protected her from all earthly power and made her powerful over others, and which in the words of Ahmed the Elephant would make Fatmatta inviolate although 'she would be desired like a miracle'. She wore the glass beads which her father had immersed in crocodile fat as a protective charm against the brutality of men like Andrew McKinley and the voracity of other slave breeders. In that way she had aged and managed to avoid the circle of bringing mulatto children into the world, who themselves would be slaves.

Enervated by the rigours of physical work, deprived of the geography of her ancestors, she lived with the private satisfaction that she was in communion with them and that this new world was merely a transition from one life to another, from one journey of re-enactment to another, and that certain images were daily telegraphed to her. Sometimes, she would be seized by the feeling that the cotton was obeying a command of authority to fall before her, to pile up into neat bundles that were the envy of other slaves, and once, when she had seen a large turkey in the field, flexing the muscles of his neck, Fatmatta knew that it was not a turkey but a vulture that was trying to speak to her. 'You are going home,' it said. Her eyes met the eyes of the bird and she saw a long ancestral bridge with a lot of people crossing frrom one end to the other, and suddenly everything was clear to her. Cut off from that coalescence of man and spirits, burdened by servitude, she had merely been fulfilling a destiny circumscribed by fate, by an old animated life rhythm that went round the universe like a great flame and then she knew that she would not die in the land of leeches but that she would return, shed all signs of degradation and abuse. Because by the persistence of its look, by the grave and reverential distance it put between itself and other turkeys, the great bird had come to take her home to that land where her navel string was buried.

3   The Sweet Potato Plague

One note of interest that caught the attention of Pedro Almerado, when he called at the Kasila coast in 1462 on his way to Cabro de Casa to begin a reactionary tyranny that was to last four hundred years, was that the inhabitants of the place did not resemble any other he had encountered since he left Portugal. Tall, agile, dark and fearless, they were secretive and suspicious of strangers to the point of being treacherous, and possessed of a warlike character. Three hundred years earlier, they had lived under a monstrous and bloody tyranny south of the present town. A succession of bloody revolts finally won them the freedom that they cherished and were prepared to die for. Soon after that they had moved through the unbroken terrain of dense forest, crocodile-infested rivers and valleys that had changed little since before the first men to walk on earth, to settle down to a prolonged period of exerting their freedom. For fifty years they fought off repeated attacks by surrounding clans and marauding bandits, beat off the panthers and hyenas that stalked their cattle. Hemmed in by the sea, surrounded by high mountains, plagued by repeated bouts of malaria, they managed to build a prosperous town where the itinerant Tuaregs came to swap their salt, cotton and Arabian asses for monkey meat, gold and coffee. It was during a peaceful interlude from wars that the six galleon ships pulled into the harbour; but when the sailors attempted to come ashore they were assailed by such deadly spears and arrows aimed with frightening accuracy that they sailed off to the island where they built the fort in which, four hundred years later, General Tamba Masimiara would spend a year talking to the dugongs, trapped in the hourglass of his former glory, before he was hanged in the national prison a hundred miles away, with the comical name of Meriweather Palace.

Three hundred years after the Portuguese had fled, the four English ships sailed from Plymouth Harbour on a morning of unimaginable excitement with four hundred passengers inspired and determined to settle there. They did not suffer the same fate as the Portuguese. Being a man wise to the ways of foreigners, the captain of the flag ship took the precaution of first warning the tired travellers about the risks they ran if they rushed ashore before being cleared by the natives.

'First, I go in and see if they will let us. Failing that, we look for another place.'

He had hoped to make enough money from this expedition to be able to give up his former life. First a pirate, he was then a slave merchant until, bitten by remorse brought about by the death of a beloved son who had gone off to live among a prehistoric Indian tribe in Guyana, he had renounced the evil trade and offered to lead the expedition to the Guinea coast. He had nothing to do after that, and he was looking forward to a life of sedate living in the Dorset of his beloved England where he had built a splendid brick house furnished with the plundering and profit of his former life. That was why he did not want to jeopardise the chance of taking his ships back intact by any premature assumption about the friendliness of the natives. Accordingly, when he went ashore, although he was accompanied by six fierce-looking sailors he made sure that they were unarmed because of the suspicions that guns might have aroused. He had been on many expeditions before to hunt men and whales and to sell gold, but never before had he been on a journey for the salvation of others, for the bestowing of munificence upon those who had been robbed of everything: so that was why he found it difficult to begin. The king of the town put him at his ease. He was an old man who was not easily excited by gestures. Contrary to that universal belief that men grew wise with age, he had been born wise, a king among men, a seer in the madness and conflicts of his age, who had been born without a single black hair. When he was forced out of his mother's womb after she had been in labour for two weeks he had the unmistakable projection of a tooth so that he was older than speech and had known at what time Sulaiman's prediction about the coming of the blacks from the other side of existence would happen; how they would look like bedraggled cranes after a storm, how they would bear the signs of the adulteration of the blood, but driven by the implacable will of conquerors determined to build a community.

Sebastian Cromantine who, because his father had given him a rudimentary description of the place knew more than the others about the terrain and the inviolability of the custom of the people, spoke on behalf of the newcomers. He told the king about how they had fought in a war without meaning or glory because it was not their war although they had had no choice in the matter. He spoke of the bitter disappointment they had experienced when contrary to the promise of good land on which they could live after the retreat of the colonial army, they had been given land not fit for the cultivation of animals in a country of ice and marshes. Which was why, inspired by the primordial light of their forefathers, they had returned, and would the good king welcome them and give them land which they were prepared to farm, and pay him back from the harvest?

'Here, no one owns anything, not even the stones,' the king replied.

'In that case,' said the captain who had suddenly become alive, 'we will have to go somewhere else.'

'No, you may stay and have all the land you need, provided that you respect our laws and the men keep off our women.'

Sebastian Cromantine promised the king that they would obey the laws and keep their hands off the women. They had brought some gifts from the ships: the king was presented with a trunk full of silver spoons and ceramic jars that looked like reposing Buddhas which had belonged to a rebel soldier who had died clutching a portrait of St George slaying the dragon – whose religious symbolism Sebastian had not understood when he had taken the loot from a deserted camp. Then those determined men and women began the journey up the river to the land they had been given, aided by guides. Captain Thomas, considering his work done, left the next morning.

That evening, Sebastian Cromantine obtained permission from the king and buried the bird-woman, oblivious of her spotted navel or of the incredible tales of Sulaiman the Nubian and the desert albino. The people who had come off the boat had not had time to keep a proper wake for the dead woman but, now that she had finally been accorded a burial as she had requested, Sebastian Cromantine made coffee and passed some biscuits around. While the women sang for the repose of the dead, Sebastian Cromantine sat facing the sea, thinking that death was not so much a question of going back in time but a revelation of things to come, because this world was merely an extension of the past and death was like a mirror into the future. After the wake was over, Sebastian Cromantine tried to sleep on the beach using his old sailor's coat as a pillow. He was bothered by the rhapsody of the crickets and the singing of the mosquitoes which made the first night of the travellers in the tropics unforgettable. When he finally drifted off to sleep he dreamed that he had been in that country before, and that he knew all its history so that nothing was hidden from him, and he could retell all that had happened before. It was thus that he saw a large elephant charging through the woods, rushing to the sea out of the sand. Sebastian saw a scorpion rush to the elephant, circle it and wait. They started to dance as if they had known each other in another world. When they were exhausted, the elephant kneeled down and let the scorpion climb on its back and, gently this time, the great beast went back to the woods, trumpeting the memory of former times when he had seen the proverbial eyes of the woman, who no longer tormented him as he bore her triumphantly into the silver light of morning.

The reality of being in a new environment brought about a discernible change in the spirits of the voyagers. The grey clouds that the death of Fatmatta the Bird Woman had created over their lives gave way to an inordinate optimism which, in the brightness of that world, in the reaffirmation of creation before the naming of things, pushed them on. Cramped inside canoes, they went up the treacherous river that was the heart of the country into the breath of a universe that was dense and terrifying, because they were surrounded on either side by an impenetrable jungle. They almost suffocated because the air was impregnated by the poisonous fragrance of a motley fauna that had changed little since creation, and by the decayed mass of animals that had manured the region. Encumbered by the dense vegetation that blocked the passage of the river, they lost all notion of time so that they seemed to go slower than they thought they were. Sometimes they lost the light and were engulfed by a fearsome darkness, which was made more menacing by the crescendo of sounds and the cries of the animals and wandering spirits of the region enraged that their paradise had been violated by people whose smell did not merge with that of the vapour of the earth. It was a region of snakes, and Sebastian Cromantine relived once again the horror that he had felt in the swamps of Georgia. He tried not to let the others know about his fear by talking about the beauty of the region, about the great prospect that lay ahead.

'Think of what we kin grow in dis place,' he said.

Helped by the guides who had remained at the heads of the boats to steer them through the difficult passage, they soon emerged from that area with its sulphuric drowsiness, and its smell of iodine that had induced a potent laxative in the bellies of those newcomers.

When he saw the land beyond the jungle, Sebastian Cromantine did not grasp its size and potential. It was better than he had imagined. Straddled on the one side by a rugged mountain of green and golden forest and on the other by a coast of white sand and rocks, it was peaceful and bore the signs of a recent earthquake so that the land was black and fertile, and the banks of the river shone with the brilliance of precious metals like stars in a moonless night. Much later, when the Arabs from North Africa became tired of hawking coral beads on the Kasila coast and decided to move into the interior region, to persuade the children of the settlers about the practical use of balsam ointment and the magical result that could be obtained from the recitation of the verses of the

Damascus sage Farouk Baraka on the treatment of rheumatism and neuralgia, they discovered the precious minerals in the river beds and built large houses of glass windows and Moorish porticoes, with Italian terrazzo and marble tiles covered with expensive Moroccan rugs, from the profitable smuggling of the gems.

Among the travellers was a bachelor named Gustavius Martins. He was about twenty-five, strong with powerful muscles. He was shy but not diffident, and was not averse to letting people know that he had killed in self-defence during the colonial war. He had been one of the first to consider the possibility of making the crossing, because he was a man for whom the adventure was more than just a journey to an unknown region. Malagueta was in his blood. Many years earlier, as a young child, he had been taken out of the region south of the place they had landed, and although time, suffering and the war had worked havoc on his memory, they had not completely obliterated all the lines of the country from his heart. So he could remember that there were men who came out at night, once every year, wearing clothes that covered their entire faces, and whom women were forbidden to see. He had not forgotten that the region was swarming with some of the deadliest reptiles ever known to man, or that there were people whose only pastime was to make music, who tapped a special tree that yielded a sweet, white wine which was especially potent to monkeys.

Partly due to his childhood experiences, he was the first to insist that they survey the place well before deciding where they were going to build the new town. He could still recognise the smell of primal herbs and insects, and he could tell which tree was good for medicine and which yielded the best wood. Also, because the area was still reported to be infested with bandits who came trying to kidnap people, Gustavius Martins was not taking any chances.

'We gotta be very careful we don't go too far apart, because dem tiffs be everywhere.'

They listened to his advice and by common consent Gustavius Martins, together with Sebastian Cromantine, became the recognised leaders of the new settlement. At first they let the women and children roam all over the place, because many were still unable to believe that they had left one life where eternal happiness had seemed out of reach, and were now in a land all their own. They were as awed by the immensity and darkness of the area as they had been frightened of the cold and misery of the other land. Then after a while, the two leaders decided to organise the men into working parties. Some of them were put to the task of cutting down trees without adversely affecting the environment, because in their blood they had a reverence for the earth, which had welcomed them and which they had to obey. While Gustavius Martins mapped the outlines of a town, how many houses it should have, where a general market should be, how many streets should run vertically and so on, and whether the town should face the sea or run parallel to it, Sebastian Cromantine went up into the hills with a party of twelve men to see whether they were being watched, and to hunt for food before their supplies ran out.

Soon an area of wooded land was transformed into a settlement of neat log cabins with kitchens and outhouses behind them. Each household had about two plots of land to grow vegetables, and there was an agreement all round that when the entire area had been cleared people could have as much land as they wanted. Linked by a network of narrow streets, all the cabins faced the sea, and they had neat rows of flower gardens in front.

Every day they made new additions or alterations, reinforcing their rafters so that they would be well prepared for the first rains, which they had learnt were destructive in that part of the world. About half a mile from the centre of the town, where they had been told the people of Kasila used to confine the lepers and burn people suspected of communicating with evil spirits, they decided to build a cemetery in a quiet spot on a hill, so that, as they put it, the dead could keep watch on them and keep an eye open for their enemies. Later, when they had been there for over three months, Gustavius Martins led a delegation to the nearby village to exchange some of the things that they had brought off the ships: from those rudimentary cabins came pans, pots, cutlasses and hoes traded for chickens and goats and other necessities for the first Christmas they were going to celebrate as free men and women. It was during one such mission from Kasila that Gustavius Martins, deciding on a walk on a road that took him past a stream, came across the woman who would change his life for ever. She was a young beautiful woman, bathing in the stream, several layers of brightly coloured beads round her waist. Gustavius Martins stood there, held by the brilliant gold of the woman's skin with its polish of an onyx, with her long and graceful neck. He watched the woman as she soaped her firm and round breasts with an art that suggested an age-old custom, and in that instant Gustavius Martins realised that whereas they had given themselves over to some barely understood and irrelevant notion of original sin in that faraway country of damnation, stamped for ever by the grave impression that they had to wear the makeshift clothes of the whites to cover their nakedness, and while their women took their baths in washhouses and barred all men from seeing their bodies during the day, the women of Kasila had raised the act of bathing into a graceful art, and he knew there and then that he had been cheated of the most god-given right: the right to enjoy the beauty of a woman without shame or lust. Suddenly the woman turned around, sensing that she was being stared at. Their eyes met, and in the instant when she held his with her look that spoke of mysteries and exotic gardens, Gustavius felt as if he had been struck by a vertiginous power and he could not tell what involuntary motions of his legs took him home. He was the most exploring of the young men among the settlers and he recalled memories of the smell of wild flowers which the women emanated, of the henna they applied to their lips and soles, and that night he knew he had to have that woman to heal the ulcers she had given him in spite of the conviction that the women of Kasila were beyond his reach and that he could die haunted by her lingering fragrance.

$\diamondsuit$

Life went on more or less according to plan for the settlers in the first years in Malagueta. Through hard work and perseverance, the town began to take shape. The more enterprising among the settlers, wishing to double their landholdings, asked for permission and received more land so that they could grow rice which they had discovered was preferred by the people of the surrounding villages over the cassava that other settlers had begun to plant.

One day, a young man arrived from 'somewhere beyond the forest' with a chimpanzee that when commanded could dance on its head and go round removing the hats of the spectators, which it then proceeded to toss in the air. Fascinated by the antics of the animal, the people of the town gave its owner permission to stay. His name was Gabon Kawalley, a trader in exotic birds who had been left behind by a ship after he had ventured deep into the forest in search of his game. He had lived on wild berries and cassava until, almost dying of the heat, he had been rescued by some woodcutters who had taken him home and nursed him back to life. They had given him the chimpanzee to pass away the time but, being a man wise to the ways of making money, he had taught the animal the tricks. So that no sooner were the newcomers settled in the area than he thought of introducing the acrobatic animal as the answer to a bout of homesickness which some had complained of.

Some were indeed homesick for the people that they had left behind. Sebastian tried to hide his loneliness from his wife. Since coming to Malagueta, he had set up a trading post on the waterfront where the itinerant Moorish traders from beyond the mysterious forests brought spices and other condiments which they traded for salted fish and the skins of animals. Soon the shop became the place where the men of the town met every Saturday to drink the rum which Sebastian Cromantine obtained from the schooners that had begun to call at Malagueta. Although he hated the idea of being a trader, he nevertheless had a business acumen and in a short time had begun to register a healthy profit.

One evening, after a profitable day at the shop, he decided to go beyond the fringes of the town to be alone. Things had begun to happen to him. Once he had come across the head of a sheep in front of his shop; another time someone had hung a bat on the door of his cabin and, being a man who believed in the power of the occult, Sebastian Cromantine had regarded the two incidents as signs that someone was trying to do him in. That was why, without telling his wife, he was going into the woods to shake off the feeling of evil, of bad omen, that was eating him up. It was the first time that he had ventured beyond the last house of the town. As the neat gardens with their smell of jasmine and gardenia gave way to the unruly growth of the wilderness and the cries of the creatures of the evening, he suffered a momentary loss of confidence. But he knew that he had come this far not so much because of a voluntary desire but because the hand of fate was pushing him to it. For the first time since he had left the other country, he thought of the old woman who had been his owner, of the war in which he had fought and the journey across the ocean that had taken them to London. It was a lovely evening: flocks of crows flew overhead blanketing the sky with their black plumage. Going deeper into the forest, he heard the sound of a bowharp which brought back memories of the days in America when he had attended the dances of the blacks. Someone would play the banjo, and afterwards the men would disappear into the fields with the women where they pressed their bodies together before going back to their separate cabins and owners.

It was getting dark. Loud thunderbolts rolled in the distant heavens and Sebastian Cromantine turned back from the forest. He felt lighter, though the illusion of happiness did not buoy him home. The clarity of his mind was still as elusive as when he had first entered the forest, but he no longer felt he was hearing things in his head. Suddenly, he heard a rustle in a tree nearby. A large green snake inched its way down from a branch, dropped to the ground and disappeared into the grass of the approaching night. Sebastian Cromantine experienced a terrible fright. He tried to shout but he felt that being afraid of a snake made him a coward. Yet he was afraid, for the snake had awakened memories of the past. His whole being shook with a tremor that was as strong as any he had known, and the memory of the other time when he had seen the snake came back to him with a clarity that unnerved him further. Suddenly, Sebastian Cromantine began to run and did not stop until he reached his cabin.

$$\diamond$$

Soon after her husband succumbed to the snake fever, Jeanette Cromantine woke from her life of a woman raised to be above the drudgeries of life, to face the urgency of their situation. It was not that this woman who was beautiful and well bred was unprepared for the predicament of any hardship in life. But twenty years of sheltering in the Bible-saturated home of the pastor did not altogether afford her a clinical idea of how to cope with life in the event of something happening to her husband. Thus, the gravamen of her depression over Sebastian's condition seemed greater than whatever material goods they had. One day, however, while she was serving him his soup on the porch where he sat all day breathing in the fresh geraniums, getting old with fear, Jeanette Cromantine suddenly found the answer to their plight. The rains were not too far away, and soon they would have to replenish their stock of food and other essentials. Whatever money they had had been eaten up by the building of the cabin, and because Sebastian could not plant the seeds that they had brought on the *Belmont* for commercial uses, their stock was reduced to a few weeks' supply, supplemented by the poultry in the back yard. So that if they were to survive the rains and she keep her husband dry and well in the transition of his life, she had to do something. Fate had brought them together, and it was fate that put the idea into her head to start making dresses with the large quantity of materials that she had managed to save from the ravages of the war, and to turn her small cabin into a business house. The cabin itself was appropriate for her needs, built on a gentle slope overlooking the ocean. It had a great view of the jade islands where the native boys dived for pecten shells, of the sublittoral creatures in the south thrown up by the great tidal waves, and the luminosity of the sun setting in the evening. At night it was cooled by the mountain breeze, by the shade of a large jacaranda tree and by an underground stream which, according to one of the labourers who had helped Sebastian build it, had a djinn that kept the water running all year round. Fired by a demonic strength, she set about fixing up the place in readiness for her business. When the sun looked into the parlour, it showed a floor that was stained with mango bark, brilliant with a polish of soap, wax and oil. Next, she made matching curtains of soft green for the windows of the parlour and assorted ones for the two bedrooms, and put plants everywhere. The world was still peaceful when the Cromantines moved to Malagueta, and Jeanette indulged in the ancestral worship of plants as a source of driving out evil spirits and of beautifying her cabin so that it was transformed into a paradise of living foliage of emerald green: the fragrance of caladiums, of diffenbachias, the uncontrollable greenery of the monkey-favoured spider plant, of anthuriums and assorted violets. Being a practical woman, worried about her husband and prone to a fear of insects and lizards, she planted lemon grass around the cabin, which she had been told kept mosquitoes away during the suffocating heat of summer. Much earlier, she had induced Sebastian to part with some of the gold coins he had taken off a dead soldier during the colonial war, and invest them in a Jacobean chair, a highboy chest of drawers and a set of landscape paintings that a drunken sailor was willing to part with. She also acquired a set of highly polished chairs and a sofa of flamingo feathers with a high back shaped like a lion's head to complete the furniture of the cabin. After three weeks, Jeanette Cromantine was satisfied that the place gave the impression of being the home of a woman used to good living. It was after this feverish preparation that she felt ready to instruct the women from the nearby village in the delicate art of sewing, and to start making her dolls. One morning, she put on one of her best dresses, combed her hair into an outlandish coiffure, threw a shawl over her shoulders and walked the quarter-mile to Kasila. There, in the shade of a tamarind tree, she explained to a group of twenty women who had come more out of curiosity about the elegant woman and her refined manners than because of what she had to say, how to hold a pair of scissors, how to cut a line straight, how to cut patterns and how to sew buttons on. They were fascinated by the intricacies of the art; they liked the delicate way she manipulated the vicious-looking daggers, and were enthralled by the soft tone of her voice, by the way she sat on the grass with her legs folded, almost touching her bottom, and also by how she smiled at them all the time.

When she went home that evening, satisfied with her efforts, she told

Sebastian about what a nice day she had had, how she was going to start a small business in dolls and dressmaking.

'Don't go gettin your spirit too high,' he said. 'What you think dey gon do wid dem American dresses of yours?'

'Dey could wear 'em, and besides, am teaching dem so dey can sew better, and we gon make some money someways.'

'You go ahead, just so long as you don't have too many people here 'cause dey be bringing dem snakes here. Shucks, before you know it dey be crawling all over de place.'

He was slowly coming out of his terrifying delirium. Rum and bay leaves had worked a miracle, and when she looked at the man who was not too frightened now, she wept silently and put his melancholy down to the shock Sebastian must have suffered when his father, tired of wandering in the swamps of Georgia, came to visit him that night. She seldom thought about that place and had not bothered to pray since their arrival in Malagueta. Now, she felt the need for a little prayer to restore her husband's spirit. Much later, when her clouded head had cleared a bit, she remembered she had not worn the glass beads of Fatmatta the Bird-Woman because of an unconscious fear of the power of that mysterious woman. Instantly, she found herself going back, like some mesmerised crab, to the corner where she had kept them, glad that she had that link to another presence and being, now that her husband seemed so far removed from the present.

Just as she had hoped, the women from Kasila came one morning soon after she had been to see them. They had dressed beautifully in flowing gowns as if to complement the foreign woman, painted their lips with henna, and wore large gold earrings. For nearly all of them, it was the first time that they had been inside the home of a settler. They went from room to room looking at the curtains, at the patchwork bedspread, the antimacassars with their embroidery of seabirds illustrated against blue skies, and at the wall paintings, noting that in one of them a beautiful woman was standing naked over what looked like a waterlily floating in a lake, surrounded by two men whose feet were hanging in the clouds. Jeanette Cromantine served them rice bread, cake and ginger beer, asked about their children, made them feel comfortable, and in a short time had them talking about sewing and asking to be instructed in the fashionable art of making dresses.

That was how Jeanette Cromantine became one of the most important women among the settlers, and how in later years her business acumen would extend her trade to Fernando Po, Forcados, Lobito and

Calabaro. The women who came regularly on Saturday not only learned how to sew but were soon procuring expensive materials for Jeanette Cromantine to make elaborate costumes and gowns in readiness for the numerous festivals the people of Kasila delighted in holding all year round. There were festivals for sun and river gods, festivals for births and deaths, rain and thunder and there were festivals for when important people were setting out on long journeys. Nothing was ever left to chance and Jeanette Cromantine, who had begun to grasp the importance of being well dressed for the right occasion, soon had her hands so full with orders that soon she was compelled to take in two of the women she herself had trained, as apprentices. It was at that time that a completely new development happened that would change her life, make them rich for a while and eventually lead to the surprise attack that would wipe out the settlement.

One morning, a sailor who had gone fishing up the river for crocodiles and had been left behind by his ship came to Sebastian's house because he had been drawn by the smell of ham cooking in pineapple sauce. He was young, with a shaggy beard, and green eyes that kept going all over the place. His right arm was tattooed with a replica of the Queen of Hearts, while his left bore a reproduction of the dragon of Indonesia. He spoke a language which was not exactly Portuguese but which was understood nonetheless as having something to do with the language of Portugal spoken by bandits and pirates. Sebastian, who had encountered sailors before, recognised the harsh intonation of a man brought up in Brazil from where most of the sailors who were then frequenting the place came. They fed him, let him wash himself, and that night he was allowed to stay in the guest room while Sebastian kept vigil in front of the room with his old war gun. He was gone the next morning, after thanking the Cromantines for their kindness. But they refused to accept the gold coin that he offered as payment. Jeanette Cromantine noticed however that the sailor had looked at some of her dresses on her worktable with fascination, that his eyes lost their liquid vagueness of his first day and became almost a pale grey as if the sight of the dresses reminded him of something painful in the wild ocean of his life.

Jeanette Cromantine's business prospered so much that she hardly had time for her husband except for the rudimentary duties of a wife. In addition to her dresses and dolls, she had one day hit upon the then foreign idea in the village of making puppets which, thanks to the mice-like propensity of the women of Kasila to produce children, soon became hot items in the village. As soon as they had grasped the provocative

79

possibilities of the puppets, the women rushed in with their orders. They wanted them made to resemble mothers-in-law they did not like; husbands who talked in their sleep, and women who were perceived as witches and had goitres. 'Make one for me that resembles an owl. It's for my mother-in-law when she visits us at night,' one of her customers said. Everyone wanted the ubiquitous caricatures, saying what they had always felt for their bitterest enemies so that it wasn't long before Jeanette Cromantine became known as 'the judgement woman' because her creations were, to those people, pronouncements that only God could have inspired, and meant to convey the right message.

Although she was making money, try as she did Jeanette Cromantine could not forget that the primary reason she and Sebastian Cromantine had come to Malagueta was to make a home, raise a family and, hopefully, prosper. Tired of waiting for him to recovesr his old self, she decided to resort to a hedonistic trick that she hoped would take Sebastian's mind off other matters and entice him back to her. One Sunday night, when he had been looking at the sea for almost four hours, Sebastian suddenly found himself surrounded by six nubile girls bearing fruit trays and inviting him to eat. For a while, he seemed to come back from that country to the one of prolonged laughter that the faces of those young girls represented; to the idea of an infinite tenderness and caring that such lovely and splendid animals promised.

'Let's see now if he won't come back to his bed,' Jeanette Cromantine said to herself.

Later that night, after the girls had gone, Jeanette Cromantine drew the curtains together, put some incense in an urn in the bedroom, sprinkled some lavender water on the pillows, combed out her luxuriant hair and felt her naked, tremulous body glowing with warmth and desire as she waited for her husband. He came like a great horse, encumbered by an age of accumulated burden which made his legs ponderous, fixed to the ground, and his hands felt useless and weak like the extinct wings of a great pterodactyl bird as he tried to remove his clothes and put on his night shirt. Looking at the landscape of brown nudity lying in his bed, Sebastian felt like a little boy who had come upon a great treasure whose value he found hard to comprehend. A conglomeration of joy, desire, happiness and conquest flooded his being, urging him on, but at that moment when he wanted so much to expel the fearsome and relentless demons that had possessed him, he felt the strength of his manhood going out in him and he collapsed into the arms of his wife, crying like an orphan.

Unable to restore Sebastian's appetite for a taste of marital enjoyment, Jeanette Cromantine went back to her work. Times were good, business was booming and she was able to expand the poultry, and add two cows to their animal stock. The dark clouds of rain that had hung in the sky disappeared and gave the place a most endearing look, and she felt it would not be long before her husband was able to shake off the illness. To help him along the way, she took to sitting with him on the porch, cutting patterns out, and singing some of the songs of Fatmatta the Bird-Woman.

Then one evening, while she was heating ginger tea on the coalpot in the porch, the young sailor returned. He looked healthier and happy, dark like a Moor. He had trimmed his beard short, and the former look of vagabondage that his rough sailor's clothes had given him had been replaced by one of civility with his beige cotton suit, his office clerk's collar, his high cordovan boots and the white straw hat on his head. Hanging from his left shoulder was a large, worn bag of coarse and indeterminate leather that contrasted sharply with the general air of neatness about him. He came up the steps of the porch with a timidity that was at once noticed by Sebastian, removed his hat, bowed and said, 'Evening, Mister, evening, Ma'am,' and began to speak in a formalised manner.

'Kept thinking about this place after I left. How you good people took me in, gave me food, a bed and kindness, and you don't even know where I come from or if I am a thief or pirate, even if I robbed one of your kind before, which, as God is my witness, I never did. When I left here, ship went back to the place they call Madagascar, which is the most beautiful island in the world, and I know what I am saying, because I have seen many islands in the world. The people there are beautiful and gentle like monks, and they got birds the colours of twenty rainbows grouped together, and one the size of an elephant that lays eggs big as a coconut, and monkeys that are so tamed they could steal the clothes off your back if you let them. A man could get spoiled there, Ma'am, with all those dark women inviting you to stay and eat crabs cooked in coconut milk and wanting to take you home to their grass huts, where a man could believe that Adam and Eve were still alive in paradise. Never been so happy before, because a sailor's life is harsh. "Enjoy yourself, Rodrigo! Life is too short!" I told myself. This is not your Brazil where the priests are telling all the Indians to put on white man's clothes, and collecting their precious images of solid gold which they replace with useless images of Christ that the Indians never heard of. Also, the

Fazendeiro farmers from Portugal are stealing all the land, the native women, and even the cattle.'

'So why you come back?' asked Sebastian.

Rodrigo was a man not accustomed to the idea of permanence. The thought of the familiar and constancy was like a ship wrecked in the middle of the ocean. While it lasted, he enjoyed the pleasures of the women of the island, its primeval creatures, its smell of prehistoric times, and its clocks that had been stopped two hundred years before so that the people could be happy without having to resort to the remembrance of past labours or anxieties. But he missed the freedom not so much of the sea but of his own creation. Paradise was a spectre of creation stamped with its own eternity, with its own order and with its own solitude. So he had found the idea of an unbroken happiness in Madagascar frightening, and left one day and went on another boat to Brazil. There he had worked as a miner among the Indians of Roraima. It was a vast area, rich in minerals, where men died from malaria and succumbed to leprosy. Others were condemned to waste in the sulphuric future of their hearts or to die in the beds of Indian women who sold cheap jewellery and blankets during the day and their bodies at night.

A renewed passion for the sea finally drove him away from the mines. His heart was never really in it, and he had gone down more to make money than for any other reason. Every day he came face to face with the insatiable greed that gripped men once they were faced with the possibility of increasing their wealth, with the limitations of kindness, with the brutish command with which the overseer bullied the Indians, the parasitic exploitation of the earth by men forsaken by time, and with an innate cruelty for other men. Thus, when he finally left, he swore never to be among such men again, never to confuse the desired attainment of happiness with the quick and rapacious pursuit of that happiness. As he sailed through the Straits of Magellan, past the emerald islands where the Spaniards had begun to destroy the tombs of the sungods, the idea of revisiting Malagueta began to take hold in his mind. Life was just beginning there, he felt; the land was rich and there was much to be done in that burgeoning world of men and women who, like him, had escaped from one form of terror in search of freedom. Accordingly, he brought samples of a crop which he intended to introduce to the place, that he thought would grow, while he could always come back at any time he chose.

'Just came back so as to see you and bring something to help out, plus presents for you and the missus.'

Jeanette Cromantine looked at a glittering blue stone, round like an egg dotted with green and white marks of transparent luminosity. She felt at once that Rodrigo had brought a stone with magical powers to protect her, like the glass beads of Fatmatta the Bird-Woman.

'Ain't never seen de like before, so you gon tell me what it is,' she said.

'It's lapis lazuli, and you can wear it in a locket on a chain.'

She had never heard the name before, but she thanked him, and promised to wear it on Christmas Day when she was sure 'all de new womens come to town will see me and Sebastian is gon be mighty proud of his woman'.

The solid gold watch that Sebastian Cromantine got was to be his parting gift to his son many years later, before he died. The watch with its hands that never failed to fascinate him also came to symbolise his attachment to this first settlement before it was wiped out by the plague, by the degree to which the ticking of the mechanism with its anatomy of the future served to help him to regain his bearings and a sense of the clarity of time.

But it was the crop samples that interested Jeanette Cromantine more than the expensive gifts that Rodrigo had brought for them. When she saw the reddish-brown crop, Jeanette Cromantine at once perceived the possibility of doing what she and Sebastian had not thought of before they sailed on the *Belmont*, and which needed less time to grow. Now, regarding the omission as part of the confusion that had overwhelmed them when they had first conceived of the journey to Malagueta, she tried to bring back the lost years, the agony of her husband, the neglected land that was there for the asking. But she knew she had time on her side and felt that it was Divine Providence that had sent the stranger to them. For that reason, she did not mind having to work in the field, despite her upbringing, despite her pastor foster-father, and that long, long nightmare about fields in the other country.

'If ah have to do it all alone, ah gon do it, God willing,' she tried to reassure herself.

It was a reassurance she did not need. Next morning, Rodrigo was up before the Cromantines. He had cleaned the parlour, lit the coalpot and was drinking tea when Jeanette Cromantine came into the parlour. Although she was only a few years older she felt like a mother who had neglected to feed her son, seeing the Brazilian sitting there.

'Poor man,' she said, 'let me feed you some nice brown bread, honey and bacon; dat is if you ain't no Moslem.'

'No, ma'am, never met a Turk in my life.'

'You got any mama?'

'She died a while ago,' he replied.

'My mama died when I was a big girl, just before we come on de boat to dis place; but I sure do miss her, yessir, she and ma old pa.'

It was the first time she had thought of them jointly: the old pastor whom she had regarded as a father, and the big mulatto woman who had come frequently to his cabin, bringing things from the big house where she worked. A tear escaped from her eye and sailed down her smooth, light brown face, but she quickly wiped it away, because it took her into an avenue where there was no beauty, no love or sunshine. She fed Rodrigo, listened to the kingfishers on the jacaranda tree, went out to fetch some water for Sebastian and sat down on the porch to contemplate the unfathomable extremes of happiness.

The digging of the holes for the potatoes commenced the very next morning. Rodrigo worked from morning to dusk making them round, three inches deep, and in a straight line. Next, he constructed a channel that wound its way round the holes, allowing each to be irrigated with water taken from the stream of eternity running under the Cromantines' house. When he had planted the young of the potato plant, Rodrigo felt a certain exhilaration take hold of his mind. Sitting with a cup of strong tea, he reflected on the story of the man who had planted his crop in fertile ground and reaped accordingly. But if he was going to reap anything from what he had sowed he hoped it would be in the nature of a secondary pleasure for him, because he had, by coming to Malagueta and seeing the Cromantines, already experienced a great levitation. He recalled an incident in his childhood when his father had gone fishing in a river near their village, and had come home with the biggest fish any one had ever caught. In that village of prehistoric nostalgia, of women who waited for men whose ships did not come back, of children who sold macaw feathers for food, Rodrigo remembered the kindness of his father. When he brought his fish home, during a period of great want, his mother, a tired and bitter woman aged by the circle of childbirths, funerals, baptism and the paganistic adoration of saints whose figurines she kept in her room, wanted his father to keep the fish for themselves.

'But I can't, Emelia, we must share and trust in our faith for more.'

'Think of your children, they are growing in the streets because of your waywardness,' she replied.

'There, they receive love, here they hear nothing but recrimination and your talk of saints.'

He gave most of the fish away. Many years later, when he was crippled by sclerosis, his wife and the other children abandoned him. It was Rodrigo who came round every day to lift him from his bed and put him in the wicker chair so he could sit, wrapped in an old Indian blanket, on the wooden porch. The son never grumbled, emptying his chamber pot and bringing him food from the store. Rodrigo was happy and did not wish to gain anything for himself. He was part of mankind, and that was enough reason for him to be optimistic and grateful.

Things went on according to plan. The potato crop responded to the care and attention given it by Rodrigo and Jeanette, who had temporarily suspended the making of puppets and her dressmaking lessons. The women from the village came to lend a hand with the dresses. They would spread their fine loose garments on the parlour floor and let their children roam all over the place, while they made the rudimentary outlines of dresses for Jeanette to complete later. But just before it was time for them to harvest the crop a great hurricane almost blew Malagueta off the face of the earth. It had been coming for days; the July heat had been oppressive and humid, the air tasted of sea salt, and a great fear hung over the place as everyone tried to reinforce their doors and shutters. It came in the night when Jeanette Cromantine felt the foundation of her cabin shake with the force of a conglomeration of earthquakes, threatening to renounce the validity of the settlement. She heard the thunderous disorder of the winds tearing into the sheaves of the roof which threw Sebastian, lying next to her, out of bed. Then, as if from some large pyramidic dam, she heard the violent lamentation of the stream under the cabin, and the rush of a tormented season bearing the stones of the intemperate flood.

'De crop! De crop! Sebastian, de crop, Rodrigo!' she screamed.

They rushed into an avalanche of people in a confused stage of awakening and despair. Men were groping around looking for their wives who had come out in various stages of shock; the children scrambled to climb the trees to escape the fury of the water, raising the panic of the dogs. Jeanette Cromantine did not lose her courage as she found herself deep to her knees in a whirlpool of water, threatening to drown her. She dug her feet deep into the mud, while the world shook with the force of the hurricane. They had never experienced anything like this before and had no idea of how to deal with the disaster. Then, from some great instinct, born out of the immediacy of danger, Rodrigo had a lucid idea.

'Gather the stones,' he yelled. 'We have to divert the water.'

The great rush of water pounded the cabins, and knocked down the trees. Nothing seemed to be able to withstand the onslaught, but the instruction from the Brazilian suddenly fired everyone out of the fear that had gripped them. Freeing herself from the quagmire, Jeanette Cromantine waded her way towards the path of the stones brought down from the hills. Suddenly, she felt a pair of hands lift her as if she were a leaf and drag her out of danger. It was her husband. He had thrown off his shirt and, in a demonic rage that matched the rain's, Sebastian Cromantine was hauling stones towards Rodrigo, attempting to construct a dike. He worked with the strength of ten men to pile the stones on top of each other, reinforced with the mud of black earth. Both men battled against the force of the universe which seemed determined to drown them in a lagoon of untimely death; using all the strength that they could command, they pushed the stones in the path of the water, which in turn knocked down the dike as if it were a useless object.

Deep in the belly of the hills, they heard the murderous cannons and the gigantic roar of cavernous gods. It was as if they had enraged the rulers of all the eternities who were demanding sacrifices, and that only the death of those two men foolish enough to fight against them could prevent the disaster from reaching its climax. Then, when all seemed almost lost, Sebastian Cromantine saw a multitude of hands reaching down to pick up the stones. He heard the great and unified cry of his people: those brave men and women who had already crossed one frontier to come to this unruly and treacherous land. He perceived through the window of another time the primeval certainty that the key to all creation lay in endurance, that God had endured to create the universe and to create man, and that he wanted man to endure and to create. Like a great raging elephant, he picked up a large boulder and hurled it in the path of the water, and the liquefied tongue of death was forced to part into two paths. The men resumed the building of the dike, and several hours later, exhausted, with their feet deep in the mud, looking like mad men, they heard the distant rumbling of the thunder in the mountain which when it had died down was succeeded by the flow of the stream, now charting a new course on its way to the sea.

The potato crop had been saved, no one had died and everyone seemed happy that they had survived their first baptism in Malagueta. Everyone except Sebastian. Ever since that day when he had collapsed like a sack of rotting corn, he had shut himself up in a world that was silent except for the spiders in the dark. When he managed to escape from that prison, he saw himself on another stage; he was an actor in a play where he was the only performer obeying some instructions from a director whose hands were white, whose face was black but whose voice was indiscriminate. It was this feeling of not knowing where or what he was that was the nadir of his life in these trying times. He lived in a vast cave of loneliness, dejected and trying to hold on to the last threads of hope that had propelled them on the crossing across the ocean. How bitter it was that in this Arcadia he should feel so enervated! He thought of his father, of the night the old man had visited him, dragging his impermeable bones, and thirsting not so much for water but for some final release from his century of wandering. Now, it was as if having brought his father's bones to rest in Malagueta, Sebastian was at some crossroad where nothing was clear, where existence was puerile. And all he wanted was to be a man, to make Jeanette happy, to create in that void dug by centuries of exploitation. Sometimes, out of earshot of his wife, he brought his lips to the songs he remembered from the plantations; the songs of chain gangs, the songs of revolts that never got off the ground, songs that helped to relieve the anatomy of suffering and promised to accompany them to freedom. But it wasn't the quality of the freedom that bothered him as much as the listlessness he felt in this new place.

Looking back at the near disaster that they had experienced with the potato crop, he felt that perhaps it was because conquest had only just taken hold of him in a moment when all seemed lost, and which was common to all individuals, to all humanity, that he had felt so alone, adrift, like his father. He could no more wish to be free of the filial debt he owed the old man than to wish he had some scheme about how to work out the equation between being alive and being happy; but he was glad that the woman whom he had married understood and put up with his idiosyncrasies. His gloom lasted another three months. He gave up spending too much time on the porch with the pungent smell of the geraniums, went out for walks on the hills, came home rather late and tried to sleep. Then one night, while the mosquitoes buzzed over his head, he had a dream. He was shipwrecked on some remote island in the company of a family of malachite kingfishers. In that world of dazzling luminosity he felt a certain gaiety, listening to the melodic voices of the birds, to their morning serenade. And because the island had no inhabitants other than the birds, Sebastian found it easy to sleep. In that idyll, his father came to visit him for the first time since he had left America. Cured of wandering, spending his days as a fisherman who came occasionally to the island, the old man was surprised to see his son.

'You have come a long way from the west, my son,' he said.

Sebastian told him about his unhappiness and how he had been unable to work, but the old man did not let him continue. 'Dat's de trouble wid you young 'uns. You think of time; life is change, change every day. Go back home and enjoy.'

Then he told his son how happy he had become, fishing only for what he needed to eat. He had found himself a woman and they were so happy that she would sing like a barbet while he fed the lugubrious seacows and taught the herrings how to avoid the kingfishers. In the evenings, they had nothing better to do than to listen to the poetic birds settling down for the day, while she played her bowharp. 'Life is so peaceful, son, dat I feel like a young bull,' he said.

Once again, the old man touched him and disappeared. When he woke up from his dream, Sebastian Cromantine also felt ten years younger, like a man who had dyed his hair and was about to marry a young new wife. He got out of bed, lit the coalpot to make some ginger tea and chased away the persistent mosquitoes. Jeanette Cromantine had always made her husband's tea, served it to him on the veranda, and left him to his melancholia. She could barely conceal her surprise when she saw that he no longer looked morose and was, in addition to drinking his own tea, whistling a soft tune.

'What done happen to you?' she asked.

'Life ain't one season,' he said. 'Gotta change, change, change, whichever way you look at it.' The change was coming faster than she imagined.

One day, his friend Gustavius Martins came to visit him. While Sebastian had been struggling to find himself in Malagueta, and having visits from his father beyond the border of the living, the other man had not only adjusted to the new environment but was now so much a part of it that no one remembered that they had come only recently to this place or that he had quietly given up the habit of wearing his long gabardine trousers in favour of the loose, long gowns favoured by the men of Kasila. The change had not been unexpected, for although he had prospered as a mason and had built himself one of the best cabins in Malagueta, in one way, however, he lacked recognition. He lacked a woman he could call his own. Since that day when he had seen the woman bathing in the stream, he had undergone a slow transformation.

He wasn't the only womanless male among the settlers but while the others hoped to have one if and when new women arrived from the other country, Gustavius had decided to have that woman and had been planning accordingly. Unknown to Sebastian, he had been learning the language of the people of Kasila, adopting their food habits, and the wearing of the long gown was merely an extension of his preparedness. Abandoning his normal practice of visiting his friend when they would talk about the past, he fell into a state of unhappiness brought about by his failure to find love with that woman. He went about like a man who had become the victim of some kind of fetish and felt that if he could not have that woman, he might end up like his brother who had died without continuing the line. So many weeks later when he decided to call on Sebastian, he was thunderstruck to see the woman there in the group of women learning to make the puppets with Jeanette. With a solemnity unusual for him, Gustavius Martins told his friend how he had come upon the woman in the stream, how he had gone back there several times in the hope of finding her there and, not doing so, had stolen into the village at night disguised as one of their men, going from yard to yard, taking care not to disturb the hens or alarm the dogs. He had seen other women bathing in the stream, but not finding her among them, he consoled himself with the ephemeral amnesia of rum, only to wake up the next morning more desirous of the woman, and going back in search of her. He sought her in the musical variations of the women pounding rice, and in the twilight atmosphere of story-telling round the open fires, in the tormented insomnia of rainy nights, and here she was when he thought he would never see her again.

Sebastian was aghast, 'You gone crazy, my friend,' he said.

'Ah may be crazy, ole friend, but dat is what life all about; a little craziness.'

'You don't know what you doin,' said Sebastian. 'You goin bring de king out here, and we be thrown out of dis place.'

Gustavius Martins did not consider that a serious possibility. He reasoned that with the growth of the settlement, the new skills that the settlers had brought to the development of the whole area, he could take his chance with the woman by asking the king for permission to marry her. Failing that, he threatened to put an end to the matter by kidnapping the woman and going off into the woods to live with her.

'Do dat, and you gon start a war,' Sebastian said.

'Leave him, he ain't a chile no more, and every man be wanting a woman in his life pretty soon 'cept you,' Jeanette said, speaking up for

Gustavius. She was a born optimist and had never once swayed from her conviction that Providence had brought them to Malagueta. Unlike her husband, she had adjusted and believed she had a chance to survive and prosper, and her optimism showed in the delicacy of her smile, in the unselfish manner in which she let the wives of the men in the nearby town take up her time. It was she they came to for advice when their children came down with measles and influenza, and when they caught their feet in animal traps she made poultices for them. After the potato crop had been saved, she had resumed her puppet business with a restored vigour, and soon practically every home had one form of it for the numerous festivals of each year. With some of the other wives of the settlers, she had become a teacher of not only their own children but of some of the children of the surrounding village so that her esteem was high and her advice much valued. Although she had not succeeded in dragging her husband to her bed, Jeanette Cromantine nevertheless believed in love as the ultimate goal and happiness between men and women. Thus she was pleased that some woman had aroused the fire of desire in the heart of Gustavius, whom she loved like a brother, and made a secret promise to bring them together in her house if possible.

A week later, when she was having some ginger tea with her husband and Gustavius, she told the lovesick man, 'She will be there, where you first saw her; she sends you a basketful of fruits that are in the kitchen.'

He found the woman, whose name was Isatu Dambolla, waiting for him by the stream that evening, listening to the nostalgic cicadas. She sat with her knees clasped together and her head resting on them, and with such a calm beatitude that the ripples she made in the stream with a small stick seemed almost a part of her beauty. She was surprised that he had mastered her language and could converse in it about even the smallest details of life, and that he was as shy as a jerboa. That evening they talked about her growing up frightened of witches, of his growing up among the pine needles of hate and death in a country 'without tenderness'.

After that meeting, Gustavius Martins lost his bearings. It soon became obvious that he was suffering from an obsession, which was how to ingratiate himself into the heart of Isatu Dambolla. He conceived of the most beautiful ideas, translated them into creative expressions with which to express his love. Labouring in his workshop, he made figurines, carved large wooden elephants and many other objects which he sent to her family. Not being a poet or a man who went out of his way to find pleasure in nature, he had never been aware of the intrinsic and lovely music of weaverbirds, of the enchanting courtship dance of ostriches. But now, he found pleasure in not only those creatures, but even in the most commonplace of things.

Around that time, the people of the town were getting ready for the annual harvest festival, which always ended in a parade. On the afternoon of the parade, the whole town would begin to line up in the streets to watch the main event, which was the crowning of the beauty queen of the year. In addition to receiving entreaties from all the available young men, she was guaranteed a large portion of the harvest.

Gustavius Martins decided to get in on the act. Emboldened by the certainty that his gifts would be accepted, he thought of the then novel idea of building a wooden lantern to look like Noah's Ark. He worked on it for a whole month, and completed it just two days before the parade. Jeanette Cromantine, using all her skills as a negotiator, persuaded the shy Isatu to ride in the lantern. So on the afternoon of the carnival, the astounded people saw the most spectacular creation ever to pass through their town. They saw a large wooden ship with dens for lions and caves for hyenas. Saying that the man who could make such beautiful things must have received his inspiration from God, they had difficulty taking their eyes away from the aviaries for the birds which chirped, chirped and tried to outdo each other preening their plumages, while the primates danced to the music of the xylophones and turned their bottoms on anyone who annoyed them.

But the star attraction was the queen herself. Although she was undoubtedly the most beautiful girl in town, Isatu Dambolla had never looked more lovely as on that late afternoon of the ship of the enchanting animals. Sitting on a high throne made of polished mahogany with gold armrests, and surrounded by a dozen attendants dressed as Moors, she waved to her admirers like an empress, while two women fanned her with fans made of ostrich feathers. Lions crouched in front of her, and a chimpanzee dressed as a sailor rang a bell and smoked a large cigar.

Isatu was crowned queen of the festival that evening. But in spite of her triumph, she found the attention lavished upon her by the Malaguetan rather puzzling. Being a woman not yet wise to the ways of men, especially foreign ones, she viewed it as merely the fascination of a man for what was then a local girl he barely knew.

Urged by Jeanette Cromantine, she went twice to the stream to meet Gustavius Martins, but behaved with the utmost discretion and sobriety. During those stolen moments, she was aware of the demons she unleashed in him, the way his hand shook when he tried to hold her own, the roads of the many odysseys he had taken just to get to Malagueta and to her.

They would have gone on like that, meeting near the bullrushes, but for the fact that Isatu Dambolla felt that in that town where gossip grew like a wild bushfire someone was bound to discover their idyll. Confused and tormented by the feeling that she could not give up this man, while at the same time she was frightened to give in to him, she went to Jeanette Cromantine to ask for her advice.

'He ain't like de others,' Jeanette Cromantine said. 'And ah sure he means to treat you nothing but proper.'

In spite of this assurance, Isatu Dambolla did not relax her guard. She continued going to meet the man at the river, though the visits were becoming infrequent. As in the past, these meetings brought new discoveries. She learned more about life in the country without names. She wanted to know whether the women looked like the ones in Malagueta, if they had to work on farms and had too many children. When Gustavius Martins told her that some of the women he knew were so afraid they would become ugly after giving birth that they hired wet nurses for their babies, she replied that they were not women but scarecrows.

The long wait for an answer was beginning to have a noticeable effect on Gustavius Martins. After months of trying to get Isatu to relax, and to let him hold her in his arms, he broke off one evening from her and went to have a drink in the only rumhouse then in town.

His friend Sebastian Cromantine found him later in the night, lying in a gutter with a cut lip. When he had left Isatu Dambolla, Gustavius had not cared where he was going. He wanted only to be away from that woman who was causing him so much pain. It was a prison he found unbearable, because after the dark furnace of the life on the plantation, he needed the illuminating power of love to live and have children. So that when he put the first cup of rum to the parchy roof of his mouth, he was driven by the longest grief ever known to man, and his groans came from the farthest country of despair.

Sebastian Cromantine washed his lips and put him to bed. Being of a different temperament, he felt no woman deserved that kind of suffering. He resolved to talk to his wife, to get her to intervene on his friend's behalf.

'Ah may not like de idea, but if dat woman gon let ma friend suffer so much, den we gon kidnap her, and ain't nothing her father kin do,' he said.

Jeanette Cromantine did not give him a reply. She was expecting her friend in the evening. When Isatu Dambolla arrived, laden with all kinds of materials to make new dolls, Jeanette Cromantine noticed that she kept her eyes fixed to the ground during the sewing of the first doll. The colour of her skin that had made Isatu so lovely had lost some of its lustre, and her face wore the look of a woman who had not slept for days. Then, with the insight of one woman peering into the heart of another, Jeanette Cromantine deduced that her friend was also suffering. It was the opportunity that she had waited for, and she seized it.

Lifting the chin of the younger woman, Jeanette Cromantine looked deep into the large eyes, filled with tears.

'Ah gives ya ma word,' she said, 'dat if he gives you a child he gon act like a man.'

That night, Isatu Dambolla found it hard to sleep. She sat by a window in her bedroom, biting her lips, and watching the stars in the sky. When she was sure that her father was fast asleep in the room next door, she threw all caution to the wind, unlocked the main door and ran to the stream. Praying that Gustavius Martins would be waiting there for her, she told herself that she would do anything he wanted. When she saw him sitting with his back turned to her, she ran up to him and threw herself into his arms. Her voice trailed into a longing that was so painful as she started to kiss him that he let her drink the raw wound on his lip.

'Love me,' she said, as she held his hands to her breasts, guiding him like a child.

Gustavius Martins did not let his inexperience thwart the fire in his heart. He stretched the woman out on the grass, and felt a storm raging in his body. When he entered her, a wild cry escaped her lips, disturbing the egrets nearby; the pain and pleasure that accompanied the flow of her warm blood raced through her legs which she wound round the waist of the man. Then, knowing that he was entering her innermost secret, Gustavius Martins felt himself carried on the crest of a tumultuous sea where the woman was a mermaid; and he did not resist the coils of her legs which were tightening round his neck, pulling him down into a deep whirlpool, where she was searching for the fabled conch. Her last resistance gave way as she carried him on his first journey of love trying not to reach the bottom of the sea, because it was becoming hard for her to breathe. She clung passionately to him, called his name in all the languages of her people, and as their bodies merged into one, they clawed each other like sea-anemones, as she surrendered to the tempestuous rhythms of his homecoming.

A week later, over the furious protest of her father, who threatened to expel all the settlers from Malagueta if she went ahead with her decision, she married the man who had given her a taste of happiness, standing in front of a man wearing a white collar, who intoned the words of a God she had never heard of before but was prepared to meet through her husband.

The morning after the wedding, the newlyweds rode in the float where Isatu Martins had been crowned queen. So as not to let any other person use it, they drove it into the remotest part of the forest and walked back to the cabin of the man. Nine years later, Thomas Bookerman and his men, trying to find the spot where the first Malaguetans had established their settlement, were to pass through the region. Hacking their way with cutlasses through the forest, they followed the sounds of the chattering birds who had made their home there, and discovered the lantern intact. They saw the lions crouching in the same position, waiting for Isatu Martins to come down from her throne, and they readily understood from the look of happiness in the eyes of the first primate sailor that he would have gone on wearing his uniform for ever, because he was waiting for the ark to start sailing with the million birds that were nesting in it. To protect the creation that the lovesick man had built, Thomas Bookerman sealed off the area with a high wall of granite stone.

Jeanette Cromantine did not expect the immediate effect that the love between Gustavius and Isatu would have on her husband. He who had spent weeks cloistered in a prison to which only he had the keys, he who had entered a world of premature impotence, letting the cobwebs grow in his mind, suddenly found the impetus to live a normal life again, as he watched the growing relationship between his friend and the young woman from Kasila.

'Life has no meaning if there ain't some idea of a place,' he said unexpectedly one evening as his wife came out into the veranda. For the first time in months, he found the appetite to eat. Shocked at his own state of dishevelment, he washed and changed after having gone without a bath for a week. It was while he was washing himself in the backyard that he discovered the new addition that Jeanette had made to their livestock. During his illness she had added a cow, two goats, lots of hens and a sheep from the proceeds of the puppet business. She had also hired a young man from Kasila to take over the upkeep of the garden now that she was too preoccupied with the puppet business. Sebastian came out of his shell just in time. He had been inside so long that he had not noticed the obstreperous atmosphere the town was assuming. Suddenly, everyone seemed to be busy, to be doing something as if they were preparing for a great occasion. He decided to find out from Jeanette.

'Why is everyone running about?'

'Because it's Christmas next week, you fool.'

He entered into a new phase. The news that Christmas was just around the corner did much to revitalise his spirit, and to give him a new concern for time. Suddenly he realised that much had to be done. He had not visited the spot where he had kept his father's skull and he shook in mortal horror at this neglect. He had to talk to it and return to work; but he did not have a clear vision of what he had to do, now that the shopkeeping business was over. Though he had intended to farm, he had let the seeds that they had brought rot during the first rainy season. However, with his spirit restored, he knew he had discovered the new enlightenment in his previously clouded life. Gone was the anguish that had paralysed his senses, that ambivalence he felt for this place although he did not want to return to that other country. He realised that he had come home to this sanctuary, with its mystery, its malarial womb and its claustrophobic and sweltering heat. And the more he came to accept that life offered some sort of plenitude here, the more he accepted the idea of the existence of another God who had made it possible for them to come back here, to start all over again. It was then he remembered that three months earlier, while he had been exploring the hills above the settlement, he had discovered that coffee grew there in abundance. The climate was similar to that in Georgia, and he was familiar with the crop from his days on the plantation. But before now, Sebastian Cromantine had not thought much about his discovery. Snared in the labyrinth of the past, in the illusory power of snakes, he had been unable to think straight and look through the window of inertia to future endeavours. If he had kept his discovery a secret it was not because of any idea of entrepreneurial gain which he knew nothing about at that time, but because coffee like cotton brought back memories that he wanted to forget. Who could blame him? For that reason, his new vitality was real and promising, and he shone with a glow that was so warm that it was apparent to everyone that what had restored his life was not so much the realisation that Gustavius had found love, but that Sebastian had rediscovered the terrifying power of his love for his wife. Everything that he heard or saw was affected by his intense feeling for her: the freshness of Easter lilies, the soft aura in the cabin, the smell of the bread that she baked, the perfume of geraniums in the flower pots, the songs of the sunbirds. The petals of love that he had not noticed in the past were suddenly opened for him to see, by that woman who when she looked at him now left him with an uncontrollable desire to fecundate her womb. Later that night, inspired by the memory of his father in that distant happiness of the other world, Sebastian Cromantine came silently towards his wife as she was undressing in the bedroom. He made her put on the lapis lazuli so that he could see its reflection on the graceful lines of her neck. When she touched the unbelievable evidence of his preparedness, Jeanette Cromantine gasped.

'Is it real?' she asked.

'Let's say it been wantin you too long,' he replied.

He blew out the oil lamp, pushed the window wide open to let the wind in. When he came into the warm tranquillity of the woman, Jeanette Cromantine swooned in the passion of a breathless man thrusting with the force of a bull and inspired by the primordial music of creation. Nine months later, she was to give birth to a son who was the first man to shoot a white governor.

They celebrated their first Christmas in style. All the heads of the families that had come to found the settlement met and decided that because they were all like one big family, there was to be no ceremony. Everyone could drop in on everyone. Later in the evening, they would all come out to the centre of the village, bring their food and musical instruments and enjoy themselves. A makeshift church had been built, and on Christmas morning all the men, women and children who could squeeze in came to worship and relive the magic of the birth of the baby Jesus. Thinking about the baby Christ Jeanette Cromantine prayed she would soon become a mother herself.

The excitement about Christmas and the knowledge that they were cooking for themselves meant that they did not have to be punctilious. There was no need to put aside some amenities for tomorrow, and because they had worked so hard during the first year in Malagueta, December found them with enough to eat. The potato crop of the Cromantines had done well and the sweet variety was especially suitable for puddings and cakes. Other settlers had planted corn, okra and beans, and raised turkey and guinea-fowls. Gustavius Martins provided the drinks; he had not planted like the other settlers but he knew how to brew corn, molasses and ginger, which after a short period of fermentation became a highly intoxicating drink. Afterwards, when the children were enjoying themselves, sucking on the delicious bonbon of happiness, an old man who had come on the journey alone, and who made shoes with goat leather, brought out a fiddle and began to play. Then, in that pastoral laxity that only those men and women rescued from the fumarole of despair could feel, they began to improvise a dance. Responding to the fiddler, they danced singly at first, then, as if to confirm the closeness they felt to one another, they linked their hands in a beautiful revelry which erased all memories of their past individual fates.

Much later Isatu, whose people had not lost the ancestral practice of celebrating an occasion with a masquerade, insisted on going to bring one. She came back with a man with parrot feathers in his hair, with a red cloth wrapped round his head. In one hand he held a horse's tail and a mirror in the other, and coming up close on his rear was a large figure completely covered in raffia grass that looked like a bear. Ten men who had accompanied the bear began to play an exotic music by rattling the bottom of calabashes with their fingers bedecked with rings. When the masquerade started to dance, the settlers were so astonished by its gyrations that some of them began to cry. It was a new discovery for them, this dance which was part of a heritage that they had forgotten but was nevertheless in their blood. Not to be outdone, an old settler disappeared from the crowd and returned later wearing red overalls and sporting a white beard that almost reached down to the ground. He came with a large bag that was hidden inside his overalls and told the children to close their eyes if they wanted to see the great wonders of the world. When they opened their eyes, they saw in front of them replicas of the manger, of the ships in which they had made the journey, of the banjos their grandfathers had consoled themselves with during their days of bitterest rancour, and of the drums that the colonial soldiers had carried as they marched through the towns during the last war. He distributed the gifts and told them they had come from a man called 'de Lawd'. The children had seen their first Father Christmas, whom they thought was an angel, and they were disappointed when he picked up his empty bag and walked away. They had wanted him to fly to 'de Lawd'.

The beginning of the new year intensified Sebastian Cromantine's optimistic plans for the coffee plantation he had been dreaming of before Christmas. Now that the terrible lassitude that he had felt before had been replaced by a prodigious expansion of energy he wanted to work and felt time was short. He replaced his solitary walks on the beach with trips to the hills. There, working to feverish pitches at times, he cleared the bush round the trees and after almost two weeks made a path that wound its way from the boundary of the town to the hills – thus doing away with the necessity of having to walk through elephant grass and encountering snakes. He gave up drinking rum in the evening and it wasn't long before his wife became suspicious about his daily trips in the mornings, his bouts of excitement and the feeling that he was hiding something. However, when she heard about his plans, Jeanette Cromantine responded in a manner for which her husband had not prepared.

'You don't know de first thing 'bout dis place,' she said. 'So how you gon grow coffee, if it ain't some craziness seize your brain?'

Sebastian Cromantine conceded he did not know much about the place. But he did not consider that a major obstacle, especially as no one else knew about the coffee trees, or seemed interested in them. He was not to be put off, and tried to seduce her with the prospect of selling the beans to the ships that called at Kasila, with dreams of expanding the house.

'Think of how much money we gon make. Ah knows ah kin do it. Also gives your man some respect. A man ain't a man if he ain't working.'

He had worked it all out and, in some curious way for someone who only recently was lost in the shadow of former times, dwarfed by the mirage of ancestral feasts, Sebastian Cromantine showed a strong temerity when it came to the one point that he felt could restore his credibility to his people and his sense of place. It wasn't pride, but more a matter of belief. He had seldom felt so sure of himself, so determined to prove that destiny had finally opened up the gates to success for him. Feeling that he already had some advantage over Jeanette, because of their recently restored love that had indeed been blessed with the promise of new life, he pressed on with his point.

'It's not as if ah trespassing; is only dat no one smart 'nough to think 'bout it, and soon you ain't supposed to be working lest your veins tek to swelling.'

Jeanette Cromantine was not a woman to argue with her husband who, from past experience, she knew to be as stubborn as a mule; but nor was she a woman easily won over with simple and dangerous schemes. She made him promise one thing.

'Promise me, Sebastian, dat if your coffee ain't doing well, you ain't gon be sick one more time, and ah kin get on wid ma potato business when de child done come.'

He went back to work. Each day brought with it new surprises and new discoveries: the waterfalls hidden in the mountains falling on black luminous rocks, giant dog-faced mandrills, intelligent chimpanzees that led him deep in the forested mountains. During breaks from tending the young coffee trees, he was surprised at how little he missed solitude, how unavoidably preoccupied he had become with his relationship to the earth so that he could not stop thinking. He would see how his coffee trees did, then, perhaps, avocados, oranges, tangerines; he felt elated.

Rain came to Malagueta early that year and he seemed to be the only one working hard at that time. The nights, which were humid, seemed unnecessarily long; people slept throughout the day, played draughts and cards in the evening, and generally tended to complain about pains in their joints, migraine and a loss of appetite. The only thing that they found edible was the sweet potato that was resilient enough to grow in all weathers. Jeanette Cromantine, growing heavy with her child, surveying their land, thought they had done well. Sebastian did not experience the lethargy of other men at this time. But nor was he aware that the air of prosperity was soon to give way to a most lethal development. Suddenly, by some involuntary movement of a mechanism that had been wired to their brains, some of the settlers began to suffer from a strange fever, passed a yellowish-green urine, and felt dizzy like flies trapped in oil. Unexpectedly, the first deaths struck. They claimed Rodrigo and the old fiddler. That afternoon, while Sebastian Cromantine and his friends buried the two men who had brought some happiness to Malagueta, Jeanette Cromantine wept bitterly, put the lapis lazuli and the glass beads of Fatmatta the Bird-Woman on her neck, and prayed for her unborn child. At first, Sebastian Cromantine was not alarmed. He assessed the situation and viewed the distemper of the dogs, the spate of diarrhoea and the loss of appetite among the people, the uncontrolled vomiting of the children, as a sign that they were suffering from the lassitude brought about by the oppressive climate, or that worse, they were experiencing a scourge that was new to them. He sought to calm them down, and went from cabin to cabin to advise people.

'Ain't no need to panic, it's only a little boderation, and it gon pass.'

He told them to mark their windows with white chalk, keep their hens and dogs inside, and to turn their mirrors to face the wall at night. The precaution was as useless as it was unnecessary, because two days later more people died, and Sebastian Cromantine could not resist the conclusion that it was something larger than what he had imagined. They had succumbed to the malaria scourge that would kill off many of them just as Sulaiman the Nubian had predicted many years earlier, when he had foreseen that, stamped for ever with the mark of their tragedy, ignorant of the legend of the scorpion woman who had married the stuttering albino, the evil wind of the anniversary of that marriage would blow many years later, when only a few would survive because the memory of that albino made all strangers suspect.

Going against his first instinct – which was to stay at home – Sebastian Cromantine went off one morning to see his coffee trees. He had not been there since the day Rodrigo had died but he was comforted by the inexorable feeling that this was his life, second only to his dedication to Jeanette. He had carved out a place in this mountain and he knew its pulse and its smell, the rich aroma of his coffee beans. He concluded by the pungency of the smell that they were almost ready for the harvesting. Now, he had to think about where to store them, how to transport them; his worries had started.

The evil wind of their misfortune began to blow as Sebastian was carried away by the anticipatory notion of success. He heard it rising with a tremulous fury from the mysterious solitude of the epistolary mountain that Pedro da Cintra had written to his king about. He perceived it in the frightened and ejaculatory cries of the rhesus monkeys on his beloved coffee trees, and in the ominous moment when a great snake appeared behind him. But unlike former times he did not run from that horror. Seizing his axe, he attacked the serpent with a prodigious strength in the hope of finishing it off with a single blow. The snake kept on coming, trying to raise its head, to strike the enraged man, but Sebastian Cromantine did not lose control. He let the snake exhaust itself, then as it tried once more to strike, Sebastian hacked its head off. He was no longer terrified of the images of the past.

A luminous bolt of lightning shattered his triumph, brought him back to the present. In that bright night he saw the ravenous tongues of fire shooting up in the village. Dropping his axe, Sebastian Cromantine began to run and he did not feel the sharp thorns that lacerated his body or the stones that blocked his path. A second bolt rang out in the mountain and it was as if he felt it in his belly which was another's belly, where the sperm of his ancestors had fertilised the egg of the woman. A great fear swept him up and he knew that he could not go on living if anything were to happen to the pastor's daughter. He found her huddled behind the bedroom door. 'Jeanette! Jeanette!' he cried. 'Everything gon be all right.' It was then that he heard the noise. A great horde of enraged men and women from Kasila was pillaging Malagueta, and

Sebastian Cromantine, crouching over his wife, prayed that Malagueta would not go up in flames. The plague that had been killing the settlers had spread to their neighbours. At first, they had not thought much about it. But when their children succumbed to death soon after eating the sweet potatoes which the foreign woman had planted, they deduced with an age-old logic, contrary to reason, that the seed of the settlers' misfortune had been planted in their world, which not even the totemic power of their gods could halt. Sebastian Cromantine ran out with his wife towards the hill. Trying to get away from the conflagrations, he did not see the sad dead eyes of the man haunted by the unmistakable proof of his estrangment. He did not hear the voice of Fatmatta the Bird-Woman guiding them through the now perilous forest, because at that moment, resounding so that it was heard in the bellies of the fleeing pilgrims, the last cabin of their claim to that world had fallen into the catastrophic furnace of their misfortune. The last fires of the memory of Malagueta were extinguished later that night by the unrelenting power of the rains so that their names were erased for ever from that place in spite of the voices begging to be understood, as the Cromantines and a few lucky ones rushed to the lacerating solitude.

4   Ballad of the Twelve Virgins

The morning after he lost his left eye in the colonial war, Thomas Bookerman thought he had lost everything. He felt a bitter rancour against the world, against the white men for whom he had fought and against those he had fought. Surveying his chances in the world, he viewed the prospect of life without his faculties intact as the worst tragedy that could have befallen him. He had never married, had run away a year before the war so he was a free man, and was prepared to kill to defend that freedom. But to have fought for others who did not deserve to be alive, left him numbed and desolate. It came therefore as a surprise to him, when two years later, in spite of his infirmity, he found himself at the head of twelve hundred men, women and children ensconced inside their tents on the shoreline of a great ocean, looking at their new country. They were a tough lot, frontiersmen and women who had trekked all over the face of the world and knew how to fight like bloodhounds; messianic and determined like crusaders, and with the fervour of priests who had sworn to build a new temple, because they had seen the face of the devil and defeated him in battle. At dawn they folded their tents, thanked the sailors who had brought them there, and set off on their journey.

Inspired by the fantastic tales of the incredible Malaguetans who had founded a town, Thomas Bookerman and his team had resolved to cross the ocean after a drunken sailor had told him about the place, somewhere in Africa, where they could live unharassed by white men.

'They have a paradise there,' the sailor had concluded.

At first Thomas Bookerman put the enthusiasm of the sailor down to the effect of a prolonged indulgence in piracy, in loose women and gambling. History had taught him to be wary. Life was a battlefield in which only the strong and the cruel survived, and although the present was merely a vague improvement on the past, he viewed the temporality of their situation as an opportunity to think, dream and hope. Through perseverance, he was finding the courage to come to terms with his disability, with the possibility that all was not lost. If only there was some pointer about where to turn, some unequivocal statement about destiny and exploration, he would feel better and ready for greater things and regeneration. If only he did not feel so distrustful. He found it hard all the same to forget about the image of that distant land that the drunken man had aroused in him. He would trust his instinct.

Thomas Bookerman had heard of the revolt in Santa Domingo, of Macandal the Left-Handed whose name and that of Toussaint L'Ouverture were associated with the most fearsome tales of demonic powers and cleverness that their race had created in the hearts of the French. When he was a little boy he had dreamed of those men in the distant country of the blacks, and in some invincible corner in his heart he carried their memory. Inspired by the irrefutable evidence of the exploitation of his people, now eking out a threadbare existence in the marshlands of Canada after the colonial war, he could dream anew of an exodus, of a country with an even more fearsome and turbulent mountain, where they could settle. The idea became an obsession, and he went out one night and knocked on all the doors of the wooden cabins, bent on persuading the men of the merits of his idea.

'We must leave here, and trust in Providence to get us there,' he said.

He pointed towards the ocean and tried to win them over with the prospect of unlimited land beyond it, where they could build better cabins, raise families, and be able to defend themselves against their enemies.

'Think of it,' he said. 'There we ain't gon have no more flames in our hearts 'cause of dem white folks.' The men who listened to him sat in stony silence. These were not men to be played with, because they had fought and killed for their freedom, and were accustomed to betrayals at the hands of former masters and prophets.

'Look at dis place,' Thomas Bookerman told them. 'It ain't no place for man, woman or chillum; what de white people don't wan dey give to us and you gon be happy to take it?'

An old black man with the look of a fearless African warrior spoke for the others. 'But how we know dis ain't some kind of trick? We free here and we ain't going back to no Africa where dey ketch us in de first place.'

'Ah knows how you feels 'bout dem brothers of yours,' said Thomas Bookerman, 'how dey done let you down before. But what you 'fraid of, what is freedom, if you ain't willing to test it, wipe away de humiliation, dem tears from your eyes? You ain't never gon be men and women in dis place fit only for dead folk. All free men gotta go to a new place to become new people. And we gon be armed so no one gon mess with us.'

The men looked at one another. No one bothered to speak, but in the eyes of their wives and children, huddled in the frightened dark corners, they saw the mercury of grief, the long and hard surfaces of the roads of malediction, the peripheral nature of their present existence and, prodded by their deep and penetrating silence, they relented and agreed to join the one-eyed man in his mad expedition across the ocean.

A year later Thomas Bookerman, at the head of those twelve hundred men, women and children, put down anchor on the Kasila coast. Leaving the rest of the party behind, where the bewildered local people offered to look after the newcomers but could offer no news of the whereabouts of the first Malaguetans, he set off with some forty-two men in search of the paradise that the sailor had told him about. He was convinced that it was all a bad joke, but he hoped to prove himself wrong. They kept to the caravan route taken by the salt Arabs on their way from the coast, alongside the great river so they were guided by its thunderous noise and by its reflection of blue light. When they had gone only about a mile, they were surprised that the world smelled of the earth, the sun came out of the morning and they saw the magnificent reptile-eating birds that looked like giant fish, and that had lived in the region since the beginning of time. Being men of adventure, they tried to cut their way deep into the dense and talkative jungle but Thomas

Bookerman and his men came across a foliage oozing a green and poisonous moisture that brought about an instant feeling of hunger. They were now tasting the salt of a country without a map, which they had not known was so great and awesome. It was there, to his surprise, that Thomas Bookerman discovered the lantern with the acrobatic animals and the splendid throne of Isatu as it was when she had kept Gustavius Martins under a cloud of confusion.

At the end of the first day he stopped to let his men rest near a waterfall. They had brought some food with them – stock fish, bread, corn and smoked alligator meat – which they ate with relish, and drank the clean water from the falls. Much later, while most of his men slept, Thomas Bookerman and two others who had elected to keep watch began to ponder on the nature of existence, and on why they had come on this journey. To the big man who had lost an eye trying to save his commanding officer from the jaws of death, the nature of man's existence had to be understood in terms of the absolute surrender of his own desires to the loftiest of ideals: the elevation of the spirit to the apotheosis of good work for mankind. He felt that nothing was beyond man; neither theosophy nor redemption, for both were in the nature of the first principle in life which was a belief in the importance of time. It was time that he had believed in as he had waited to embark upon the expedition a year ago. He was convinced the universe was orderly, and man would cease to oppress man once he was free of his own fear. In the silence of that night, punctuated only by the sound of the water falling upon those prehistoric stones, Thomas Bookerman tried to think of the world that he was going to create: free, just and humane. He had come on this journey to make that a reality and nothing was going to stop him.

His companions dreamed of a mysterious and absolute God whom they felt had created them for the divine purpose which was a great challenge to them. The trip to the unknown territory was part of that challenge. Suddenly, their reverie was broken by a feeling that something was moving towards them. While they had been dreaming they had not realised that the peaceful breathing of the night had given way to a multitude of sounds as if the earth itself was waking up from a long sleep, and surrounding them with the nocturnal regiments of the tropics: iguanas, ratel badgers, vipers and mongooses attracted by their camp fire.

The watchmen frightened them away with flame torches, trying not to disturb their sleeping comrades. They were at that moment terrified of that world: of its imponderable face, its many animal lairs, its creeping darkness and immensity, its eerie and primordial voices of restlessness, and of the tremulous and uncontemplative surface of its womb. But after some time, their nocturnal visitors left them to pass the night in a state of tension.

When, according to their calculation, they had spent three days in the jungle without seeing other humans, some of the men began to despair of ever reaching their destination and voiced their reservations.

'We come all dis way to find dem brothers and sisters,' urged Thomas Bookerman, 'and we gotta trust in Providence to find 'em.'

The next day, they were out of the jungle. Once again they saw the river which they had lost on the first day. As they were now covered with the slime and vapour of the jungle, they decided to wash themselves.

'Be careful of dem crocodiles, dey maneaters,' said Thomas Bookerman. They dived into the water and washed away their first contact with that mysterious world. Because it felt so good being there, the men soon forgot about the crocodiles and, much later that afternoon, while they were relaxing in the river, one of them was pulled down by a great reptile and was never seen again. It was therefore a sobered and sadder group that continued their search for the first pioneers. Because it was March, they did not have to worry about the rains or the hurricanes which, unknown to them, had plagued the first exploration to that part of the region. But the sun blazed down mercilessly on them, necessitating a slowing down through the unknown wilderness. Sometimes, a leopard or a hyena would emerge from the depths of the strange world, fascinated by the noise of the travellers, only to disappear again. Then one day, they found their path completely blocked by a herd of wild elephants which mercifully did not attack them.

After twelve days, they reckoned they had covered a long distance in that nameless tenebrous world of unbearable loneliness, dwarfed by tall monumental trees and home to a wild assortment of plants, reptiles and other animals. The men absorbed their plethora of smells and colours in a state of bewilderment, fear and fascination. It was a mad journey which only those men driven by a demonic fate and ignorant of the globe would have made. Two days later, when they had almost given up all hope of emerging from that monotonous darkness, and thinking that it was only a matter of time before they were eaten by wild animals, the jungle gave way to a rich and fertile valley on the slopes of the mountain from where the dark maze of a smoke cloud wound its way to a clear blue sky. They had spent two weeks in their determined search for the first Malaguetans, and after a good night's sleep Thomas Bookerman woke up the next morning in search of the source of that smoke. There, on top of that mountain, possessed of that inordinate loneliness which only conquerors feel, he was shocked to discover that the wide and savage ocean of their recent tormented history was clearly visible against the skyline with the fifteen ships still anchored in the bay.

'To think we have only gone a mile,' he wept. The realisation that it had taken him and his party the best part of two weeks to search for the lost Malaguetans when they could have done so in three days if they had travelled on the river, came as a terrible shock to Thomas Bookerman. Henceforth, he was to remember this day as the time when he resolved to build a settlement covering the entire length of the area they had mapped out, taking in all the coast to guard against the pirates, who he was sure would make attempts to attack the place. But first, he and his party had to find the Malaguetans.

They pressed on for two more days, groaning and moaning as the fiery sun blazed down at them with its red eyes. Sometimes one or two would succumb to the heat, fart, curse and momentarily recall the satisfaction and taste of entrails in the cabins, now regretfully left behind. But when they thought they had finally kept their appointment with death, a large tree, unlike any they had seen before, caught their attention.

Perched on its branches were large birds, which looked ghoulish because they had lost all their feathers round their necks. The prehistoric creatures seemed engaged at a feast and, making one last effort, Thomas Bookerman and his men walked to the tree and were shocked to the roots of their hairs. What they found at that site was not what they had been searching for all along.

Instead, he found a group of unsmiling people who looked at the newcomers with mistrust. These were the survivors of the early Malaguetans who had passed beyond the frontiers of life. He put their withdrawn mood down to the remoteness of the place, the fact that they seemed to be cut off from all human contact and most certainly did not know of their coming.

Once again, Thomas Bookerman had the difficult task of persuading people to move. He expostulated on the numerical strength of the new settlers, arguing that they 'could deal with any human or beast attack', and the danger of death in the prolonged exposure of the windswept mountains. He tried to persuade them with the sop that among the new settlers were midwives, priests who had brought entire congregations, and men who knew a lot about farming and were going to grow all sorts of delicious fruits.

106

'We want to share all we got wid you,' he said.

It was this last piece of news more than anything else that persuaded Sebastian to move. Though his coffee trees were doing well, he felt trapped in their pervasive smell, in their tenebrous shadows, in the warm, sweet aroma of the beans that impregnated his house because he was unable to sell them, and the prospect of doing business on the coast, protected by the undoubted reserve of the new settlement, finally mowed down any reservation he might have had about going back to the ruins of Malagueta. A week after Thomas Bookerman had left with his crew, Sebastian Cromantine told his wife to start packing.

'Do we have to go?' she asked.

'Yes,' he replied. 'Because dat's where we made our son.'

The first Malaguetans did not like the look of the newcomers. They resented the fact that their hideout had been discovered. Eight years earlier, when they had fled from the rampaging horde, they had come to this place, led by Sebastian Cromantine, and had resolved not to flee again from any enemy. Working with sheer determination and tenacity, they had cleared a new but smaller area and were now on their way to regaining a modicum of their former way of life. It had not been easy. At first they had survived on wild roots, monkey and lizard meat which churned the insides of their stomachs so that after only one month they had lost five of their dwindling number. Nor were they helped by the fact that when they had fled they had only the clothes on their backs and a few odds and ends. Everything had to be done again: the making of tools, the discovery of dyes, of the right sort of animal skins, the building of makeshift dwellings, everything necessary.

Isatu, who had been in bed with Gustavius when Malagueta was attacked and who fled with him, saved the settlement during those trying days. It was she who taught the women how to cook new foods, who showed them how to preserve meat with salt and thus do away with the habit of killing animals whenever they had to eat. Being a child of nature, she identified herbs with which they were able to survive during the languid torment of their flight.

With his assiduity restored, and his mind no longer locked inside a prison of shadows and illusions, Sebastian Cromantine had resumed the cultivation of his coffee crop. He worked with a feverish concentration, like a man running against time, responding to a summons, and he had to get to a shore frightened by the ominous current of failure. He did not really think he would fail because he had never failed at anything in life. But he did not know this country or what invincible enemy lay waiting in a treacherous ambush, to snatch his prize away from him. His beans were his alpha and omega, his passage through a channel at whose end he could already discern light. Because of the change in their lives he had to abandon the idea of an immediate trade with the white traders, but as soon as the first beans were ready to be harvested, he cleared the back room of the makeshift house of the little they had accumulated, reinforced it with a double door and prepared for his crops.

During the first year of their mountain retreat, Jeanette Cromantine, shaken by shock and anxiety, but in generally good spirits, had given birth to a son. It had been a difficult pregnancy; the result of her arduous work. She had done washing and cleaning, trying to make some sort of new home in a violent and untamed wilderness. She had kept her good looks, her ebullience and courage, but her body showed the signs of undernourishment brought on by the high carbohydrate diet proffered by the place. In the last month of her pregnancy her varicose veins became so hard and painful that she could barely walk. Confined to bed and consoled by her friend Isatu Martins, she felt miserable for the first time since their arrival in the new home. In the throes of her first signs of pain, she had almost forgotten about the man, her husband, who had been standing there all along.

'You ain't got no need to worry to much, 'cause we gon get outta dis. And once we over de hill, ah gon build you de best cabin dis side of de mountain.'

She was worried that her baby, because of lack of nutrition, would be born sick. 'Look at me, Sebastian, tell me you ain't 'fraid.'

He was not afraid. Fear was a contingency he had made plans for since they arrived. Looking at her, he was resolved that in spite of the humiliating circumstances of their lives, in spite of the fact that they slept on a mattress of rough and prickly grass, thrown on a hard bed of cheap wood, his wife and child would be spared any further hardship. If he had to drive himself relentlessly through that dense, mysterious forest so that they would not go hungry, he would do so. He had not been afraid to die on the battlefront in Virginia when he was fighting for his freedom, he knew how to fight.

One day before her son was born, Jeanette Cromantine woke up with a fever which left her prostrate and threw her into a day-long delirium. Isatu Martins made her drink a concoction consisting of the roots of a sacred tree she had dug in the enchanting forest, of lizards that had been soaked in the egg whites of tortoises to guarantee old age, the crushed beaks of eagles to make the child fearless, and the eyes of vultures to give him the power of seeing things in the dark. Jeanette's labour lasted twenty hours. It began as she was standing in front of the woodburning stove, cooking Sebastian his dinner.

'Go get the old granny,' she had said to the man.

The old woman, named Rosa, had delivered quite a lot of babies in her time. She herself had produced a son who had been lynched for looking with desire upon a white woman in Alabama, but his death had left her without the bitterness of time or the senility of lost memory.

So that when Jeanette Cromantine's pains started, Rosa got her to lie on the hard bed, while she prepared the paraphernalia of midwifery. Jeanette Cromantine discovered, during her ordeal, that her senses were not tuned to the pain she was feeling. A great cloud enveloped her, and she felt her body go limp. Then, as she began the long road to knowing how the real side of womanhood began, she saw, as if in a dream, a woman of exceptional beauty coming to lie beside her. The pains that had begun to tear at her insides stopped, and Jeanette Cromantine saw the celestial face of Fatmatta the Bird-Woman. She had lost the premature wrinkles of old age, which years of labouring in the fields and in the kitchens of supercilious brides had left on her face. As if time had not kept up with her, she had the body of a girl of sixteen, the hands of a woman who had never known what it was like to work. She barely gave Jeanette Cromantine time to wonder where she had come from or at the astonishing power of her transformation, before the pregnant woman began to feel the child in her belly moving into position.

'Move over, sister,' said Fatmatta the Bird-Woman.

She held the hand of Jeanette Cromantine; then, as if she was transmitting her strength to the woman who was losing hers, Fatmatta the Bird-Woman began to rub the belly of the woman, who was thrashing on the bed. Large beads of sweat broke out on Jeanette Cromantine's face, but they were mopped by the gentle hand of the other woman. They were two women who were completing a journey they had begun a long time ago. 'Wear my glass beads for me,' Fatmatta the Bird-Woman had told Jeanette Cromantine many years earlier. Now, as the labour reached the high seas of childbirth, Fatmatta the Bird-Woman removed the new set of glass beads from her neck. She rubbed them gently on the forehead of Jeanette Cromantine, and muttered some sort of incantation.

'Now, you goin to deliver,' she told the raving woman.

A loud shriek escaped the lips of the labouring woman; the snakes of her varicose veins uncoiled, and in that terrible moment between life and death, between joy and sorrow, the pelvis of the woman was relaxed, and the sweat that had clouded her brow trickled down her face, which like a priceless ancestral mask shone with a brilliant effulgence. Jeanette Cromantine fell into a deep sleep, and when she woke up, she saw Rosa standing next to her holding her baby. Then she remembered her friend.

'Where is Fatmatta the Bird-Woman?' she asked.

'No one been here, just you and me, and you got a nice, woolly-haired boy, just like de daddy.'

She handed Jeanette Cromantine her son. The mother looked at the baby, who had been cleaned of all the blood from her insides by the midwife. Then she thanked God for the other woman who had been there, who had ridden on the difficult road with her. Suddenly she knew that never again would she be lonely, because there was someone watching over her, and, besides, she had her son. She gave the baby back to the old woman and was about to fall asleep again when Rosa admonished her.

'De child gotta eat; what you got dem breasts for?'

The sun was breaking through the clouds and an oriole came and perched on the window sill. Looking out into the sky, Jeanette Cromantine saw the rising sun, looked at her son a second time. A prodigious happiness possessed her, and the new life at her side felt good.

It was an auspicious beginning. The birth of the first son among these dreamers who had been toughened by the sea and the treachery of the misadventure in Malagueta restored their fortitude. They had always looked upon their women with concern because they seemed fitted more for outdoor labouring than for the natal bed, but Jeanette Cromantine now commanded a new respect. A day after he was born, the boy was inspected by his father in the room where Jeanette Cromantine had been lying drinking rice pap and consenting to her belly being tightly tied with a large piece of cloth and smoked guava leaves by the old woman, who muttered something about useless husbands as she went about her duty.

'You gotta lie down and let me fix dat belly of yours, it ain't never gon be de same again,' she said.

Jeanette Cromantine felt the air of post-natal lassitude being pressed out of her belly. Although it was a little uncomfortable, she was glad in spite of herself, because she now possessed a claim to the world in that bundle of flesh that was lying next to her. She felt his breathing, and when he yelled she picked him up and performed the first rite of motherhood, and she did not mind that in giving life and love, her breast hurt a little because it was heavy. When he was allowed to see his son, Sebastian Cromantine kissed the woman on her cheeks with his awkward lips, and thanked her for ensuring the continuation of his line. Then, with his feathery hands, he picked up the little wonder, wept for his happiness and for his father, and felt his burden of debt lifted off his chest as if by the wings of a great bird.

'Soon he gon be running all over de place and saying mama, mama,' he said.

'Not dat one,' said the woman. 'He ain't gon be saying ma name alone. He gon go places and make us proud cause he de first born.'

A week later, when Sebastian was touched by the angel of inspiration, he named his son Emmanuel and, over the protestations of his wife, and after the killing of a bull and the downing of fermented liquor, he had him circumcised by the oldest settler among them, who claimed he had magical powers. To prove his point, he made a small incision in one of his nostrils, passed a leaf over it and next day showed that there was no sign of the wound. Sebastian Cromantine was impressed.

Jeanette Cromantine watched over her son like a hawk. She smiled when he tried to put his big toe in his mouth, and worried when he fretted and had indigestion. Soon, however, when he began to walk and catch tadpoles, throw stones at mangos and could stand and pee like a man, she missed the poetry of his infancy and thought of having another child.

The Cromantines passed eight years in exile in that relaxed atmosphere. The place assumed a spectre of permanence as the men built new cabins and planted crops. If the recent disaster was ever mentioned it was lost in the smoke of the fires that rose in the chimneys of their prosperity. It was in this climate of recovery that Thomas Bookerman found them. They would have attacked his party but for the discovery that the newcomers did not look like the lowland people who had been the cause of the exodus, and that they spoke a language very much like theirs.

◇

Nothing was left of the first settlement except for the smell of the bones of the dead whose wounds had not healed, the goital lament of those searching for water in the crypt of the underworld. In that putrefaction of dead eyes, a large fire glowed every January, around which a man and

111

a woman who wore the clothes of runaways came to warm themselves, looking for their former home.

'We hope dey gon find some peace some day,' said Thomas Booker-man, as he and his party planted a lime tree to drive away their spirits before they started clearing the land around the spot.

It took two weeks for the newcomers to unload their possessions and for them to overcome the whirlwind of predicament and mishaps that had plagued the first lot. Whereas the first Malaguetans had relied on a combination of hope, faith and the benevolence of others for their survival, the new settlers left nothing to chance, and had come better prepared. From the bellies of the ships came metal trunks and cases of that brief period in Canada, and an amazing assortment of equipment and materials: fierce-looking tiger-toothed saws, axes and adzes, brass candelabras and moccasin shoes, wooden food boxes and chamber pots, spikes and cutlasses, large kegs of poultices and vegetable oils, salted moose meat, broken lowboys and demijohns. They were a hetero-geneous lot whose only semblance of common interest was their wish to get out of that land of unbearable cold and put as much distance between them and the past, and in their elected leader they had found a man with the right blend of fanaticism and pride to lead them.

Thomas Bookerman parcelled out the land. Drawing up an arbitrary map of how much land there was in the vicinity, he marked with a red pencil all the land bordering Kasila, past the route of the gold and salt camels in the east, and to the west he marked with a blue pencil all the land to a small town where a group of white men had set up a post trading in guns and animal hide. By so doing, he had an area of some twenty square miles of prime land and for the next three years the place became noisy with the cacophanous sounds of tools as men felled trees, sunk wells and built houses. 'We must build for the future,' he said. The town which they conceived was a beautiful one. It rose from the sea with its breath of moist and humid air, towards the rolling green hills and golden plateaux, overshadowed by the great forested mountains, so that on one side lay the swamp which they had to cross to get to the river, and on the other the residue of a volcanic age of rocks and dunes.

Deprived of the names of heroes of the place and the worship of djinns, Thomas Bookerman named the twelve streets of the town which faced the sea after the months of the year, while the twelve which ran vertically from the sea towards the mountains were named after the twelve disciples by two settlers who hoped to establish their churches. It was thus that in later years, when the American and British sailors began to call in the town looking for something other than okapi wood, ginger and palm oil, the town came to be known as The Town of the Twelve Virgins and the Twelve Whores. Living on the streets facing the sea, emancipated from all notion of damnation and hell, were the young men and women who had not married, putting as much distance as they could between them and the melancholy and grief of their past, in those houses with their windswept verandas, where they grew African violets, geraniums and anthuriums, fanned by the tropical sea. On the other twelve streets, the men who had married, and the women who did needlework clad in starched stiff black gowns, mourning for lost husbands and sons, set up their homes, which looked into each other so that everyone knew what the other was doing and they were forced to maintain a regimented form of propriety and decency. On the third street of the virgins they started work on their first church, named The People's Church, and several years later on the ninth street, a rival sect built their own church which they namd after the mad king George.

Never having married, Thomas Bookerman built himself a small house at the end of January Street, which was the first street facing the sea, at a spot where the land curved into a bay. There, he tended a lush garden of mimosas, poinsettias and bougainvillaea, and held court to the men and women who trekked down to the sea in a kind of pilgrimage to ask for his advice.

He did not miss having a family because he was one of those men whose random nature of life sometimes imposed a terrible burden upon him, and it was enough that in the drama that he had chosen to act out, whether for good or for bad, he did not have a son who would be condemned to bear his name. Yesterday he was a man without a country, now he was a leader who had founded a town far away from the hardship of his former life. From the very start, they treated him with a kind of reverence that he found puzzling. It was to him that they came to talk about the remedies for the new fevers that they were contracting, to settle their quarrels about where to situate a church or a school and for the rights to acquire more land to farm if no one was going to be hurt in the process. It was a peaceful world at the beginning, and because they were all motivated by the same idea – to keep Malagueta safe from bandits and to make it one of the best towns that would attract more people in the future – the early anxiety that had hung over them when they first arrived soon gave way to a great bout of optimism. So much so that in the first five years, the jungle and swamp that had blocked the exploration had been replaced by a thriving town, noisy with activities and people.

Because of its proximity to the sea, some of the women tried their hands at shopkeeping. They persuaded their husbands to build small shops that smelled of rich mahogany and bamboo, where all the fruits of the tropics were bought from the dealers of the surrounding region, and household goods from visiting sailors were offered for sale or in exchange for services. Cooling themselves with fans made of peacock feathers, middle-aged women revived by the breath of the sea and by the hoped-for good prospect of finding husbands among the many young men for daughters whose husbands had perished before Malagueta was founded, haggled with the growers to make as much profit as they could.

'We making money today so dat we can enjoy our grandchildren tomorrow,' said one woman who had a most desirable daughter she wanted to marry off in style. For a future that held much for their children they were prepared to make any sacrifices. On rainy days, it was not unusual to see these traders, protected only by broad cocoa leaves, coming from the wharfs, where, after having stood for hours with their boots stuck in the mud, they came home triumphant with goods, lit the coalpots and cooked meals for their husbands. They were great pioneering women.

Others opened floral shops and bakeries, or became seamstresses so that in time young girls were instructed in bridal etiquette and homekeeping. Not to be outdone, the few men who were not masons or carpenters went into the shoemaking business; and on the corner of Thomas Street, dragging his clubfoot to the music of his grandfather clock, old Theophilus with the instinct of an apothecary experimented with the wild herbs of the region, and hung a notice on his door with the letters of his profession written on it.

◇

Rescued from their mountain exile, thrown into a world of diagrams and speculation, Sebastian and Jeanette Cromantine did not initially fit in with the new lot. Being of a different temperament, drawn by the mesmerising power of that land whose subterranean womb promised so much, Sebastian did not find the prospect of opening a shop much to his liking, especially as in the world of nostalgia, with its aged and ossified beauty, a town of shopkeepers and theologians seemed out of place. It was this latter group that he had begun to detest the most in the first year of the nascent settlement. He and his wife had set up house in a small cabin on January Street because Sebastian felt a poignant sense of history: 'We were de first to get to dis place so we gon live on de first street,' he told his wife.

A month after they had been living there, a woman from one of the surrounding villages turned up at the house, saying she remembered Jeanette from the days of the Malaguetan women's puppets. Her name was Binta and she wanted to help the Cromantines settle in 'like my own family,' she said, and asked whether she could stay.

'Is all right wid me,' said Sebastian. 'One more mouth don't make no difference.'

His son was now eight and the responsibility of looking after his young family forced him to think of what to do while he waited to return to his fields.

'Let's raise pigs,' offered Jeanette. 'We could buy some from de Jordans, then, when dey multiply, we could sell 'em to de white people coming now.'

'How much money you think dat gon bring us? Everybody be thinking of de same idea, now.'

Times were indeed hard for some of the Malaguetans. Those who had opened shops had to rely on the arrival of ships to buy goods and then try to sell them to the people from the surrounding area who came weekly to shop and to see how the settlers were coping with their new environment, and also to copy their strange examples in house building and carpentry. The only exception to the rule of anxiety were the women who had opened schools, convinced that as well as conferring the benefits of learning, schooling could also be a profitable business. It was for this reason that many of the older women had come to Malagueta. Accordingly, great store was laid on the type of schools to be built, on how many children of all ages were to be enrolled and when the instructions should start. So in the vast solitude of a new world, in that town of merchants, the feeling that everything was possible was sometimes hampered by the problems of growing enough food to eat and building new homes.

The Twelve Virgins met for the first time three years after Thomas Bookerman first saw the land and parcelled it out. They assembled in the house of the oldest woman among them who was called Beatrice and who had offered to hold the first classes behind her house. She was a widow with a daughter who was somewhere 'among God's chillum' in Canada. The younger woman had not wanted to leave her husband whose left leg had been amputated, but had promised to join her mother 'when de good Lawd sees fit to show me de light'. The widow kept a clean house, neat and meticulous, on James, now renamed George Street. Age had not dampened her enthusiasm for work. She had a tough, spirited attitude to life which belied her seventy years. Doing nothing was a torment for her, not because it filled her life with gossips or mirages but because it cordoned her, left her useless with her hands when what she wanted was to be out in the open, to turn the soil and thresh corn in addition to her religious vocation. Gifted with a keen intelligence, she could read and write with an astonishingly clear mind, and she was one of the few people who had a modicum of idea about nursing as she had cut and applied bandages to white and black soldiers during the infamous war – men who otherwise would have died but for her skills. Some grateful soldiers taught her how to read and it was this new skill that she was about to apply now that she was home away from the skulduggery and brutality of the human slaughterhouse.

The favourable response that the Virgins had hoped for did not materialise. Not all the parents who had been asked to attend their meeting came. Sebastian Cromantine who did not trust religious preachers, spoke for the other sceptics and freethinkers when he voiced his objections to his wife.

'Ain't as if ah don't want our boy gettin de alphabet, but ah don't want dem women in black teachin him.'

'But how he gon learn if dey don't teach him?' asked his wife.

'Look at dem virgins,' he said. 'You think dey know de first thing 'bout men, 'bout pain, 'bout de way we gon grow in dis place? Shucks, dey ain't even had chillum of dem own, so how come dey gon teach ma son?'

But in spite of the objections of men like him, the first school class took off a year later. It was a simple session, with learners of all ages sitting on rough-hewn benches under a large mango tree, while Sister Beatrice instructed them in grammar and what she called 'sums'. Jeanette Cromantine, who in spite of her husband's opposition was a woman with her own mind, enrolled her son in the class.

The rest of the Virgins seemed to have come from the same background. They were tough and serious, preaching hell and damnation against men who drank liquor and talking about 'women living in sin' every time they passed through the district on the waterfront. It was as if their chosen vocation had removed all feelings of being women in them. What was left was a driven spinsterly rurality, which made their views on everything from the rights of women, which they did not believe in, to the presence of the devil, which they did believe in, rigid.

God was a sombre figure who was to be feared, and was unreachable. So they viewed their school as part of a long process of finding the right path to his mercy, and they themselves as the angels helping those children in the backward frontier to get to him. In addition to the grammar and sums, they instructed the students in a strong dose of the Old and New Testaments.

It was there in that infant school, on those benches made by Gustavius Martins, that Emmanuel Cromantine heard the story of the twelve men who had given up everything on earth to seek a paradise in heaven, following a bearded priest who claimed he was the son of God, although he had another father who was a carpenter.

Such complexities threw the young Emmanuel Cromantine into a state of confusion; he found it hard to imagine a man with two fathers, especially as his own father, to whom he was drawn, was the embodiment of all the waywardness that the Virgins preached against in church. At that time, he was beginning to show the same anxiety over how the world around him worked, over light and darkness, that his father had shown when he was much older, fighting off the invincible hand that touched his shoulder at night. Such teachings as he received from the Virgins mercifully did not have a lasting impression on him in later life.

The only Virgin who did not conform to the image of the Amazons was a young woman, the first person ever to appear in Malagueta wearing spectacles. Her name was Sister Louisa Turner and she was easily one of the most beautiful women in the town at that time: fine-boned, willowy and graceful. She had such fine manners that every time she entered a room, everyone commented on her felicitous manner, on her delicacy of walk. Nature had endowed her with the gift of pleasing people, and she did not conform to the idea of original sin which was a badge worn by the other Virgins with an irrevocable rigour. No one knew how Sister Louisa had become a member of the league of Virgins, but it was rumoured that she was the only survivor of a family that had tried to escape from the plantation of a sadistic farmer in Mississippi who got drunk every night and, protected by his dogs and armed overseer, raped the prettiest slave girls tied to the back of a great stallion, while the frightened slaves played the banjo and sang the blues. While trying to flee from that degradation, she and her parents had gone into a region infested with poisonous snakes and deadly lizards whose bites had killed her parents. She had been rescued from her shock and delirium by some antediluvian Indians who initiated her into the ancient mysticism of Torlino, the priest of Hozonihatál, into the origins of death, and the poetry of the lamentation of the fox. They taught her how to mourn for the dead without being sad, how to be stoical and passionate without fear and cowardice as no one could escape death. Scarred for a time by the trembling memory of the brutality of her former master, Louisa had lived in a world in which every white man on a horse was coming to rape her, where the sight of a dog filled her with the greatest terror, until she had been brought back from the intransigence of death by the affections of the Indians, so that she could live without being haunted by what she had experienced. Two years of living with the Indians not only restored her vitality, her natural goodness and hunger for life, but gave her an insatiable passion to help others who had been marred by the scars of exploitation. So that when she was taken one night to see some wounded black soldiers who had sought refuge among the Indians before going to join the men and women who were sailing with Thomas Bookerman, she resolved to go with them, to help in any way that she could, and in that way pay back the gratitude she owed to the divine mercy that the Indians had shown her.

Accordingly, her teaching was filled with love and devotion for the upliftment of the soul and less with the intoxication of biblical allusion and the abnegation of the desires of the flesh. It was her purity of mind, her beauty and warmth that accorded her the image of a virgin rather than any reference to her lack of sexual knowledge. What went on in her mind as she taught the final year of the five-year period to eager young men and women was a secret that no one guessed at except Emmanuel Cromantine who, by that time sixteen, was only four years younger than Louisa. While the other Virgins spent years bringing their children to God, on the wonders of geography and with the personification of women in the image of Mary the Virgin of saints, Louisa represented a much more temporal figure. She taught her students about the beauty of love, about the dimensions that sacrifice for love could take, and the beauty therein of the surrender of all other ambitions to the great cause of loving your fellow man. On those soporific afternoons, she held court like a queen who had regained her crown, like a woman who knew the brightest corners of love. Thus, it was inevitable that when Emmanuel Cromantine began to take an interest in what she was saying and asked questions about how such a young woman had found herself among the Sisters of Charity, she would blush and try to avoid his eyes. Although he was dimly aware of his own influence on his teacher, Emmanuel Cromantine took to staying behind after classes to talk to Louisa. He wanted to know about the history of the region, about the fallen woman Mary Magdalene, about the black revolts and the kind Indians.

'You is too smart for your age,' she said to him one afternoon when he had been staying behind over a period of three months.

'Just wanna know more 'bout ma people, if it ain't no crime.'

'What you gon do with all dem knowledge once you git outta school?'

'Gon be a teacher like you, make 'nough money so ah kin marry a nice girl like you, Miss Louisa.'

She found it hard to sleep that night. For the first time in a year, Louisa missed the obligatory evening prayers and meditation before meals in the newly renovated mission house with its Portuguese porticoes. During the night, she begged God that she might be strengthened against the temptation to yield to the sensations of her body over the power of her mind, and she read the psalms of David for enlightenment and for the beauty of their music. But love was like an ivy climbing on the trellis of her heart, and the ghost of the rape of the young women that she had witnessed on the plantation no longer troubled her. Worn out by the ogre of insomnia, Louisa began to pace up and down her room. She had changed into her nightgown and the glow of the moon came into the room to reveal her as a woman of exceptional beauty standing by a window. Suddenly, she saw the figure of a man strolling in the garden, holding a book in his left hand. It was Emmanuel Cromantine who, unknown to Louisa, had been out birdwatching as he had done for the past three months. She quickly pulled back from the window so that she would not be seen, but his appearance, coming on top of her confusion, had unsettled her and weakened her resolve.

Standing on the chest of drawers in her room was a figure of a Black Christ that the Indians had given to her as a parting gift. Barely conscious of what she was doing, Louisa removed the figure from the top of the chest and began to caress it with her fingers, placing it on her breasts. She was startled that it came alive with a vibration that shook the arteries in her heart, making her quiver like a frightened child caught sucking her finger. An involuntary hand guided her to the narrow bed of her maidenhood, laid her gently and began to fondle her breasts, that were taut and ripe like enlarged pomegranates. Her blood flowed like a stream from a great dam, flooded her being, and parted her legs like a broken earthenware jug. Out of the depth of a dimly perceived desire like hunger, she felt her hand curving like a bird with the figure of the porcelain Christ into a darkness that was soft like mushroom, that had never been watered before, but which at the unbelievable pleasure of the implantation shook her body like a hurricane. She screamed and shuddered with the realisation that this was what had been promised to woman by Christ on the other side of Golgotha, to Mary Magdalene, and which, despite the image of the girls on the big stallion on the plantation, and the arbitrariness of the misplaced glory of the cloister, had been growing in her heart of hearts. When she realised what she had done, she cried with happiness because she had loved Christ as she had always wanted, and could now love man.

Alarmed by the shriek from Louisa's room, Sister Beatrice came rushing up the steps, thinking that the young woman was being attacked by a man who had climbed through the window, or by a snake. She pushed the door open and saw Louisa lying down, with the face of a celestial angel, but with the languor of a mistress. When she saw the porcelain Christ between Louisa's legs, it did not take the older woman long to realise what had happened.

'My child!' she exclaimed, 'De devil done took your mind, but you gon come down and pray to de Lawd to drive him out.'

Louisa did not move from her position. She was still enjoying the discovery, wishing that the moment would last, that it was not all a dream from which she was terrified of waking up, to return to the cold reality of living in the cloister. Christ whose blood had flowed on the cross, confirmed that it was real, because she felt her own blood trickling down her leg, warm and beautiful. She felt miles and miles away from the child that she had been only a few moments before so that the woman standing there seemed not like the avenging angel of former times who had the power to return her to the flock, but like a cuckoo that had landed among the precious eggs of her maturity. She looked at Sister Beatrice with a smile that was like a flower opening up on a summer day, proud of herself, like a beautiful peacock, and replied with the calm of a young celebrant:

'I thought it was Sunday, and that he was showing me his paradise.'

One week later, when Phyllis Dundas fought with one of the older Virgins in front of the church, Louisa left the House of Surrender Your Soul to the Lord, and went to live with her. There, warmed by the breeze of the sapphire sea, rescued from their past supplications, they sat on the veranda every day, making kites with the rainbow wings of the Senegalese butterflies.

◇

By this time, some of the people were beginning to drink too much, yellow fever and malaria were taking their toll, and the least pious of the men who lived on the ecclesiastical side of the town had begun to stray into the 'nest of evil', as the Virgins called the part of the town facing the sea. In that atmosphere of suspicion and gossip a clash seemed inevitable, and the pretext came on a dull Saturday afternoon. Returning home from working on the city market, Gustavius Martins went through January Street where the gay young people lived, and was soon captivated by the unmistakable sound of a fiddle. It had been a long time since he had heard a fiddler, and as the unknown musician peeled off layers of a tune that seemed to come from the depths of a prolonged unhappiness, Gustavius felt an involuntary spasm in his heart. He experienced a deep feeling of cerebral animation which made him want to dance to that slow, bitter and tragic music. His soul responded to a far distant time when from the dark cabins of their desolation he saw men coming on to ships in pursuit of a dream. Moved to tears, he danced for the aloe distillation of that dream, the trapezoidal dimensions of their lives in Malagueta, for the frogleaping quantum of benevolence bestowed upon them, and the quadrumanous martyrdom of those who had been humbled, humiliated and insulted, but who had made the settlement possible in spite of all of its imperfections. The music merged with the sound of the waves in the evening amidst the rustle of coconut trees, which completed the effect. The possessed man surrendered himself to the flexible movements of his long legs pounding the hard belly of the soil as he gave himself over to a sensual abandonment that pushed his chest skywards to the heavens.

'Come on inside, brother,' a voice rang out from a top-floor window of one of the houses. The owner was a tall, dark, beautiful woman, with eyes the colour of topaz. She wore large earrings of cheap brass plating, and a long tight-fitting dress with wild flowers patterned all over it that revealed a luxuriant bosom. Her blackness was of a kind that shone, like mahogany, and she gave off an emanation of oils and perfumes from the enchanted market of Marrakesh, and seeming like a woman who had knocked around the world but could, in any emergency, take care of herself, although she lived alone. Gustavius went up the steps and looked at the splendid figure at the top of them. Since their arrival in Malagueta, he had not directly looked at any of the immigrant women, so that when he went up, beckoned by this one, it was not with any intention to be seduced by that majestic cleavage, but because he wanted to share the mood of enthralment that the music had induced in him. Moreover, he was quite happy with Isatu, who was fast learning how to cope with the strange ways of his people: their habit of calling old men Daddy, old women Mammy and their children pikin. She had refused to be baptised, insisting that she felt she already had a religion that was powerful enough, and that, no thank you, she wanted nothing to do with his God. Thus Gustavius's mind was far from enticement as he looked round the room that was small but beautifully decorated. A large door opened into a wooden veranda, allowing light to come into the room. Pots of petunias and marigolds shone in the light. An old chest of drawers with an oxbow front took up almost an entire wall and, right next to that, a small bed adorned with a beautiful Indian quilt formed an L shape to the chest. Two well-used cane chairs completed the furniture in the room.

'Drink some rum?' the woman asked. Sugar cane had been introduced by some of the more enterprising settlers and a small distillery was producing rum and beer made from corn. Gustavius nodded his head and accepted a glass. He eyed the woman, whose name was Phyllis Dundas. She earned a living by making wreaths and kite paper adorned with the coloured wings of butterflies and no one could understand why such a beautiful woman had resisted all attempts by men to get her to take a lover, except that perhaps she was not yet ready to commit herself to any man who did not see relationships as part of the struggle against not only the merchants of evil but against those hiding behind the power of the church. Malagueta had grown in population and there were all sorts of new arrivals flocking to the town every day. Because her establishment was on the waterfront, Gustavius was sure the woman had arrived with the second group of pioneers. Had she left a man, did she have children somewhere in America, and why had she come here? These were questions that ran through his mind as he drank his rum.

He waited for an answer to his unspoken questions, but those eyes that flashed a kindness and warmth did not betray anything about her past. Instead, she appeared determined to keep her past secret, until she was ready to talk.

'Sometimes, ah feels like dancing too, when am feeling low,' she said. Gustavius Martins found it hard to believe that this woman could be unhappy: she was too much of a woman, a desirable woman whose gentle manners suggested a not too brutal life in the past.

'Why you come over here?' he asked.

'To find ma self, and make something outta ma life.'

'You alone in de worl?'

'You ain't never alone if you knows who you be, or where you come

122

from, and if you never let people put you down. Like you is a kind man, ah kin tell by de way you sitting down, all quiet and proper, and you dying to find out 'bout me but you ain't askin, least ah put you down. But ah gon tell you all de same.'

Gustavius Martins took a sip of his rum and waited. He watched the woman as she went to a window, looked at the sky which was turning grey in the twilight of the day. She came back and sat close to him and started to talk.

'Ma and Pa be slaves on a plantation in Virginia. Ma died before de war, 'cause she wuk so hard in de kitchen; dey wuk ma Ma, 'cause she don't let de master of de big house bring no foolishness to her. "Georgina, you ain't cook 'nough cabbage," de master says to Ma every time she done put him down. "Georgina, de pork too damn hard, floor ain't clean and stop dem chillum hollerin or ah gon do you mighty harm." But she don't fear him none and she knows he frighten of her. Ma old Pa been sufferin from pneumonia 'cause he be drivin white folks to all dem parties dey fond of giving. Pa ain't no young 'un and he ain't dress proper either 'cause master says Pa ain't a young buck no more, and de way it be, ain't no white man be spending money on a negro who gon die. Pa was a good man, never hit ma Ma, and if it ain't for de fact dat he ain't nobody's man but he own, Mama sure come down from dat big house with a mulatto chile; dat is if ma Mama don't kill de master fust.

'Pa got to marry Mama when he too old to enjoy hisself. Been sold so many times dat he change name every five years, Lawd have mercy! But he ain't no onnery black man. Said his papa come from town in Africa dey call Oshogbo. Dem people got gods bigger dan de white man's God and lots of prayerhouses where dey keep ivory and bronze 'cause dey gotta workship dem gods real fine. Pa says he got tiffed by man come to town on iron horse. De man tell ma Pa he kin teach him how to ride de horse, but when Pa follow de man down de driver, a big boat waiting there and a whole lotta white men come out and take ma Pa to de boat.

'Pa never saw his Mama or Papa agin 'cause dey brung him to de white man's worl on de big river, and dey make him do all de wuk in de field. Time de war done come Pa is old man, same as de master, and de master be selling his slaves 'cause he too poor to keep 'em. Master got one son who be real bad; de way it be he so bad he done gamble all de money and ain't long before he drunk always and done molest some coloured women and Injuns and he ain't sleep none at night 'cause he done see some coloured men and Injuns come kill him. Dey coming all de time, and de dream keep on a-coming and de man be real scairt.

'So one time he done go off and open a saloon called de Silver Bullet and 'cause he be making money he feels he gon mess wid de sly bordello woman of a real mean man. So de man says, "Tom, if you gon mess wid ma woman ah gon blow off your head." Tom ain't one to lay off a woman so one night he calls de man. He says, "Harry, ah gon have dat woman and ain't nothin you kin do."

'Harry, he comes and tells Tom to come out and let dem shoot it out. Master son comes out and before you kin say jack rabbit he lying there wid dem holes in his body and he dead. Master done took to drinking too much, forced hissef on his missy who he ain't looked at in years and gives her a girl chile. Missy took to her bed where she reads Bible and says son comes visit her. Tell her war is coming, better move, 'cause de way it be, slavery time done pass; master don't belief he wife been seeing her son, but he sold off de slaves all de same 'cept for ma Pa and Ma, me and Joshua, master son by some mulatto woman, 'cause now he true born son done die, Master say he gon keep his coloured boy 'cause it ain't Christian to sell his own blood.

'Time war comes Ma ain't fit to do no scrubbing or picking; been wukin since her bornin' day for dat man and ain't never took care of herself 'cause de way it be, slaves ain't got time for demself; she done come down wid dis sickness de white doctor says is wasting away, and dey lay her flat on her bed and Ma starts to die real fast. Skin turns blue, eyes turn grey and her hair de colour of sawdust. One time dey let me hold her hand ah feels ah touching corn 'cause it so hard. "Phyllis," ma Ma says to me, "you be a good girl now and look after your Pa; ma time ain't long in comin, gonna meet ma Master." Ma ain't one to sing but dat night she done took to singing, says it de partin of de ways, she done see de big river over yonder where de black people be waiting wid de big bell and dey ringing de bell, and a whole lotta people coming outta de forest, outta de huts, down de mountains and dey all goin to de river where dey take off de cloth and baf.

'Ma says, "Ah sees de land and you all goin home 'cept for your ole Ma." Sure 'nough Ma die when people start talkin 'bout a place dey call Canada. Dey bury ma Ma under de birch tree where dey hang one black man who done kill horse dey ketch black man wid.

'Pa soon took to his bed and ain't long before he die and ah is all alone in de worl 'cept for Joshua who don't trust his papa none. One night Joshua come and says, "Pardon me, Miss Phyllis, ah don't mean no harm, but seeing you is all alone, ah bin thinkin we kin be friends." Ah gives him something to eat, and he come to my cabin a lotta time after dat. He never treat me anything but proper and tells me 'bout some white folks come from place dey call England, fightin dey own kind which don't make sense. "But ain't none of our business, Miss Phyllis, if dey is killin one 'nother," says Joshua, "but ah hears ma Pa says de white folks from England done promise freedom to de slaves who gon fight for dem. So ah bin thinking of joinin."

'Ah got me a fine man in Joshua, so seems but natural dat we gon sleep togeder, but he ain't happy, 'cause his mind ain't in dat place no more; war done enter his brain; but ah loves him so we run off togeder one night and join de war where dey kills ma man. Ah ain't one to complain, but after dey kill Joshua ah feels empty 'cause God done took ma Pa, Mama and Joshua; and de war ain't goin de way suppose to go. Many people dying and de slave driver ketch some slaves and took 'em back. Us slaves be mighty afraid to go back if de Americans win de war, but one night a whole lotta wagons pull outta dat place and start to move on; we come to place name of Canada where de people same as white folks in America, but dey don't have no slaves, but ain't kind either 'cause dey done give us land ain't fit to grow nothing: marshland and swamp, and when de winter come, oh Lawd, it sure is cold!

'Us blacks begin to hear more people talk 'bout going to Africa. Preacher man comes round all de time and talk 'bout de chillum of Israel, 'bout Moses, and how God done brung dem outta de land of Pharaoh to dey own place. Preacher man says de way of de Lawd is mighty strange; he lets his chillum suffer so dey gon know he can do anything. Preacher man says ain't no difference between dem dat gits husband and dem ain't; between womens and mens; we all chillum of de Lawd, and we be goin to Africa. One time preacher man says, "Sister Phyllis, come to de house of de Lawd tonight." Ah go there and preacher man tells me he loves me and is a burnin shame he don't have money to support me, but he a good man and aims to do proper by me when we is in Africa.

'Ah gives him some love, ah takes him to ma breasts; ah says ah gon serve dat man wid ma body and ma heart, and ah serves him 'cause ah needs a man too. But he ain't no man; he a coward. One time, one of 'em Virgins come to de church at night and done see me and de preacher lying on de floor, and she tinks she done see de serpent of Eve and ah done mess up de mind of Brother Adam. He bin walkin like a dog wid his tail 'tween he leg since dat time. So ah says to him, "Brother Adam, you ain't a man, you is a sissy, and ah never goin to de church ever!"

'So ah comes to Africa on ma own 'cause ah done tell white man ah kin cook real fine, which ain't de case, and ah done live in dis house some white man done build afore he gone back to England. But ah ain't never goin to de church ever 'specially as Brother Adam be preachin in dat place.'

The idea of building a church had been one of the reasons why the founders of the town had been working hard against the coming of the rain in the early years of the settlement. As the dark woman ended her story, Gustavius had an idea of how deeply she must have suffered; he was touched by her story, by her sincerity and goodness of heart, but especially by her courage. He felt that if he had been faced with such hostility he would have reacted differently, and he wondered how far from the spirit of founding a peaceful town the settlers had strayed in response to the tyranny of the Virgins.

'Dis ain't de way it supposed to be. We messing up de place before we fixin it up,' said Gustavius Martins.

'No, we ain't; jus dat some people done let de Virgins turn de church into dey own.'

The first church that the settlers started building soon after they arrived was a large stone one, beyond their immediate needs. They conceived of a cathedral where each stone would one day bear the inscription of the carrier of that stone; where each supporting beam in the ceiling would have come from the choicest wood. The ambulatory arcades would be wide and high. Asbestos sheets, the windows of the clerestory, the stones of the triforium would be ordered from England through the agency of white coastal traders and special attention would be given to the ownership of pews.

Because they were creating a society where they hoped to establish a high level of propriety, the founders of the church would have a virtual veto over who would become members, and would turn away all those who might dare to break their sanction by placing sextons with the look of avenging angels at the door, under the cinquefoil of their achievement. In the event, however, the mighty edifice did not materialise for some time, and they were content to settle for a temporary church: a small white building, sad and lonely on Bartholomew Street, dwarfed by a large jacaranda tree placed in a disadvantageous position to the sun, and which because of the suffocating clothing the church members insisted on wearing was a most uncomfortable place to worship. They had not given much thought to large windows and the ceiling was low and threatened to fall at the first signs of a hurricane. But that did not diminish the fervour and organisational ability of some of the Twelve Virgins who ran the affairs of the church like Amazons.

Next to Sister Beatrice, the woman most involved in gathering the pious to the church was Sister Caroline. Unlike her leader, her vocation did not come from any sense of devotion or ecclesiastical calling, but from a desire to fill a deep gaping hole in her life. Years of growing rice in the swamps of the Carolinas had left her a sullen and unsmiling woman, with the countenance of a rainy day. Like the rest of the other Virgins she lived in a large house from which they emerged to go to church, shop in the open market and to fetch water. Men were barred from entering the place except for the fathers of the church and a crude inscription on the front of the house warned: Surrender Your Soul to the Lord or Burn in the Fire of Hell.

When she had seen Phyllis in the arms of the pastor in Canada she had felt a pang of envy and regret swell up in her. No one had desired her sexually, not even the old master who had brought her and then freed her later. Her body was a mass of rhinoceros flesh, hardened by the sun and rice powder, unresponsive to her desire. It was that body and not so much her soul that she had offered to the God of her conception and to the incubuses that came at night to lift her slip, fondle her, and give her the pleasure of the woman in the pastor's hand, but left her stroking the rigid evidence of her depraved womanhood when she emerged from her dreams. Unable to kill her torment, she had developed an irrational hatred for the young women who could entice the men from the work of God, and it was she who had spread the rumour that Phyllis was a lewd woman and husband snatcher who was under no circumstances to be allowed in the church.

Angry because of what Phyllis had told him, Gustavius Martins decided to go to church for the first time in his life, and he was going to invite Phyllis and bring his woman. The prospect of their being turned away did not enter his head as he felt he could deal with any ugliness from the Virgins. But when he told Phyllis of his decision she did not welcome the idea of being in the same building, especially a house of God, with those Virgins. She called them animals who had lost all claim to humanity and who were so sick of themselves that they wished to drag others down with them.

'Ain't going to no church least ah spit in dey face,' she said with a wave of her beautiful hand.

'But you is coming wid me, and 'nother thing, de church ain't their property, it's de house of everyone done pay for de building and it's free.'

When he said that he did not realise what a raw nerve he had touched in her, how close to the truth of her relationship with the preacher his words went. It was the same idea of the freedom to give, at the behest of God, to the idolised representative of the tree of salvation that had plunged her into a confused state of mind: on the one hand exalting in the fact that she was being seduced by such an important man while on the other hand being unsure about the limitation of passion and enjoyment with the overpowering image of the master watching them. That she was later abandoned by the weak-livered priest did not do much to settle the doubts about what was free in the external for Phyllis. Now, she trusted only freedom as defined by her needs, and she felt she did not need the church.

'Dem womens ain't no Christians,' she said, 'and ah don't want to be mixin wid no cowards either.'

'Ah know how you feels,' said Gustavius. 'But you and me gon be friends and togeder we gon change dis place.'

The next Sunday, although still protesting, Phyllis let herself be taken to church by Gustavius who had also brought Isatu. The African woman and the American woman experienced an instant feeling of discomfort when they saw the people who had gathered in front of the church to wait for the doors to open and for the service to begin. They saw in front of the whitewashed building a cross section of all the admixture of races and colours that was the make-up of that settlement; they saw the infusion of the blood of the gospel in the faces of that stony crowd held in anticipation of the entry into the Divine Presence. It was a reservoir of so much fevour, of so much piety and chastity that the two women were left with the stale impression that something was impure about those faces, that a great wrong had been done to them; that in that submission lay the root of an impurity that was menacing. When the doors finally opened, the crowd started going in, more unsure than prepared: the men went in first, then the women, followed by the children. Gustavius and the two women moved behind the children, prepared to sit on any available seats. Suddenly, they found their way blocked by one of the Twelve Virgins. It was Sister Caroline, dressed in the black of someone in perpetual mourning. She positioned herself squarely between the two frames of the door so that she seemed like an ox, and she had about her the hissing preparedness of a cobra.

'You can't come in here,' she said to the trio. Gustavius did not let himself be disturbed by her attitude; he did not know that she spoke more for the benefit of Phyllis than for the other two. He advanced forward with the two women behind him, but the woman blocking their way did not shift her bulk. 'Ah says you can't bring dem women in here,' she said in a voice that was loud and designed to carry.

He pushed her aside and walked in, but when Phyllis tried to follow, she felt a strong pair of hands grab her from behind, and then push her down. Struggling to maintain her balance, Phyllis saw the swift movement of five claws of a hand that was strained by its magenta veins, by its laundry-woman hardness trying to pull her hair; she saw a demonic creature looming over her, threatening to swallow her. Swiftly, she manoeuvred her way out of the spot where she had fallen, kicked the shin of the big, vituperative woman so that she crashed with a thud which was heard in the front pew of the church, and which forced the worshippers to turn around. Phyllis did not let her advantage slip her. She sat on the big woman and pummelled her. She hit her for the cerebral unhappiness that her badmouth had caused Phyllis in America. She held the Virgin's mouth in her hands, which for a delicate woman were strong, and she began to squeeze it tightly, while under her she felt the enraged power of a tigress, but she did not let go. Increasing her pressure on the big woman's mouth she forced it open, and with her left hand collected a heap of dirt and pushed it inside Carolines's mouth.

'Now, you gon eat dirt,' she said, 'because you is dirt and you ain't fit to be livin cause ah gon kill all you virgins.'

Only the timely intervention of Gustavius prevented her from carrying out her threat when he pinoned her arms behind her back and gave the big woman a chance to escape. It was a bad omen for the church. Now that the sanctity of the occasion had been broken, the service could no longer be held. Brother Adam interrupted his sermon and the worshippers soon filed out, giving the three newcomers menacing looks as they did so. Later that night, while Gustavius, Isatu and Phyllis were enjoying a quiet evening on the porch of the house, in the fragrance of caladiums and aphelandria, a noisy mob attacked the house and tried to set it on fire. The would-be arsonists did not escape, however; from the houses of the twelve streets of the single men and women an even bigger crowd of people came out and engaged the religious fanatics. A great divide had opened up between those who came to escape the intolerable loneliness and hardship in life in the New World and those who came to impose a most severe form of Christian rigidity and morality. It was to be some time before the ugliness of that

129

bloody day would be erased; when on the site where the white church stood, two women had pointed the way to those who would be insurrectionists and patriots, and those who would place their destiny in the hands of the white men in flannels who at that time were assembling somewhere in England with plans of their own for Malagueta.

BOOK TWO

5 The Day of the Feast

Sebastian Cromantine had been unable to overcome his dislike of the
conditions into which they had been thrown by the involuntary removal
from the mountain. He finally devised a way whereby he could keep the
flames of his dreams alive and maintain a family. He decided to start
building a 'House for the Dead' where he could cast in stone and bronze
statues the living image of the dead. Though he found the prospect
exciting, he had experienced some difficulty finding a suitable place.
But after one year of trying, Sebastian Cromantine was finally established in his new business, and his dream of a prosperous coffee
plantation if not altogether jettisoned had been shelved for the time
being.

The new house was on January Street, then a busy, boisterous place
with bars, rum houses and shops that offered an amazing variety of
excitement against the occasional tedium of a new place. The proximity
of these places to the sea made the street a natural favourite of the sailors
and pirates who came there to rest and look for enjoyment while their
ships were being repaired or while they themselves were treated for
wounds sustained during shipwrecks and attacks. Trade was picking
up, shops and stalls lined the sea fronts, and the old bamboo houses had
been replaced with more permanent wooden structures while the more
adventurous members of the community were beginning to journey into
the interior to explore the land and to test the limits of their fascination.
When he had thought of his house where he could work with cement and
clay to make his plaques and statues, Sebastian had not anticipated the
strength of opposition to his plans from some of the men who had come
on the second expedition with Thomas Bookerman. The idea of a place
where they could go and watch the likeness of their loved ones being

131

created in stone and painted white before they were put at the head of a grave did not please them. Up till that time, they had buried their dead in simple graves, with simple crosses tied with palm fronds, placed in a vertical position, and they were quite happy with that arrangement, especially as it did not distinguish between rich and poor. So Sebastian's idea was viewed with suspicion. The poor among the settlers thought he had received money from the well-off citizens to start his business, and in return would set up an oligarchy in the cemetery whereby the rich would decide about where they wanted their dead buried. To the fiercely independent-minded men who had risked their lives to tame that place, fought off the leopards, snakes and impetuous traders who sometimes wanted to cheat them, tombstones sounded like the first step towards a tyranny.

Sebastian nevertheless persisted. One night in his house he met some of those opposed to the idea. Jeanette Cromantine welcomed them graciously, served them ginger tea and rice bread, showed them the lovely trellis that her husband had attached to the porch so that she could grow beautiful vines of jasmine, and as a support for the bougainvillaea shrub that she had begun to cultivate. She asked about their children and left the men to talk. Clearing his throat, Sebastian Cromantine told them how he had discovered the coffee trees, 'guided by an invisible hand', how he had dreamed about a life as a farmer before the terrible plague that had wiped out almost the entire first settlement, God bless their souls, and how he was now turning to this new endeavour because he wanted to give the settlers a means whereby they could remember their dead, as they had loved them, because there were so few of them anyway.

'You can't make money outta de dead, Pa would strike me dead. And 'nother thing you gotta know where dey is buried before someone else comes and removes de bodies.' Such clear thinking was to form part of his argument every time he had to deal with the settlers. They were a stubborn lot: men determined to go as far as the possibility of conquest would allow them, but always ready to fall back on the idea of permanence. For this last reason, they saw some sense in what Sebastian Cromantine was saying. Many years earlier, when they had made the crossing from America to Malagueta, some of them had died and had been buried at sea, and since coming to their new town, others had lost wives and children who had been buried in graves with only crude crosses as means of identification, which had been blown away by the persistent terror of the winds in that place. The next rainy season was only a couple of months away, and they had to plan for Christmas when they would all have a big feast, and for New Year's day which was the day they would visit their dead. It was appropriate, therefore, for them to invest in tombstones as they were already investing in the big new church which, since the day of the fight between Sister Caroline and Phyllis Dundas had taken on a new significance.

Sebastian outlined to them his method for making the tombstones. He told them that since there was no method of capturing the faces of the settlers as they would reflect in a mirror, it was important that someone should draw their pictures. When no one offered to draw their pictures, he volunteered to go round to each house where there was an old person and draw the pictures himself, using a piece of charcoal which he would apply to a cardboard. Then he told them about the large reserves of red laterite clay close to the river and how he was going to chip away at the material and then soak it in water. By mixing it with luminous sea pebbles, dirt and sand he hoped to achieve the right degree of hardness, and when that was done, the magical transformation of capturing the brave men and women who had cleared the land and planted seeds would begin. He needed time to work out the process of shaping the tombstone: how big or small he wanted the letters to be and whether he wanted them festooned with angels who had delicate hands raised upwards as if urging the dead to hurry up and go to heaven, or whether he wanted to imprint the four sides of the tombstone with images of the dead man's or woman's trade. With the modalities out of the way, he reassured the settlers that as far as payment was concerned they could pay him by instalment.

'Ah knows ah won't be goin round ringing a bell to bring debtors out.'

Equipped with a brand-new toolbox that his friend Gustavius had made, Sebastian Cromantine opened his workshop on a brilliant, sunny June morning. First, he swept out the dead lizards and wayward rats that had given the place a most noxious smell. He went out, picked some guava and lime leaves, put them in a mortar and pounded them with a pestle until he had produced some juice. Then he added some carbolic acid which he had obtained from a sailor. When he had achieved the right smell of a strong disinfectant, Sebastian Cromantine washed the place clean and felt a great exhilaration; that he was going to own a business filled him with a profuse anticipation; one that he could feel would be as great as that morning when he had opened his eyes on the preacher's bed and had seen the bright, warm eyes of the woman staring at him. Next, he tried to think of where he would build a large slab of stone on which he would work, and settled for the centre position of the shop, with his back to the mountain so that he had a most advantageous view of the sea, and could see the ships as they arrived. While he was waiting for the air to clear in the workshop, the need to have a sign suddenly took hold of him and he stretched his mind beyond the limits of fancy, thinking what he wanted to call his shop. He thought of simply putting his name on it but that was not likely to draw the people who did not know who Sebastian Cromantine was. When he had tried all conceivable possibilities, he settled for the sign: Sebastian Cromantine's House for the Dead. I Helps You Remember Them as They Was. Give Me a Try.

He resolved to make the sign as soon as he got home and to hang it over the door the next morning. Later, he bought some paint and painted the shop a bright blue so that prospective customers would not have a morose feeling when they came to discuss business. When he had exhausted himself with brush and bucket, and had put his ladder away, Sebastian Cromantine threw himself on the newly polished floor and slept for a long time. It was already evening when he woke up, the sea smelt of minnows, the first cicadas were beginning their vigils, and the bread and honey hawkers were just making their rounds when Sebastian Cromantine hung a large padlock on his door, satisfied that he had taken the first step towards providing for his family. He went home, walking past the large church on which the stonemasons were busy at work, in front of the bay, where many years earlier the ship on which he had come had landed. The church was a dream of those who had a vested interest in Christianity and, as Sebastian was not a very religious man, he was drawn to the church by the beauty of its architecture, by the intricate formulae of cutting the stones into the right sizes, by the wizardry of the carpenters who had built huge scaffolding to get to the ceiling and planted their beams in nicely chiselled grooves. He went on his way convinced that he had hit upon the right method for the preservation of his line which at that time was limited to his only son.

◇

He found him in a state of high fever, with Jeanette trying to calm him down by applying a wet towel to his brow.

'What happened to him?' Sebastian asked.

'Dunno, just started coughing and next thing ah know he doubled up and says his head feel like fire,' said Jeanette.

'How you feeling, son?' Sebastian asked him.

Emmanuel was then a taciturn and lanky lad with a tendency to spend a lot of time collecting insects and dissecting them. He knew the town and surrounding countryside very well, as he was inclined to wander off for hours in search of the many species of butterflies, grasshoppers and hornets, some of which he caught and kept in large jars in his room. Because he spent so much time alone, his mother was worried that he was growing up lonely; but the truth was that Emmanuel was happy though he was not a demonstrative person. He enjoyed the lessons in school, where he had confounded the Virgins with his quick intelligence, with his ability to solve mathematical equations. From the little that the Virgins could teach, he had deduced that there were other parts of the world, that Malagueta was surrounded by other lands where people spoke different languages and dressed like fairies. He had earlier been introduced to the beauty of those people, to the festivals of the area. One day, drawn by the pulsating rhythm of the drums and the deep lamentation of the violins, he sneaked out at night to the surrounding village where a festival was being held. It was a wedding, and Emmanuel was held spellbound by the coloured fabrics, by the elegance of the dance which they performed by raising both hands to the rhythm of the music of the harp players, by their painted lips and by the gyration of men who seemed to dance as if they had no limbs. On another occasion, he saw a masquerade: it was a strange sight. First, he watched the menacing figure of an apparition coming towards him, then it slowed down in response to some strange words that a man who commanded it uttered. Suddenly, the apparition started to grow in height and Emmanuel saw the bewildering parchment of colours and a brilliant kaleidoscope of glasses, beads, shells, horns and cowbells clashing in the reflective glare of the sun, and he experienced such a strange sensation that he rushed back home thinking he had seen the legendary demon that had the power to prolong its life by changing itself into a man and sleeping with women who chanced to go down to the river to bathe at night.

But it was the world of nature that fascinated him and held him in the intense probing of his youth, and made him seem almost strange and different from other boys about his age. He had an unusually big head for his body, and he seemed to possess a certain waywardness when it came to matters of the heart which Louisa had aroused. He was not interested in Sunday school where boys and girls his age went to get acquainted, and he lacked the force of will to be part of the groups that organised bazaars and outings, went into the mountain and camped out. That was why he guarded his privacy, his love of animals, the unutterable pleasure that the sight of an armadillo gave him with its scaly skin, that a bush hog brought to him with its ugly beauty, and the mellifluous voices of barbets. One day he came home smelling of wild mushrooms and sweet basil and Sebastian Cromantine, thinking his son had been sampling the pleasures on January Street that the women there promised, exclaimed: 'You have been with dem whores!' It was the first time that Emmanuel had heard the word whore expressed by his father, who though not a prude did not want his son led astray by the hypnotic music that the women in the area sang. The seafront had changed over the years: more and more traders came to the harbour drawn by the fantastic tales of the pirates and traders who spoke of the rugged beautiful coast, of the availability of gold, iron and timber, of small coastal rulers who collaborated with the pirates and sometimes mistakenly sold their own relatives for gunpowder, rum and mirrors. But it was the story about the women in a yellow house that was giving the place its name: there were glamorous women who wore raffia skirts and alligator beads round their waists, women with breasts like ripe melons, gregarious women from the high plateau of the Foutah Djallon who could talk like starlings and who promised instant satisfaction with their spidery fingers, exotic women who sang lugubrious blues about the plantations and who drank raw cane juice, pale white women who turned scarlet-chested when exposed to the sun and who thought they were going to the court of the King of Morocco when the ships sailed from Plymouth, women from the length and breadth of the Guinea coast, whose reddish-brown skins glittered like ruby, women with beautifully elongated necks, women who met at the crossroads of humanity and who could arouse even a dying man with the delicate caresses of their beautiful hands, and whose glassy Guereza eyes could tempt even the most dedicated married men to go in and sample their special offerings. Emmanuel had not yet been seduced by such a promise, and it was to be a few years more when, tormented by the wish to leave Malagueta, he would drift like a reed into the tempestuous lagoon of desire that Louisa had opened up for him.

Sebastian felt like a stranger to his son. He felt he was an intruder witnessing a secret pact between a mother and her son, and as Jeanette applied the cold towel repeatedly to Emmanuel's brow, the father made his person felt.

'Put some guava leaves on his brow,' he said; 'it's better than de towel.'

'He don't know you, he sees me too much so he thinks his fader don't love him and he sick; maybe it's malaria,' said Jeanette.

The obsession with the coffee trees, the interlude on the mountain when Sebastian and the few others who had survived the scapular of the storms while they worked hard to find a new life through the jungle of the new experience, had robbed him of the crucial relationship with his son when he was growing up. Now, he felt the words of his wife like fangs biting into his skin and he resolved to make up for lost time. He ordered his wife to go to bed, offering to sit up with Emmanuel all night until the fever had broken.

It was a night of shadows and a terrible dream. He saw on the walls a family of giant spiders emerging from a dense and vaporous growth, and he perceived the outline of a country where all the men had the same faces and where the women had torsos the size of elephants. He felt that the spiders were coming to take him away from his son and that the women were tossing him from breast to breast. As he sucked at those breasts his lip began to assume the shape of a spoonbill; he became a prehistoric bird, losing its body in the atmospheric listlessness of another time. He had not dreamed in ages, and the violence of the transformation filled him with its alarm. He shook his son and called his name, thinking that the asomatous nature of the dream prefigured a disaster in his house. Emmanuel opened his eyes and saw his father as he had never seen him before. Seeing him like that, he felt drawn to the pathetic looking-man whom he reached out to touch. He wondered what had frightened him while he himself lay feverish on his bed. He had no notion of his father's dream and what symbolic attributes it called up for the older man. He was as much of Malagueta teeming with people who were free, assertive, deliberate and determined to go places as Sebastian had been part of another world where they could only dream of being free.

Next morning, the fever broke and Sebastian saw the clear sign of it on his son's brow; he was sweating profusely but the colour had returned to his eyes, and he asked for some soup. Seizing the opportunity to talk to his son, Sebastian went into the kitchen to make the soup and came back a half hour later with a bowl of lentils, mushrooms, garlic and chicken gizzards. He watched his son as he drank the soup and resolved that never again would he allow the great scheme that he had for Malagueta and its future to interfere with what he now perceived as his first duty. If he had a mountain to climb, it would be for this boy with whom he and Jeanette had hidden in the mountain, and consequently, Emmanuel's name would have to be engraved on all future enterprises.

Sebastian decided to tell him about his heritage. Although lacking a formal education, he had nonetheless acquired a rudimentary form of learning about the history of his people, about the ongoing conflict between the various European peoples who were beginning to show signs of being more interested in staying and causing trouble than in trade and raiding. Sebastian told his son about how he had fought in the war in America. He described America as a place of horror and damnation. 'There is too much evil there, son. De devil made a pact with men, white men, black men, and he eats their souls, warps and breaks their spirits.' He went over the torturous injustices, the horror of women who watched while their children were taken away from them. Distance and time had not lessened his bitterness but he felt more sadness than anger as he went back to the unregenerated history in his bid to teach his son. 'Dey put you in chains, hand and foot, son, and dey let you eat worse dan their horses: entrails, horse radish, onions and potatoes; but we is God's chillum and we learnt to cook chittlins, spinach and sweet potatoes real good, and your granny, God bless her memory, was a fine cook, and your mother done took after her.'

'And why we don't mix too much with the people in the next town?' Emmanuel asked.

'Because some is good, and dey come here and brung us food Tuesday, Thursday and Saturday. Dey learn us how to grow cassava, rice and beans, and before you was born your mother gives 'em lesson in crochet and make puppets for 'em. But the others bad, bad; dey attack us and burn down de first place we build, and sometimes dey come with white men to us, so we gotta fight.'

'But Gustavius married one of dem, and I call her auntie?'

'Dat is what we want, son, dat one day we all marry each other, be de same people, speak de same language, and build up de place; because your grandfader told me before he died, he come from dis people and he asked me in a dream to dig up his bones and bring 'em back.'

'Is that why you goin to open de workshop, for him?'

'Yes, and for others, for us, for de future; so dat we gon feel we belong here. Look at us. We come here from different places, every day more and more people be arriving and many are afraid or lonely, like Beatrice, because dey have no relatives, so we all like one family and we gon grow togeder, die here and we want to stick togeder.'

The idea of one family in Malagueta fascinated Emmanuel. History

138

was his favourite subject and, unknown to his parents, he could distinguish between those he perceived as outsiders in their idyll: vagrants and idlers who came from faraway countries and the peoples of the immediate towns and villages. In his young mind, the possibility of travel was already beginning to take root, fuelled by the bits of learning that he had received in school from the Virgins. The more he thought about the other lands and people, the more he conceived of a day when he could leave to go and explore those lands and come back later to continue the work of the women whose limitations were all too obvious. Thus it was that he decided to ask his father whether one day it might be possible to travel out.

'When ah make enough money you kin go anywhere; but you gotta promise to come back.'

He promised to come back and later that night, touched by his father's attempt at closeness and concern, assured of his mother's quiet love, Emmanuel sat on the porch and watched the opal brilliance of the sun going down over the vast expanse of the sea, thinking of the day when he would leave.

Satisfied with his son's recovery, Sebastian Cromantine went back to the workshop the next day. His mood was lighter and his head much clearer about the project he was embarking on. Whereas the day before he had been at a loss about how to start, and his formula was merely a list of vague ideas about faces, masks, bronze and portraits, he now had a sort of working manual about what he was going to do. Quickly, he built his slab with a mixture of stones, clay and sand. First, he mixed the sand and clay, then arranged the stones so that he had two supporting pillars. Then, by cutting short staves and planting them in the ground between the two pillars, he nailed a flat piece of metal that looked like the base of a trunk, which he had retrieved from the sea. Next, he mixed the concrete and constructed a five-foot-by-three slab, which was then left to dry in the chilly harmattan winds. Then, overcoming the fear of the unknown and relying on the notion that the principle of creation rested on the idea of perception, he set about creating his first bust. He moulded the ball of clay, big as a large coconut, which was rubbed over and over on the floor so that all the lumps were crushed. While he waited for the right temperature to harden the ball, he brought out some of the charcoals and paper from his bag, intending to sketch a face which would serve as an example for him to work on. He did not want to sketch anyone who was alive nor was he keen to offend any of the members of the community by inviting them to sit for him when his workshop was still in a chaotic and crude stage. The idea of giving away his method of work, his perceived advantage over others, as he was the first to have thought about the idea, meant that he preferred to work alone. Unable to think of anyone whom he could sketch, he went out for a walk, hoping that the fresh, clean air would restore his sense of perception. He walked past the waterfront with the giant flame trees from which the towns-people had not succeeded in driving away all the monkeys that were harmless as monks and only interested in the nuts that the young girl hawkers carried in trays on their heads. He reached the extreme end of the town, passed a cluster of houses that were thatched and arranged in a circle, with a large one in the centre, and surrounded by a small palisade.

Since coming to live in the house on January Street, he had scrupulously avoided going away from the perimeter of the town, not because of any perceived danger but because he had sworn never to go near anything that reminded him of former times, of his coffee trees. Because in some inexplicable way the intense but quiet war between the religious members and the free-thinking people of the community provided him with more than ample relief from his work. As he wandered now to what was certainly beyond the limits of his world, he felt struck by an irresistible lure to the house, by its smell of beef roasting, by the persistent odour of the tamarind drink which filled the air. Coming nearer, Sebastian Cromantine experienced a disturbing ambiguity that although the place looked new, he had been there before, and felt urged on by an invincible force to go even closer and enter all the houses.

Then he was lost in a different sphere. He was entering a city with a fabulous and mysterious past, where he had once been a visitor in the company of a beautiful woman dressed in silk and wearing ermine and onyx, and they had been accompanied by a tall man who could change houses by heating dirt clay which then became wood, and by affixing a sticky cement to the roof which made them inviolate in thunderstorms. The floor of each house had golden Tuareg rugs, while in the corner of the parlour of each house stood a cupboard encased in glass, storing silver, brass and enamel dinner sets. All the men of the houses in the circle had the same number of wives, the same number of children and donkeys, and kept the same size of goat and cow herds. But it was the house in the middle that opened up to Sebastian, like a valley to a past. It was like the painful reminder of an affair that had been short-lived and bittersweet. He stood on the last incline of the hill that led down to the valley of those houses, fixed his eyes on the big house and the effect was as if he was seeing it in a looking-glass. Its hexagonal shape was reflected in every movement of the mirror.

Something like an eagle's talon lashed out and smashed the mirror of his confusion and Sebastian perceived the twelfth realm of reality and the unambiguous certainty of the globe that was this big house. It was the house of the first king of Kasila who had initially welcomed them. The realisation that he had come to the place of his former anxiety and of how he must have struck the king as being unfit for life in the new country brought him back to why he had gone for a walk in the first place. Thus it was that he had a clear idea of who his first bust would resemble. He was going to make a bust of the king, because he felt that his destiny had been circumscribed by the proverbial meaning of the return of the prodigal son. He was returning, chaste and wiser, more determined in his endeavour, and he felt that it was some invincible hand that had guided him back so that he could renew the threads that had bound him to this place, in the name of his father, of his ancestors. 'Dey will see,' he murmured. 'Ah gon show dem what ah kin do.'

Next morning, he brought out the skull of his father, which he had kept in a bag in the room with him to the consternation of his wife, and which he now spoke to for guidance. 'Give me de fire and ah gon give you glory,' he said.

The bust of the king began slowly the next afternoon. He tried to sculpt him as he had seen him that day, reverent and dignified, surrounded by his courtiers, with the high forehead which was like a dome of great wisdom. Sebastian remembered that the eyes had been clear and kind, despite an unmistakable look of authority. He hammered away at the stone, working with a frenzy that more than compensated for the earlier period of ennui when he had been content to sit on the geranium veranda and face the sea, while Jeanette worked long hours trying to make the ubiquitous puppets. Soon, he had carved the outlines of a face, the deep and aged lines of the brow and the thin lines of the cheeks, without losing the perspective of the living that he wanted to convey.

He worked on the stone, carried away by an obsession, of logic seeking the ultimate perfection, which only his dedication and love could produce. After more than two weeks, he succeeded in fashioning the face so that the nose and mouth were discernible, and the bald pate of the old man shone with a veritable smoothness. When he made the eyes so that they had the penetration with which the king had looked at the captain on that memorable day, Sebastian Cromantine broke out in a warm sweat. He was not sick but the fascination with his own creation was giving rise to an unbearable sensation. It was twenty years since he had come to the place. A lot had happened; more streets had been opened up, and some of the settlers had even drifted away into the interior and to some offshore islands where they had set some small plantations raising pineapples, tea and piassava, married native women and raised families. There had even been some attempts by pirates to attack the place, but none of that had meant anything to Sebastian because he had been living in a sphere more remote than time in Malagueta.

Ever since that day when he had come back from the mountains, in response to the pleading of Thomas Bookerman, he had lived with a nebulous feeling that instead of going forward like everyone else, he was going forward with one foot and backward with the other. It was this feeling that engulfed him now as the bust responded to his strong hands. Those hands which spoke more for him than his heart, as if it were the hands that were glad that the stone was the master who must be loved. It was six in the evening when he finished the bust, and because he had worked for almost three weeks on it, during which time he had not been anywhere, he decided to go down to Phyllis's house, have a drink and then go home. He walked past the giant flamboyant flame trees that stretched from his shop to the new church, saw that business at Theophilus's apothecary shop was doing fine; and he noticed without being moved that a bunch of mulattos had suddenly appeared from nowhere and opened a dance school in a dilapidated house on the corner of James and January Streets. Suddenly, he heard the dull thumping of hooves, and as he approached Andrew Street he came face to face with a procession of mourners. They were about fifty men and women wearing heavy, dull clothes of a solemn summer. From the look on their faces, he perceived that the dead person had died suddenly and they had hurriedly made a coffin because of the stifling heat. He noticed that among the mourners was an old woman who looked nearly eighty, and that it was she who led the procession in singing. She sang in a rich contralto voice which came from a body that was astonishingly strong for a woman her age. But it was the lyrics of the songs that held Sebastian rooted on the spot. He was not a churchgoing man but had always responded to the great songs of the plantation that had helped found the black church. Thus he let himself ride in the River Jordan with the woman's voice, which was leading the corpse on his final journey. He let himself be embraced by Moses pleading to God to let his children go, and in some poignant way, which had a throwback to an event in the past that he tried desperately to remember, Sebastian Cromantine climbed on the sweet, low chariot oiled by the molasses of the old woman's voice. Then an instant miracle occurred; he saw the dead man trying to sit up, bothered by all the attention he was getting. Coming closer to the cortège, Sebastian Cromantine wondered whether the dead man had left a family behind, how he had died, and whether they had given him a proper bath before they had dressed him in the stiff black suit with the starched white shirt. The old woman kept on singing of the vanity of this world, of those who would have a lot to answer for when they met their Maker. Two white doves circled overhead, came and rested on the coffin, and while the pallbearers tried to shoo the birds away, Sebastian Cromantine was filled with the most terrifying desire to shake the hand of the dead man.

'Look at dem birds, he is going to heaven,' he said.

Thinking he had gone mad, they pushed him out of the way of the coffin because the living were afraid of madness. Soon, Sebastian Cromantine was left standing there alone, watching the slow thread of the procession disappear. Then, in that terrifying power of aloneness, he understood what had happened: that all men belonged to another realm of existence where they would be washed, to become light and innocent again. Larger birds flew this time and his body was filled with such a new power that, like a man waking from a long spell of forgetfulness, Sebastian Cromantine remembered that it was twenty years since that journey when Fatmatta the Bird-Woman had sang the songs of lineage to pass the time away. And it touched him that through the present dead, man was alive, and going with his doves. Sebastian realised that toiling in Malagueta had blighted his senses to tell his wife to continue to leave a meal on the table every year, on the anniversary of the death of his father, so that he could come with his feet of the living dead man and visit them.

Little wonder he had not been able to see straight, to perceive that the nature of life in Malagueta depended upon the remembrances of those who had been there before, and who demanded respect. He decided to remedy the situation. When he got home late that evening, he surprised Jeanette with the determination and earnestness in his voice as he announced:

'We gon have a feast.'

'What for?' she wanted to know.

'It's for Pa and for your friend Fatmatta the Bird-Woman,' he said.

Jeanette Cromantine found the idea of having a feast thoughtful. She was glad that her husband had remembered her friend. But she worried about where the money would come from for the necessities.

'Don't worry too much, ah got some saved,' he said. Prudence learnt from the hard days had taught him to put some money away when he was selling his beans. They had not celebrated before, not even when their son was a year old. She was so busy thinking about the feast which had already begun to occupy the yard, that she forgot to ask her husband about his work.

''Nother thing,' he said. 'Ah finish de bust today; made a face of de king, and we gon have a feast like de one he gave when we come.'

Malagueta was hot then. March came with its dry eyelashes and dusty hairs; the corns roasted in the fields and hens dropped dead in their coop, while beneath the grey clouds the brown mountains looked woebegone with their emaciated trees and the sea promised little in terms of a breeze.

Sebastian Cromantine was lucky that, in choosing to give a feast at that time, he could rely on the benevolence of some of his neighbours, and on his own acts of prudence. They had stored up against months like the one they were experiencing, so that they had quite a lot of groundnuts, eggplants, carrots, salted meat, and the rice they were beginning to take a liking to after they had been introduced to it.

Like all people unaccustomed to having guests around, Sebastian Cromantine had not thought about the details of numbers, or of the parade of pots and pans.

'Ah will have to see to dat,' said his wife. 'Lots of neighbours sure to help wid dem pots.'

She was right. On the day of atonement, large pots of food rested and smoked on equally large mounds of rocks, while the warm taste of rum made the work easy and light for the stout women who supervised. The whole community – or what was then the community nearest to the Cromantines – was there. Sebastian passed around glasses filled with rum, to reconcile people who had gone apart, because the Cromantines were a peaceful couple and the dead were peaceful and demanded honour at their gatherings. It was thus that Sister Beatrice and Sister Caroline came to be invited along with Phyllis and the wife of Gustavius Martins, Isatu.

Men not hitherto seen, but who qualified because they had just begun to taste the salt of the earth that was Malagueta, were there, and welcomed civilly. There were the brothers Orlando and Septimus

Blackstone, entertainers who could do things with their feet and with bowler hats and canes, and who were going to open the first dance school in the town, because they did not believe in the power of the Virgins to stop them from getting to heaven.

All the children of the twelve families who had survived the potato plague came, more to commemorate that anniversary than the other one they had been informed to attend. In that gathering also, because they had not seen a feast before, were two mulatto brothers, Richard and Gabriel Farmer, who had arrived quietly on a timber ship, wearing the expensive gabardine suits of their class. They spoke perfect English, had civilised manners, and were diffident about their worth, but, in all, respectable men. Next school session, they were going to open a high school for the smarter children.

But the guest of honour was Thomas Bookerman. Since that day he had parcelled out the land to the enterprising settlers and built himself the small stone house near the sea, with a lush bougainvillaea and mimosa garden, he had shut himself in a frustrating attempt to write a book about the road his people had taken to get to their present position. Malagueta was ready for such a book because it was beginning to assume the proportions of a growing town. The old men who pulled their carts laden with fruits and wood, the women under the baobab trees who picked their teeth with straws of broom and who sold condiments for all types of meals, the clerks who were learning to perfect their signatures in the logging warehouses, the butchers who came face to face every day with the slow bovine dignity of cows, would have a place in that book. They were content to live without haste and greed, without fear and torment even at those moments of trial when the strong winds of August ripped through their cottages and emptied their paltry belongings into the streets. Thomas Bookerman had come to respect them in the long glow of perseverance.

At forty-five, he lived alone, cooked and tended his garden and, except for the weekly visits that he allowed members of the community to make for consultations about exploring new lands and building new cabins, he imposed a strict ban on callers. So the community came to respect him, and had elected him a kind of unofficial sheriff, but not over matters of their lives, which would have provoked a revolt.

When he arrived at the Cromantines', they greeted him with the respect due a leader but not with fear. The Cromantines laid out a great feast and the sky was black with the smoke from the skewer where the pigs were turned by the grateful celebrants, while rivers of chicken blood ran through the yard. When they had finished the cooking and laid out the tables with the rest of the feast, the bread and cakes brought in by the neighbours, Sebastian Cromantine raised himself to the task, as he had been told to do, and made a speech.

He spoke of his father 'wanderin 'cause his son done forgit howta tell him to come on home and bring us his blessing; but he sure knows ah means well, and ah knows he comes 'round 'specially dat time when dey done drove us outta our homes and we hafta go to de mountain'.

He was unaccustomed to the riddles of speeches. They were new myths he had to learn but, having spoken in public for the first time, Sebastian Cromantine was overcome by the solemnity of the occasion; he felt the warm flow of his tears down his cheeks, and was grateful for the piece of white cloth his wife handed him so that he could dry his face which was alive, and touched by the grateful hands of the dead father.

The guests turned their eyes away from Sebastian Cromantine to look at the one-eyed man. Then, with the dignity of a man accustomed to making speeches, Thomas Bookerman, with a glass of water in one hand, spoke to the dead, pouring out libations of welcome. He told them they had been good to the settlement, which could afford to be generous in the person of this son who knew his duty. Small mounds of earth had been excavated beneath the eaves of the roof, and when he had finished speaking Thomas Bookerman put morsels of meat and bean cakes into the holes, where he hoped the wandering living-dead would come to feast, and be at peace with the celebrants, at least for that day.

The bad blood between Sister Caroline and Phyllis was all but forgotten when the schoolteacher made a rare joke about stuffy women who had a lot to learn from women who had given selfless love to men who were not worth the corns on their toenails. Much later, when they had eaten and drank a lot, some of the guests crowded round the mulatto brothers to talk to them. They were handsome men in their light blue gabardine suits; breezy and optimistic, hoping for acceptance by these tough, suspicious settlers. They had been born in England of an African father who had been one of a group of boys taken to Europe to be baptised and attend school as a means of silencing public outcry over the mistreatment of blacks. He had acquired some level of education which permitted him to work as a clerk for a clergymen, and had later married one of his parishioners, a respectable young woman who kept a bird menagerie, and who had always wanted to travel because of her beloved birds. She had raised the boys with the help of the clergyman after their father had died from pneumonia. With the money that she got from exhibiting her birds to bemused English ladies who considered her 'coffee-coloured' sons 'fine African gentlemen', she enrolled them at a Quaker school where they were instructed in Latin, History, Greek and, at the pastor's insistence 'so that they would be prepared for the greedy world', in the practical subjects of commerce and book-keeping. While the prospects for her sons did not seem good in England, she had never on the other hand considered the alternative option of living with them in Africa very desirable. Avoiding the missionary fervour which was then the vogue, and not having the money that would have given her freedom to act, she clung to the belief that there were strong enough men of goodwill whose minds had not been twisted by the perverted and distorted ideas about race that were then drawing-room topics of conversation, and which she believed were eating the very foundation upon which the civilisation that she cherished was built. She had introduced Shakespeare, Byron and Blake to her boys, and they had come to love Blake, especially the master's belief of souls being joined by the fibres of brotherhood in his Jerusalem. To add to what she called their 'religious education', she took them to concerts where they heard the music of Purcell, Corelli and the Germans Haydn and Handel; one of whom she said had written some music about water for the king, while the other wrote oratorios and some 'big music' called symphonies that she found difficult to understand. One night she cried in church during a performance of Purcell's double-choir anthem *Hear My Prayer, O Lord*: at the solemnity of the music and because of the deep invocation addressed to the divine. Through patience, diligence and love she moulded them into good young men with exquisite manners and good taste and, at fifty, when the first signs of the consumption that would carry her off began to have an effect on her energy, she considered her work done.

Gabriel Farmer had left the atmosphere of that protective existence. He had put the yokes of his mother quietly upon the white stones of disconnection, like the wreaths of parting, and the webs of entrapment that his mother had woven had begun to wither. He moved with the ambulatory idealism of a released son, and was glad of the opportunity to be a man among the ripe suns of other women, who had drunk the juices of the sun to nourish their brown skins. At twenty-five, he was younger by three years than his brother and inclined towards taciturnity, though solicitous and good-natured. His mother had succeeded in moulding his character, taught him to be diffident and generous, but he was an essentialist where the finer points of man's relationship to his fellow men was concerned. When his mother died, he had gone off on his first bout of heavy drinking, and had been picked out of a gutter by his brother who washed his mouth with salt and put him to bed. Later, he tended to drift.

But the sun of his mother, his protector, had shone and he was pulled back from the snare of unhappiness, and remembered his father, the black man, as resolute of being. In the London of that period were shopkeepers, merchants, sailors and bankers: the sort of men who were in general ignorant of the music of universal brotherhood that his father had cherished, and for which he himself had been prepared by his doting mother. Yet he felt neither dislike nor contempt for these men; hate was expensive. If he felt anything, it was a deep compassion for the destitute, the poor and the prostitutes who had the souls of goodness but had been refused the bread of equality of all men and women.

Sometimes, the winds of adventure lashed against his own brown face, touching his youth with the invocations of dreams, which books had suggested. Ships came and sailed out of the ports, unloaded tobacco, and took on the deadly kegs of liquor, which he knew was prized by the brown people, who also prized mirrors. Gabriel Farmer lived in those dreams for a few years, until one morning, convinced he had outgrown the mornings full of the unknown, he sailed on a schooner, accompanied by his brother.

Being of an English temperament, he had not found the boisterous people of Malagueta initially to his liking, their habits oblivious to discretion. But he was a man without the permanence of prejudice, and four months later, sitting down to his beans and chicken, it was the unexpected disturbance that Phyllis was causing him which was paramount in his mind. He found it hard to think of anything other than the chair where she was sitting, thinking he would like to get to know her, without being familiar, which he was by nature disinclined to be, and which he felt she would have rejected.

Thomas Bookerman was observing him, noting that the mulatto was not obsequious as others had been in his association with them. He particularly liked the way this man in his fine English suit of excellent cloth said 'my lady' to the hostess, and was hoping, it was clear in his brown eyes, the blacks would like him. Thomas Bookerman decided he liked Gabriel Farmer.

Being a man who believed in predestination, he couldn't help feeling that Divine Providence had a hand in the coming of these refined gentlemen and that somewhere in the grand scheme of things for the enlightenment of Malagueta he could trust them to lead, though he had never trusted any mulattos before. He could afford to be friendly, because they did not threaten the settlement that he had founded. They were not conquerors.

'What you think you gon do for us here, seeing dat you is different?' he asked, speaking to both of them.

'Don't know yet, sir,' replied Gabriel, 'but my brother and I have some idea we could teach.'

'We done all de teaching we need here, ain't we, Phyllis?'

It was the first time he had acknowledged her presence there, though it was clear to everyone by the deep penetration of his look that he had been aware of her presence there all the time, because she was not a woman that even Thomas Bookerman could avoid acknowledging in public. His question was thus a preamble to great things to come between them. She rose to the occasion: 'Some people need all de teaching dey kin get, seeing we is all beginners here.'

She spoke more for Gabriel Farmer than for Thomas Bookerman. Like the rest of the women in Malagueta, the image that she had of the founder of the place was that of a womanless man who had put behind him all notions of companionship. But because she believed in the ultimate happiness that was possible between a woman and even a man as redoubtable as the founder, she was not averse to disagreeing with him in the hope that she could soften him up a bit. The young mulatto smiled shyly, pulled up his collar in the wind and spoke. He called her 'my lady', and said that if Thomas Bookerman would forget his youth, he would try to convince him that there was much to be done.

'Out here, we are happy, we have found a place, untroubled by the men of evil, though we have to be careful because there are always enemies; but look around us, at how much we have got. It is true you have built cabins, a church, markets, shops, roads have been opened up, and the jungle has been pushed back. But we need more schools, nurses, for your children. How do you know that what you have is enough, that you are not more than what you think you are?'

Then, in the same manner that over a hundred years earlier Sulaiman the Nubian had kept the gold merchant spellbound with incantatory declarations, the young mulatto, using the benefit of his learning in England, spoke about events in the past.

That day they heard about a country called Abyssinia where there was a Christian tradition older than the one they had found in America, where the monks went for months without food, and where they had reached such a high state of meditation that pilgrims came as far away as China, which was itself a great country, to test the limits of their endurance. And did they know that there was a black general called Hannibal, long before that Christian mercenary Prester John, who had invaded Europe, or that black people, travelling in boats made of plants, had travelled to America and returned to their country?

It was the first time that Thomas Bookerman had heard about a black general other than Toussaint. Throughout his campaign in the colonial war, he had lived with the feeling that short of starting his own army he could not hope to advance beyond the rank of a sergeant. Six months after the feast, when he would attack the British garrison of Captain David Hammerstone who was trying to impose a most despicable and unacceptable tyranny upon his people, Thomas Bookerman led a small army whose men treated him like a general.

Now, more vultures came to perch on top of the trees, and were promptly thrown morsels of meat so that they could intercede on behalf of the celebrants with the people in the other world. Sister Beatrice prayed for peace among the settlers, and got Phyllis to shake hands with Sister Caroline; they exchanged drinking cups hoping they would know each other's secrets. After his long speech, Gabriel Farmer felt that all eyes were on him. He had come to the feast to stake his claim to some sort of recognition, to strengthen that tenuous link that his father's memory had left in him, transmogrified by the dubious quality of his upbringing. Now it was that ambiguity, that by-product, which had given him a certain esteem among these people. Jeanette Cromantine – who, in spite of her having been awake all night to see that everything went well – was as punctilious as a hermit crab and, tactfully neglecting her other guests, she kept on filling his plate with food.

'Thank you, my lady,' he said, 'but I can't finish all of this.'

'Sure you can, ain't no woman be wanting you with dem skinny bones you got, despite de fact that you knows so much; and we want you alive, don't we, Sebastian?'

Sebastian Cromantine had not been too surprised by the expostulation of the mulatto. Somehow, deep inside his heart, he had imagined that there had been a better life in that part of the world before they had arrived, because the smell of the place was ancient, organic and transmutative. For some time now, he had felt like a distant creature that had survived the saltpetre ravages over the centuries of changes, in another life, in another body. That was why he had been drawn to the earth, by the prospect of reliving his birth in that ancient world, by the apocalyptical discovery of his coffee trees; and that was why he knew that one day, he would go back to them, even if it meant leaving the settlement, so long as he could convince Jeanette about the terrible nostalgia that lived in him. 'Give de teacher all he kin eat,' he said, 'because he ain't gon be alone for long.'

Gabriel Farmer found himself trapped inside a web of confusion. He was experiencing something that he had never felt before. Except for his mother, he had never loved anyone before, so that the transparency of his feeling for Phyllis was something he tried to hide. He tried to fight against the clamour of his heart, to steady his hands that were trembling, but the attempt was useless, drawn as he was by her mesmerising aura which made him want to be near her, to live for ever in her lingering fragrance of a exotic woman of the plantation, to hear her tell about life there. He had not been to her house, but now he felt an uncontrollable longing to go there, to be invited by her; that woman who had raised his blood pressure, who was in his pulse, and who when she looked at him produced the hiccups that not even the hot peppers that Jeanette Cromantine had mixed with the garlic in the chicken stew had produced. He tasted the salt of his own tears and was about to ask for some water when the great mast of a ship appeared beyond the fringes of the tamarind trees, in the distant solitude of the sea that came alive with the resounding thunderbolts of gunfire, which drowned the frenzy of the fluttering vultures and the excitement of the celebrants listening to Isatu Martins telling the story about a proud girl whose face had been twisted to the back of her head because she had laughed at a cripple, a prince in another form, who wanted to marry her.

6   Anatomy of a Riot

Captain Hammerstone sat in the comfortable living-room of his English country cottage. He watched the logs burning in the fireplace, and his Great Dane lay at his feet. He had just had another jigger of rum to chase away the cramps that he had begun to suffer during the winter. Except for that dog, he had no other companion and did not feel the need for any. He was himself an old seadog, exiled from the tempestuous wave of adventure, and he viewed his present condition in temporary retirement from the oceans with a little displeasure. When he had been made to give up command of his ship six months earlier, because of an acute case of nervous disorder brought about by the effect of blackwater fever, he had rejected the offer of a job in an office preparing export documents, in favour of a retirement at forty-seven. But after twenty-seven years at sea, he felt like a seal out of water in the pleasant meadow where even the gentle nature of life and the splendid bulls did not compensate for his former life. He missed the turbulence of the great oceans, the freedom and music of the waves, the conquest of that livid animal terror that tore at even the most seasoned sailor's belly when faced with a giant whale, and the chance of being fêted by the natives of enchanting islands.

Now, in the cold nimbostratus of his world there was no glory to be had, no battles to fight and, above all, he found the puritanical bent of the women not to his taste. Those that he had known on his voyages, the women who had swooned at his breast, belonged to another life and knew how to arouse him. Fate had removed him from the clutches of Englishwomen who wrote lifeless poems about flowers and attended meetings at the local church, and viewed marriage as the pillar of respectability and morality without any allowances for the desires in the wilderness of a man's heart. Not wanting to end up with one of those representatives of English stability and gentry, he had fled to the sea, to the call of the waves and the glamour of the undiscovered, where his character had been changed, and where he had learned how to make love in several languages. He never lacked women and had fathered a son by a Tamil woman in Ceylon, and lived with a bewitching woman in Calabar. So that to come back to this nothingness, this tyranny of inertia, this life of a country squire without meaning, urgency or a palpitation of the heart over a new conquest, produced the utmost dejection in him. The flames roared, the Great Dane growled at an imagined threat outside and the captain rekindled the permanence of his nostalgia. He did not belong to England and he felt as a dying man feels, rethinking his last will. If only he could be given another life, another chance at the plenitude of living, unrestricted by the arbitrariness of solitude in England. He had known how to live and only needed another chance.

It came unexpectedly. He had been reading the exploits of the missionaries, about the omnivorousness of the Bible for all men and women. Going into the deepest resources of the Bible, he concluded that God had arranged it so that they could blaze the trail for empire builders and explorers in Africa. He had not sinned in practical matters in the stormy seasons of his past, because what he had done during those extremes of passion was to reshape the caciques of the human race. What could not be done to those birds in their paradise, in their wilderness of trust and acceptance? he had asked during one of his moments of female conquest. Once again, he saw himself as a captain, flying the ensign of a new ship, behind the liturgy, to the ends of the world just to get away from England. He was ready when during a break from his exile in the countryside they told him about Malagueta.

He had gone to London to see an old uncle who was dying, childless, and wanted to sort out his papers. Captain Hammerstone was the only relative he had. The old man had not approved of his choice of a career nor of the neglect he had shown his parents' memory by not erecting large tombstones on their graves. The captain did not believe in loud remembrances, and their passing had been like a small knot in his emotionless life, not an upheaval. He had buried them with the simple dignity of country folks in the village where they had lived and known everyone. They had frozen to death during one particularly cruel winter and, when the ceremony was over, he thanked the pastor who had more than a clerical interest in the deceased because the church had been bequeathed the small cottage in which his parents had died. Later, Captain Hammerstone walked away, reminding himself to remove the precious silverware which he had been left before the bishop's emmisary got there. He felt enervated by death and, not waiting for his funeral leave to end, fled to the only sanctuary he knew.

It was therefore with a little trepidation that he had gone to see his uncle, who had been a bookseller most of his life but whose prosperity had come too late in life for him to enjoy the pleasures of moneyed old age. Nonetheless he was an epicure in the matter of collecting rare books and music. He kept leatherbound copies of Virgil's *Aenid*, the epic of *Beowulf*, the theoretical obscurities of Thomas Aquinas, the *Paradise Lost* of Milton, the divine purpose of Spinoza, the *Republic* of Plato and the tragedies of Sophocles in a large wooden bookcase with a glass door festooned with large flowers. Surprisingly for an Englishman, he had immersed himself in the wisdom of *The Vedas*, and was an acknowledged authority on *The Rubáiyát* of Omar Khayyám. What he had not found in other spheres he found in music. He was one of the first to recognise the greatness of Haydn long before the composer agreed to travel to London, and he had original manuscripts of Corelli's *Concerto Grosso* and Handel's *Flavio*. Once, to compensate for his lack of a family, and feeling that life was like a journey through an underground tunnel in search of happiness, he had paid for a performance of Gluck's *Orfeo ed Euridice*, and had often given money to charities. So that what he was leaving was a world that had been shaped by his vision of beauty and fulfilment and, in that sense, his life had been meaningful and productive, and he was not afraid to go. He believed that beyond the present there was some sort of eternity, some everlastingness, where he could partake of a spring festival. He was ready to meet his maker.

'You have not missed the sea, I suppose,' he said to the captain when the former sailor arrived.

'To us who have spent our entire lives there, the sea is like a mother always beckoning us to go back,' the captain replied.

'Not even a business of your own could compensate for that?' the old man asked.

He was imagining the captain among the tapestries of a sedate life, loving his books, paintings and the Byzantine relics in the house where his heart would no longer be lit by the inflammable passions of tropical loves. He saw the sailor growing old and content, like an aged crab, satisfied that he had achieved all that was possible in a lifetime, secured and protected by his inheritance. But the old man knew that his nephew was a man without a country, a sailor without a ship, and much as he would have loved to die with the certainty that all he had worked for would receive the same cherished attention that he himself had given them, he knew that he would have to be content with the hope that they would not pass into the hands of strangers, although in so many ways he was bequeathing them to a stranger. It was the first time that they had talked in years and the discomfort that the two men felt at the inevitable meeting was all the more obvious because of a disinclination on the part of the old man to talk about money, though that was precisely one of the reasons why he had sent for his nephew.

'There is the matter of some stocks I have in the bank. That plus bonds and the contents of the bookshop, and this house, amount to some ten thousand pounds.'

It was a staggering sum of money, far more than the captain had assumed the old man possessed. In all his travels he had not been able to save more than a thousand pounds, and the bulk of it had gone into the purchase of the small cottage. The prospect of someday inheriting a large sum of money had never entered his mind, but now, the credulity of that moment was no longer far away, although he was resolved not to let the old man set any condition to the terms of the will, which he would be forced to reject.

'I am an old man now, David,' said his uncle, 'and I suppose you could say I have had a good life. Your mother and I were the closest, bless her soul, dying in that cold. But we have to go, all of us, one of these days and the manner of our going is no longer as important to me as when I was young. Then, we were afraid of God, his infiniteness and remoteness; such a force and creator, an enigma to us. I found a clearer, less abstract God later in books, music and in philosophy, though I don't know whether that has made my understanding of the world better. But I mustn't bore you, because you young ones tire of listening to talk on a subject that you find unpleasant. I have made my will and nearly everything is yours, being my closest relative. However, there are some papers that need looking at, and my lawyer will help you with them; not the most interesting thing to do, I dare say, but you should find them interesting while you are making up your mind about what you are going to do.'

Captain Hammerstone went to a pub after visiting his uncle. Death did not seem to be in too much of a hurry to claim the old bookshop owner, and the younger man, the more to drive away the pernicious spiders of death that he had seen creeping in the room of the old man, hurriedly drank two small glasses of gin. The sight of the old man lying on his bed in a jungle of books with the smell of damp leather and the faded illusions of past glories had accompanied him to the pub. He did not know what he would do with the house, though he admitted it was much better than the cottage that he had bought in the country, and nearer to the power and the glory of his former life. He ordered another gin, sipped it slowly and took a closer look at the people in the pub. They were men like himself, veritable strangers in their own land, who were experiencing the abnegation of glory and the disconsonance of joy, betrayal and conquests which patterned their faces. Cigar smoke rose towards the high vaulted ceiling, the logs creaked in the fireplace, and a gale threatened outside. It was the first time for a while that he had been among other men who were themselves wearing the last garments of their adventures and he felt rather awkward because he did not seem to belong anywhere at present, being a fossil from another age. He felt he looked it, what with the look of curiosity that the other men gave him. He felt lonely, like someone needing to be loved. Suddenly he found himself thinking about the son that he had fathered ten years earlier, whom he had not thought much of leaving in Ceylon among the mellowed tea plantations, the meditative dignity of monks, to grow with the coffee-coloured girls and chanting snake charmers. He had left him with his sarong-clad mother with her brilliant copper beads and monsoon eyes. Although he sent money regularly, made sure they had supplies from the shop owners there, he had not seen much of them in the last four years. Sitting in that pub with the dead-living men, he made up his mind that at the first opportunity he would go and see them and, if the mother would allow him, arrange for the boy to be educated in England. It was while he was coming to terms with the responsibility of his paternity that he overheard a conversation about a place where 'a bunch of blacks had established a republic where the earth had not been explored', and for which the British government was looking for men with experience to go out and set up businesses, backed of course by a garrison to protect their interest.

Six months later, in March, Captain Hammerstone, at the head of sixty men, sailed for Malagueta to establish a British garrison. He had obtained a commission from the Colonial Office which had been pleased to find such an enthusiastic man willing to go out to a place when others had baulked at the idea. His instructions were to build a fort, protect the new traders who would follow on his heels to build warehouses and shops, guarantee peace and stability, and to put down any rebellion or uprising by the founders of the town, though he was warned against antagonising the citizens. It was two months after he had buried his uncle, and he had, as an afterthought, given away most of his inheritance to a library devoted to the education of Sisters of Charity preparing to go out to India to try to convert Hindus to Christianity. By disposing of his property, Captain Hammerstone hoped to atone for the pain in his heart for not having loved his parents too much. He went out with a conscience that was clear, and with the impetuous notion that his new life had already been sanctioned by Divine Providence. Being a man utterly convinced of his own worth, he sailed, determined to impose his rule.

◇

When they heard the sound of the cannons, Thomas Bookerman and the others who had been enjoying the feast did not immediately discern the danger that was coming to Malagueta. Although they kept weapons, the firing of guns was something that had died in another time, and ever since they had built the new Malagueta they had by some unwritten rule banned the use of guns except for the hunting of game. No one had seen a white man with a gun on the streets in the time they had been there although they were aware that the countryside was full of bandits

156

looking for people to snatch. Thomas Bookerman told the women to go into the Cromantines' house and lock the doors. When they had gone, he spoke to the men.

'We got some visitors and dey sure don't look friendly, coming here disturbing our peace when we remembering our dead. You all know how we came here, why we here. Dis place ain't anything till we opened up dem roads and cleared de jungle, built schools and let de Christian folks build their church; so we ain't going to be lettin no one mess up wid us, least of all, no white men, cause we gon fight if dey want trouble.'

Captain Hammerstone came up the stone steps of the bay. It was a warm salty day and he noticed a dead shark on the sand. He considered it a propitious sign that the sun was up, and that the air was filled with the drifting smell of cooking. In the past, when he had entered an island he had done so cautiously, checked by the temporariness of his stay. Now, he moved with the arrogance of a conqueror, like Attila leading the Huns. As such, it was inconceivable that a legion of men could be in that wilderness which, according to what he had been told, had only a group of people who were living a life of lassitude, and who he was going to drive out. England seemed like a bad memory, and he had forgotten the pain he felt about the son he had abandoned in the enchanting Indian archipelago. He checked his revolver, saw that it was loaded, and led his men inland.

Of all the people who had listened to Thomas Bookerman warn about the sinister look of the Englishmen, Sebastian Cromantine was the one who found it hard to conceal his rage. It was his feast that they had interrupted, his libation. He had been expecting his father to come and be present, cured of wandering through the forest, so he wondered why God, if he was alive, had sent this plague, this circus show of fifty men armed with muskets, who looked as if they were going to camp on his land. If he had to expel them singlehandedly he would do so because he was resolved that never again would he and his family have to flee from their homes, never again would he give up his dream of an eternity and joy in Malagueta. His inclination towards chasing off the newcomers was so strong that his hands began to shake and he felt a tightness in his heart. There had been too much pepper in the chicken stew, and he was mad enough to realise that the only thing that lay between him hurling the big stew-pot at the incoming men was the massive figure of Thomas Bookerman.

Sebastian Cromantine and the other men lined up behind Thomas Bookerman. There were thirty of them, and most had come on the second expedition and had a deep respect for the Cromantines who had survived the first attack. That tragedy, they realised, had stamped Sebastian with a solid courage and ambition. Except for Thomas Bookerman, they were simple men who for the most part had achieved what they set out to do: bring their ships across, farm, raise children and plant new roots. What they had to uphold was not so much a vision but a present, the pillars, the structure of an organic world in which they had established some sort of order, with their own nameplates, and where they hoped to die in peace. So that although they were prepared to fight if anyone threatened their lives they were less incautious than Sebastian Cromantine, and were content to take their cue from Thomas Bookerman.

Captain Hammerstone advanced on the crowd with his men. The smell of cooking that had filled his nostrils when he had landed was all over the place, and he saw from the silent faces and the cold eyes of the black men that they had been surprised at some important gathering. Protected by the superiority of his number, he did not feel threatened, and when he came into the compound of the Cromantines, so that he was in the shade of the trees, he spoke the words which he had rehearsed several times during the journey.

He told them that he was a representative of a king who already controlled a large portion of the world between the islands of the Nordic tribes and the ancestral grounds of the aborigines of Australia, and with a vast trade in sugar, cotton, spices and gemstones. How they had pacified the warring peoples of Borneo and sent an expedition to crush a rebellion by dogeaters in China. The black men listened stonefaced and the captain, thinking that he had their attention, continued:

'This place is good for trade and we are going to build a garrison, new shops and a tannery, a distillery and other business; and what we produce we can sell to other people. You can work for us any time you want, just so you know that we intend to stay and run our business unmolested.'

Brushing aside the arrogance with which the newcomers had come to their land, Thomas Bookerman moved forward to stand squarely in front of Captain Hammerstone. He raised himself to his full height and although the other man was tall, the big black man towered over him and seemed not to be aware of the numerical superiority of Captain Hammerstone's men. In a voice that was made louder by rage, Thomas Bookerman spoke for his group, and the earth bore the tremor of that voice, which filled his being, translated into an echo that rang in the valley behind them, where many years earlier he had seen the smoke that was the first sign that some sort of life was going on in that part of the world.

'You done come like a tief 'mongst us, and you gon tell us how you gon steal our land, how you gon build factories, and take our women and chillum for your bed and workshop. Ain't never known any king be good to black people. We all come here 'cause de king done lie to us; tell us to fight for him and he gon give us land, gon give us respect and we gon be safe. And we done believe him, but he gives us land ain't fit for man or animal. People dying there 'cause ain't nothin you kin do wid dat land: marshes, swamps, thorns, thistles and it's cold. So we come here and make dis place real nice, and we got a little happiness, and our women ain't afraid no more people gon be taking their chillum. Now you want to live here, but why you don't stay where you come from? Because we ain't gon be letting you do nothing to us now we free. We is our own men now, dem chains no longer round our necks and we ain't gon let you, you hear, Mr King?'

Thomas Bookerman did not wait for the captain to reply. Life had taught him many things, and one was not to let his enemy know his hand. While he had been speaking he had simultaneously gone over the nature of his first attack against the invaders without letting them know when it would come. Going home that evening he felt more at peace with the beauty of nature than at any other time of his life, because the coming of the invaders had not upset him as much as he thought it might when he had seen the men coming up the steps. He heard his own footsteps on the stones that were strewn all over the laterite road leading to his house, and he saw as he went by that people were putting out their palm-oil lamps and pulling down their shutters for the night. But as he entered George Street he heard the choir of the church reciting the music of the twelve stages of the crucifixion and, suddenly, the solemnity of that drama that had been re-enacted for nearly two thousand years became the solemnity of that drama of the invasion. Daydreaming, he saw all the men of the village walking towards crosses which they were not only afraid of but which were also sinking into the earth. The soil had become soft like quicksand, and only the hands of his men were left struggling to escape drowning with the feverish eyes of their women looking on. He was not a practising Christian, and the fact that he could think of life in terms of a struggle between the crucifixion and salvation upset him greatly, but he was resolved to think of it in the nature of a struggle against all tyranny. Henceforth, beginning with the one that had just landed, he would keep his eyes open for tyrants, all tyrants.

He turned the corner of January Street, caught the whiff of the jasmine in season, saw the bright red colour of the poinsettia in the moonlit gardens, and inhaled the smell of minnows in the drifting saltiness of the sea, before he saw the figure of a woman sitting quietly on the stone steps of his small house. It was Phyllis. When Thomas Bookerman had told the women to go inside the Cromantine house, she had gone in with the others, but, excusing herself to go to the toilet, had gone to the back of the house, walked past the hen house and the pig's enclosure until she was within earshot of what transpired between the newcomers and the settlers, hidden by the outhouse. Of all the women who had arrived in Malagueta, she was the one who felt deeply the loss of her parents, the transitionary forces in life and the vividness of her past life. She remembered how during the colonial war she had been pursued by the persistent hounds of the soldiers, by the crude assertion of their desires. But being a woman who understood men, she had survived by being able to play one man off against the other, by promising to keep the flame alive for the soldier who went off to fight, not so much because of the glory of war, of which there was none, but to make herself worthy of keeping such an exotic woman as his mistress. In that forlorn wilderness where each day brought a new hope, where each tragedy replaced that hope, she knew that the desires of men were more like tea leaves that were fresh before boiling water was poured over them, giving way to a lamentable discoloration a few cups later. So she had managed to live in a world of faded flowers with the shadows of her nostalgia, making kites with the myriad wings of her elusive butterflies, until she had caught them flying over the head of the one-eyed man who had ignited the charcoals of her heart, because he was a man unlike other men who, without knowing it, needed to be cared for; and standing there, facing the enemy sailors, Thomas Bookerman had produced a most endearing tenderness in her heart, being a leader without a ready army, a prophet without disciples. When she heard him speak to Hammerstone, Phyllis resolved that she would go to him that night, to be at his side for ever if he wanted her because he was a man with a cause and Phyllis could conceive of love only for a man with a cause. He had opened the floodgates of her desires in a way no other man had. She felt certain that they believed in the same things as she waited for him on the steps of his house.

She rose when he came close to her, with his collar turned up to keep out the bitter tongues of the ocean winds, his hands in his pockets. In the dim light of the moon he seemed larger than when he had poured the libation at the Cromantines', and Phyllis put that down to the miraculous transformation of being founder of a town in one day, and assuming the responsibility of protecting it the next. He did not seem surprised to find her there. He had a score to settle with Captain Hammerstone but for tonight at least he did not mind being a man without struggles, a warrior without memories, sheltered in the passionate arms of a beautiful woman.

◇

Captain Hammerstone and his men camped out for the night in the churchyard. They had come prepared for this mission down to the smallest details, assuming the people to be without the barest trace of civilisation. They had brought ample supplies of food: corn, raisins, smoked beef, biscuits, lard, dried asparagus, beans and vegetable oil that they hoped would last until they had explored the place and discovered the abundance of its resources.

Undeterred by the threat of Thomas Bookerman and by the ambiguities of the instructions from his superiors, Captain Hammerstone resolved to explore Malagueta to have a first-hand knowledge of the place, to be able to defend his position in the event of an attack. Early next morning, after they had eaten, he and his men marched through town, noisy as a storm. They walked towards the school where men, stripped down to their undershirts, were making extensions to the building so that the Farmer brothers could supplement the teachings of the veritable Virgins, past the town's main market where the Yorubas were displaying their wizardry by offering to turn sand into gold for the price of only one guinea coin, while an old Fulani had tethered a cow with ten udders that could supply enough milk to nurse a dozen babies each day. Going towards the house in the town, they felt oppressed by the silence, the mask of mourning, by the weight of their own uncertainties, and by the pounding assertiveness of their boots on the streets. For Captain Hammerstone it was merely an extension of his importance into a new corner of the world, but his men were drawn into a territory as murky as their entrails, because already they were beginning to feel a tightness in the dark of their bellies which belied the bravado of the expedition. A young soldier who had gone on an expedition to locate the fabled King of the Aborigines of Australia, and who considered himself a man of the tropics, commented on the heat.

'Is like they say in the Bible, Captain. This place is like going to hell.'

'Not exactly, but a man could smell like roasted coffee living in this place,' the captain replied.

Trying to save time, he divided his men into four groups of ten, with orders to go round the entire town and to knock on each front door, and to tell the people that they were representing the King, and planned to build a garrison. 'Use your weapons, if you are threatened,' he advised. It was thus that one of the groups came to the house of Gustavius Martins. He had been present the previous night when the noisy sailors had arrived, and marched arrogantly towards the house of Sebastian Cromantine. Although he had not shown any visible anger over the announcement that they intended to stay, for he was slow to anger, he had also, like his friend, resolved that they would only do so over his dead body. So that when the leader of the ten sailors walked up the steps, he came face to face with a man who had the implacable look of an enraged bull.

Gustavius Martins did not let him speak. Raising his head high, and making sure that his voice would be heard by his neighbours, he barked at the young lieutenant.

'Don't come in here or ah gon do you harm,' he said.

The young blond lieutenant hesitated for a while before responding. Although he was frightened of the place and thought the whole scheme mad, he was not going to let the angry black man make him look impotent in front of his men.

Telling his men to keep back, he went up the steps, filled with the sensation of his own power, which were cascades of rain on his body. He had almost reached the door when a shot rang out and missed him by an inch but raised his temper as he rushed for the door. A great thud sent it flying off its hinges but the lieutenant paid no attention to the pain in his right leg which would have shamed his importance. He grabbed the black man and tried to drag him out of his house, as he would have a corpse. The indignity of being accosted in his own house produced a murderous desire in Gustavius Martins. He had killed before when he had to, during the lacerating moments of the colonial war when he had come face to face with the anger that had urged him on. Now, he was in the grip of a greater desire that was fuelled by its own uproar of vituperation and he made for the throat of the blond man, determined to stop him entering his house. He was saved from certain death at the hands of the lieutenant's men who had raised their guns and were aiming at him, by the timely intervention of his woman.

'Neighbour, neighbour,' Isatu screamed from the rear of the parlour, 'dey killing my man.' He relaxed his grip on the lieutenant's throat, but he did not give any ground to the blond man, whose face flamed with the red of fright.

'Get outta ma house,' barked Gustavius Martins.

Later that night, the lieutenant told Captain Hammerstone about his experience with the black man. They were eating a meal of wild boar meat, corn and spinach under a bright sky in the yard behind the church, where they had set up temporary camp. Between great mouthfuls and an explosion of healthy wind, the captain listened to his subordinate, while eating his meal with relish. He belched loudly, wiped his mouth with a large handkerchief, and then lit a cigar with a piece of coal from the fire in front of him. When he spoke, his men were surprised at his attitude. 'I like these people,' he said, 'they are no pushovers, but we don't have to worry too much about them for now.'

Next morning, when he felt they were safe from any immediate attack from the Malaguetans, Captain Hammerstone gave the order for the building of the first garrison in Malagueta. He chose a site in a wooded area of land behind the cemetery on the hilltop where he felt they would have a good view of the town. At first, no one seemed concerned when the foreigners started hacking away at the trees because nature was plentiful and allowed them to fight their way through dense forest. For the most part, Captain Hammerstone and his men kept to themselves.

During the day, the site came alive and trembled under the hammers of men who worked their muscles into position to give permanence to their ideas, and risked hernia, while they suffered from snake bites and malaria, until their skins were burnt by the silver fires of the sun and the gaseous humidity of the place. Of the fifty men who had arrived with Captain Hammerstone, five died in the first three months when they had almost completed the garrison. It was a small building shaped like a table, built on raised wooden pillars. The floor was made in such a way that there were gaps betwen the planks so that at night the building was cooled by the dampness of the ground below. When it rained, the goats and sheep took shelter there, and the frogs, disrespectful of the laws of men, entertained the men with their concerts at night.

Several times during the building of the garrison, Thomas Booker-man went to the hilltop protected by the forest and had a look at it. Unknown to Captain Hammerstone, the men who had seen him and his crew coming up the stones of the seafront had been meeting secretly in Sebastian Cromantine's workshop, not because they were afraid but because they judged themselves superior to the foreigners. Under the guise of ordering tombstones for the dead, during the nights of wakekeepings, six men and one woman discussed the presence of the foreigners, argued about the best method of dealing with them, and of the possibility of mobilising enough men to drive them out of Malagueta. When they met for the first time, Thomas Bookerman had already decided to drive the foreigners out but, except to Phyllis, he was resolved not to tell any one about his plans until he had heard from them. The Farmer brothers who, because of their upbringing in England, had not had a taste of war, were reluctant to fight when Gustavius Martins raised the possibility of an attack. They were brave men who were decent to a fault, but the ideal that had sent them sailing from England for Malagueta precluded the shedding of blood. They had already opened their school, where they taught proper grammar so that they could correct the impurities in the speech of the Malaguetans. Although different in character, they had the instinctive respect for reason and discussion possessed by men brought up on a daily dose of Quakerism. Because of their attitude to other men, they felt that with time the foreigners would see the wisdom of behaving without antagonism towards the Malaguetans and live like everyone else because there was room enough for all men in the place.

Their caution was interpreted by Phyllis as a lack of resolve.

'Here ah am thinkin am de onliest woman in de house, but seems as if there be others,' she said. She looked round the room and when her eyes came to rest on Gabriel Farmer he thought he detected deep anger in them.

'We'll talk 'bout dis later,' said Thomas Bookerman. Two hours later, without resolving anything, they broke up.

The incident that changed the attitude of even the most reluctant members of the group from a position of coexistence to one of outright hostility towards Captain Hammerstone occurred one afternoon soon after the garrison had been completed. The Virgins, who had kept aloof of the disturbance brought about by the presence of the foreigners but who in some ways welcomed their presence because they felt they might instil the fear of God into the men who had stopped going to church, received one day a visit from Captain Hammerstone. Ever since the 'sinning' of Sister Louisa, they had added several more layers of fortification to their lives so that only God and his messengers were allowed to enter and stay at the Mission House. She had been their brightest star whom Providence had sent to them, and who in some ways made their vocation tolerable in a blighted world. If she had fallen, they felt themselves in danger of falling and, lacking the vigour of youth, or the mutation of disposition, they pulled up their drawbridge.

Consequently, the group of men who came knocking at the wrought-iron gate in their Sunday uniforms, holding their caps in their right hands, did not receive the immediate welcome they had hoped for, in spite of their trepidation.

When they were shown into the stark, pious living room with its pictures of Christ, its parched solitude, its blinds drawn, the pots of lantana that were put to sun twice a week, the large Chippendale table laden with rulers, slates and the books of Common Prayers and the Holy Bible – the matrix of the education the Virgins gave at school – Captain Hammerstone and his men felt a little uneasy. It wasn't being in the presence of God that overwhelmed him but the symbol which in its representation was commonplace rather than revelatory; those women who sat in comfortable sofas with their hands folded in their laps had about them an air of usurpation and fear. He felt that they were as remote from the present as their dresses were marked by an antediluvian rigour. If these were the messengers of God, then he was glad of a little waywardness which made him unfit for redemption or salvation.

'What would de captain be wantin'?' asked Sister Beatrice, when the wick of the kerosene lamp was turned up for a better illumination.

'We are paying our respects, Sister. If you need anything you can rely on us as even non-churchgoers can serve God,' he said.

'No one but de good Lawd hissef lives here, Captain, and he sure gon bless you if you want to serve him. We sure be needin' books and ink and paper so we kin get on wid his mission.'

He promised to write to England to ask for supplies; to recommend the mission to the right authorities whom he was sure would be glad to help, because they were hoping for influence in that area, which they hadn't had since the shortlived occupation by the Portuguese, before the time of Sulaiman the Nubian, when they had built the fort. The visit itself afforded the captain the important first link he had tried to make with the people of Malagueta. Through the exegesis of the church, he felt he could establish contact with a wide section of the community, so that he and his men would not have to go around explaining why they thought they could bring progress to the place. But the intransigence of Thomas Bookerman and his men was always at the back of his mind, though he could think of nothing in the present to deal with that, until the future opened up with new possibilities.

Thomas Bookerman heard about the captain's visit to the mission the day after, but he did not let the information trouble him. Although he did not hold the same hostile opinion of the Virgins that Sebastian Cromantine and Gustavius Martins had, he had concluded a long time ago that those women were content with the charities of God in their lives; that if they had a cause it was circumscribed by their desire to recruit more people among the young to serve him, and to turn the clock back on the progress that the town had made so far. They had not succeeded in attracting as many people as they would have liked but already they were having some sort of influence over the new arrivals from other towns, who, drawn by the idea of prosperity, were coming to Malagueta. Then one morning, Thomas Bookerman was shocked to hear that Captain Hammerstone had tried to recruit men to work in the garrison. He had offered them the tantalising prospect of not only having enough money with which they could build nice houses but favourable concessions with the rationing of sugar and other essentials that were then only available from the garrison.

'Now, dey gone too far,' Thomas Bookerman raged that night. He was in the parlour of his house, talking to Sebastian Cromantine and Phyllis.

'Dey trying to force our hands,' Sebastian Cromantine said. 'Any time you say, and we kin attack dat place.'

'No, dis ain't de time yet. Dey know our blood be boiling so dey gon fire and kill; first we gotta organise and wait 'cause ah know dey ain't finish trying to provoke us.'

He was right. In the sanctuary of his garrison, Captain Hammerstone felt elated by the response to his attempt to recruit men to work for him. They came slowly at first: big-bodied men who spoke a harsh language, rescued from the icy jaws of death after they had been lassoed and readied for transportation across the ocean in ships that stank of the putrefaction of other times. Men stamped for ever with the scarifications of heritage, who liked neither the old Malaguetans nor the white men who had hired them, but who, pushed by the voracity of hunger, came to the fortification. At first the work progressed slowly; they built school benches and tables for the Virgins, made furniture for the rooms of the captain and his officers, and stables for the horses that they had succeeded in rounding up in the countryside. Impressed with their assiduity, Captain Hammerstone doubled their ration of sugar, flour and cooking oil, and toyed with the idea of building warehouses on the seafront for the merchants to whom he had sent secret messages in London about the prospects of trade in Malagueta. Trade was indeed

166

the reason for the frenzy with which he had pushed both his officers and his men to finish the garrison in record time. His idea was to provide storage for the goods bought or plundered in the country north of Senegal, in the markets of Onitsha and Forcados, for the control of the region against others who like him might have the same idea of wanting to establish a foothold. When he felt sufficiently strong, and considered the likelihood of any opposition to him somewhat remote, Captain Hammerstone began to issue decrees through the Virgins to the people of the town. He instructed that the livestock roaming the streets of the town should be restrained by their owners.

'Explain to them, Sister Beatrice,' he said during his second visit to the mission house, 'that it's unhealthy for the place.' Next, he ordered the nightsoil men to go by a route that avoided the vicinity of the garrison, and that the practice of leaving food by the graveside of their beloved be stopped.

So it was this that they had planned, when they had come that evening upon the feast, thought Thomas Bookerman. This time, when he heard about it, he did not let his anger show. Rather, he went back over the history of Malagueta in his mind, from the time of the great crossing, through the eternal forest with its suffocating air, to the instance of when he had stood on that lachrymose hill and seen the sea back at the point where they had started. He relived once again the longevity, the pain, the tensions and weariness brought about by the laying out of the streets, the pushing back of the jungle and the discomfiture of vigils suffered by the founders of the community to keep out intruders. The coming of the new black men and women had brought about a most heterogeneous note into the town, but towards them he felt the same concern that had sent him knocking on the cabin doors in Canada. So if they had gone to work for Hammerstone, it was only the turning of the wheel of life that had assumed a measure of momentary permanence, greased by the oil of adventure which made it possible for man to entertain the idea of engendering his race. If he was going to stop Hammerstone from taking over the running of Malagueta there was no point frightening away the men and women who had only just begun to comprehend the immense beauty of life. There was room in his kingdom for all of them.

'Life can be beautiful,' he said to himself, 'if it ain't for dat scorpion who done come 'mongst us.'

That night he decided the time had come to move against Hammerstone. Someone was having a wake for a relative at which he was not expected, but the three men who were closest to him, and had an inclination of his plans, were there. Sebastian Cromantine – who since the evening of Hammerstone's arrival had been filled with a rage, and who was fighting against a virulent desire to set fire to the mission house because he suspected the Virgins of passing on information to the captain – was talking about the menace of the new situation with Gustavius Martins and Gabriel Farmer, while the wake-singer intoned about the virtues of hard work and self-sacrifice. The corpse lying there, with his nostrils stuffed with cotton wool, was being preserved with salt so that decomposing would not begin before the funeral.

Under a moonlit sky, inspired by the sonority of the singer's voice Sebastian Cromantine and the other wake-keepers began to file past the coffin to have a last look at the face of the dead man, and to imagine the radiance of his life in the world after.

'De brother done finish his time in dis sinful world, and he gon start a new one in de other one. Amen.'

Thomas Bookerman moved among the crowd. Mankind was this, he thought: this contexture of the living and the dead, the triumphs and the sorrows for which he, like the others before him, and those who would come after had suffered and would suffer. Life was worth fighting for, and he owed it to the dead man that the freedom they had struggled for would not die with him.

The funeral procession wound its way through the narrow streets of Malagueta, which had become a confusion of corrugated sheets, timber and stones, when the sun was setting the next day. The shopkeepers came out of their shops and removed their hats as a sign of respect for the dead. It was a small crowd at first then, like the leaves falling from a tree, the dead man drew the people out of their houses; and they cut bunches of flowers to put on the coffin, and threw coins at it so that the corpse should never be in want of money. As the numbers swelled, voices rang out here and there to speak to the departing man.

'Don't forget your chillum, a parent don't sleep,' someone said.

'Speak to de angels so dat ma business gon be good,' another man said.

Thomas Bookerman walked at the head of the procession, accompanied by Phyllis, Sebastian Cromantine, Gustavius Martins and the Farmers. The horses groaned going up the hill and to get to the cemetery they had to pass in front of the garrison, which stood like a pyramid in that solitary surrounding. It had been painted brown, a flag flew from a post in the yard, and on its wide terrace armed soldiers marched up and down from opposite directions. Captain Hammerstone was just sitting down to his dinner when he heard the deep resonance of Thomas Bookerman's voice leading the mourners in a funeral dirge. He came out to the terrace and saw the crowd which was nearing the gates of the garrison. He saw the largest crowd of black people that he had seen since he had first encountered them during a stop in Louisiana, picking out among them the tall, one-eyed man who was holding the reins of the mule, and who epitomised at that moment the menace that Captain Hammerstone felt was imminent.

'Stop them,' he ordered his men on the terrace.

The young lieutenant who had tried to enter the house of Gustavius Martins several months earlier was the first to respond. He moved with a swiftness that surprised even his captain, so that by the time the other soldiers were opening doors and rushing out of their rooms to join those on the terrace, the young lieutenant was already at the gates of the garrison behind the captain. With his men behind him, Captain Hammerstone came out of the courtyard, and gave an order that he expected the mourners to follow. 'You can't pass here,' he said.

The funeral procession moved slowly on its way to the cemetery which was only about two hundred yards away now; the mules pulling the cart bearing the dead man staggered going up a small hill and, as if they had not heard the captain, the mourners kept on walking towards him, led by Thomas Bookerman.

'Stop, or I shall shoot,' warned Captain Hammerstone.

A hawk circled in the sky looking for a chick. Somewhere in the distant quiet came the echo of a thousand feet marching like a trained army. Captain Hammerstone raised his revolver to shoot. He aimed at Thomas Bookerman with a hand that trembled with the anxiety of not wanting to do what it had been commanded to do, and he squeezed the trigger and waited for the resounding evidence of his action. But instead of Bookerman, he saw the most beautiful woman he had ever seen, looking straight at him with the deadly eyes of a scorpion. He heard the bullet ricochet against the shell of an animal that had swam in the deepest rivers, over the longest resources of time, before surfacing to the shore to torment men like him and others who had the temerity to interfere with the dance of the spirits on their journey to a different home.

When he saw that Bookerman had not been killed by his shot, Captain Hammerstone grabbed a rifle from one of his men and fired into the mourners. The bullet hit a young child in the shoulder,

169

frightening the mules and enraging the crowd, so that when Thomas Bookerman told the crowd to attack the garrison, he was met with an immediate response.

'Let's go clean out dis slavehouse,' he said. He rushed at the armed men as if they did not exist, and the soldiers of the garrison found themselves engulfed by a wave of emotion, fuelled by its own force and constancy, because the mourners were smashing the place out of the love for all men and women who had rejected tyranny and had been born free, and were determined to die free.

Thomas Bookerman led his people through the rooms of the garrison. He saw in one the arsenal of weapons that the captain and his men had brought from their visits to the ships that called at the wharf, and the crateloads of crocodile skins that they had bought from the animal killers. Attracted by the massive padlock on it, he kicked open a door, and looked into a room where, arranged in neat rows, brilliant even in the evening, were bars of solid gold.

'So dis is what dey bin doing. Coming here tiffing our land and gold,' he raged.

When he and his people, sated and tired, finally left the garrison, having cleared it of all valuable objects, it was burning wildly, lighting up the sky, while Captain Hammerstone and those of his men that had not fled from the enraged mourners tried desperately to put out the fire in a tiny section of the building. Much later that night, protected from the hyenas and other scavengers prowling about, they slept uneasily before disappearing from Malagueta chased by the shadows of their burnt dreams.

7 The Awakening

The school of the Farmer brothers had opened at the same time as the building of the garrison. Richard Farmer had written to an old friend of his father's in England, requesting textbooks, and in time the first consignment arrived, followed by others, so that by the end of the first year, in addition to teaching the practical subjects of maths and bookkeeping, he had a prosperous bookshop where students came not only to buy but to exchange love letters between the pages of the books.

Among the first to attend were the two sons of Theophilus the apothecary, who up till then had been taught by their mother, a strict disciplinarian who nevertheless loathed the 'churchianity' of the Virgins' school. Other students were the sons of the merchants who had transformed the waterfront into an area of flourishing commerce; the children of a few Dutch and Portuguese shopkeepers who, having given up all notion of proving the superiority of the word of the venerable Erasmus over the belief of the barbarian races, had closed their shops in Europe and come to that part of the world in search of their fortune; and Emmanuel Cromantine, then experiencing the first signs of excitement over the discoveries of the ancient mystics, the works of Wordsworth, Shelley and Keats, the demonic genius of that degenerate and lecherous poet Byron, the metaphorical oratory of Demosthenes and the military wizardry of Alexander the Great. To that youth, listening to Gabriel Farmer enunciate the virtues of learning, the wonders of some theories that had only just been tested in parts of Europe, a new world was opening up. What was life, if it was not the power of words to uplift men, to open vistas to unknown territories and for the transformation of the weak into the strong? If only he could accomplish something in his life so that one day he could make Malagueta something other than what it already was. If only he could . . .

Confined in that space of limited possibilities, Emmanuel Cromantine nevertheless became aware of the special enchantments of other times, of the beatitudes of history which had come down to his time, and of the extremes to which men would go to circumvent the laws of Divine Providence and of nature, to impose their own laws.

'Men had been so perverse in the past that they confused their desires with their rights, which are two separate things,' said Gabriel Farmer to him one evening when he had visited the teacher's house. 'But for the wrath of their bishops, men would have canonised the devil because they have always been attracted to him. Which is not to say that bishops have not experimented with the ideas of the devil, once in a while.'

Emmanuel Cromantine did not always understand the philosophical vagueness in what Gabriel Farmer was saying, but it was enough for him to feel that he was living the life of a different man. It soon dawned on Jeanette Cromantine that the son she had raised and whom she loved so much, and felt loved her in return, was experiencing the first surges of a profound animation with things that his own father had not been able to give to him. While Sebastian Cromantine and Gabriel Farmer had been occupied with the details of the construction of the garrison and with the jubilation of the newcomers who had been working for Captain Hammerstone, Emmanuel Cromantine virtually lived in the small library of Gabriel Farmer.

Worried that her son would turn into a bookworm, and that nature had endowed him with too serious a countenance, Jeanette Cromantine sought to be close to him, to anticipate his wants, to see that he ate well and drank root potions which she kept in bottles and put in the sun to ferment. Although he was now a big-shouldered lad of nineteen, and the profits of the tombstone business had made the Cromantines a fairly prosperous family, he did not seem affected by their new status in life. He was the first to question the wisdom of spending too much money on expanding the family business into the newly opened up parts of the country. Palm oil, rice and pineapples were being added to the items that Jeanette Cromantine bought from the planters. After many years of persuasion, she had got her husband to build a shop for her on January Street, and every day Jeanette Cromantine sat in the ginger aroma of her shop and watched the carts of grains being unloaded, and the drums of oil being rolled in. She bought all year round so that she was sure of supply for all times. She made contacts with the tobacco-chewing farmers who knew when it was the best time to plant which crops; with the men who knew where to get the best spices in the right season; the chiefs who had land that was too big to be farmed, who knew where to find the men to dig the canals for the irrigation of that virgin land. Jeanette Cromantine was propelled by an ambition.

When she had been carrying Emmanuel in her womb, she had sometimes felt her guardian angel near her. She bore the spells of morning sickness and inertia with a fortitude and calm that surprised Sebastian Cromantine. During her worst days when she was forced to lie down, he would bring her salted snapper soup and warm tea, and when her fancy took to eating the fruits that were not in season, he combed the bush of the neighbouring hills, and knocked on every door asking for the opiate. It was his child and he wanted the woman safe and happy. Jeanette Cromantine was happy during the pregnancy. Later, she defined her womanhood giving birth to that child, with the miracle of breast feeding, with the dark nipples thrust into the red lips, with the lime smell of soap and with the blood of her placenta wrapped in banana leaves buried under the pomegranate tree where it nourished the earth.

Soon after Emmanuel Cromantine went off to the school of Gabriel Farmer, Jeanette began to put large sums of money away not so much because she felt it would be needed for his education, but because his maturity was a thing that was beginning to creep into her mind like a new season. One morning, realising that he was fifteen, she had stopped cutting his hair with the old pair of seamstress scissors and sent him to the barber's; she ordered new clothes from the asthmatic tailor, tripled his supply of underwear, and relented over the order forbidding long trousers, so that his masculine legs showed a new confidence as he strode over the lawn into the kitchen. It was there in that room that Jeanette Cromantine first conceived of the necessity of saving as much money as she could for this son who was also a man, and almost the same age as the Malagueta that she had mothered with her hands of a toiling woman.

For Jeanette Cromantine was determined to have her son move centre stage in Malagueta where there were so many sons already stamped with the competing ambitions of their parents. There were sons training to be clergymen who tried to coax their flock to give more to the church by preaching fire and brimstone and whose faces rose and fell like the sun at the altar where they administered the sacrament; there were the surveyors who made the unknown country more accessible to planters; there were builders who tried to capture the splendour of the Portuguese in the imitation columns and porticoes of the houses built by the new rich; there were men already practising the dignity implied in the white wig of the law and the rewards hinted at in the defence of the weak; there were men, touched by the dying and the suffering, who wanted to heal and prolong the gift of life by taking the Hippocratic oath; there were men whose mothers never tired of the search for the right daughters-in-law who would give their sons the right sons to keep the family trees alive.

Emmanuel Cromantine had been at the new school for about six months when he decided he wanted to be a doctor. At that time, the sick had to make do with the skills of the herbalist and the potions of Theophilus the apothecary. Death had not come often to Malagueta, but the bodies of the men and women losing the wax of the new world did not always hold out well in their new country. They came down with ague, with neuralgia, and their brittle bones needed massaging with goat fat; the poor women who did not have shops or sons to worry about knitted cashmere stockings which they sold, and then bought rum to fortify them against the coming of the cold that was old age. Sometimes they were struck by illnesses whose origins they did not understand. They developed goitres in spite of the abundance of salt in the air and the ocean of fresh fish. They suffered from swelling stomachs and the discoloration of the eyes. Worried old men and women who still had their teeth kept watch over young people dying from a disease that frothed in the mouth and made death swift and terrifying.

'Don't know what it is, but sometimes ah feels dis place too full of evil,' complained Theophilus when he was defeated by some illness.

Emmanuel Cromantine was introduced into the divine nature of the occult soon after that. One evening Binta, the old woman who helped to look after him, suddenly came down with a terrible seizure of epilepsy, never having given any signs before of being affected by the disease. It was she who had raised the boy while his mother was busy in the shop. Through her, Emmanuel Cromantine had learned to kill lizards, make imitation fires where he could pretend to cook the reptiles, and recognise the sounds of all the creatures of the region. She had a large store of do's and don'ts: how not to sweep your house at night, how not to thread a needle at night because it was like plucking out the eyes of the dead who saw only at night, and why only dogs with black mouths were to be kept as guards. By burning the peel of onions she had rid the area of snakes. Very little was known about her life before she came to the settlement from her village ten miles away, to teach the women of Malagueta how to thread their hair with beads. She had arrived at the Cromantines' house with only a large bundle on her head, asking to be allowed to practise her craft. But when asked by Jeanette Cromantine why she had come, she replied, 'Because you need me, and I want to help you raise your son.'

She had changed nappies, cleaned nostrils and checked bowel movements in the intervening years and, because she loved that family, a quiet but firm routine was established, so that life seemed less complicated for the Cromantines. Her meticulousness did not inhibit the husband's or wife's vocation. Meals were served punctually, with days fixed for certain specialities. In that way it was she who knew which guests were coming to dine before Jeanette Cromantine could think out aloud, leaving her free to indulge in the powerful cult of businesswomen.

On the floor where she lay trembling in a fit, Binta was shadowed against the wall in the evening fire, and her contortions were repeated over a wailing that seemed less human at each interval. Jeanette Cromantine did not know what to do. She sent Emmanuel to get Theophilus. When the old apothecary came, he took one look at the prostrate figure of the old woman and announced that the prescription of his science could not deal with her.

174

'She is in de power of dem spirits whose names I dunno.'

Frightened, Jeanette Cromantine went out of her house looking like a mad woman. She did not know what she was looking for or whether she was running away from a bad omen, but it was enough for her to have heard the diagnosis of the apothecary to be reminded of that afternoon years earlier when she had seen a baboon giving birth in front of her house. That incident had preceded the terrible moment of the shattering evidence of the enraged crowd looking for the sweet-potato woman. If Binta was convulsing in her house at that moment, it was the sign that the wheel of fate was turning inward again and that Malagueta was doomed. She ran until she came to the house of Gustavius Martins and asked for Isatu. When her friend heard what it was, she pacified Jeanette Cromantine and offered to go with her to see what she could do.

Emmanuel Cromantine was fanning the old woman with a large peacock feather fan when his mother and her friend arrived.

Isatu asked for some cold ashes and a spoon. She was as composed as a priest as she faced the sprawled figure of the distraught woman lying on the floor. Gently, holding one of her hands, she began to anoint the sick woman's head with the ashes, and forced the spoon between her teeth. From the raging storm of her demented world, Binta began to respond to the touch of the healer. She stopped thrashing about, a calm look wrapped her face, and her life was called back from the inscrutability of a world that favoured only the few who had been invested with the power to use sorcery by the simple exegesis of coaxing the devil out of his spell. 'Give her some honey, and rub some guava leaves on her forehead, and she will be all right,' Isatu said before she left the house.

Emmanuel Cromantine was to remember that day as the time when he decided to resume his long walks to be near the world that possessed the miracle that had cured Binta. Much later, as he framed and reframed his life, as he confronted every obstacle, during the solitude of his bitter exile, he would extend his being into that atmosphere which was the only one he felt comfortable in. When he went for a walk the night after the miracle of the ashes, he did so with the disturbing fervour of youth, experiencing the pleasure of watching the sun, and listening to the elysian elegies of birds. He saw the men who were returning from the fields with their cows and the lighting of the evening fires in front of the houses in the poor quarters of Malagueta, to warm off the harmattan. Somehow, he could feel already the winds of his separation from that place blowing, and he perceived in those fires the sparks of his own ambition and the difficulty of leaving his mother one of these days.

'Mother,' he said involuntarily to himself, 'your boy must leave.'

Emmanuel Cromantine was thinking about his mother when he came to the house shared by Phyllis and Louisa, the young refugee from the House of the Virgins. In the salty windlaced parlour of their house which was lit by the sun during the day, they had become sisters of a kind; happy and understanding of the anxieties of others. The older woman only partially lived there because her mind, which moved and commanded her body, was enraptured by the paradigmatic world of Thomas Bookerman. With the combination of an intelligent and adoring woman and a good listener, a woman who did not demand, who did not nag, and who without being asked knew how to equivocate the wants and the desires of men with their unspoken minds, she had all but set up home with Thomas Bookerman. But she came back to her own place every other night because, as she said to Louisa one night in response to her question, 'You been living there so long why don't you move in?'

'It ain't dat ah don't loves and respects him, but a man like dat is married to de world and ah loves him like dat.'

Louisa was putting some stitches to a dress when the young man looking like a saint walked in. Since leaving the House of the Virgins, she had seen Emmanuel Cromantine quite a few times. She knew when he was taking charge of the tombstone shop because he had to pass in front of her house, and though she was dying of love for him she would hide behind the curtains, biting her lips to repress a desire to invite him in so as not to frighten him. She lost weight, ruined some fine kites, and developed ulcers trying to kill the gnats of her desire. She avoided looking at him during the church bazaars where the young people met to exchange letters of love, steal passionate kisses and arrange rendezvous, while the stout matrons sold pudding, lemon pies and toffees and gave away their old shoes and dresses to the poor so that they could appear decent in church at Christmas. She was privy to his fevers because Jeanette Cromantine would close shop every time her boy was sick and the tombstone father went home early.

Emmanuel Cromantine did not know why he had come to the house but somehow for a long time he had carried a weight in his heart which was the oldest burden of man: that of being drawn to the woman who had thrown away a vocation presided over by God in order that she could find herself in the enigma of desire. As he laboured over the hieroglyph of the masters in the house of Gabriel Farmer, as he tried to walk through the minefield of the English language and tried to understand the digestive habits of birds, Emmanuel Cromantine could not keep the woman out of his mind.

The wooden floor creaked under his feet when he moved slowly to the table where the disorderly artefacts of her vocation lay. He felt giddy in spite of the breeze from the sea which cooled the heat in his bones but his timidity in front of that woman was so noticeable that he almost knocked the table over.

'Let me take your hat,' she said.

Emmanuel Cromantine gave the woman his hat. He noticed that she too had perfected her language, and that she was removed from the generality of most of the people who had stuck to the speech of their former life. She had kept her smile, the charm of a well-bred woman, and he saw that her hands were still soft and gentle and that her eyes were kind in the yellow light of the evening. Offered tea and ginger bread, Emmanuel Cromantine sat looking at the room with his eyes of a seacow. His breath was laboured and he felt a tightness in his neck because of the starchy collar he was wearing in spite of the heat. When he saw how relaxed Louisa was, he secretly hoped that Phyllis would come so that he wouldn't have to say anything, but he also hoped she wouldn't. Yet he knew that his conflicting emotions made him feel ridiculous because he had come for the oldest reason known to man: the desire to have a woman.

To hide his confusion, he decided to indulge in small talk.

'I have been studying hard because I want to go away,' he said.

Louisa felt a sudden change in her body temperature. She wondered why he was telling her this; whether it was because he wanted to see what she would say, or if he was trying to hide something from her.

'But you are too young to be going anywhere,' she said.

'I am nineteen and Gabriel thinks I am ready to learn more than he can offer.'

Her belly tightened against her dress but she was held back because she felt that she could have him, that he could be made to change his mind.

'And your mother, Emmanuel, are you going to leave her?'

'She wants me to go if I promise to come back as soon as I have become a doctor.'

Lousia decided that the bold talk of Emmanuel Cromantine was merely a subterfuge for avoiding what he really wanted to say. Although she knew very little about men, it was not for nothing that she believed that even men with the pristine idea of a vocation, with a fierce and

177

stubborn sense of duty, could be made to see that life without a woman was meaningless. She had been aware of the way Phyllis had so manipulated and arranged her affairs to look as if she was serving Thomas Bookerman, that the leader who was so wise in the ways of the world had not noticed that it was he who had changed a little. 'Men are such babies in the hands of a woman,' she said. Nor had she left the House of the Virgins only to sit and hear the man that she loved tell her he was going away to rot in the cold of a foreign land, and possibly be ensnared by some white woman. If she could help it, he would be made to stay, or at least postpone his departure. She did not consider herself a scheming woman, and she viewed her desire to delay him a little motivated only by the purest idea which was love. She wanted to send him away with something to remember her by, even if it meant having to pay for it later. The fear that she might be rejected did not enter her mind, because she knew that she was older and wiser, and that it was she who had helped to inspire the desire for learning in him and coaxed him out of his timidity when he was merely a boy in the shirt-tails of innocence. If someone was going to send him out into the world among the experienced women it was she, not because she was afraid he might not come back but because she had already given up so much for him.

'Will you be coming back to Malagueta?' she asked.

Emmanuel Cromantine still felt troubled by the heat in his head in spite of the salt winds that whistled outside. Although he was fascinated by the picture of the world that Gabriel Farmer's books had opened for him, he knew he had to come back not only because he had already promised his father he would, or that the bonds that bound him to his mother would in the end drag him back to her, but because he could not conceive of a man without a country, or a life without the familiarity of history. The tendrils of ambition to own something in one's own country were already encircling him. Even though it was his ambition to go, he would come back and practise medicine among the woolly-headed urchins of the shacks of smoke and mud, and in the fire of his hallucinating dreams and the contentment of sacrifice.

'I shall come back. Will you miss me?' he asked.

Louisa sensed she could have him because he had exposed his heart of a caring man. She felt that if he loved his mother enough to want to come back, he could also come back if there was a woman waiting for him. She decided to put him at his ease and to wait for the appropriate moment before showing him the gift of woman.

'There is something I want to show you, Emmanuel, if you would stop by tomorrow in the evening.'

When he arrived home later that evening, Emmanuel Cromantine was greeted by the news that someone had broken into their house, using the back door while his parents were out at a christening. The thief had escaped because he had disturbed the hens in the henhouse and roused the attention of the dogs which had chased him away. Scattered all over the yard was the evidence of the haul that the thief was trying to make away with: the suit that his father had ordered for him for the coming Christmas, the chess set that Gabriel Farmer had given him for his last birthday and which he had not yet learned how to play, the notes that he had made on the geography of the area, of the species of reptiles and on the frequencies of certain illness in Malagueta. No doubt it was not an ordinary thief who had broken into the house but someone who was like himself an intelligent man, who wanted to thwart his ambition, an enemy among the young men with whom he had been attending school. That he had an enemy came as a bitter disappointment to him.

Emmanuel Cromantine was not close to the other young people with whom he had grown up, except for the two sons of Theophilus the apothecary. These boys, considerate to a fault, had a goodness of heart that made people like them: they were bright, energetic and good with their hands; they had helped their father extend his shop, and looked after their mother when she came down after the labour of keeping pigs that had weakened her heart. They rose and ebbed with the tide of their fortune, went to school and sang in the choir. They fetched wood from the forest, slaughtered pigs and salted pork, sliced the bacon, and seemed destined to succeed their father in the shop until the elder, Moses, had drifted away to live with a 'native' woman in a town far from Malagueta where they raised millet, rejecting Malagueta as a place of hypertension.

The loneliness that had accompanied him throughout the day was aggravated by the theft and, having gathered his things, Emmanuel Cromantine went to his room to be alone.

He tried to think about the strangeness of the crime but his thoughts were interrupted by the prat-prat of his mother in the parlour berating his father for not securing the doors properly. The fierce bellowing of a neighbouring cow and the pugnacious war of the dogs added to his discomfiture. Suddenly, Jeanette Cromantine knocked on her son's door.

'I want to be alone, Mother,' he said.

'What's wrong wid you dat you won't let your own mother know?'

Allowed to enter, she sat on the bed and folded her hands in her lap. She was proud of her son, glad of his friendship with Gabriel Farmer, and pushed out her chest in appreciation of this gift of a son and wanted, in a strange way, to take him back to her breast.

'Ah am only your mother,' she began, 'but don't ah have a right to know if something bodering you?'

Emmanuel Cromantine looked at his mother. She had remained beautiful, for she was one of those women who grow beautiful with the advancing shadows of age, which flowered her face and held the lines back, despite the insolence of a streak or two of grey that somehow added to her preservation. Between mother and son there had always been a warm relationship. While Sebastian Cromantine experienced the travail of cultivating the coffee trees, while he lived at the border of anxiety during the exile on the lacerating mountain, while his father came to visit him in his shop and shaped the figures with his hands of a dead man and made his son prosper, Jeanette Cromantine watched over her son like a lioness. It was to her that he owed his respect for the things pertaining to the laws of absolute return for kindness rendered, his distaste for bright clothes, and his unconscious habit of putting all women on a high pedestal. Although he was still a virgin, he was aware that the sons of Theophilus, men wise in the ways of women, had been meeting them behind the school room where they made love, because one of the women had become pregnant by the younger son, and the baby was due any time now. But he did not feel smothered by his mother, only that in the way that he had been brought up, she had come to symbolise all that was good to him, and he wanted to be good for her.

Now that she was in his room, he tried to evade having to confess that he had been to see the woman who had encouraged him to study, and was now arousing such desires in him that he had not experienced before.

'Nothing is wrong with me, I am just tired,' he said.

'You expect me to believe dat? You been coming home looking like you don't remember where you live, and not eating after ah spent de whole afternoon cooking.'

'I am not hungry, and I am only very tired.'

'Then it's a woman. You in love?'

Emmanuel was shocked at the clairvoyance of his mother, but he did not let it show. He felt that it was a private matter for him that he had just come from Louisa's, and that his mother, like all mothers, would turn the privacy of his emotions into a family affair. While it was growing in him, he wanted to savour the beauty of it, because he was unsure of how far he had travelled on the straits of love.

'Go away, Mother, and leave me alone,' he dodged the question.

'Then it's love, ma son. There are lots of girls about, and ah don't mind because you a man now, and about time you were going out; and remember, mothers always know, and you can always talk to dis one; but find de right girl!'

Jeanette Cromantine went out of the room with the solemnity of a mother. Behind her, she left a bewildered man flooded by his own emotions which were patterns that he had been trying to sketch, but without any idea how they should look. His landscape, which only a few years ago had been small and untroubled, was now big with a lot of foliage in it. Yet he felt he was not quite ready to traverse that landscape, to be a man on it and to see what was on the other side of creation. Fearing that he was becoming too engrossed in the affairs of the heart, he sought a diversion in carpentry by trying to finish a bookcase that he had been working on for some time. But the more he sought to get away from the disharmony in his heart, the more he was brought back to look at the figure that had appeared in his mirror.

Sometimes, the long shadows of night found him hard at work into the early hours of the next day. They would stay with him, guiding his hands and shaping his perfection. Tonight he was putting joints together, hammering and nailing the rough pieces of wood which he would polish later with resin varnish. Eventually, when he had exhausted himself, he fell asleep and had a dream. A woman took him by the hand and led him to the extremes of his confusion, which was what he should do if he had the choice. But it was a luxury that had been taken away from him, for the woman was going down to the cool water of a river, between the hyacinth, and the inescapable fragrance of her love silenced his protest. Next, she was kissing his lips and eyes and stroking the flanks of first love, which was a rite that he had to perform to become the son of man. He woke with a stir, opened the window and let the morning rays of the sun in; the weaverbirds had a concert which made the trees loud with wings, and he noted with pleasure that it was one of his botanical days when he must go out and tend his plants, change the water in the lily ponds and take note of the latest growths in the fern boxes. Sitting down to breakfast about an hour later, he wore the mask of the last days of his adolescence which was disadvantageous to his mother, because she knew that she must share him now with another woman who would take him to her breasts not like a mother but like a lover. But she was glad that in spite of her clinging there was a second man in the house. As she passed him his pancakes and watched him pour honey over them, Jeanette Cromantine sensed with a mother's instinct that it was only a matter of time before she would know who the woman was that was eating the heart of her son.

Emmanuel Cromantine went to see his teacher after eating his breakfast. It was a Sunday, but he had not thought of going to church with his mother. In the past, when he had felt troubled by things other than matters of the heart, it was to the teacher's house that he had gone, as if it were a well from which he could drink and water his own sprouting seeds in that garden of knowledge. He loved its tranquillity, its living room with the rows of bookshelves alive with the eternal voices of the masters. But it was a womanless house, so that sometimes the curtains were drawn, the begonias not watered while the orioles shat on the windowsills and the silent furniture gathered dust. Gabriel Farmer was just cooking himself a meal when his young friend walked in. Ever since that day when he had seen Phyllis at the feast, he had fought against going over to see her, not because he was afraid of Thomas Bookerman, but because he was content to love her without possessing her. A reverence and respect for what the leader stood meant that he could never hope to win her. Consequently, he lived in a world where cobwebs were growing in his soul and his hairline was receding from trying to hide among the tormenting books of his nostalgia.

On this Sunday morning, they were two men in different countries: the one needing the other, because he was presumed wiser, and the other not being able to deny the other what he wanted, because he could hide in the boldness of his talk the pain that was growing in his own womanless heart.

'You are not in church,' the older man said.

'Tell me, my friend, why don't you go yourself?' asked Emmanuel.

'Because I am not one of the chosen ones.'

The pork whistled in the frying pan and Gabriel Farmer stepped back from the sizzling of oil that mercifully fell on the floor. Remembering his cloistered upbringing by his English mother, he wondered whether she would have approved of him standing there on a Sunday morning, turning his back on God. For Claudia Farmer had been a woman married to the eternity of God, and her faith was sustained by the luminosity of his power.

'How can you tell the chosen?' asked Emmanuel Cromantine.

182

'By the way they confront pain: not by running from it, but by facing up to it like men.'

In spite of his friendship with Gabriel Farmer, Emmanuel Cromantine did not know of the poems his teacher had been writing to express his unrequited love for the woman in the butterfly house. At first it was the poetry that expressed the most abject kind of dejection. In page after page, he had created the image of a woman who had rejected him, although she herself was lost. He wanted to rescue her and tend her wounds in the peaceful sargasso of his love. Because unlike Byron, the poet whom he most admired, poetry was a meditation on women for Gabriel Farmer; a sonnet that he composed in a filigree of admiration and caring.

But the more he wrote about the woman, the more she remained distant. Out of his dejection, he let his heart sink into a state where he took to drinking when he was alone. Tormented by not being able to forget her, he created an image of a woman who had gone away, but whom he was condemned to love for ever. Sometimes it was the poetry of a passion without hope. She came and went back like the waves of the sea, leaving him running on the beach to breathe the air perfumed with her oil of pachouli. Some herons would come to feed on the plankton washed on the beach, but Gabriel Farmer was not aware of their presence. When he was spent, he went back to his room where he covered the naked anguish of his night with more poems: poems that had grown on his sleeves, poems that permeated the voices of the nightingales, which like him had known the bittersweet taste of love.

Emmanuel Cromantine was not a poet, but he too was experiencing the torments that only love could produce in man. When he walked into his friend's house that morning, he had come to find a way out of his solitude and suffering. As they sat down to their breakfast, Gabriel Farmer ate without relish, while Emmanuel Cromantine drank a cup of white tea.

'I must not be one of the chosen, then,' said Emmanuel Cromantine.

'What makes you say that?' asked his friend.

'Because I am running away.'

'From what? Here the world is beautiful, it is new; the world has colour, but it has not yet found its metaphor, the sound of its voice or the smell of its future. But Malagueta is the nearest thing to paradise.'

'But paradise without love?'

'So you too are in love? I should have known, as you have not been yourself lately.'

'Yes, my friend, I am in love, and it's frightening. Not because I don't desire it, but because of its power over the intellect. You have taught me to be a man of words. You know some of the great men intimately and make their world real. You say knowledge is a thing of pristine beauty that must be obtained at all cost.'

'But which does not preclude love; not when you are young and can afford to make mistakes, learn, suffer, and bounce back.'

'And you are suffering too?'

'There was a time when I thought that knowledge was a treasure all by itself: books, literature, astrology, philosophy and religion; man among the beauty of the elements, pursuing with a clarity the fulfilment that only those things could give. I thought it was possible to create without possessing, to love the universe and be soaked by the falls that rush down from the mysterious hills. Ideas would get us where we wanted to go, especially in this place now that we are beginning to feel we have made something of it. When I came here, the dirt road behind the cemetery led into a wilderness of ignorance, but it has been explored and nothing can stop us now to conquer more of that wilderness and make it ours. But are we merely educators, conquerors, builders and traders? The smiths, the tillers and masons, are they not more superior to us and are we not becoming prisoners of the intellect? Yes, I am suffering too, my friend, suffering for the love of a woman who is unobtainable because the master has her heart, and he is a better man for not being a book man.'

Emmanuel Cromantine listened to his friend, but he did not make any visible move at a response because he was shocked not only at the discovery that his friend was in love with Phyllis, but also because he had masked the face of Gabriel Farmer with the infallibility of the celibate. Only now did he realise that the venerable teacher was, like everyone else, subjected to the regulation of the heart, which was more a matter of the influence that other people had on you and not dominated by the abstraction of ideas. And because he had been privy to his beloved teacher's suffering and confession, Emmanuel Cromantine found it hard to conceal his own grief. Beginning slowly, he poured out his heart to the other man. He told him of how he had first been inspired to learn, not so much by him, but by the beautiful woman whose hands had sometimes touched his while turning over the pages of the elementary primer book. How a glance from her, a touch by her hand meant more to him than an entire volume of poems by Byron, how it was because of her that he had come to understand the languages of birds and keep alive the nostalgia for life as it had been lived before the time of the expedition. It was she who had opened his eyes to the possibility that love could be attained when a man and a woman surrendered a little of each other for the other. Because by the tremulous assertion of Louisa's lips when he was there the last time he was sure that she loved him, and wanted to express that in a special way.

'Then go, my friend, and become a man,' said Gabriel Farmer.

Emmanuel Cromantine left the house of his friend late in the evening, and he did not see the tortured face of the albino who had spent a lifetime searching for someone to love and understand him, or the woman who, as she had done for many years, was riding on the back of a great elephant towards the mysterious forest where they had lived in peace without anyone disturbing them. They were creatures endowed with the gift to inspire anything that they touched with love, and had the equally beautiful power to defeat any attempt by man to regulate the rhythm of the world in which they lived.

A small trickle of rain began to fall, but Emmanuel Cromantine did not feel it on his face. He was borne by a different heat that had disturbed other men before, and which he knew would torture him until he was able to find some release in the house facing the sea. This time, instead of pausing to watch the ducks in the waterlily pond, where he had spent many contemplative days in the past, he hurried towards the house. He was a man bitten by the scorpion of desire and his whole body felt the lacerating tongue of love. He wondered whether Louisa felt anything for him, whether she liked animals, because as God was his witness, he was going to marry her one of these days and build the finest botanical garden where they could both stroll. Such was the depth of his feelings for Louisa that Emmanuel Cromantine forgot that he was suffering from a toothache and was supposed to have got some cloves which his mother would grind for him to smoke in a pipe. Suddenly he was near the house.

Emmanuel Cromantine expelled the bad wind of fear as he turned into January Street. He saw the men who were playing draughts under the flame trees before going to check on their nets; he heard the boots of the white sailors going by, hugging the mulatto girls, who wore carnations and roses in their hair and smelled of cheap pomade and brandy. At the same time, he caught the voice of a woman in the throes of labour pains, heaping curses on the man who had made her pregnant. She swore that if God went along with her on this journey, she would never let herself be taken again by sailors who knew how to make love but seldom stayed around to look after their children.

When Emmanuel Cromantine finally began to climb the steps of the house where Louisa was making the kites, he prayed that they would collapse under his feet so that he could explain to the woman that he had been sleepwalking and had found himself at her door by mistake. He hoped that she might be out, but at the same time he knew that his wish was false, because he had come that far, propelled by a pestilential disturbance in his head. When he knocked on the door, a voice inside his head told him he still had time to turn back, but he knew that it was useless. He was no longer in control of his life.

Louisa the ex-Virgin was just putting away the bottle of lavender water that she had sprinkled on her breasts when she heard the timid steps of Emmanuel Cromantine. Ever since she had asked him to come to see her, she had known with a woman's instinct that he would come back. But although she had experienced sexual pleasure in the abstraction of the embrace of Christ, she had at times been inclined to a certain feeling of doubt about the completeness of her womanhood. That was all in the past, as she felt no such thing today, believing that love was now a thing complete in itself. All day long, as she tried to make the butterfly kites, the colours of the insects assumed the colours of her love: malachite, brilliant and flaming torquoise. In anticipation of when Emmanuel would come, she was carried away by her own luxuriance of spirit, by the quiver of her arms that she wanted to throw round the neck of Emmanuel to confirm her place among the divine and the splendour of women.

When she heard the three faint sounds on the door, Louisa straightened the patchwork on the bed, pulled the curtains together and walked barefooted to open the door. She saw a man whose face was marked by the timidity of a virgin, who smelled of trampled jasmine and seemed discomfited in the shadows of the kites. Coming into the flowery room, Emmanuel Cromantine felt that he had taken the long step into an unknown territory where the vegetation was dense, and where he needed guidance to explore the profusion of its inflorescence. He felt lost in the presence of the woman who seemed to him the epitome of the mystery in that jungle of brilliant colours, and he was trying to call his voice back from the territory of the dumb when she took his hand and led him to the patchwork bed.

With her other hand, Louisa put out the lamp and began to strip the coat of his innocence off his back. Like some great insect climbing up his legs, he felt the fingers of her exploration travelling in search of the proverbial animal. A cold wind blew through the shutters and he shuddered in the cold. Then, like a tremor in his stomach, Emmanuel Cromantine felt the prison of his childhood break and the vertiginous awakening of his animal shake inside a dark radiance where his trembling was steadied. A great pleasure engulfed him as he was warmed by the secret flow of its juices until, like the dew of morning, the last drips of his first rite of manhood had fallen into the womb of the woman, while Louisa prayed that they would find fruition there, and join the man to her in the timeless miracle of creation.

8 Garbage

No one believed him when he said he was leaving Malagueta to go and live in another town. No one believed him when he closed his builder's shop. But when he started putting his belongings in crates to be stored at the Cromantines', auctioned his animals that he had devoted time and love to, Gustavius Martins's neighbours thought he had either gone crazy or that the 'native' woman he had married and who had not been fully accepted by anyone, except by the Cromantines, had put a spell on him to abandon Malagueta.

'Dat's what he gets for marrying dat woman who done bring him a lotta harm and no chillum,' said an old woman who had recently moved into the neighbourhood.

'Mama, dat ain't no Christian thing you be saying 'bout Mr Martins, after he built you a house pretty cheap,' said her daughter, a vivacious nineteen-year-old girl secretly in love with the bookseller Farmer brother.

The truth was, Christian or not, Gustavius Martins was one of the happiest and most successful men in Malagueta. Years of hard work, initiative and good luck showed in his house, in the fine cut of his clothes and in his business. During those years, he had become the master builder in Malagueta, but his prosperity was something he wore with the concern of a man for whom other people's lives mattered. From money made from building houses, he had supported the life of the church, although he was himself not a churchgoer, by ordering from a

Liverpool merchant the stained-glass windows with the replica of Christ rising on Easter and Mary Magdalene kissing his feet. At the request of Sister Beatrice, he had made a mosaic of the Last Supper behind the altar; his beneficence was given by others, for ever since the day when Louisa had gone to live with Phyllis, he had arranged for the women to receive supplies from the butcher's, the baker's and from the coal vendor without their knowing who the donor was. Being a man of a non-complex nature he had arranged his business with life so that his routine was regular. He went to his shop each morning after eating the porridge, bean cake and whatever fruits were in season that his woman Isatu had prepared. After closing his workshop in the evening he would stop in one of the bars on January Street where he drank port, smoked a cigar and engaged in the desultory talk of tradesmen, many of whom, unlike him, boasted of their mistresses, and had begun to scatter their names in the polyglot community of children.

Gustavius Martins went home every night to the reassuring warmth of his wife. He was happy he had such a decent and strong woman who respected the supernatural extremes of her world and had bridged theirs together. When he had married her, she had brought with her not only the resources of a heritage to which he had lost all claim to knowledge, but also the bright fires of her enthusiasm for life and adventure. During the time of exile, when he had begun to doubt the possibility of any future for the survivors of the potato plague, she showed such a resourcefulness for doing practical things, for inventing new methods of doing old ones that she had virtually assured the survival of the exiles. No sooner had they arrived on the mountain than she was organising the men and the women into two small groups to comb the surrounding forests for the right materials to build temporary huts, and showing them how they could avoid coming down with the diseases of the region by eating only those fruits that she recommended, and by drinking prophylactic herbal potions. She taught them how to sleep on floors with their ears awake to the sound of the creatures of the night, how to mimic the noise of wild fowls so that they could be lured to eat out of their hands, and how to forget the transience of present grief by being alive in the happiness of former times.

But in that woman who had exchanged the comfort of her father's house for the early years of vagabondage that had characterised her marriage to the man who said strange things when she had first encountered him, in that woman who had cooked and recooked beans and spinach so that they would not starve, who had ruined her beautiful hands by doing too much laundering in a brook but who now had all kinds of oils to bring back the soft feel to them, that woman who had applied dung to the floor to keep them warm in the cold while he went out to hunt but who now lived in comfort because he had worked hard to provide it for her, in that woman, something was missing. And, although most people were not aware of it, she was prepared to trade all the comforts that years of hard work had brought them in favour of what she dearly yearned for: a child.

In the splendid house with the large porticoes flanking the gardenia porch where they sat in the windsor chairs in the evening, in the kitchen where she cooked on the iron-wrought stove that Gustavius had bought from a Dutch sea captain, in the parlour with its exotic atmosphere where she kept expensive silverware in the Gothic cupboard, and served ginger beer and cake to her guests sitting in wing chairs, and even allowed the unheard-of indulgence of a chimpanzee to have the run of the room as a pet, Isatu moved about like a woman who had been cheated by fate. Soon after their first lovemaking by the stream, Gustavius had discovered that she had a voracity for love that belied her small figure, and which even in the bleakest periods of their early lives she used in a subtle manner. But Isatu Martins was not a prisoner of love in that body, nor did she aspire to martyrdom in the marital bed. Although she had been quick to conceive in the early months of the marriage, and had been glad, and thanked God that there were eggs inside her rather than the stones of infertility, many years later after four miscarriages she came to associate the bed with a mixture of desire and a livid fear.

Gustavius Martins was never a better husband than during those times of his wife's post-miscarriage woes. While she knitted bootees and gloves which she would then put away after each disappointment, when she came home from visiting a new mother only to throw herself into his arms and weep, he would embrace her and remind her of the many blessings that life had given them, of how fortunate they had been to have stayed married when, because of their different backgrounds, few people had initially given them a chance; how he had not married her so that she could become a breeding cow, but because, when he had seen her by the river wearing those glittering beads round her waist, he had wanted nothing else in life but to call her his wife, and just in case she had forgotten, he had always loved her, and she was his Queen of Kasila, and when the next ship came calling he was going to order a coach so they could ride through town together as she had done during the lantern parade.

'Don't worry too much, 'cause we don't need chillum as dey will stop me enjoying you all by maself,' he would conclude his ministration to her because he was not only her husband but also her best friend whose reassurance she needed to survive.

'But all dem women are saying am a bad woman 'cause al de pikin die before dey born, and dey say ah kill 'em.'

'Dey jealous! Dat's why; dey wan me to send you away and bring 'nother woman come enjoy what you and me done wuk like mules to build. But ain't no one gon come between us, you hear, ain't no one!'

Isatu Martins was swallowed up by the love of her husband. She blossomed and flowered in the permanence of that love so that the mysterious child would appear in the azure morning when he kissed her goodbye, and went off to work, while she busied herself about the house, trimmed the flowers and waited for him to return in the enchanted evening bringing the freshly baked bread of that love. At that time, they had new neighbours: the Farahs, who were of a mysterious ancestry, and were beginning to keep animals with a view to teaching them how to dance; and the Savannahs, the husband a rice-grower, the wife a beautiful woman from Fernando Po who still spoke a little Spanish but was of a sickly disposition. Gustavius Martins would sometimes take his wife to see these people, who were not envious of them because the incontinence of sorrow sometimes came among their neighbours who were decent people and relied on Divine Providence to apportion each man his lot.

Once, without letting her husband know, Isatu Martins went to see a diviner. His name was Modiba, a man with a medieval look who wore the clothes of the possessed, the feathers of an eagle in his hair, gyrated in his room, sang and plucked a thumb piano when he was communicating with the forces he claimed gave him powers over men. He had come quietly one evening to the town bringing a large dog that went everywhere with him and which carried a bag round its neck. No one paid any notice to him until he had begun to clear a small plot of land near the cemetery, built a shack and installed himself there. Because he seemed harmless except for the brute, they had allowed him to stay. Then someone had seen him one evening, naked on the beach, holding what looked like a small axe in his right hand, dancing, and going into a trance until he was licked out of it by the faithful dog. Later that night he went through the town ringing a bell which sounded like the beginning

190

of doomsday. Before they chased him off the streets, the strange ragged man had told those who cared to listen that a double invasion of Malagueta was coming; that in the region beyond the country, men were assembling to march on Malagueta to try to seize all the businesses in the town, and that soon after that, though it could be five, ten, or fifteen years later, although it did not matter, as it was written in the planets, a monstrous horde of coral-bead sellers would be coming, and nothing was to stop them from changing the face of Malagueta, when some names of the people now famous would disappear, as if they had never even lived there.

Large ugly cracks appeared in one street after that. Soon there were others in the earth which became unfriendly after gusts of wind blew and raised a red dust which settled on the trees and made the atmosphere unpleasant. Removing the dirt from her chairs, Isatu Martins some-times wondered whether fate had decreed that she and her husband would have almost everything in life, but she knew she was waiting as a child waits for her own child in her tormented arms. Being married to Gustavius had made her aware of things that would otherwise have escaped her: the equal role of women in the building of a community; the importance of believing in individual efforts for the good of the community; and how it was possible to arrive at the conclusion of an idea without having had a clear understanding of the idea in the first place. Since that morning when Gustavius Martins had brought her to live in the then wooden cabin, she had been going around thinking that the people among whom she was living were not like any other that she had heard of or met. She wondered how in God's name they had come to that place, and whether the Almighty had not made a mistake in grouping them together. One day, she wasn't sure when, they were going to give up all façade of unity and start fighting each other, because they were already beginning to talk of the poor and the 'aristocrats' among them and develop serious notions of class. They seemed to her a people not given to the idea of love and happiness in any one place on the surface of the globe, because they had appeared like ants after the rains and as likely as ants to disappear once the weather changed. Mean-while, it was enough for her to live among them and not try to understand them, because there was such madness in their ways: trying to speak a language which every day was receiving new words as more and more of them appeared from all parts of the world with their accounts of wars, famine, kidnappings and revolts. It was through them that she had become acquainted with names like Lobito, Jamaica,

Mississippi, Congo, Angola and the ocean that was so great that it took almost a whole season to cross it. Never having left that part of the world before, she was sometimes mystified by the stories of the strange countries where the ground was covered with a whiteness for months, of the brave women who went off into the hills to give birth alone, of the lionhearted old men of the country of the 'bronze kings' who went off to die in groves where they were never seen again. But it was their tales which, like the dust on their boots, had made their lives real in Malagueta, and given meaning to the names of their children, and a place in the universe of mankind although they seemed not to be aware of it, which fascinated her.

The afternoon she went to see the diviner, Isatu Martins already had the name of her child sewed into her memory; she had rehearsed it over the years when she had yearned and yearned to trap the miracle in her womb, giving the unborn child a face in the labyrinthine world of its own absence because her wish had been pervasive and enduring in the long nights of her marriage.

'I dunno why all de chillum die before dey born,' she said to the old man, when he had relaxed her and got her to sit on a goatskin rug. She told him how she had been trying for years to retain the child in her womb, how she had been overjoyed every time she discovered she was pregnant, only to lose the baby before the fourth month; how the women had come to regard her as a witch, and how she was going out of her mind just thinking about her plight, because she was sure that although he loved her and seemed content, her husband, who was a good man, and not one of those useless drunkards who as soon as they received some money went to one of the houses on the waterfront and hired women, she was sure that he wanted a child, because it was in the nature of men to want children especially sons as that was the law of mankind. What had she done to deserve this curse? No, she was not bitter, but sometimes she felt that God made mistakes: there were women who had so many children, their men only had to *touch* them once and *bam!* While there she was all these years praying to God that she might keep only one, but they had all ended up feeding the roots of some tree that she felt was only waiting for more.

'That husband of yours, where is he from?'

'He is from here,' the woman replied.

'I meant who are his people, his group.'

'Well, he is one of those people who came to settle here some time ago.'

'You mean he is a foreigner, a man without any claim to this soil?'

'But he is my husband.'

The old man remained still. If he had heard the woman, then it was in the soft folds of her gown. Years of practising his art in the small hamlets and villages beyond the forest that almost encircled Malagueta had not been without their favours and problems. When he had embarked upon the venerable profession of telling the future, he had been met with distrust and even open hostility among the people in those parts of the world where they had ceased to believe in the workings of miracles since the time of Sulaiman the Nubian. The name of that sage had gone out with the last of the Tuaregs who had switched from hawking their wonders to settling down and raising families and becoming common stall owners in the Saturday market. The freedom that they had possessed to roam over the vast desert, the incantatory verses of Omar Khayyám that they used to read and the jars of ointments from the bazaars of Istanbul were replaced with the rolls and rolls of cheap Indian cotton, the cooked entrails of salamanders and other reptiles guaranteed to drive out evil, and by the aromatic smell of Arabic coffee and the gastronomic condiments of the Moors. When he had tried to preach the laws of abstinence, the rights of women, and the responsibility to the divine, Modiba found himself among non-believers. He discovered that whereas men were willing to sell their daggers which they had once worn proudly as symbols of power and virility, they were not prepared to compromise their taste for the good life with their fear of God or the belief in individual destiny. That was why he was glad to have come to Malagueta, where in spite of the first hostile response of its people, a few were beginning to come to him with their problems.

Sometimes he got the dog to dance for him, wearing a chain. He had trained it to dance to the song of initiation played on the bowharp, to the music of how to catch the thief by holding a pot to his belly, and to the song of the returning hunter played on the thumb piano. But Isatu Martins's problem, he concluded, did not require the dance of a dog. She was a woman whose heart was as transparent to him as a piece of glass, and he could say to her, when she had finished her story, that she had not had a child because she had put a lot of distance between herself and her parents as the dead 'was crying somewhere in the wilderness' for the lost child.

'When were you last home to visit your parents?' he asked the woman.

'Over two years,' she replied.

'Then you realise you have not kept in touch with the news.'

She was immediately alarmed. If anything was wrong with her

parents she would have been informed, although she blamed herself for having stayed away from them, and she was certain that the magician was merely saying there was something wrong back home to extract some gains from her. He soon dispelled her suspicion.

'I don't know how to tell you, but I see a procession of men, no women. I see a white shroud, and I see a house where the light has gone out, and the women sit in a group oppressed by a terrible silence.'

Isatu Martins was no longer in any doubt that what the diviner was talking about was death. No one close to her had died in all the time she had been married to Gustavius Martins; but if something terrible had happened or was about to happen, she did not want to know because she was afraid of premonitions, afraid of revelations which triggered off her asthma. She had almost forgotten why she had come to see the diviner in the first place, when he continued in a voice that was reassuring.

'Go back to your village, take that husband of yours with you, and when you are pregnant the next time, you will see what will happen.'

Isatu Martins had to persuade Gustavius that they should go to her town for a visit. 'Time flies and we lose touch wid those we love,' she said one evening when they were having dinner.

'What you talking about?'

'That ah ain't seen Papa in two years, and maybe ah won't before he dies.'

'But he ain't come to see you either, what kind of father he be if he don't come to see his own daughter?'

'Maybe he dead already, maybe he roaming all over de place and we don't know.'

'Then you go home. I'll make arrangements for you tomorrow.'

'I won't go alone. You married me so dey be wanting to see their son-in-law 'specially as dey got no grandchild from us yet.'

'You blaming me for dat?'

'No, just ma bad luck; but ah feels like going home for a visit, but if you won't come wid me, I won't come back here.'

One week later, after he had sold off his animals, closed his shop and put their belongings in large crates which the Cromantines promised to store so that thieves would not break into their home, the Martinses hired three horses and went off to visit the parents of Isatu who had moved away from the coast and lived in Bolanda, a town some two days' journey from Malagueta. In the past, when she had visited them alone, she had considered each visit merely as a social obligation which she had to perform, take whatever she could from Malagueta to the old people, reassure them that she had not married a rat, and that all was well. To questions of when they were going to be grandparents, she had always replied:

'When we find the right formula.'

Now she was sobered by a doubt which was giving a new dimension to her life, to their marriage. The man riding beside her seemed even more than ever a larger part of the world that they both had created but she was, as a woman, receding into another world where the threads that she had sewn intricately, and which over the years had seemed so reassuring, were beginning to come off. The town she was going to now, seemed less the home that she had once known, the family where she had once counted herself as a member. It was now a vacuum. The goods that they were taking this time suddenly became more an act of atonement for some unmentioned crime than the gifts that a prosperous son-in-law and daughter were expected to bring on their regular visit. The rainy wind of July blew into her face, and Isatu Martins was taken back to her childhood when she had played with the rainflies which would appear in their thousands, and how the servant girl had cooked them and taught her how to eat them with honey when her parents were busy in the house. How she had come down with chickenpox when she was fifteen, and still carried some of the scars which Gustavius, bless his heart, had said, added to her lovely complexion.

When they were nearly in Bolanda, she had a strange feeling that something had changed. The brilliant light of sun was trying to break out after the long period of rain but the noisy urchins who used to play everywhere in the past had disappeared; the meat hawkers who roasted goat and cow meat alongside the road lined with baobab trees wore a terrible and frightened look, which even the presence of the stranger Gustavius did not alter.

'Good grief, dis place is dead,' Isatu Martins gasped.

She wasn't far from the truth. Soon after her last visit, the angel of death had visited the place; a great flock of killer bats flew out of their caves in the mountain one night and attacked the men, women, children and dogs. Every house was marked by the remorseless suckers of death which had sucked the blood of the living, and terrified even the peaceful dead in their graves under the tamarind trees. When the bats had gone, the extent of their destruction was such that Bolanda became a town marked with the cross of a plague. Travellers coming from all parts of the world, who got lost in the haze of speculation, avoided it so as not to come in contact with the mysterious disease the bats had supposedly brought to the town. And its citizens were marked with the solitude of men and women who had been dosed by the salt administered in quarantine. Among those who had died but whose death had not been carried by the post of the dead was the father of Isatu Martins.

Although life had brought him many favours, it was his perceived misfortunes that he had taken to his grave, including the loss of two brothers during a regional war, and the fact that he himself had not had a son. When his daughter had married the foreigner, he had hoped for a grandson so that he could leave his vast holdings in rice, coffee, oranges and ginger to him. In his field with the smell of the permanence of cow manure, in the orchard where monkeys chatted on his coffee trees, on the orange trees where the iguanas sunned themselves and chased the flies, in the warm glow of afternoons, in the rice paddies where the cobras waited patiently for the frogs, two generations of men and women had come and gone. They had worked there in return for a share of what they produced and for the security that they derived from such a large community. Floods and hurricanes had not dampened their faith and their courage. They had fought off attempts by neighbouring communities to take over their farms, and by foreigners, who smelled of varnish because they had the blood of albinos, to settle among them. But his prosperity had not brought him happiness, and at the time of the invasion by the carnivorous bats, Santigue Dambolla was a man tired of waiting for the son that his wife had not been able to give him.

'Shit,' he said just before he closed his eyes on the world, succumbing to the poison that a dozen bats had injected in him, 'building all of this so that worms can inherit it.'

Gustavius and Isatu Martins arrived at the house of Santigue Dambolla when the dead were beginning to come out for their walk; the streets were filled with the tracks of the dead looking for their houses of former times, for particles of clothes they wore in past life, for the stables where they had last seen their horses. Being a woman attuned to the noises of the region, Isatu Martins heard the bleating of the goats as they struggled to get out of the mud of death, of the last of the wandering Tuaregs who were trying to find their way, through the rush of the dead, back to the desert. It was a house of mourning they had come to, and when they knocked on the door, they heard the movement of someone removing the mortars, pestles and brooms which had been put against the door to keep out the dead of other times who might want to come in. They saw where the nocturnal spiders had built webs large enough to trap the moths in the porch, they smelled the wetness of the hide of a bull that had been killed to mark the forty-day anniversary of a dead man. It was then that it dawned on Isatu Martins that her father had died, and that the conversation she had recently had with the diviner was a premonition of the events to happen in Bolanda.

'He thought he had lost you when you did not come in two years; this was what killed him, not the bats; it was not the first time that they had come, but this time, they seemed to laugh at everyone, and they sucked blood everywhere for a whole week. Your father waited for death as if for a lover,' said the dead man's widow.

Isatu Martin's mother had to be restrained from banging her head against a wall when she was recounting how the disaster had happened. She was in the white of mourning: white chalk circled her brown eyes, white shawl draped her entire body, and white slippers covered her feet which she dragged across the floor of the parlour.

'There was no way of letting you know,' she continued, ignoring the husband who had come with her daughter. 'The caravans did not pass through here and the paths were blocked anyway; it was a siege.'

So Isatu Martins remembered her father only in profile as he had been among the turfs of grass. Through the maze of former times, she saw him throwing his seeds to the porous earth, shooing away the fowls, and being glad of water which was plentiful. In the liquidity of sorrow she recalled the tall man in the white of his caftan, strolling across the lawn of his yard, coming from the mosque where he made his Friday peace with God, thanking him for his crops and for the men who worked on his land, and for holding back the plagues of locusts and rats. As he was a generous man, who never forgot the birthdays of his workers' children which were recorded on a slate, he would sometimes buy expensive fabrics for their wives, give them enough so that they could be men among their own wives, while he became rich on the bounteous and peaceful terrain of labour. But if the peace had been counterfeit, Isatu Martins did not know and did not try to think about it. She dreaded conjectures which left her terrified of her own mortality and her nakedness which she had been trying to clothe with the children of the seeds of her husband.

Gustavius Martins remembered when he had come for this woman during the lantern parade of another season, how he had summed up the best instances of his own humility and humanity to become worthy of her. He remembered in particular how he had dreaded meeting her father, and had hoped that his 'foreignness' would not be held against him, because he was himself a son of the man of that soil, and the knife of the sea which had cut the bloodknot had been sheathed in the first thanksgiving in Malagueta.

Now that Santigue Dambolla was dead, he wished he had known his father-in-law better beyond the mere gestures of courtesies, which had been returned in like manner by a man who had been kind enough to let his daughter go and live in the wilderness of a new settlement, among the babel of humanity. He was grateful to the memory of the man and Gustavius Martins felt lonely in the presence of the dead.

'We will have to wash you and your husband,' said Sawida Dambolla when they were sitting in the kitchen drinking some tamarind pap in the evening glow of fire. Gustavius Martins did not immediately grasp the point of being 'washed' and looked at the face of the woman he had married to get him through this new terrain.

Then the voice of the widow spoke softly about the dead man:

'Before your father died, he went to see a diviner, a maker of medicine. I don't know what your husband's people call them in Malagueta to which they brought the junk of that place where I am sure they shaved their heads of all memories of the divine purpose. They have a dubious notion of freedom so that man is perceived as living in a world where he is independent of nature. Space is a thing they have not learnt how to deal with, because they are pulling down everything: trees, groves, shrines; insulting the souls of the dead. Rites that help us into adulthood mean nothing to them, the spiritual is suspect, and very little thought is given to the relationship between what we bring into this world and what we take with us to our graves. Or for that matter to the little things that are much more important than the big ones in our lives. Well, we still have medicine men here, and when your father consulted one, the diviner saw you in a grove where your child was imprisoned among other children with hairs that had become entangled in the roots of the trees. No woman, the diviner said, could hope to bring forth a child from that confusion of limbs. So that although you had not told us about your repeated miscarriages – not that you young ones tell us anything these days, how different it was in our time when your mother examined you every morning to see whether you were pregnant – so although you kept it a secret from us, we knew about your problems. When your father came back, he thought about what the diviner had told him, for a very long time. He gave up spending too much time on the farm, and sat for hours on end in the wicker chair on that porch and sucked on his pipe. Sometimes he went out among the almond and lemon trees to be alone, but although he did not talk much then, I knew what was troubling him.

He was arguing with himself over the nature of the divine purpose; whether it was right that goats and sheep had heirs while he was deprived of a grandchild. 'Don't jump before God's time,' I said to him; but I am only a woman and he did not pay too much attention to me. He used to say that life was only important if it led you towards a fuller understanding of the supremacy of sacrifice over all other objectives. He saw the willingness of Abraham to sacrifice his only son as the ultimate example of selflessness of man. Then he would think about you as the daughter he had sacrificed to what he called the Oporto, the white/black people, and as recompense he expected sons from you. He wanted so much for God to give him a grandson with whom he could sit on the porch in the twilight of his years, inhaling his beloved jasmine. He would have told him about our greatest king, Farama Borea, who could make himself invincible, about his son Kilsano who could wake up the souls of the dead by holding a mirror over their graves and by talking to them. Your son would have been instructed in the teachings of Mahmud Kati of Timbuctoo who wrote the Tarikh al-Fattash, and to whom we owe so much of our history. But it was not to be. So your father waited for death dragging his feet of a dead man long before the bats came. When I found him he was lying next to the banana grove where we throw the garbage, as if he himself had become a part of what decays and rots in the vegetation of man, trees and plants.'

Santigue Dambolla was buried with bits of rags and bottles hanging from his neck as part of the ritual of his people, the afternoon after his death. When her mother had concluded her story, clasping her arms the way widows do, Isatu Martins's own youthful hands went to the atlas of her belly in search of her lost father, thinking that she could reincarnate him as her child. If she could have pinpointed the country where he had gone, she would have cajoled him to come back, to bear witness to the child becoming the man; but the lines of the country were blurred, and she began to doubt her ability to find the right tracks. So she thought of hunchbacks and dwarfs, not as they begged on those Fridays of supplication, but because they had conquered fear, hate and death. When she was young, her mother had told her that they had come among the fortunate since the time of man and, in spite of their infirmity, had learnt to cure with their hands and their spittle all those who suffered from desires, greed and lassitude. They were the men and women who understood the frailty of man, his weakness, and the terrifying cold that he feels despite the heat of not only his body, but of the sun that had ripened the earth.

Suddenly she found her burden unbearable. She wondered if she had given up laughing because of her obsession to possess what was not hers to give to the husband; if she was not destined to add to the cradle of man, then it was enough that she was alive in the world of other beings and that the man loved her.

Later that night when she cuddled up to her husband in the strange bed, she made love with a passion that surprised him, and awakened such heat in him that he wondered whether it was the same woman who had only recently been afraid of the marital bed.

'We must not get too anxious over these things,' he said, after they had stayed awake all night, and she had exhausted and brought him to a new country of love.

It was the beginning of a new life for Isatu Martins. As soon as a respectable mourning period had passed, she opened all the windows of the house to let the air of the green hills come in. She got her mother to stop wearing the mask and colours of mourning, to talk about what her father had said in his last days, about the business of running the farm, how to get the cows producing milk again after they had stopped when Santigue Dambolla died, and how to eradicate the lice popping out of the damp ground. When Sawida Dambolla came out of mourning, she saw a house in which her daughter had washed the curtains, painted the walls a brighter colour, turned the pictures back from the wall, rolled the mats on the floor and got rid of the candles and incense which had been lit every night since Santigue Dambolla died. The neighbours were scandalised when they saw her walking around with a broom at night, sweeping away the ubiquitous cobwebs that her mother had let grow in the place. They prayed that such an indiscretion against the dead of the town would not bring back another plague on their heads. After the house had been given its lustre of former times, Isatu Martins persuaded her mother to open the trunks of the dead man so that they could sort out his things.

'There are people out there, Mama, who do not have anything, and you are going to keep these locked up for the cockroaches to eat,' she said.

They had to get a diviner to come and open the trunks as they were afraid they might contain things not meant for their eyes to see. When they were opened, the trunks contained the symbols of glory and love of an ordinary man: the expensive, embroidered gowns for the splendid festivals that he had attended; the cordovan shoes of the first white man who had gone to that part of the world and exchanged them for a pair of

200

Moroccan slippers; the twenty pairs of worsted woollen trousers that he had seldom worn because he was a man of the farm; the sword of Modibo of Timbuctoo; the leatherbound volumes of El Omari of Cairo about the Mandingo king who had caused a run on the gold market because of his profligacy; the golden tapestries and brass ornaments made by the eunuchs of Kano, which he had bought from the wandering Tuaregs; and the porcelain jug with the drawing of a woman being kissed by a creature with the body of a man and the bottom of a lion. Wrapped in a beautiful black box inlaid with pearls, they found one hundred gold coins mixed with cowrie shells and withered red pepper, which Isatu Martins recalled was used to drive out evil spirits.

Santigue Dambolla sat under the leaves of the banana plants, watching his relatives rifle the contents of his former life. Now that he had shed the baggage of his mortality he felt light and happy. After years of being regarded with awe, he could walk freely among the living and the dead, among the beggars who no longer bothered him, among the street vendors who were returning to the town now that the plague of the bats was over. He had passed through the byways of haste and desire, and had given up the human habit of being driven by time. 'That was what I hated most about my former life, being governed by time,' he said one morning when he suddenly found himself with too much time on his hands. Now, he thought he could encourage his wife to go for walks without someone coming up to them to ask for money. Sometimes, he would come and sit beside her on the porch where the rainflies had fallen, to hold her hand and talk about their early days of deprivation: the days when they had only beans and mushrooms, the times when the locusts came and ate up everything. He would take out her grey hairs, guide her through the labyrinth of solitude caused by his death, and give her a role in life other than that of being his wife in this or that life, when she had said, 'No, thank you for your help, but understand that this is woman's business, you get out of the kitchen.' From the tedium of one life Santigue Dambolla was preparing for another life because his death had left him the freedom to live without the transcience of commanding his wife, so that if she wanted to get rid of his stuff, he was glad of her charity and was prepared to help her. And because he was content to be a man of all ages, to come back to this house, it was Santigue Dambolla who got rid of the lice, after Isatu Martins had given up trying to douse them with oil.

The first time they heard him going through the house, they saw the doors of all the rooms open and close behind him, they saw the pictures on the wall shake with the force of a hurricane and the wicker chair on the porch move into position so he could sit down as in the suffocating afternoons. When Sawida Dambolla tried to pour coffee into a mug and take it to him, she saw his own mug filled with coffee, right next to his chair, after it had been missing since the day of his death.

As soon as they had grown accustomed to his presence in the house again, they left the doors open, put food on the table in the dining room so he could go and come as he pleased.

Gustavius Martins was the only one who did not see the dead man moving about the house. Years of being in the wasteland of America had stripped him of the power to make contact with the dead, but when he was invited by his mother-in-law to choose some items of Santigue Dambolla that he would keep for himself, he chose the sword of Modibo of Timbuctoo, the porcelain jug with the voluptuous woman, and one of the white-laced gowns which he could wear on his castaway body.

Sawida Dambolla, smiling at her son-in-law, said: 'He would love you for that. Welcome home, son.'

Because he was reconciled to his presence among the people of the town, Gustavius Martins did not mind that they were beginning to stare at him, or that because of his strange outfit, his stiff collar and gabardine trousers, he was arousing interest in some of the young women who were coming to the house ostensibly to pay their respect to the new arrivals.

Without anyone telling him, he had concluded that it would be some time before he and his wife would return to Malagueta. The rains that had fallen for six months were over and the state of the orchard was alarming: the combination of the prolonged rain, the plague of the bats and the death of Santigue Dambolla had forced his workers off the fields, destroyed some of the coffee and orange trees, and driven away some of the cows. Drastic moves were needed to restore the trees to productivity, to get the men to come back, to harvest what remained of the last season's rice and corn. He was therefore not surprised when his wife, as if reading his thoughts, suggested to him that evening that she would like to stay a few months with her mother, to help her get over the shock of the recent tragedy, and to find her bearings.

'It's all right,' he said, 'the clock is ticking in Malagueta, but it has stopped here, and we gotta wind it up again.'

The winding of the clock to signal the beginning of a new day got off right away. Through word of mouth, the men who had fled from the fields emerged from their huts and were persuaded to go back to work. They came slowly at first with their cutlasses, and began harvesting what was left of the crops. They were not accustomed to working for strangers, but when Gustavius Martins's mother-in-law told them that he was part of the family, and was the new boss, they regarded him with the same respect as they had given Santigue Dambolla. Then it was that the couple from Malagueta became farmers in the translucent world, surrounded by the ghosts of some of the founders of that town, who had achieved a permanence among the trees and the fields, and who made the burden of the transformation easy for the Martinses.

Six months later, when the dry clouds had sucked up the rain, they looked at the field and were content with their labours. They had restored the trees to good health, planted three varieties of rice, got the cows milking again, and had the potatoes, yams and corn ready for the harvest.

The pleasure derived from such a happy conclusion to the hard work did much to push the period of the plague into the remotest corner of memory. Now, they wanted to celebrate, to give their relationship a new meaning because their natures had become one, and their humanity had been confirmed by the dirtying of their hands to keep the earth alive. Sawida Sambolla had come to love Gustavius Martins like a son so that it was she who fretted over him, who worried about whether he was happy 'away from his people', whether her daughter was feeding him well. 'Look after him well, Isatu. Men like him are hard to find,' she advised.

'Don't think I don't know that, Mama,' Isatu Martins replied.

But in spite of the happiness that she felt at the closeness of her daughter and her son-in-law, Sawida Dambolla was also aware that such happiness would be temporary, because they could not stay for ever. She tried not to think about it but she dreaded being alone without her husband, without the young people, because she realised that it was also in the nature of man and woman to hold on to others for ever. That was why, when she was sure that Isatu and her husband were still asleep in the early hours of the morning, she would sometimes get up before the cocks started crowing and before the bread and cashew nut hawkers came round to her house, and go out into the porch with a glass of water. There, after pouring some of the water on the ground, she would talk to her husband, thank him for giving the children the wisdom to rebuild the business, for not letting the neighbours laugh at her, because she could now show off her daughter and her son-in-law. 'What a son-in-law you have, Santigue. But don't forget that you can see better than any of us now, you have gone to meet my father and your parents. How are they? Tell them that six months from now when I have a big feast to mark the first year of your death I shall also be cooking for them.' She asked him always to warn them about any dangers before they happened, because 'you know there are enemies everywhere, and I am all alone in this house, that is why I want you to show me the way to keep Isatu and Gustavius here for a while. Let her become pregnant again, Santigue, and this time, talk to God that she has the child and can keep it.'

When he finally showed his wife the way, Santigue Dambolla did so in the most unexpected manner. One day, without warning, two small dwarfs, one of them also a hunchback, appeared in the town. They were colourful little creatures with large heads and noses that were too small between glassy eyes. Although they insisted that one was male and the other female, it was hard for people to tell, because they wore the same type of wild, brightly patterned clothes, sported moustaches, laughed and swore and wrestled together until they both became exhausted. Gifted with acrobatic skills and wiles unknown in the town, they soon attracted a lot of attention, on the hot afternoons of summer, after they had set up camp under a large baobab tree.

Referring to each other as brother-sister so as not to give away which one was a man or a woman, they promised they could bring back some of the early wonders of the world, reduce the sizes of all the bad people in the town to their small ones, and bring back the twins who had been driven away from land as possessors of evil. This time, as bringers of fortune to whoever would have them, they claimed they could get a person to do anything they so desired. When Gustavius and Isatu Martins were finally persuaded to go and watch the dwarfs, they arrived just as the hunchback was trying to touch his bump with his right foot, and trying to balance a calabash of water on his head. Succeeding in that feat, he bent over, and let his brother-sister climb on his hump, and then, with each of them balancing on one leg, they began to dance a wild dance, which threw the crowd into a state of hysteria.

'Now that you know we are special,' said one of the dwarfs, 'show your appreciation and we will continue.'

Wanting to see more, the crowd started tossing all kinds of coins, small gold pieces and other objects of value into a calabash which one of the dwarfs had produced from a small bag. When they had collected all the offerings, the dwarfs dusted their clothes, made faces at each other and began to fight. Brother-sister without the hump threw the other down; sat on him and began to kick him with his small legs. Then, seizing him by the throat, he announced to the crowd, 'I am now going to show you how you can trap your enemy inside a bottle and keep him there for days.' He produced a small bottle of grey powder from a pocket, sprayed some of it on the hump and, after spreading it all over his victim with a horse's tail, he started dancing round the fallen man. A grey cloud of smoke rose from the ground, and the body of the victim contracted into the size of a newt, whose tail had a red tuft as of a cow's. The crowd was just about to see the dwarf put the newt in a bottle when Isatu Martins fainted in the arms of her husband.

'You there,' said the dwarf. 'Take me home with you so that I can revive your wife.'

Stunned, Gustavius Martins nevertheless carried the figure of his wife back to the house, with the dwarf coming behind. The small man had succeeded in trapping his brother-sister in the bottle, which he announced as the last wonder of Sulaiman the Nubian who was still roaming in the area one hundred years after he had last been seen being dragged by the primates. Sawida Dambolla saw the unconscious Isatu Martins in the arms of her husband. She was about to scream but was restrained by the appearance of the dwarf behind her son-in-law.

'Don't look so pathetic,' said the dwarf. 'We have travelled a long way to get here, all for your own good.'

When he had smashed the bottle on the floor, his brother-sister came back to his original form. Afterwards, they related the story of how they were the last members of a race of dwarf children who had been trapped in a grove by an evil spirit, which had once been a beautiful woman who had consorted with the devil. By so doing she had sold her soul to him, and promised him all the children of the region. Teaming up together, the children had found a way out of the grove, and discovered the herbs that could prolong life, shorten the forms of people, and allow them to be in several places at the same time.

'Each of us represents several lives in the intrepid kingdom of children forced to live without mothers, but once in every twelve years we recognise a woman who has suffered, and in whom one of us chooses to be reborn. That was why your wife was touched by the power of the sect, because she was one of those women whose children had been stolen from them, in their sleep, by the devil which has the shape of a seahorse.'

The hunchback went up to the prostrate form of Isatu Martins and rubbed his hump against her forehead, after which she regained consciousness and was no longer terrified of the dwarfs.

'But we are suspicious of those who have lost the power to understand the origins of man, those who can attest only to a certain concept of creation, without the taste of the salt of this earth, this world.'

When he had finished speaking, Gustavius Martins knew right away that he was referring to him. He was about to go out of the room, when the dwarf stopped him, 'But you and the woman, tainted by the garbage of your union, possess a single spirit that is eternal, and your purity of minds can release you on one condition.'

'And what is that condition?' asked Gustavius Martins.

'That you be washed with the sap of the leaves of the grove where the foetuses of your wife have been trapped for years.'

'Agree, my son,' said Sawida Dambolla. 'Do anything he says. Let me tell you, this is as it was before your time, because we are all segments of the dirt of the world, and an inescapable part of living is recognising our relationship to spirits, to nature and these creatures of the underworld.'

A week later, Gustavius and Isatu Martins stood naked in front of a boiling cauldron, inhaling the pungency of leaves and roots which the dwarfs had gone to the forest to find. Spirals of smoke rose from the pot, and the senses of the man and the woman were filled with a vapour that made them innocent and childlike in the baptism of their second coming. When they were beginning to feel their feet moving into the territory of their regeneration, the dwarfs touched them with the tails of horses soaked in the cauldron. The voices of the dwarfs spoke as if in a dream, and the woman felt the encrustation of the dirt and garbage that years of marriage to a man without the roots of the forest had imposed on her, while the man felt the garbage of the world across the sea of blood rubbing off his body, so that they were one again, cleansed of all impurities, and could touch each other with their feathery hands which had been anointed, and with their bodies which had been repossessed by new seeds, so that the fecundity of the woman could respond to the male-power of the husband.

The dwarfs were gone the next day, but not without making it clear that if the woman became pregnant, the child, when it came, must be thrown at the foot of the plants, near the garbage, where Santigue Dambolla was found dead.

When Isatu Martins became pregnant once again, she lived with the hieroglyph of the dwarfs. She took out the symbols at random and tried to find meaning in the writings, but there was none. So she grew in the nascent state of her pregnancy with a mixture of happiness and concern. As in the past when she had been pregnant she insisted on getting up every morning to prepare breakfast for her husband, iron his clothes and now, in their new home, go out to the hens to relax her varicose veins that were beginning to appear.

She felt old, not so much from age or from labour, but from the repetition of this demonstration of womanhood, this expansion of her body which harboured the mystery that the semen of her husband had planted there. For the first time since they left Malagueta, she thought of her life there, about when they would return to be among the familiar substances of their lives, and to breathe the air of the ocean. But thinking about other things was an excuse for her not to think of the one thing that was paramount in her mind: the fear that she might suffer the same fate as in the past. The anxiety brought about by such a possibility was greater than the mystery of the baby among the banana plant, because she was sure that if all went well with her pregnancy, when the time came, God would send a sign to tell her what to do. Gustavius Martins lived with his wife's fear of losing the baby, but he was reconciled to the instruction laid down by the dwarfs. He considered it part of the penance for the neglect of Santigue Dambolla during his lifetime, for not giving him a grandson who would have built the stones of his grave with the mortar of his hands.

Nine months later, when her labour pains began, Isatu Martins had grown to twice her figure. In the room where she lay, surrounded by her mother, Gustavius Martins and the midwife, she begged God that she might be spared the curse of the childless woman. She called upon her father across the country of the dead, bit her tongue, cursed and loved her husband for this journey across the unknown sea, where she thought she would drown. When she felt the rough hairs of a head forcing its way out of her, she screamed in a voice loud enough to frighten the other children in the grove, watching this passage of their chosen one. The child and the mother gave each other strength because they were linked in a secret pact that prohibited others. When eventually the child appeared, it cried with the woman because they had completed a journey which they had begun not nine months but many, many years before, which had exhausted the woman, so that she fell into a deep sleep while the midwife picked up the child and cleaned it of the blood of the woman.

Isatu Martins slept for twenty hours. While she was asleep, she had a vision of her husband and mother taking her child to the banana grove near the garbage. She saw them throw the child there and then walk away. When they had gone back to the house, Santigue Dambolla appeared with his feet of a dead man, and picked up the child. Suddenly they began to fly above the fire of the flame-trees, like two birds. She saw the big bird plucking the feathers of the small bird as if they were useless. Miraculously, in the glare of the fire that lit up the sky, the skin of the small bird was stripped of the feathers of past seasons, and its body was smooth and clean like the skink's, with the smell of fresh leaves.

When Isatu Martins woke up from her long ordeal, she saw her son lying next to her, wrapped in the ornate silk that Santigue Dambolla had worn when he was himself a child. Her eyes met the happy face of her husband, the man who had given her a claim to the earth, and who in turn she had given a son to bear witness to his final homecoming.

'He is a beautiful animal,' he said. 'What shall we call him?'

'Garbage!' she replied. 'So that he will not forget his roots.'

BOOK THREE

9   War and Loyalty

Thomas Bookerman worked on his *History of the Founding of Malagueta* for five years before completing the first volume. Since driving the forces of Captain Hammerstone out of the area, he had paid little attention to the details of running the town, turning it over to the Farmer brothers and a committee of ten men, believing that affairs of state needed those who had nothing better in life to do. But he did not entirely turn his back on the running of the town. Recognised as the sole arbiter in all matters, he saw to it that no one was subjected to any law that was unjust; that no one was forced to go to church against his will because, as he put it, the 'Lawd hisself ain't ready for all of us'. If anyone tried to get too rich selling or buying anything, he was quick to remind them: 'You behavin like we wus before, selling and buying sawdust.' Priding himself on being able to command respect among the people without being tryrannical, he had got the men to form a people's militia to defend the town against another invasion. For those who committed any crime against their friends or neighbours, he had the people from their own 'judgement committee' consisting of six men and six women to resolve the matter involved. The greatest crime that was committed in the first years of the founding of the town was that of a woman pouring hot water on her husband because he had fallen in love with his mother-in-law who was only three years older than he was. The women members of the jury, having considered it unusual for a mother-in-law to fall in love with her son-in-law, but not unnatural for a younger man to fall in love with an older woman because that was the only way boys were brought up to be men, prescribed the punishment of the wife: 'lending her husband to his mother-in-law for three months', cooking for them both, while they repose during his convalescence.

He held great store for the future of the town and, in all, was pleased with the way things had gone so far. He had not been disappointed by the men and the women for whom he was prepared to wage a protracted war against anyone: black or white. But it was the history of the people that interested him more than the idea of war. So he immersed himself in the study of some of the materials unearthed by newcomers to the town while they were clearing the land to build their new home. The clay pots, jugs, beads, combs and other archaeological objects revealed a most interesting past to him. He was fascinated with the idea that some form of organised life had gone on before in the area; that, contrary to what he and others had been told and had believed, Malagueta was not a land inhabited in the past only by men who hunted warthogs and guinea hens; unknown to outsiders, those men had achieved a high degree of leadership. The tombs that were unearthed in some of those explorations were encrusted with a dust that was of a dark orange colour, with the smell of fossils. When they opened them, they saw the skeletons of men and women whose feet were the size of giants. Thomas Bookerman concluded that these giants must either have grown tired of living or exterminated themselves, but that their race would come back to life if the newcomers made a mess of their opportunity.

'We are trampling upon de graves of people who are only waiting to rise up and throw us out of here, if we ain't careful,' he told Phyllis one evening when he had come home exhausted from examining the bones.

That possibility, plus the feeling that he had to delve more into the past to understand how the region had been before the coming of the Malaguetans, was to occupy his mind for a long time. So that armed with the telluric evidence, he sought written evidence to enlighten him further. It was thus that he came across the documents in the house by the sea, which according to the legends of the area had once been the home of a hairy mulatto and his black woman over a hundred years before his arrival on the scene. The house was now a home to lizards and snakes; a dense forest of weeds, vines and creepers grew there, the windows had been blown off the hinges, and the rust of the sea had made the doors impregnable. It took him and two others the whole of a day to break them down to get into the house. When they walked in, they saw evidence of a life that had been full of luxury: they saw the two fine chairs where the couple had sat, the golden pelicans that the bugs had begun to devour, and the flute with the silver mouthpiece which, according to the people who lived by the sea, the man used to play to attract the dugongs to the shore. They saw the brass four-poster where they had made love, the china plates with the pictures of the dowager queen, the silver candelabrum which had lighted the living room when the house had looked like a ship anchored at mid-sea, the torn paintings of the caravels that had sailed across the seas, spreading the power of the King of Portugal, and the empty boxes in which the smoked herrings had been packed and which they had not bothered to throw away. No one in living memory knew how they had died, but the last man to have seen them alive had told his son, who had told his son, that the happy couple had been in the habit of walking around naked in their house, in view of passersby, that they had enjoyed eating out of each other's hand, and had been known to stand by a window for hours looking at the sea, and kissing each other, until one day they had just disappeared, and nothing was heard or seen of them again.

'Dey sure must have been happy, and ah bet dey still walking about,' said Thomas Bookerman.

The documents had been left in a trunk with some other things owned by the woman: emerald earrings, gold bracelets and necklaces that Antonio the Mulatto had given her over the years during the long, lazy summers of their life. But the most interesting items of their life was the bronze figure of a woman holding a bird in her hand with a snake round her body. Thomas Bookerman decided it was the symbol of a paganistic rite that only people madly in love kept. When he had dusted off the eggs of the cockroaches and restored the scripts to some form of legibility, he read with interest the fascination with which Idirs Aloma had con-cluded that the first men and women to inhabit the region spent three months every year trying to prove the existence of God in all his manifestations. Strange things had happened: crops grew without being watered even in the dry season, death would pass over them during that period and it was enough to wish for anything for one to get it. Thus, if a man wanted to erase all bad things from his memory during those months, it was possible for him to do so by simply saying, 'Erase'. They had learnt how to connect gold with spiritual properties, how not to refer to some evil things directly because they could appear and carry you away. He grew excited over the insistence of the mystic Aloma that it was because of their privileged relationship with God that those men and women had grown to the size of giants, but that the men had gentle hands. The women were so beautiful that, after having one child, they were forbidden to do any other thing but to remain in a perpetual state of happiness. They had enough time away from men, and the world was so orderly that everyone could go to bed at the same time during the three months of happiness and wake up at the same time until they started to manipulate the balance in nature by prolonging their happiness beyond three months.

'Dat's it,' said Bookerman. 'Dey was a bunch of greedy bastards!' He leafed through the rest of the documents and came across the name of one Sulaiman the Nubian about whose life Aloma was vague. However, he deduced from the fragmentary evidence that Sulaiman the Nubian had been a mystic with a remarkable power of premonition who had seen the destruction of the area that was now part of Malagueta because the town was in the direction of a cyclical wind that blew once every fifty years, unleashed by the imponderable hand of a remarkable king. The knowledge that everything proceding the founding of Malagueta was repeatable convinced Bookerman that he and other men were engaged in a task that was a farce, because life was circumscribed by pathos. He saw that all he and others had laboured to build would one day be destroyed not only because of greed but because it had been laid down that although Divine Providence had blessed Malagueta, it had also given it some of the most unfortunate people on earth whose children would make the bones of their ancestors tremble in their graves because of their greed and servitude in the face of tyranny. The real heroes and heroines, he concluded, were those not arrogant enough to see themselves as conquerors or builders, but who had been engaged in only one pursuit in life: making others happy.

Accordingly, when he sat down to write the first chapter of the *Founding of Malagueta* he gave less emphasis to men and women like himself, and more to those who had made them laugh during the lugubrious afternoons in the new region. He recalled vividly the journey across the ocean when Fatmatta the Bird-Woman had sung the bittersweet ballads of Simon the Blind who had lost his right hand because he preferred playing his banjo to working on the field. He created whirlwinds of pages for the girls who had been rounded up from the four corners of the world to come to Malagueta, and whose breasts and eyes tormented all types of men in the yellow house, and who knew all the secrets of some of the leading men in Malagueta. Although he was himself not a practising Christian, Thomas Bookerman nonetheless put down for posterity that it was the Virgins who in spite of their horror at what they considered the loose behaviour of some of the young women in town, took in the pregnant girls who had no home of their own but insisted on keeping their babies.

He spent so much time on his work that Phyllis thought he was becoming a hermit, 'Go out and get some fresh air,' she said to him after he had been home two weeks writing.

And she protested that while he had been killing the mice and cockroaches in the dilapidated house of oblivion, the paint had been peeling off the walls of their own house and the roof had begun to leak, and it had been some time since they had entertained in their home. He told her that was for the merchants who wanted to rise in society. 'We have almost become the exception to what you preach,' she cried.

Which was that there were to be open houses so that people could come and go as they like because in spite of the time when Emmanuel Cromantine had discovered the theft in his room, there had not been any other report of people breaking in. Women could go across their backyards into their neighbour's kitchen to borrow a pinch of salt, and fish from the barn where they smoked fish. Everyone kept watch on everyone's children and could punish them, because 'what would your mama say if she knows ah saw you misbehavin an' ah did not whip ya behind?'

After a few years of living with him, Phyllis had come to understand that Thomas Bookerman was not a man given to great theories or abstractions. While she had worried that the continuous arrivals of new members to the community would rob the place of its original flavour, while she had fussed over the undisguised air of superiority that some members were beginning to feel because of their commercial success, Thomas Bookerman had not seemed bothered by such illusory developments. He viewed with contempt the beginnings of the rise of an oligarchy: men who only yesterday were shopkeepers with bad teeth and could barely read now ordered evening jackets in black Venetians and hopsacks; women who only yesterday were content to wear hand-me-downs and keep clean houses had taken to buying gold and parading in silk and brocade at church services. 'Dis is inevitable,' he told Phyllis. 'Dey over de hill, and now dey want to have balls and parties like their masters in de other place.' Nor was he surprised by the awe and respect with which some of the Malaguetans were beginning to recall the place which only a few years ago they had been only eager to escape. Sailors who called at Malagueta looking for whores spoke of the women of England as being the best dressed in the world; of the rich who could afford butlers and chambermaids, of the latest types of furniture, the invention of the steamship, the advantages that could be had by going there for a while to give their skins the right colour, away from this mosquito town. How it was not such a bad idea if some of them sent their children there so they could learn how to speak 'the king's English' and dress like English men and women.

'Dat's de nature of men,' said Thomas Bookerman to his woman. 'Dey love de things that dey hate so much dey prepared to pay for them.'

Pay for them they did. No sooner had the news leaked out that Emmanuel Cromantine was considering going to England to study to be a doctor than the sons and daughters of other merchants began to pester their parents to send them away. The resources of the school of the Farmer brothers, the books in their bookshop, the catechism and Sunday school lessons which the Virgins gave had been nothing but preparations for what was inevitable: that men and women who had laboured to build the shops, turned the jungle back, built wooden houses and raised solid and healthy children would sell all they had to send their offspring away, because they were ashamed in their hearts of hearts of being men and women without the fine graces, refined speeches and manners which not so long ago they had laughed at when practised by their spurious masters. They were people who after all lacked family trees stamped with an authenticity that could stand the test of time. They were pioneers who after all had no names in the history books, no armoury, no plaques or monuments in their town, but who failed to see that they were among the chosen, among the salt of the earth; that men and women were distinguished not so much by what their fathers had been but by their singularity of mind, of success, by their integrity and an implacable insistence to be respected in their time by their enemies. Malagueta was about to change, and Phyllis, watching Thomas Bookerman immersed in the history of the town, was to recall that day when looking out of a window, she saw Gustavius and Isatu Martins, she holding a child by the hand, coming to the house of the founder of the town, looking as if they had seen a ghost.

They had bad news. Two years before, when they had become parents, they had been so overjoyed with the change in their lives that they postponed the idea of returning to Malagueta. Sawida Dambolla was overjoyed. She kept her daughter in bed like an infirm old woman, sponged her brow with a towel soaked in guava and lemon juices every morning for a week after her delivery, brought her milk from the cow, burned incense for a whole month, hung dried cassava leaves on her mirror and prayed to her husband to protect his grandson against evil eyes.

Gustavius Martins was dutiful to his wife now that he was a father, just as he had been when he had seen her by the stream many years ago.

214

Unencumbered by the necessity to prove anything now, and content with the life of a country squire, he sent word to Sebastian Cromantine to hold on to their property for a while yet, saying that Malagueta was for people determined to grow ulcers trying to pave the streets with gold, which he was no longer interested in. Watching his son crawl on the floor, he figured, was better than building houses. No one had fussed over him as a baby or sang songs to him. Although he had never been told, he knew he had come into the world under different circumstances, and he remembered that he had cried for his mother when they had taken him away from her at an early age. His son therefore was part of the future that made the anguish of the past bearable. When Isatu Martins would gently push her pendulous breasts into the mouth of the infant, Gustavius Martins sometimes touched them and marvelled at the love of the woman for her son, and also for the man who had built the lantern for her. He was at peace during this interlude, surrounded by his family but also by the enormous range of forest where every night he could see a bright light illuminating the sky as if from a mysterious object.

It was an illusion. For many months, beyond the fringes of that forest, five hundred men had been training for an attack on Malagueta. They were the forgotten remnants of the forces of Captain Hammerstone, backed by four hundred recruits from the rugged region of the Foutah Djallon mountains: men for whom the idea of profit from the pillage of cities and towns served as the only reason for fighting a war. Captain Hammerstone, fleeing from the enraged horde attacking his garrison, found a sanctuary in the mountains beyond the forest after a three-day journey across some of the most treacherous territories in the world. He had cut through a part of the forest where no one had been since the time of the first Arabs who had been trying to locate the source of the black gold, and had been eaten up by wild animals. While re-examining his life, he had transformed his humiliation into an austere martyrdom, stayed away from women and drank less, and his sublimation helped him see in his defeat only a tactical human error. He concluded that not only had he misunderstood the determination of men other than his own kind to maintain the image of conquerors, but that he had been blinded by one of the worst sins of men: a reliance upon your own judgement of other men to help you in times of danger. He had thought that his men, being white like himself, would stand up to the horde with the greatest valour and determination because that was how things were, as they had been told in the grammar school: standing up for king and country, showing the flag and upholding the reign. Now he knew better. He was resolved never again to go in search of allies solely among his own people, and blamed his defeat on his past neglect of the men and women who had given him the only pleasure that he had known in life, men and women among whom he had tested and confirmed his manhood and his courage. Thus, in looking back at what had happened, fleeing from Malagueta, it was his women in Calabar and Ceylon that he remembered: the dark women who had covered his whiteness with their love; the one in particular who had given him a son, and for whom he suddenly felt a fierce and protective kind of love. He would have swum across the ocean to get to the exotic island, to tell the woman with the enchanting eyes to forget about Buddha, the jasmine-scented gardens and the snake charmer, but Malagueta had an urgent claim on his life. If he had found a new enlightenment, Captain Hammerstone wanted to be with other people, and that was why he could see his flight not as a defeat but as a revelation. Henceforth, he would know that men and women were judged according to what they could do and give, and not according to any false notion established by men like himself. He had been used as a guinea pig, and for that reason he felt he was one of the few martyrs of the age, and resolved to do better when he returned to Malagueta.

His plan was to recruit men about whom he had heard: black men with a history of courage, and some degree of fanaticism who would help him bring his new enlightenment to the people of Malagueta, especially to that one-eyed man who had led the attack against his garrison. Two years later, Captain Hammerstone had organised his men and was marching like a desert warrior.

Isatu Martins was getting ready to put Garbage to bed at seven o'clock in the evening when she heard the street shake with the tremor of an earthquake. Holding her son to her breast she stood by a window, and saw the unmistakable face of Captain Hammerstone leading an army of tall black men through Bolanda. Fierce, determined and possessing a brutal solemnity, they were barefooted animals who trampled the thorns in the grass as if they were leaves, their feet raising the dust into a cloud over the graves of the victims of the plague. Laden down like mules, they marched with an ease that produced a tightness in their intestines, and she felt a chill down her spine looking at their weapons: lances, old-fashioned muskets, clubs, daggers, and a large artillery gun mounted on a carriage.

Captain Hammerstone trusted those men: mercenary dogs-of-war

216

who could kill with their bare hands; men who individually could throw a bull to the ground and cut its throat with one slash of a knife. They were hardened ferocious warriors who knew how to strangle a panther, break a constrictor's bones and throw a dagger with a deadly accuracy. They kicked and lanced the dogs that barked at them, raided the rice granaries to replenish their stocks and camped on the outskirts of the town for the night.

When she guessed their destination, Isatu Martins knew immediately what she had to do. Terrified by their presence, she felt an even greater horror about their intent, but she was not so paralysed by their preparedness that she lost all notion of her own ability to thwart them in any way she could. She knew that they did not know the country too well, that the heavy packs on their backs would eventually wear them down, and that being bandits of the worst kind they would plunder and rape all along the way so that they would be forced to slow down. She turned to her husband who had come to the room attracted by the uproar outside, and said to him with a certainty born out of a familiarity with the history of those tough men, 'They are going to invade Malagueta.'

Gustavius Martins was not alarmed. He was himself a man of steel and the sight of the troops had not unnerved him as they had done his wife. Many years earlier when he had fought in the colonial war he had concluded that only two types of men fought in wars: those who fought for the glory and honour of a country and those who fought to increase their personal worth. He had fought for the second reason because, although he hated killing, he had been witness to several deaths when the victims had been men like himself: obstinate to a point of naïvety about the uselessness of war. Forced eventually to kill, he had done so not without a good deal of remorse; so that he had lived for many years with the implacable look of death in the faces of those men who were surprised that he could kill with such accuracy. Malagueta had made him a man of peace despite the time when the blond lieutenant had tried to force his hand, and the attack on the garrison had not really been regarded as war by him, but as a legitimate act of expelling a pest. Now he found himself feeling the flow of anger churning his entrails. He experienced a disgust not only for that pirate leading the men but an even greater contempt for what he considered the treachery of the men marching behind Captain Hammerstone. He looked at his wife who was still holding Garbage, and said in a sad voice, 'De idyll is over. Start packing. We are leaving tonight by a back road for Malagueta before dey get there.'

When Thomas Bookerman received the news of the march of the invading army he did not show the slightest surprise. He closed the book that he had been reading when the Martinses walked in, patted the head of Garbage whom he was seeing for the first time, and commented on how well the mountain air had agreed with Isatu Martins before expressing any opinion on the recent development. 'So he had balls after all, dat captain. Now we gon show him how not to mess with our lives.'

Early next morning, he held a war council with some of the important members of the community who had been secretly summoned to his house. 'Dis is a matter of secrecy, men, because we want to have a good plan before we tell others,' he said to them. His plan was to recruit two hundred men from all the families who had a stake in the building of the town 'Dat way, we sure of total loyalty.' Over the years, the Malague-tans had bought guns from sailors or exchanged goods and supplies for them. Those, plus the weapons they had discovered in the garrison when they had driven Captain Hammerstone out, were enough to arm the men, he said.

'Of course you know we ain't going to be telling everyone 'cause we don't know who be for us, and who be for Captain Hammerstone.'

'Let's say wars produce strange bedfellows, so we gotta be careful,' Thomas Bookerman replied.

When they had worked out the mechanics of the plan, Thomas Bookerman asked his second-in-command and three other men to stay behind, and sent the others away after they had sworn to secrecy upon their mothers' curses on their heads. The men who remained were Sebastian Cromantine, the Farmer brothers and Gustavius Martins. Not only were they the ones who had also met at the time of the planning for the march on the garrison, but they were the ones Bookerman felt he could trust and who over the years had demonstrated their commitment to the progress of Malagueta.

After many years of running his school, Gabriel Farmer had become one of the most widely admired men in Malagueta. By sheer devotion, love and patience, he turned out men and women like Emmanuel Cromantine who dreamed of a future in the wilds of England, and instilled in them a taste for the fine arts. The gatherings that he held at his place drew the sons and the daughters of some of the most important members of the community who went there to hear him read lyrical poems of Coleridge, discuss the crimes and punishment of Moll

Flanders and imagine the ghost of Catherine haunting Wuthering Heights. He saw to it that when travelling musicians came to town, they gave concerts of the music of the English and German masters as when his own mother, bless her soul, had taken him to the concert hall. In that way, his students were exposed to and enthralled by the precocious genius of Mozart, the demonic majesty of Beethoven, the charm of Purcell and the baroque plenitude of Bach. 'Art will shape the future of man,' he told them.

His passion for the classical masters usually brought him into conflict with the intransigence of the Virgins who believed that nothing short of a strong dose of Christian teaching was good for the minds of the young, and warned their parents that his gatherings were merely an excuse for him to corrupt the minds of the children. Years of sublimation had cured Gabriel Farmer of his love for Phyllis, and in her place he had put the love of his students, and with them he tried to venerate creative gods.

Richard Farmer had built the Globe bookshop across from his brother's school during the peaceful years after the storming of the garrison. Its smell of rich pinewood, dusty rich leatherbound books and the aromatic coffee that was sold there made it a most endearing place. Its walls were covered with pictures of enchanting places, with paintings of blasé women in long evening gowns being entertained by men in military uniforms. The primers and travel books were sources of delight for the children because they associated the former with learning how to read and the latter with faraway places. Confused by the uncertainty of his love for Louisa, Emmanuel Cromantine was to spend many days in that bookshop, trying to unravel the threads of his entanglement. To him and to the sons and daughters of the important men and women in the town, the bookshop was also the place where they learnt how to write letters. Pouring through the pages of erudition in the illuminating books, they formed an idea of how to write the archetypal love letter: 'Having caught sight of your magnificent beauty, I take courage in my hands to pen you this missive . . .' Over the years, lasting relationships were formed in that bookshop, hearts were healed and broken by words born in that haven where Richard Farmer allowed the young to steal kisses and hold hands provided they were discreet.

But the news that the army of Captain Hammerstone was marching towards Malagueta turned these men away from their vocations and set them preparing for war. Throughout that first night, while a false calm reigned over the town, Thomas Bookerman and his lieutenants discussed strategies for defending it. Sebastian Cromantine wanted the defending men to block the main entrance into the town at the top of the mountain but Gustavius Martins, being a man less attracted to long schemes, opposed the idea.

'We going be killed,' he said. 'Let de captain bring his men into town where we can attack 'em from all angles.'

Thomas Bookerman agreed. Next morning, they visited the men they felt they could trust and got them to swear oaths in the names of their mothers and the preparations for war assumed a heightened urgency. Trying to keep the defence of Malagueta a secret was, however, a most difficult thing. The men who would join Thomas Bookerman had to devise all kinds of subterfuges to cover their regular absences in the week before the invaders got to the boundary of the town. Men who had been as regular in their habits as crabs, who went to work and came straight home afterwards had to explain to their wives their sudden desire to go out in the night for a 'bit of air'.

Five days after the news of the march of Captain Hammerstone was received, Thomas Bookerman could count on one hundred and fifty trusted men to fight. The names of the defenders were known to members of the war council, but not to the men themselves, to avoid leaking out the secret. Each one had been told only to get ready when the time to stand with his rifle by his window, and to start coming out when word was finally given that the invading army was only a short distance away.

Next morning, they raised the dust of the city as they marched to the garrison that Hammerstone had abandoned after his previous defeat, and prepared to make a stand there.

From there, they could see the columns of palm trees, the tombstones in the cemetery, the lines of eucalyptus trees through which Captain Hammerstone would have to pass with his men. The hills where Sebastian Cromantine and the other survivors of the potato plague had taken refuge formed a solid mass behind them, but Thomas Bookerman knew that they were impenetrable at that time of the year because of the torrential rains that had wiped out the track. For that reason, he dismissed the possibility of a surprise attack from behind. But he left nothing to chance because he was a veteran of two previous campaigns, and although he seldom talked about it, the loss of his eye was a reminder of the terrible cost he had paid in one war. The garrison was turned into a fortress, the damaged doors were reinforced with iron bars, and the windows were painted black to make them indistinguishable from the rest of the building. But keeping the news of the impending invasion a secret was proving impossible. When Thomas Bookerman and some of his men went to the shops to stock up on provisions for the war they found a town trembling with the anxiety of an epidemic. Malagueta was in turmoil: the narrow streets of asbestos-roofed houses were choked with the panic of women looking for their sons and husbands, the shops were emptied of all goods, the peace of the House of the Virgins was interrupted by the clamour of the believers demanding to be taken in. That morning, as he offered holy communion, the Reverend Adam Freeman – who had resumed his ministration after many years of praying to God for forgiveness over the way he had treated Phyllis – urged his flock to beg the Lord that they might be spared in the coming disaster. Meanwhile in the Yellow House, the women went to bed with men they believed were going off to die, telling them not to pay for their last pleasures, but insisting that if they came back they had better come with their combat boots 'to show dat you bin men at war'.

Emmanuel was one of the young men who did not got to the Yellow House to prove their manhood and to acquire a taste for war. In the turmoil of the general preparation around him, he walked with his head in a cloud, trying to sort out the complexities of his inner nature. Years of studying had prepared him for a career as a savant but as he watched the men of his generation march past his house with their weapons, his mind was riveted by the drama unfolding before him, which made his past nebulous and his future dubious. He found himself thinking about what constituted success, about the idea of valour and the virtues of sacrifice. He had been too young to take part in the storming of the garrison, but the account of that action had become part of the folklore in the seafront bars. So although he never went inside the Yellow House, Emmanuel Cromantine would sometimes go and sit on one of the slabs in front of the house of pleasure, to listen to the rum-saturated ballads about the heroism of the men who had destroyed the garrison, about the tattooed sailors who made love in all the languages of the world to women who smelled of spring flowers, whose eyes were misty with legends, and who sometimes fished in lakes and seas under green skies for trout and salmon to feed their lovers.

Waking up from such imagined pleasures, Emmanuel Cromantine would walk to the house of the flamboyant butterflies where Louisa was waiting for him. Months of making love together had not only harmonised their rhythm but had blended their thoughts. The one knew what the other was thinking as soon as their eyes met. Being of a more passionate and forthright nature, Louisa had worked on Emmanuel and got him to stop talking about the botanical garden he hoped to start. Thus, from being a clumsy beginner of the art, he had graduated into a magnificent lover. In the damp desolation of the rainy season, during the chill of the harmattan, in the insufferable heat of March, and protected by the complicity of their friends Gabriel Farmer and Phyllis Dundas, they made love most evenings and reached such heights of unbearable pleasure that she thought she would go mad if they were ever to part. During those moments, between her moans of joy and pain, she urged him to 'come with me, my love, don't let me drown alone'. When they surfaced from that depth and had rested, she would tell him to leave the windows open so that they could hear the songs of the weaver birds, and the butterflies could come and go as they like, and they wouldn't bother to get up except to go and eat. On the night they had explored all the regions of their bodies for the first time, he let her play with his majestic sex while he brought her to such a state of celestial desire that she ended up whispering in his ears, 'Let's do it on the floor.'

'Why?' he asked.

'Because love is a thing of primeval beauty and the bed is an obstruction invented by bishops, and human beings are the only animals who make love facing each other,' she said.

He led her to the window where she had seen him go by on that evening before she collapsed on the patchwork bed with the porcelain Christ. Then, like an unquartered highly priced bull mounting a cow, he sought and found the last mysteries of her being; he drank from the fountain of her voluptuous breasts, rose and flowed in the storm of her music, before bringing her safely back to rest in the drowsy calm after their exhaustion.

Emmanuel Cromantine tried not to think about Louisa while he was preoccupied with the doubts in his mind. The commotion in the streets and the feeling that he was losing a sense of his own balance did not make it easy for him to make up his mind about what to do. His father had gone to the first line of defence with Thomas Bookerman, and the absence of the older man left an intolerable burden upon the son to care for his mother.

'You are now de man of de house,' she said. 'Let's pray dat dis war will not be long, and dat your fader come back alive.'

'He should be here, Mama, and I should be the one out there,' he said.

'Don't talk like dat, son. Why? Do you want to kill me before my time?'

'All right. I won't go out there, but how do you think I'll feel tomorrow when all of this is over and I had no part in it?'

When he said that, he knew that he was saying what he had subconsciously decided, which was that although he had promised his mother one thing, his heart ached to be out there among the others who like him also had mothers.

◇

Captain Hammerstone saw Malagueta as he remembered it from his last attempt to establish his rule there. He saw the cluster of houses on the ridge with their lights spotting the verdure like broken crystal, the animals settling down for the nights in their pens, the narrow lines of streets winding like snakes from the hills to the seafront, and he noticed that the masons had almost finished work on the church except for the cinquefoil. He saw in the distance the new mansions of the rich with their sloping roofs and dormer windows, but the streets told him in one great silence that his arrival was not a surprise.

Thomas Bookerman was about to pour himself a cup of tea when a large blast of artillery fire shook the night. 'Dat's it, men,' he said. 'De time has come.' Someone touched him on the shoulder and said in a voice that was a woman's:

'Ah came along, although you didn't know.'

It was Phyllis. She had dressed as a man soon after Thomas Bookerman had left for the school to set up his headquarters and, mixing with others, had gone there.

'What you doing here?' asked Bookerman.

'We in dis togeder, General, and you ain't gon stop me 'cause ah ain't afraid to die.'

Captain Hammerstone advanced on Malagueta after a week's march from Bolanda. When he was almost at the cemetery he told his men to break up into two groups to facilitate a double attack. While he led one group to try to take the town from the south entrance, he sent the other group down a forest path with instructions to take the area facing the sea. 'Remember we are fighting this war so we can settle down to a decent life.'

Bringing up the artillery gun from the rear, he fired another blast at the garrison and was immediately met by a rapid burst of gunfire from the defenders. When he tried to rush on the building with the large gun, he stumbled on a large rock which sent the heavy weapon reeling off its carriage. Losing his advantage in fire power, Captain Hammerstone sent human waves against the garrison and, standing behind the window, Thomas Bookerman saw them coming.

'Hold your fire, men,' he said. 'Dey trying to get close to us.' He waited until the first line of Captain Hammerstone's men had approached the perimeter of the building, before making a final speech about how to defend their position.

'You know what we fighting for, men; for our children, for our wives, all de good things we built togeder; de dead and our freedom. So give dem all you got. When ah gives de command to fire, shoot, and then if dey keep on coming, hold your position until ah tell you what to do.'

A long line of Captain Hammerstone's men began to creep on the ground to avoid being detected, but they were quickly spotted by Thomas Bookerman. When they were only twenty yards away from the gates of the garrison fence he gave the order to fire, and they were completely wiped out. Then, in one of the most reckless attempts at bravery, Captain Hammerstone's men tried to take the garrison from two directions, but they came under such an intense hail of gunfire that they had to fall back and regroup.

While the men of Captain Hammerstone formed shadows in the outstretched darkness, Thomas Bookerman began to think of the futility of wars and of the mortality of all men. In the room behind him, some of his men lay wounded. Others, in supplication – as if they wanted to clear up all their debts with their God before meeting him – prayed. They were defending a cause and a town, but they were hopeless in that last outpost where each of them had to enter singly. He looked at his men, and saw that among the wounded were Gustavius Martins and Gabriel Farmer. They would survive, but death had claimed and was claiming others in an amalgamation of voices. But the loss of those valuable men did not slacken his resolve to go on fighting. Many years previously, when he had been in the colonial war, he and twenty other defenders had held a ridge against a much larger force for two days even though they were running out of supplies. What had worked for him then was an inner feeling that the men on the other side were just as frightened of death as he and his companions had been. Waiting for the next onslaught of the captain's men, Thomas Bookerman therefore assessed his chances of breaking out of the cordon that had been formed round the garrison. He wondered how he would get the wounded out, about how long his present supplies would last, but more especially about the spirit of his troops.

'We have to keep our spirits up. Dis is gon be a long siege.'

224

It was. Over the next twelve days, the fighting intensified for the control of the garrison. The men of Captain Hammerstone kept on coming in wave after wave of reckless attacks and the surrounding hills shook with the blast of gunfire. Trying to break out of the camp, ten of the defenders ran into the vicious glints of machetes and were cut down. Among the ones who managed to get away was Richard Farmer. Considering their position hopeless, he tried to make contact with the other defenders who hearing of the two-pronged attack had taken position on the waterfront. He got there in time to see a force of youthful volunteers on January Street putting up a stiff resistance as the second detachment of Captain Hammerstone's men tried to invade from the rear.

Emmanuel Cromantine, observing the course of the battle from his house, needed only to look out of his window to see the smoke coming from the shops to make up his mind. While he had been procrastinating, men had been going in opposite directions either to join Thomas Bookerman's forces or to help the volunteers defending the waterfront, until it seemed as if he was the only one left. Consumed by a sense of shame, he went out in the street while Jeanette Cromantine tried to restrain him.

'Come back, my son, you gon be killed.'

He did not hear her. He made his way through the dense crowd and walked past empty fruit carts and battered up shops until he got to the house of Louisa. He saw the first casualties of the war – men who were never going to walk again, those whose arms had been shattered by bullets in the streets which were now thronging.

'If I don't come back, look after Mama for me.'

She had not seen him for two weeks. During that time, she had prayed that he might come so that she could give him the news that she was pregnant, but now that he was there she tried to hide her condition from him. Unlike previous visits when he had taken off his shoes and prepared to make love on the patchwork bed, he was now agitated and in a hurry. Before he could say anything, Louisa guessed the reason for his change of attitude.

'You are going to join them,' she said.

'Everyone is going and I belong there,' he replied.

She became terrified for the child that was already being formed, for the happiness that was slipping away from her. She tried to be strong, not to show that like his mother she wanted him near her, and not among the ruins and the limps that men were being reduced to by the battles raging on both sides of the town. He walked to the door without even saying goodbye, and was just about to open it when Louisa grabbed him by the shoulder.

'I have something to tell you before you go, so that if you don't come back you will die happy.'

'What is it?' he asked.

'I am pregnant.'

Emmanuel Cromantine was brought back to earth from the planet of the war. If he was going anywhere he had to rethink his steps, for this was a new country, one where he had only recently passed, guided by steadier and firmer hands. And he had to learn the language of that new country. Father! The word seemed to come from another voice, not his. But yet, it was his body that experienced the sensation, just as it had been his body that had explored the woman's body which was now beginning to glow with the miracle.

'Tell me you are happy,' said Louisa.

'You sure?' he asked.

'Same as the day I laid my eyes on you in my class and knew you were the only one for me.'

'Then I am happy, and Mama will be glad.'

'You think your papa will be happy I'm making him a grandpa?'

'I don't know, but we shall see.'

She sensed that his joy at the news that he was going to become a father had been short-lived, that his heart was answering but that his body ached to be somewhere else. Now that she knew him well, she realised that it was only by letting him go to the war that she could hope to have him back, if he was given a chance to live. She knew that she would never be happy with him, nor he with her, if she prevailed upon him to stay, because he was a man who already hated tradition, who had to be free to pursue his own dreams, however confusing they might seem to her. Over the years, in spite of the intensity of the secret love that she had felt for him, during the period of their most passionate love-making, and despite the fact that she was older and in the beginning more confident, Louisa had always known that he would one day be the stronger, and that it would be because of his manifest strength that she would obey him. In surrendering to his wishes to go off to the war, she was only doing what she had known all along she would do, and the reality of carrying his child became an act of love, in which her belief in his strength and leadership had found meaning. She folded the shawl round her neck to ward off the cold, kissed him full on the mouth and said to him, 'Go, my love, I shall be waiting when this war is over.'

The war was going badly for Thomas Bookerman. The men defending the garrison, concluding that the enemy outside must number in their thousands because they kept on coming like flies, even after they had been shot down, and must therefore be part human and part some extraordinary creatures, decided to abandon their positions and make for the mountains. 'General,' they said to Thomas Bookerman, 'we can fight better in the open.' The mere fact of continuing the defence of his headquarters appealed to the one-eyed man but, telling himself that there was very little advantage to be gained by being stubborn and subjecting his men to the merciless arrows of death, Thomas Bookerman arranged for an orderly departure of his men as soon as the place was dark. While he and some of them kept up the pretence of resisting, the outnumbered defenders quietly left the building, jumping out of the windows, being so quiet that they forgot the region they were escaping to was a haven for strange animals. Thus, when something crawled over the feet of one of the men he felt an instantaneous terror but did not let out a scream which would have given him and the others away.

If his orginal idea for choosing to defend the town at the garrison had been for strategic purpose, Thomas Bookerman now found himself confronted with a new problem: how to make contact with the men defending the waterfront and bring enough volunteers to root out the invaders. Throughout the town the first three days of the war had been marked by the wildest rumours about the conflicting positions of the two armies. Women who had awaited the outcome of the first conflict with the terrible anxieties of not knowing whether they were widows or if their men were coming back with broken legs or backbones suddenly found that they could not bear the tedium of waiting for news. Isatu Martins had turned her house into some kind of comfort centre. The women met there and gave each other support, told each other that the present war was a continuation of the wars that men had always fought because it was in their bones and in their destiny to map out and remap territory which God in his infinite wisdom had given them, and which if only they had not been so greedy and obstinate would have been enough for all men to share. Then they would heap curses on the captain, feel sorry for his mother whom they were sure must have regretted giving birth to him because, in their view, he had turned out to be a monster. It was then that the first of the rumours started, which was that at night he could change his white skin into black so that it was difficult to kill him.

This was attributed to the power that one of his troops had given him, by making him eat chameleon meat, so that like the slow but inscrutable creature he could blend himself with his environment and escape capture. But no sooner was that rumour bandied about than it was being dismissed as an old wives' tale and replaced with another – which was that some of the prosperous merchants were thinking of selling out because the war was going to ruin them, and that they had been sending secret messages to their sons to desert and go back to their business. Plagued by inertia, unable to get news about the conduct of the war, Isatu Martins decided to go to the front at the schoolhouse to see for herself. She was by nature a woman who hated silences and long empty nights which filled her head with anxieties, as if the spirit of her father Santigue Dambolla the ghost, now unwilling to settle into a peaceful life tending the banana grove, had made her eager for adventure when there was none. Entrusting Garbage to Louisa, she told the young ex-teacher when to feed the child and to send him to bed before the first owls started their hooting. Later that morning, she mounted a horse and rode into the unfriendly day when there were enemy troops everywhere, in search of her husband and others who had gone off with Thomas Bookerman.

With the garrison now back in the hands of Captain Hammerstone, the remnants of Thomas Bookerman's army made their way through the quivering jungle to get to the coast. After a day's march, they came to a clearing recently made by the other division of the captain's men who had gone to take the coast, and rested for the night so that he could take stock of his position. That night, as he slept, he saw a flock of crows in his dreams. It was a bad omen: he had always associated crows with shipwrecks and floods as when he and his men were making their way up the river many, many years earlier, they had come across the noisy birds just before a crocodile had attacked and eaten one of his group. So the feeling that he had upon waking was of fighting a hopeless war, not just because Captain Hammerstone and his men were now firmly in place in a most strategic part of the town, but also because he felt he was walking into a trap at the seafront where only his courage was taking him. Had he known of the rumour that some of the rich men in the town were all for declaring a truce so that they could go on making money he would have probably pressed on with more vigour, but, as it was, he was making his way through the treacherous undergrowth with a contrary slowness of pace and a resoluteness of mind, 'War is a curse on men,' he said.

The condition of Gabriel Farmer and Gustavius Martins now

neeeded attention. They had borne their pain heroically and wanted to be left behind but Thomas Bookerman would not hear of it. 'If we have to die, we will die together,' he said. They stayed for two days in the clearing where, after some persuasion, Phyllis sterilised a knife, heated up some water and removed the bullets from the legs of the two men. When Thomas Bookerman eventually resumed his march, his progress was slowed down because of Gabriel Farmer and Gustavius Martins being carried in hammocks. Trying to save time, he ordered the fifty men travelling with him to take turns carrying the wounded. He gave orders that all unnecessary supplies were to be left behind, and that no one was to straggle for fear of being ambushed from behind. But the spirit that was being urged to stay alive in those men was gradually being drained by the remorseless evaporation of the undergrowth. Being no longer adventurers, after years of the comfort of home, the softness of the hands of their wives, the faces of their children, they were beginning to tire of the loneliness of the campaign after only a month.

They had gone in the first flicker of fire to put it out in the green light of creation. They knew and loved that wilderness and had even given the trees and animals names whereas they had none before. But they had been content with their mornings, and at evening explored the celestial for annunciation. The war was therefore not only an intrusion of mind, but an assault on some of their bodies which were no longer so young that they could expose them to the velocity of the wind and the rigour of a soldier's diet.

Thomas Bookerman urged them on. 'Just a few yards more, men, and we shall finish dis war,' he said. Soon they had made contact with the defenders of the coastal area, and learnt that the bulk of the men that Captain Hammerstone had sent down had been wiped out by a defence force that consisted mostly of young men who had been waiting for news from the other war theatre. But they had paid a heavy price for such heroism. Many of the houses on January Street were nothing more than charred reminders of their past. The Yellow House with its air of happiness, with its tunes of come-in-and-forget-your-cares looked sad because all the enchanting women had fled at the first opportunity – not because they wanted to desert their men but because they would rather die than have to sleep with the invaders. For the first time since the founding of the town, the inveterate Virgins came out of their fortress to tend the wounded and to collect the urchins who were roaming the streets. They took them home and made them a soup of guinea fowl, sweet basil and potatoes and spread blankets on the floor for them to sleep. In later years, these boys in their shorts and puttees and boots would swell the ranks of a new army chanting God Save the King.

But for that moment, Malagueta was divided into two counties: Thomas Bookerman and his ragtime army arrived just in time to see the young volunteers disarming the last of the invaders who were then left to the mercy of an enraged crowd. A lone figure watched fixed in one spot. It was Emmanuel Cromantine. His clothes were a red-brown colour from the sweat of his body, he looked tired and seemed bewildered by all the noise occasioned by the arrival of Thomas Bookerman and his men, but the truth was that he was as much a part of the triumph on the waterfront as were the other young men. Soon after leaving Louisa he had gone to the fighting just as the women in the Yellow House were fleeing. Perhaps it was the sight of those women who had managed to collect their fine clothing and cheap jewellery and were making for safety, or the feeling of a man on whom a sentence had been passed. Whatever it was, Emmanuel Cromantine, without any experience of firing a gun, had picked one up from the hand of a dead man and with no regard for his safety had fought his way into a spectre of recklessness where he punished himself for some past perception of a world that had given him wings, for the superior idea of becoming a doctor which, if they had know about it, would have made the other youths, no longer with the smell of their mother's milk about them, suspicious of him.

He lost his last innocence in the purgatory of that war, when he saw men crying and pulling out their hair. He decided that some had less courage than chickens because they had not been weaned properly at the breast, and had very little fire in their stomachs. When in the cases of a few whom he had known personally they threw the red dirt over the rigidity of their forlorn bodies in the intrepid manner of death, Emmanuel Cromantine felt his own stomach coming out of him. Then he wanted to go home, but not to that mother who he knew would be waiting at the door to drink from his sore lips the bitter goblets of battle, because her son was now a man on a new landscape where they spoke the language of fear, terror and hate. So he was back in the only place where he felt comfortable, in the listlessness of his war-torn body which was finding it difficult to answer to the old urges and the old desires. Emmanuel Cromantine found it hard to possess that body as the woman with his child had possessed it. And since Louisa lived among the shadows of another life, he walked towards the sea to sit on a rock where he could face the stardust, while the wind blew the debris of mud, sand and the bones of war behind him.

Gabriel Farmer came down with a sudden fever soon after the return of Thomas Bookerman to the house with the bougainvillaea garden by the sea. No one had seen the fever coming. He had responded to the care and gentleness of Phyllis as he lay on the couch. Their hands would touch but their bodies remained in their separate prisons of desire because he was many years away from the mornings of the poetry of his love for her. If there were leaves left on the tree where he had written his heart out for her, they had become part of the greying of the old Malagueta which was about to be pulled down. He and his brother had come quietly into that town, had loved it, worked hard and built something. He was a quiet man and wanted to go quietly without fuss and tears. So he gave himself over to one final vista where the privacy of association was sacred. He saw his father among the believers as they dragged him to church every Sunday even after the African had become disillusioned with a Christianity that rejected his identity. He heard from his childhood the voice of his mother, the English woman telling him to be careful with the few pieces of china they had in the house, after she had served the vicar tea and biscuits on the grey Sundays of atonement, and he relived once again the terror of the voyage that had brought him across the ocean. Life was going out of his arms, and the beads of sweat that the fever had made began to flood him in hot rivulets, leaving him only dimly aware of the enormous power of his own knowledge over all things in this world. He knew that the time would come when Malagueta would cease to be a small town, unable to stop the patterns of growth through its midst, and he saw already the maze winding from the town to the hill where Thomas Bookerman had found Sebastian Cromantine, the labyrinth of construction which would amount to only the carving up of the town like a chicken. It was eight o'clock in the morning, the time when Phyllis brought him his soup, but when she got to the peaceful man he had never looked as happy as he did in death, and as she began to weep she realised that in her own way she had loved him after all and wanted to tell him.

Although he was not someone new to grief, Thomas Bookerman was nonetheless stunned by the death of one of his most trusted comrades-in-arm. He respected and liked the refined man, his dignified bearing and sincerity, his courage during the most terrible moments of the war. Many years later, when he remembered him as he himself was exiled from Malagueta, Thomas Bookerman would recall how Gabriel Farmer had persevered with his self-appointed task of correcting the lapses of the settlers, how he had been patient with the most unruly of the children who enrolled in his school and how he could charm the most demanding of parents who viewed with suspicion his brand of teaching and its emphasis on enlightenment. The dead man was laid out in the parlour, which had been brightened up with an evanescence of flowers. Although he had never married, the women who had known Gabriel Farmer were inconsolable in their grief. Louisa cried for the man who had opened the eyes of her reluctant lover to the unlimited possibilities of love. Jeanette Cromantine, now turning old, wept for the man who next to Rodrigo the Brazilian had been like the brother she never had, and to whom she owed so much for her son.

Thomas Bookerman forgot about the war with its artificial truce long enough for him to bury his friend. In spite of the general feeling that the worst was over, he knew that Captain Hammerstone was only waiting for the right time before attempting to march down from the hilltop with his reconstructed army. 'Dis respite is a trick,' he told his men. But Thomas Bookerman was secretly convinced that not even someone as unpredictable as the wily old seadog would break an unwritten rule in war by attacking his enemy during a funeral. He kept the alert that had prevailed in his house, but had its doors open to all kinds of mourners. For the first time the Virgins came to his house, but it was clear from their hawk-like gaze, from the way they positioned the chairs before they sat down, that they had come more to see how he lived than to mourn.

Gabriel Farmer was buried in a quiet spot near the church. Saying that his late friend was not a Christian as defined by the veritable Virgins, Thomas Bookerman refused to allow them to pray over the corpse. 'It's all right,' he told them. 'He made his peace wid God long before he died.' A week after the funeral, the children of the town, defying their parents who feared for their lives, streamed to the grave to put flowers of love on the stone of a man who had been good to them.

Richard Farmer was so shaken by the death of his brother that not even the public demonstration of love, the knowledge that his brother's name would not be forgotten, was enough to conquer his private griefs. As soon as he could get away from the house of Thomas Bookerman, he went to the house that he had shared with his dead brother, put his books into several boxes and shut himself up in the house to be alone. Outwardly, he had always been regarded as the extrovert one of the two brothers, but with Gabriel gone, he felt lost among those pioneers who were more accustomed to grief than he was.

◇

The final march towards the coastal half of Malagueta by Captain Hammerstone came during the night, exactly one week after the funeral of Gabriel Farmer. In the first flush of his victory over the forces of Thomas Bookerman, he had begun to have ideas of how he would rule Malagueta if, as he expected, the defence of the coast proved less formidable than that of the garrison. He drew up a plan for a jail where he could keep the prisoners that he and his men expected to take. He decided that if the town fell and Bookerman managed to escape he would hang all his lieutenants as examples to others, but that he would show mercy to those who were prepared to work with him to create an administration subservient to the wishes of the King of England. But he was tormented by his own inability to arrive at a quick decision about what to do with the men who were bearing the brunt of the fighting for him. Good in battle, fearless like the untamed animals that they lived among, they were nonetheless unsuitable for the grand design he had in mind. He tried to picture them in the uniform of soldiers of the king, teaching them how to salute, how to make their beds and raise a flag. These men, he concluded, were not born for that kind of discipline. Order for them was merely a momentary password to kill, rape and plunder, and once their appetites were satisfied they would revert to their ancient barbarism. He liked those bastards, but the thought of running a town with them filled him with the deepest imagination of horror.

'Good Lord,' he thought, 'imagine me presenting this lot to a representative of the king!'

Then it dawned on him that all his attempts at fraternity with his men had been a farce, camouflaged by the desperation to live that all men feel in war. He had created them for a purpose, and now that he could imagine the end he had to destroy his own creations and look for new materials to feed the machine that he was planning to build. Time was something he could afford, so he pressed on slowly with his advance into the city. Now, however, he was surprised at the yawning empty streets that greeted him, almost as if at that moment the silent dusty houses were mocking him, as if he had become ridiculous and pretentious. Yet at the same time, the captain felt that perhaps the fight had gone out of the men in the first houses, and that perhaps he was walking into a trap.

'It's a trick,' he said, caught in an ambiguity of evidence. Captain Hammerstone could only hope that if he was to be betrayed it would not be at the hands of the men who had come like mules and zombies to fight his war, but by his own miscalculation of the degree of resolve on the part of the people of Malagueta. He need not have worried. The houses that he was leaving behind on his final march were alive with the slow fires of recognition, but their inhabitants recognised not an enemy this time, but a man they hoped to use in the game of manipulating. There were men who lived for opportunities and Malagueta had those who were only waiting for time to play their dice. They were cowards or traitors to the cause of Thomas Bookerman, but were tired of the rhythms of war that had made their feet sore, and narrowed their choices to act.

When Captain Hammerstone finally laid siege to the coast he did so savagely, thinking he would surprise the defenders. But he found himself faced with an enemy that was everywhere, fighting in the trees, shooting from behind the derelict houses blown up in the last defence. Although he had an advantage in men he considered the risk of fighting out in the open too costly, and tried to cut off the coast from the rest of the town. His intention was to advance slowly on the house of Thomas Bookerman, but he recalled how impenetrable the garrison had been, and how the unknown coast was less likely to fall as quickly as he had hoped.

Assessing his chances of holding out for long, Thomas Bookerman was surrounded in his house by the last of the men who had returned with him. They were determined to make a final stand there, to push the captain up the hill, where Bookerman hoped he could count on fresh recruits to join the war. But even as he hoped for such a possibility, he knew that he was engaged in wishful thinking. The fact that the captain had been able to get down to the coast, through the streets of Malagueta, was an indication that he had been betrayed. He resolved not to subject the brave men around him to a gruelling last stand and to escape to the nearby town over the rocky coast, but he was quickly overruled by Emmanuel Cromantine.

'Excuse me, General,' he said. 'We must try to drag the captain and his men out into the open.' Thomas Bookerman relented. Under cover from ten of his men, he tried to break the siege with the rest of his troops but had to fall back because of the captain's superior numbers. During the next four hours some of the bloodiest fighting in the conflict followed. The men of Thomas Bookerman found themselves fighting not only from the trees but on the ancient red stones, where Sebastian Cromantine and the first group of adventurers had landed with the corpse of Fatmatta the Bird-Woman. The church on George Street where some of the young defenders had taken up position resounded with the sound of heavy bombardment, and they were quickly routed. In the midst of that commotion Louisa, who had been trapped in Thomas Bookerman's house, was making her way along the lane behind the church when she was seized by two of the captain's men. They dragged her, screaming and kicking, to the arch in front of the side entrance of the church and tried to rape her. Her screams brought Richard Farmer and Phyllis who had been inside the church out into the open. Seething with rage, Richard Farmer took aim with his derringer but was stopped by Phyllis. 'Leave this to me,' she said. 'She is my sister.' With the same steady hand with which she had for many years made the butterfly kites, she shot the men and, when she was sure they were dead, walked over and kicked them both with all the accumulated fury that the last month, the death of Gabriel Farmer and the obvious loss of the war had created in her.

Having concluded that the situation was hopeless, Thomas Booker-man decided to make a break for it and to leave Malagueta for a while. In the final attempt to defend the town he had lost another thirty men, and Sebastian Cromantine and Gustavius Martins were captured when they attempted to go behind enemy lines with a few others to try to sabotage their supplies. Finding himself surrounded by only those men resolved not to give up, caught between the sea and the advancing troops of the Englishman, Thomas Bookerman realised that the hoped-for uprising would not materialise. It was with a feeling of regret that he concluded that Malagueta was a town destined to have its periods of greatness. These would produce the fires fuelled by the determination of men like Sebastian Cromantine not to be subdued in this or the next world. But it was enough to look at the powerful waves lashing against the rocks to know that despite such frightening power of creation and the temerity of men like himself to try to forge a blade from that power, the wheel of complacency would stop at its inevitable point after the forced turning of its axle. Then he recalled the clairvoyance of the Nubian Sulaiman of Khartoum whose words he had come across in the delicate handwriting of his mistress Mariamu who, in order to recall their happiness together, had burned onion peels to drive out the smell of sardines in the cottage of Antonio the Mulatto, and embarked upon her diary.

'He was a magician,' Thomas concluded. It was almost twenty years since that day when he had first seen the unruly coastline at the head of the expedition, and once again he turned towards the coast, accompanied by remnants of his loyalists to take possession of the boats which every Saturday brought fresh vegetables to Malagueta from the other side of the river. He looked into the eyes of his woman and saw the deepest proof of love in them. Hand in hand, they walked towards the first boat, as when he had left the shores of that other place in search of Malagueta.

10   Under the Volcano

Soon Malagueta had a flag. It flew from a post in the courtyard of the garrison, where Captain Hammerstone had once again set up head-quarters, and where under the heavy guard put up by the troops Sebastian Cromantine and other prisoners were held. The morning after he was firmly in control of the town, the captain went into action to reorganise the administration of Malagueta. He issued a decree forbid-ding the reopening of shops, imposed a dusk-to-dawn curfew and abolished the prosperous business in divination by Modibo the Susu on the grounds that it was subversive. Convinced that drunkenness was brought about by the preponderance of festivals in the town, he reduced the number of hours for wake-keeping and ordered that only fifty people could attend a funeral. But his most arbitrary act was to ban the forthcoming Christmas carnival, on the pretext that it was an excuse for the troublemakers to engage in what he considered the heathen practice of bringing their masquerades to dance in the centre of town, at the same time as the baby Jesus was being remembered in church. In this he had the support of the Virgins, who felt that God had finally answered their prayers and was going to rid the community of fakes hiding behind the cloak of rediscovering their roots.

When Sebastian Cromantine heard about the captain's action, he swore that one day the Englishman would pay for it. 'It's an outrage!' he fumed, but his rage was contained within the walls of the garrison where, because of his advancing age, he had been spared the humili-ation of going out to work on the project that was uppermost in the captain's mind. Fed on a breakfast of light porridge, the prisoners were marched out every morning beyond the town where a dense forest in which monkeys and crows lived was being cleared to build a jail. Stripped to the waist, unprotected in the March sun, they worked under the supervision of the guards who sometimes beat them and left the weak ones to die where they fell.

The people of Malagueta were beginning to adjust themselves to the new regime. Those who had refused to oppose the captain in the hope that once he was in charge he would grant them special favours – such as arranging for their children to go to England – soon concluded that not only had they betrayed their best friends but that they were held in even greater contempt by the captain. Seizing the advantage that victory gave him, he dispatched two leading members of the aristocracy on a schooner to London, with a letter for the partners who had commissioned the expedition to Malagueta. In the fine methodical handwriting of a man schooled in the art of flattery, he thanked them for giving him this chance to do something for king and country. Pushing his new advantage further, he mentioned the potential for growth in Malagueta, its untapped wealth and the richness of its vegetation, and made his only concession to the people by praising their kindness, concluding that they were so peaceloving they had refused to follow en masse that hot-headed one-eyed bandit to a certain death.

Saying that the people were just waiting for the expertise which could be given only by men who had created advanced tools and were already putting their skills to building industries, he urged his partners to send young men out to settle in Malagueta.

'Come out and see for yourselves what a marvellous place this is,' he implored. 'But don't bother bringing women because we have enough here.'

Six months later he received a letter from his principals in London, telling him to prepare for the first arrivals three months later.

Malagueta was indeed a town of women without men. Isatu Martins, who had escaped being captured in the liquefied forest looking for her husband, had returned in time to see the captured men being led away. She watched with anger as the soldiers demolished the market stalls, rounded up the pigs and made away with the bales of fine cotton from the shops which they reduced to piles of rubbish. When she finally made her way to her house she thanked God that her husband had not been killed, that some of their possessions had been left intact during the search for booty. But she was gloomy in the impermeable day because the men had gone off with the light. She tried to think of the other women whose men were also gone into confinement, because that was her nature and her mind was set to work organising the possibility of resistance to the occupation, while at the same time thinking of what succour she could offer them. The women whose men were held soon came together in her house.

While they chewed on rice cakes and tried to soothe their fretful children, they planned how to sabotage the transportation of goods from the other coastal towns to Malagueta, to prevent them falling into the hands of the captain's men. Under cover of darkness they worked feverishly behind their houses to bury their jewellery and money, and resolved that as long as their men were held in the garrison and made to go out every day to work on building the jail, they would wait until dark and then go out to dismantle the day's work, stone by stone.

Jeanette Cromantine, deprived of husband and son, wore her heart out trying to think of how Emmanuel Cromantine was coping with exile, though she knew that because he was her son he had her strong will and determination to face up to any challenge in life. When she tried taking parcels of food and clothing to Sebastian Cromantine in the garrison, the guards refused to accept them.

'Don't worry, ma'am, he won't be needing anything from you,' they told her. The last time she came from there, she went to the cemetery to pray at the grave of Rodrigo the Brazilian. 'How different you were from these bandits,' she cried, weeding out the grass that had grown on the edges. She stayed for a while, thinking of Fatmatta the Bird-Woman who had appeared to her in a dream when she had been labouring to give birth to Emmanuel. Then it occurred to her that she was getting old, and that the firmaments of her life had been these people who had given so much to others. Life was becoming less and less of a challenge to wake up every morning, go to her shop, put away money for her son and her old age, and more a preparation for the unknown. Now that she was alone, she found it reassuring to remember how she had fought against the obstinacy of Sebastian to start the rag-doll business, how they lost everything during the plague but had rebuilt and prospered. God had not given her the other children that she and Sebastian had prayed for, but it was enough that they had a good son in Emmanuel, although she was worried at his sudden turn towards adventure by going off to fight in the war. For the first time in almost ten years, she thought of her father-in-law whom she had never known but who, according to her husband, had been infested with the disease of wandering. She wondered whether her son might have inherited it from him.

'It's de bad blood,' she concluded.

Putting fresh flowers on the grave of Rodrigo, she asked him to box the ears of her son so that he would remember his mother and to pray that he would come back from exile. Later that night, as she was preparing to go to bed, she looked at herself in the mirror to examine the contours of her body. It had been a long time since she and Sebastian had shared her bed, and she blushed at the recollection that over thirty years had gone by since that day he had collapsed on the doorstep of the preacher's house, and she had put camellia leaves on his brow to bring down his fever, watching in awe, her body trembling with desire, as the big black man lay on the bed, his powerful muscles rippling through the layers of flesh.

Jeanette Cromantine was not the only woman worried about the absence of Emmanuel Cromantine. During the wild storm of their passion, Emmanuel Cromantine and Louisa Turner had kept their love a secret from his mother. Although they had sometimes talked about telling Jeanette when the time was ripe, they were sometimes carried away by a luxury of spirit which made their love pristine and demanded secrecy. They wondered how Jeanette would take to the discovery that her son had been seduced by an older woman. So during the closeness brought about by the absence of the men, while Isatu Martins served ginger tea and biscuits in her house to pass away the long sleepless nights, Louisa Turner, already four months gone, would have given everything not to have to tell Jeanette Cromantine that she was carrying her grandchild. But being a woman given to anticipating what the future might hold for her, she felt that fate had conspired against them by bringing in the invasion to drive Emmanuel away and to get her to face the unavoidable decision to tell his mother. The first time Louisa sat next to the older woman she did not know what to say to her. Luckily, she had worn a loose frock which hid her pregnancy, and because she was one of those women whom old women were always fond of telling had small wombs, she did not find it hard to pretend that her evident radiance was only the result of her attempt to put some colour into her cheeks, and that her upright breasts were a sign that she was taking care of her figure. Jeanette Cromantine thought otherwise. She eyed the younger woman with the clinical scrutiny of a woman who had once been young and had herself had to persuade her husband that his masculinity was guaranteed by her love, because he had found the opiate to enable him to come to her bed and give her their son. Remembering that the younger woman had once been her son's teacher, she asked her how she was, if she was going to church, and, adopting the tone of secrecy that women of her generation used when talking to nubile girls they felt were wasting their time in the intriguing world of men, she asked her why she was not married, adding that if the younger woman found that prospect too terrible, she should find a man who would give her a child.

'Have a chile, my dear,' she said. 'Dat is de greatest gift dat God can give to a woman.'

Louisa Turner decided not to waste any more time. Given advice by Jeanette Cromantine, she felt like a drowner who had been offered a line to come back to land. She decided that life was already too complicated for them to be at opposite poles over something as important as the coming of a child fathered by the man they both loved.

She chose the dress for the visit, a white cotton one with matching sandals, washed and plaited her hair so that it accentuated the lines of her face. Although she was not a vain person, she went to great lengths to see that all blemishes were removed from her face by washing it with lemon grass tea for a whole week, and creaming it with cocoa butter every night. When she went to bed the night before the visit she slept like a child and had a dream which she was to remember many years after her child was born. She dreamt that Emmanuel Cromantine was lying dead in a gutter, with his throat cut; great Egyptian vultures flew high in the clouds waiting for him to decompose. Then she was overcome by such a terrible fear that she woke up screaming, and went to see whether she had shut all the windows before going to bed. Throughout the next morning, she was unable to eat; she kept turning the dream over and over in her mind convinced that some bad omen had been revealed to her. Being someone whose imagination went beyond the bounds of possibilities and reason, she decided to consult Modibo the Diviner, in spite of the ban placed on visits to him by the captain.

The old sage brought out his mirror from his goatbag, drew four circles on it with a white chalk and looked at Louisa.

'It's all right, chile,' he said. 'You are not the first woman to see your man lying dead before his time.' Then he told her that what the dream revealed was the evil eye of a woman who hated her because 'she wants your man, and was trying to bewitch the unborn child'.

He told her to go back to her house, to kill a black duck, stick a dozen needles into it, and after wrapping it in banana leaves, to throw it at an intersection, splattered with the egg of a hen. 'That would turn her own evil back on her,' the diviner concluded. On the evening Louisa went to see Jeanette Cromantine, she was sweating from the greasy lotion given her by the diviner to 'destroy any enemy' who might try to come 'between you and your mother-in-law'. She found herself going over what she would tell the older woman, but she was buoyed by the certainty that Jeanette Cromantine, deprived of the presence of men who mattered so much in her life, would welcome the news that her son had provided her with the child who would be the succour in her old age.

Louisa Turner went up to the door of the Cromantines' house and knocked. When she was shown into the parlour, she realised that it was the first time she had been there, the house from which Emmanuel had come every time to make love to her, the house where he had his private dreams, where he laughed with his mother. She felt an instant pang of jealousy because Emmanuel's mother had so much while she was only just attempting to lay claim to a little of what life could offer her.

Jeanette Cromantine welcomed her graciously. Thinking that Louisa had come about something pertaining to the sad state of events, she served her cake and sorrel juice and proceeded to talk about how if it were not for the chicken-livered men who had refused to join Thomas Bookerman and her husband to drive the captain out, Malagueta would now be enjoying an unimaginable level of prosperity.

'Look at all de progress we made since we built dis town, and now dey want us to accept orders from heathens just 'cause some house niggers want to wear English woollen in de summer.'

She was angry that her husband had not listened to her, and had given credit to some of those cowards who couldn't even afford to pay in full for tombstones to honour their own dead. For the first time, she spoke of how wrong she had been not to have encouraged him to become a coffee planter, because she was scared he was going to be visited by the peripatetic ghost of his father who, after dying in one country, had come alive again in another and was rattling his bones in the house.

'I can hear him, my chile, every time he come here looking for a drink, but he don't bother us none, so I don't mind him. But come, tell me what is on your mind.'

'Sure you aren't going to be mad, ma'am?'

'Shucks, won't eat you up, my chile; almost as if you ma own daughter dat Sebastian and I never could have.'

Then Louisa told her everything. She told her about how Emmanuel had restored her confidence that was shaken by memories of the violent slave-owner, how he was the gentlest man God ever made, and also the brightest. She loved him so much that she had been prepared to sacrifice her career as a teacher just to be near him. She knew that he was going to

241

be somebody one of these days, and she wanted Jeanette to know how proud she was to be carrying his child.

Jeanette Cromantine went into her bedroom and came back with a candle. Blowing out the paraffin light so that they were left in the dull light of the moon, she put a match to the candle and brought a flicker of light close to Louisa's face. She looked at the younger woman as if she was seeing her for the first time, the way she and Sebastian had looked at the new land. She was searching for something infinitely more revealing than Louisa was divulging at that moment. It was as if she wanted to enter into the soul of the pregnant woman, surround her with a cloud through which, if her confession was true, Louisa would pass like a brilliant, heavenly body.

'Tell me, my daughter, dat my ears ain't lying to me,' she said.

Louisa did not know of the old custom of mothers lighting candles and looking stern to frighten away potential fortune seekers who came knocking. But she was strong enough to look the older woman in her face, and tell her that she was hearing exactly what she was meant to hear.

The two women faced each other for a while. Both were conscious of a sudden new change in their roles, such as their old pillars of strength would allow. They were elevated to new heights of courage and suddenly buoyed by the poignancy of what had brought them together towards that summit. They embraced. Louisa Cromantine cried because she was happy the older woman had received her, and she felt her child move lovingly in her belly.

'If only Emmanuel was here,' said his mother.

'Don't worry, Mama. He will be all right. That son of yours will be back soon, you will see.'

'I guess so. It's just dat thinking am gon be a grandmoder is something ah gotta get used to; and since you ma daughter now, ah suppose ah better show you de house, but first, let me turn on de light.'

She showed Louisa what years of trading on the waterfront had brought her: the respectability of a comfortable home. Sebastian had added two extra rooms to the original building that Gustavius Martins had built. So instead of entering the house through the green parlour, you came in through a side door, walked down a short corridor which was carpeted with a rich rug that she had ordered from the Chinese who had recently arrived, opened a shop, built a pagoda and showed a keen interest in all kinds of dogs. The parlour itself, where they were standing, was on the right, and when the light gleamed once more

Louisa saw the finely wrought wood of the parquet floor, the expensive sofas stuffed with ostrich feathers and draped with flowery damask, the solid Jacobean chairs, the rococo mirror on the wall that told her how beautiful she was, the golden samovar that the first Russian to come to her shop had given Jeanette, the grandfather clock with a bird-shaped pendulum, and, going into the dining room, the Chippendale cabinet where she kept her expensive Wedgwood wares. The bedrooms were large and airy, and covered with the same wallpaper that had a sea motif. But it was the chiffonier in Jeanette Cromantine's room, the solid mahogany bed, the commode and fine Moroccan rug on the floor that took Louisa's breath away. Emmanuel Cromantine's room had the musky smell of a young man's den. When she entered it, Louisa felt rather shy – although she had shared so many secrets with the occupant of that room, she was invading it in his absence, with his mother. It had just the pieces of furniture that she had imagined: the chest of drawers where he kept his clothes and his botanical specimens, the high wrought-iron bed, the Hepplewhite chair, and a table of indiscriminate wood laden with all kinds of seashells. One item above all else caught her attention: the figure of a centaur standing on the chest.

It was getting dark. Large flocks of orioles flew under the grey clouds towards their nest in the jarcaranda trees and the women went back to the parlour. They sat in comfortable chairs and talked. It was a conversation between two women who were learning to wait but who, because of the growing child, knew they could endure anything.

Even as the two women were finding out how much they needed each other, the future of Malagueta was occupying the mind of Captain Hammerstone. He was waiting for news of the arrival of the Englishmen to put his ideas into concrete terms. He needed surveyors, builders, policemen, soldiers to replace the mercenaries who were becoming more of a nuisance with their plunder and rape, and he wanted to have new mills open up for the processing of coffee and the many other exotic products. He foresaw the day when he would be dealing with the great trading houses in Manchester and Liverpool, and in time the flames of pride would leap in his heart for opening this backwater to the great cities of commerce and civilisation. For he was clever with schemes and played with the naïvety of others to make him rich. He knew without being told that because of its proximity to the equator, it must have the same riches as Ceylon – vast jungles to be explored and untold riches to be exploited. Besides being a soldier, Captain Hammerstone was a businessman.

Thus it was that when he received a telegraph from London saying that the ship with the men and materials to turn his dreams into reality was about to sail, he vowed that not one corner would be left untouched by his leadership. Work on the prison was stepped up, the men labouring in the heat and shivering in the cold until they succumbed to malaria, to be replaced by new ones who succumbed equally to the terrifying brutality of the guards. Others were put to work building new roads to take the carriages that the rich merchants had ordered, while drainages were enlarged so that the place would not be flooded during the rainy season.

The women formed a co-operative to help each other. Previously they met every Monday in the house of Isatu Martins, but as their numbers grew they decided they needed open space. In defiance of the law prohibiting large gatherings, they began to meet in an open space opposite the cathedral; each would bring her children and whatever homemade cake, pudding and drinks they could carry. There, under the watchful eyes of the soldiers, Isatu Martins extolled the virtues of their men and spoke against the injustice that they were suffering, condemning the connivance of members of the aristocracy which had made the present situation possible. One Monday, she stood on a raised platform that the women had built with their husbands' carpentry tools. Holding her son Garbage by his right hand, she asked her listeners how long they could take the humiliation of being grass widows. 'Look at ma son, growing up widout a father. One day he will demand to know what his father done to be locked up, and what will ah tell him? Dat a bunch of barbarians come here and attack Malagueta and seize everything? No. He won't believe me 'cause he would ask what happened to de women, he would demand to know what his mother and de other mothers did. So ah owe it to him, to his father, we owe it to our children, our men, to resist dis tyranny to de end and demand dey release our men.'

The imprisonment of their husbands had not made them martyrs – they had just embarked upon their suffering; but the women of Malagueta continued to meet on Mondays, and soon on Wednesdays. On those days, between caring for her son and feeling the turfs of her grass-widowhood under her feet, Isatu Martins sometimes felt the emptiness of the silent house, in the little things that she forgot, such as where she had lain a spoon, or the name of a new dog she had acquired to keep out the neighbourhood cats. Large thunderbolts of lightning would tear off the sheets of the roof, and keep her awake, afraid of the fiery tongues of rain. Then she was glad for the gift of woman which was her son, pressed him to her breast, cursed the unruly universe, when it was in fact the dawn of her unfettered martyrdom that was beginning to pour on her life.

In the vacuousness of time, she tried to remember the hands of her husband as he had touched her during the raging nights of storms, the way wood was malleable in his genius, and of the stones on which his creativity was pronounced all over the town. But she was a woman whose grief was fleeting and only drenched her when she allowed her luxuriance of heart to dwell on it. So that in the capaciousness of her spirit, the absence of her husband sometimes strengthened her and made her worthy of her father.

She kept the house as if her husband were there: her son saw to it that she was busy, because he was a growing boy who needed a father, and was beginning to sulk at his absence. In time, he took to going out, to look at the hieroglyphs of clouds, when his mother was busy at the stove, and sometimes, as if to make up for his quietness, he went behind the house to talk to the fowls, which brooded in their coops.

Garbage did not ask his mother when he would see his father again. He was wrapped up in the script about growing up in a wilderness of youth which his mother showed to him but tried to protect him from her own sorrows. Earlier, in the first weeks of the imprisonment of her husband, when she had tried taking parcels of food to him before the guards stopped her, Garbage had refused to go with her. Then she would threaten to skin his hide and cut off his ration of cakes that he had come to associate with Sunday. But he was immune to the naked flames of threats, which his grandfather, the banana-grove man, could douse with his hands.

Isatu Martins continued to address the gathering of the forlorn women on the grey days. She could conjure words of faith, which she had begun to use to soothe the grief of others. When she was filled with the goblets of concern, she would denounce the soldiers whose ranks were swelling steadily just in case the women should decide to do something unusual. To a questioner who asked her whether she was not afraid of the armed men, she replied emphatically: 'Their mothers' milk is still fresh in their mouths, so they can't lay their hands on de daughter of woman.' Such bold talk, however, betrayed an inner unease as a result of the decrees of Captain Hammerstone, which he continued to issue regularly.

But she was a bold woman, and was convinced that in spite of their brutality Captain Hammerstone's soldiers were just as terrified of the women as some of them were of the men. Matters came to a head one day, soon after there had been an incident in the garrison. Age had not been good to Sebastian Cromantine in detention; the folds of his skin under his chin sagged, and he was suddenly an old man, unaccustomed to inertia. The hands of the man who had brought love in the first flow of discovery to his coffee trees were little spiders, reduced to squashing cockroaches. He felt his life fading.

Bondage brought back bad memories that he had lost in some swamp, in the bittersweet solitude of youth. Even the war had not broken his spirit and he had not suffered shame when they had rounded them up and locked them up, but the pernicious cobwebs of inertia were playing a harsh music inside his limited space, and made him want to get out. He and the other captives had begun to tire of waiting for the captain to make up his mind about when to let them go. Months sped by, altered only by the change in seasons so that the hurricanes of August found them naked in grief for their families, who were themselves not absolved of grief for their men, because they preferred even tyrannical husbands to empty houses. When the rains were over and the land drank up the moisture, the locusts were hatched and spread their wings in the dark, which disturbed ganglions of nerves in the old man's head. 'At dis rate,' he said, 'ah shall go crazy here before ah die.'

So he conceived of how not to die in that slaughterhouse without seeing the face of his son again, or listening to the rhapsodical poetry of his wife's voice. She appeared there on his mind, pottering in the garden of their house, in the old days, before Emmanuel their son had killed some of the oleanders trying to fly his kite. She came home from the shop where she had argued with the Chinese over the price of Java prints, cooked his dinner, while her voice rose in contralto with the songs of Fatmatta the Bird-Woman. So he decided he would pay the price to regain his freedom.

When they brought his meal one evening, he threw the stuff in the face of the guard, who was a young man and did not understand the raging fires of old age. Sebastian Cromantine was beaten that night and lost a tooth, which brought the old crocodile back to life.

And he was back in the swamps of rebellion, with the voice of his father urging him on, because that father was never really far away when his son needed him. Blood was streaming all over the face of the old man, but he strangled the guard with his bare hands as he had killed a planter who was about to shoot another black man during the colonial war. When they finally prised his hands loose from the throat of the insolent guard, Sebastian Cromantine was past caring what happened to him; death was a luxury he could afford.

The news that Sebastian Cromantine had been beated in detention reached the Wednesday gathering of women, through a gardener who had been in the compound. He was a messenger who could add frills to his story, so he told of the wild blows that had fallen on the old man.

'Dey beat 'm good an' proper and broke his teef.'

'What had he done?' one of the women wanted to know.

'One of dem jailers brought him some soup Sebastian did not want, so he threw de stuff in de ground, and dey beat him for dat, like a dog.'

How could they beat him, thought Isatu Martins, where was the justice in this world? The weeks of addressing the women were beginning to tell on her nerves. Where she had been in those weeks was in a country without the details of knowledge; she had been walking in a wilderness of thorns, thrashing through the blades of despair, but being sustained by the belief that her husband was a strong man, and would want her to keep her head up, as she had done during the exile on the mountain. Garbage was there to remind her about how much she had to fight for, how much she had to hope for in the future.

So hearing that Sebastian Cromantine had been beaten, Isatu Martins mounted the dais and spoke to the stony faces in the crowd.

'Today, our hearts beatin' heavy, because we got some news 'bout our husband Sebastian. He is a good man, like his wife Jeanette. We knows how he work to build dis place, how he never did anythin evil all his life. Ah remembers when de plague come, how Sebastian run run run like he be mad, saying, "Ma people, keep your head steady, we gon get outta dis, ain't no need to panic, it's only a little boderation." You young 'uns, you newcomers to Malagueta, don't know what it be like, seeing all you labour for going up in smoke, like dey says in de Bible 'bout hell. Well, we be in hellfire before, but now is sorta like we in de belly of a volcano, like being under, you know, and de belly is kinda shaking, and the voice of de Lawd is speaking loud and clear 'cause he vexed, and he be saying, ma people, dis ain't no kinda life for you, you gotta crawl outta de belly, and we gon start now. Dey done push us too far, and now dey is trying to whup our men like dey not men. Dey brought us news 'bout Sebastian, how dey beat him 'cause he be man and gon fight. We is no coward and if dey gon kill our men dey gotta start wid us.'

They did not let her finish. Like some great hurricane, the women began to move towards the garrison. At first they lacked momentum, as if the force of the hurricane was unsure of how far it wanted to go, what the ultimate range of its destruction was going to be. Some of them cleared their throats, adjusted the babies on their backs and fixed their headgear properly.

Then, slowly, the hurricane began to gather force; the women tore branches off the trees and picked stones from the ground. What they were going to do with the branches they were not quite decided on, but they were compelled by the force of the hurricane to rip anything their hands came across. They walked past the battered shop of Theophilus the apothecary, and saw where Amadu the old Fulani had tethered his last cow before the unruly soldiers drove him out of the area. When they sighted the garrison, they broke into a song. It was a bitter song, laced with the aloes of anger they had been forced to drink by the repressive captain. Some soldiers in the courtyard were playing a game of draughts when they heard the sound of the women approaching. Grabbing their guns, they positioned themselves behind the gate of the garrison, but they did not take up firing position. It was all that the women needed to seize the advantage.

Forgetting that they were facing men who had only recently killed in battle, Isatu Martins, the mothers, wives, and sweethearts forced the gates open and entered the garrison. Paralysed by the incredible bravery of the women, the soldiers watched them as they quickly began an assault on the place. Just where most of their men were being held was unknown to them, but that did not seem to deter them from their objective. When the first sound of the wreckage began, it was already too late for the surprised guards to realise what was happening.

'Let's burn dis place down and get de men out of here,' Isatu Martins said. Minutes later the flames of torches had engulfed the building; most of the soldiers who had been reposing in another part of the courtyard came too late to be able to stop the fire spreading. The wind that was blowing from the hill fuelled the flames, and the angry, whistling voices of fire rose in the rooms as the blaze began to spread.

Captain Hammerstone's men tried to keep the fire under control by dousing it with water from the wells in the compound. But soon the sky was black with the rage that was the fire; outside the voices of the women rose as high as the flames so that they became one with the fire because the fire had started in their hearts. As the flames spread, the women saw the now useless doors of the garrison coming off their hinges; they saw the animals in the compound running in all directions to escape the inferno. Death, which they had seldom thought of, was walking in the compound, because the flames had gutted whole areas where some of their men could be, but the women prayed that the prisoners would come out alive.

'Let's go look for our men,' said Isatu Martins, when they came inside the compound.

Sebastian Cromantine heard the voices of the women as he struggled to get up. By the time he managed to reach the door of his cell, it was no longer a barrier to his freedom, as the frame had been destroyed in the fire. When he emerged in the open darkness he had to shield his eyes from the fire, but it was his legs that troubled him most. The months of lying on the hard floor had affected his circulation and he had to get used to walking again. Yet he felt a lightness in his body; the wounds that he had endured during the terrible beating had not left their mark on his spirit. Out there, somewhere, he knew Jeanette Cromantine was among the women, and he was going to make it out of that hole to get to her.

In the aftermath of the blaze, the soldiers did not try to prevent the prisoners from escaping; those who had been with the captain during the first attack of the garrison decided that the people of Malagueta were not going to allow any outsider to impose a tyranny upon them; being themselves men who had joined Captain Hammerstone in order that they might preserve their freedom, they suddenly found themselves admiring the courage of the women who had stormed the garrison to try to free their men. It was enough to think of such courage for them to realise how despicable their own duty had been. 'Let's get out of here,' one of them said. So while the women were searching for their husbands, they did not see the men who slipped out of the chaos of the night into the world outside.

When the smoke had cleared up, the women saw their men coming out. Jeanette Cromantine – who because she was getting old, had not rushed into the cells, saw the equally old figure of Sebastian coming towards her in the courtyard.

'My love, my love,' she said, 'you look so tired, but ah will take you home and make you some soup, just like in de old days.'

◇

Gustavius Martins died in the fire that night, but his badly burnt body was not discovered for some while, not until his wife, in the confusion realised that he had not come out with the other men, and went in search of him. She prayed that she would find her husband wounded, unable to walk, so that she would bring him back to nurse his wounds, bring him

249

back to life and wipe out the terrible anguish that had come into their lives since the war. The thought that he might be dead did not enter her head, because Isatu Martins was not a woman easily troubled by the supposition that things could happen to her or to Gustavius to deprive her of living in happiness with him for ever. After Garbage was born, she had gone to see the diviner, who had told her to take her husband back to her town. She wanted to thank him for his advice, and to bring him some presents. Asked by the venerable man if she had any other request to make, she replied that she had only one wish in life.

'What is that, my child?' asked the wise man.

'To die in bed with my husband, when I am seventy-five years old,' she replied.

So now she prayed even more loudly, hoping that all the angels and all the dead would come out of their graves to answer her prayers. But the further she picked her way into the burnt-out garrison, the more shocked Isatu Martins was at what she saw. Parts of the garrison were completely gutted and the fire was still burning in the one area where Isatu Martins hoped to find her husband. It was a slow fire but if there was life there, then it was the sound of the beams as they collapsed onto the floor in the blaze. The former shop of the carpenters from Calabar, the barns where the captain and his men had stored food for the possibility of a long rainy season, had been wiped out and the place smelled of the burning flesh of animals.

Yet Isatu Martins went into each of the cells, looking for the familiar face of her husband. What she saw in nearly all of them were the poses in death. She had never seen anyone dead, and had always wondered what people looked like when they died. She saw men gripping their heads as if when the angel had come to take them away they had asked him to go away and come back later because they were not yet ready to leave this world. Others had died with their arms flung wide open as if they had mistaken death for a beloved woman who was coming into their arms after all those months of being without love.

'Good Lawd,' said Isatu Martins. 'If dis is de face of death, then ah wonder what its back looks like?'

When she finally discovered the body of her husband, she did not have to turn it over as she had done with some of the other men. She was familiar with the country of the man's body, with the way he lay in bed, especially after a hard day's work. She knew the rhythm and the storm of that body better than any other person in the world, its tales of magic and rhythm to the accompaniment of the weaverbirds' songs as he had made her his; how often she had trembled in the storm of his passion, with his smell of a man, of pinewood.

Suppressing the deep surge of pain which was threatening to flood her, she sat next to the dead man and touched his face. But in her heart, Isatu Martins refused to accept that her husband was dead. She thought that death was a nasty thief who came at night to steal all that twenty years of hard work had given you but that, like some good thieves, might return some of the stolen items when they had taken the best stuff for themselves.

She raised the head of her man to see if there had been a mistake after all, especially as his face was still warm, like a young bull's, but the buzzing of the flies that had been attracted by the smell of blood all over the garrison was enough to tell her that his life had gone out a long time before she had arrived to claim it. Then from a region in her heart where they had loved each other so much, she began to bring back the moments of happiness. She saw him coming across the cornfields, shy and dark like a bronze mask, to tell her about the throne where she would sit for ever. She remembered how his hands had trembled as he helped her into the lantern where she was serenaded by the acrobatic monkeys dancing over the crouching lions, in that forget-me-not afternoon of the protestation of his love for her. She recalled how he had told her the tales of the sea with its millions of living souls fed to the sharks would be forgotten, if only she would return to his life.

Life, Isatu Martins remembered, had been good to them, despite the terrifying period when she had wanted to kill her love for him with her death, because Garbage had not arrived yet, the gift of the chimerical dwarfs, and smelling of the banana grove where his grandfather had made him immune to the pernicious eyes of envy.

With a great strength belying her now unbearable grief, she lifted the limp form of her husband and came into the hallway. The hills dwarfing the garrison were alive with the voices of the creatures of the night, but Isatu Martins was not afraid. She walked slowly, carrying the man, as she had carried him in other times, though when in the past they had reached the bottom, it was not clear who had carried whom.

Suddenly she found herself on the road leading to the town, and for once she was glad of the oppressive silent hand that had clamped the mouth of Malagueta, so that she could take her husband home without being seen. Grief, for Isatu Martins, was a private affair.

When she felt she was losing strength, she put the man down gently on the ground where all men had an ancestor waiting to claim them. She stroked his face, but his smile did not change. Gustavius Martins looked like a happy man in death, because he had died thinking about his wife. But as he lay there, Isatu Martins saw, in the faint glow of the moon, that although her huband's face had escaped the ravages of the fire his body was badly burnt.

She ran her hand gently down the hard, leathery body, felt where it had gone to sleep, where the ribs had broken out of their cage, but she was not horrified. He was her man. Once again, she saw the same beautiful man who had come to her that evening many years ago as she was bathing in the stream. Suddenly, she felt the tears running down her cheeks and she began to speak to the dead man.

'Sleep, my love, sleep until we get home where ah shall tend your wounds: you look beautiful and no one will ever know how ah found you, because it is none of their business. We was alone together and we shall be alone again in dat house where you will never want for anything, because ah shall see to it dat you are happy in dat house dat you built wid your hands.'

She asked him to 'come any time you feel like it, from de other country, where ah know you will be going for a while, only for a while; come because you know ah shall be there always, with de doors open, wid my heart waiting for you, and holding your son by de hand'.

Isatu Martins regained her strength. Slowly, singing to herself so that she wouldn't cry, she continued the journey home. In the still of the night, she was a monument to all brave women: upright and proud, so that not even the shrieks of the dog-faced baboons giving birth in the surrounding countryside disturbed her calm. Getting closer to her house, she passed the school of the Farmer brothers, and Isatu Martins suddenly remembered that other man who had come to Malagueta, in the dignity of his English suit, with the cadences of love in his voice, to find a name in the babel of tongues that was Malagueta in those days. And because she was a woman who had always admired courageous men, men who dared the impossible to make their world better, she felt a deep gratitude to her husband and to Gabriel Farmer. She thanked God that she had been given the chance to share the life of one of them, to have loved him, and to have been loved by him in return.

Jeanette Cromantine was just blowing out the lamp in her room when she saw Isatu Martins toiling along with the body of her husband. She ran out of her house like a mad woman, without a shawl to protect her in the cold. But when she realised that it was a dead man who was coming home, she cried out in anguish as she had never cried before.

'Isatu!' she wept. 'What a great pain life has given you, my sister. There will never be anoder man like him.'

Gustavius Martins was laid out in a rough wooden coffin that Alphonso the cabinet maker made free of charge. 'He was like a brother to me, and helped me to find my feet when I was starting this business,' the carpenter said, refusing to be paid by Isatu Martins. Before she opened the house to the large crowd of people who wanted to pay their last respects to the dead man, she asked Jeanette Cromantine, who had been with her all the time, to let her have some time alone with her husband.

'Before they take him away from me, let me rest my head on his chest one last time.'

She combed his hair and powdered his face, straightened his tie and adjusted the handkerchief in his breast pocket. Then she remembered that he had bought an expensive gold watch many years before Garbage had been born, but that he had not worn it because of the situation brought about by the war, when time was measured more in terms of the number of battles that were fought than by the awakening of the sun. She found the gold piece and when she opened the case, she was surprised that its hands were moving, as if someone had wound the mechanism. 'Take dis away wid you 'cause ah won't be needing it to know when you coming.'

The sword of Modibo of Timbuctoo rested at the right side of the dead man, and the Moroccan slippers that he wore were the same that Santigue Dambolla had not been able to give to his son-in-law, but which Sawida had brought with the dead cloud of her grief. She loved this son-in-law of hers and, like all women accustomed to pain, she felt it hard to cry. While her daughter sat motionless in a chair in front of the sleeping man, it was the widow of the banana-grove man who served coffee, who saw to it that all the doors were open so that everyone who wanted to come would have a last look at the man who, next to Sebastian Cromantine, had made Malagueta the prosperous town that it was.

Over the protestation of Sawida Dambolla, Isatu Martins let Garbage stand next to her, looking at his father. As in the past, when they had shared the ephemeral hours of grief, the mother and the son did not talk too much; each was locked in a secret territory of knowledge, learning to reshape their lives, in the morning after. But when Isatu Martins put her arms around the body of her son they clung to each other, and for the first time since she had come upon the body of her husband, he cried with her because they had found each other in the great eternal love that they felt in their hearts for the man and for themselves.

Gustavius Martins was carried away to the heights of his mortality by the largest crowd that Malagueta had ever seen. Sebastian Cromantine, who, when he heard that his friend had died, shook the cane chair where he sat with a volcanic rage, insisted on burying his friend.

'Those bastards drove ma son outta dis place, and now dey have killed ma brother,' he raged, while Jeanette Cromantine tried to hold him down on the dusty road leading to the cemetery, leaning on his cane.

Under his breath, he swore that one day the young men of Malagueta would organise themselves and drive out all the foreigners. He was still recovering from the effects of his confinement in the garrison, so he had difficulty going up the hill, but he resisted his wife's attempts to help him along the way. The sounds of feet marching in the solemn procession rose above the voices of the people in the crowd; young men and women turning the last corners of wisdom, asthmatic and coughing clerics from the church who remembered when Gustavius Martins had given them the money to finish its construction, turned up that afternoon.

When she saw the open grave into which they were going to put her husband, Isatu Martins stared at the limitedness of space, the solitary, red and cold void that had claimed a man who had been all warmth and sunshine. But it was not the space that she would remember later when the body was gone, for Gustavius Martins was not a man confined by the diameters of space, as much as the thuds of the earth that she put on the coffin, earth to earth, dust to dust, and the gravity of the look of Sebastian Cromantine as he shovelled the first spadeful of earth in an everlasting rite of brotherhood.

After they had covered the coffin with the last remnants of red soil, the large crowd of mourners went back to their houses; they were too sad to remember how many years earlier, at another funeral, Thomas Booker-man had led the first attack against the garrison.

Isatu and Garbage Martins moved in with the Cromantines. Although the widow had insisted that she was all right and could get on in her own house with only a little help from her friend, Jeanette Cromantine would hear nothing of it.

'Put youself in ma position,' she said to the bereaved woman. 'What would you do if it be Sebastian and not Gustavius who died?'

Death had broken a bond that had existed between the two couples since the early days of the founding of the town. Throughout the long years, in the bitterness of the first settlement, in the triumphs over the various adversities they had encountered, in the excitement of watching the town grow, nothing so terrible had happened to any of the original families. But when Jeanette Cromantine wanted to shut the windows, hang white curtains and mark the windows with white chalk as a sign of mourning for Gustavius, Isatu Martins told her not to.

'Gustavius was a kind man, always gentle wid me. Take de time when ah wanted to die 'cause ah did not have Garbage then. Most men would have been vexed, vexed, but not my Gustavius. So let me think of him as if he only gone away on a long visit.'

They opened the house, whitewashed the stones and welcomed the neighbours who came around every day to pay their respects to the dead man's widow. Some brought little pieces of lace, spices to drive out witches, a leg of lamb, chickens and eggs, not because Isatu Martins needed them but because they wanted to be one with her in that season.

Louisa Turner was very heavy with her baby when Gustavius Martins was buried; the shock of the death had so shaken her that she almost miscarried, but when she had been made by Jeanette Cromantine to chew some mustard leaves the bleeding stopped. She was pale for a few days as she tried to adjust to the absence of a man who had meant so much to Emmanuel and to herself, and tried not to think of how Emmanuel, wherever he was, would respond when he heard of the death of Gustavius. She prayed that he would come back one day to see his child, because the months of being without him had begun to fill her with anxiety. How terrible it would be if he himself were eaten up by the rapacious worms of evil which she felt were beginning to run through the heart of Malagueta.

A few days later, when she saw how the widow bore her grief, Louisa Turner forgot about the absent man and tried to concentrate on having her child. She regained the colour that had gone out of her face, insisted that Isatu Martins and Jeanette Cromantine take it easy while she did the cooking. They were three women in a house, who gave each other strength while they watched the silent figure of Sebastian Cromantine sitting on the veranda as he had done in former times. He had aged beyond recognition because the hourglass of death had begun to trickle with the sand of time on his back and he felt the presence of the women rather than saw them. For he had wanted to pay the supreme price that his friend had paid. The burden of existence in old age required a new definition, yet there was very little left for him to do. All the mysteries of life had been excavated, classified and named. In the glow of the morning, in the nostalgia of the sea, he was a refugee from turmoils and regrets, because Sebastian Cromantine had lived through enough hurricanes to fortify him against even his last wish, to see his son, before he surrendered his life to the reliquary of his bones. Everything that he had desired, suffered and lost was mixed up in that kaleidoscope that was the preserve of old age. The old rage had left him and the humiliation suffered in the garrison seemed like a small wave on what had been the turbulence of his sea so that he could await, whenever it came, the twilight of his age without fear and concern. Sebastian Cromantine was freed of the burdens of knowledge.

On the day they marked the fortieth day of the death of Gustavius Martins, Louisa Turner began to experience the first signs of pain. When she felt the child kicking inside her, demanding to be born, she tried to remember what Jeanette Cromantine had told her about the miracle of the moment, about women who pulled out their hairs and screamed when the baby was coming, but by the time the old midwife arrived Louisa's mind was past remembering all the details of delivery. While Isatu Martins and Jeanette Cromantine held her pinned to her bed, told her to push down hard, breathe so that she wouldn't suffocate the child, she felt the knives of the piercing spasm coming from the same lacerating womb where, in previous times, she had felt the jabs of the man whose child she had desperately desired. Rivulets of sweat covered her face; she kicked and raved, bit her tongue and pissed on the bed before the animal that she had carried for nine months found its way down the shaft and left her paralysed for a few minutes, like a spent storm.

'It's a girl and she gon bring good luck to her fader,' said Jeanette Cromantine when the baby had been examined, washed and given to her mother to be fed.

Seven days later, Jeanette Cromantine named her first grandchild Fatmatta-Emilia Cromantine. 'Wid a name like dat,' she told Louisa, 'your child gon be a strong woman 'cause ah named her after my friend, de bird-woman, and after her fader.' She was a big baby, dark like her mother but with the long arms of her father and a high forehead which Jeanette Cromantine said was a sign of intelligence. When the excitement of having a new member in the Cromantine family had died down, Isatu Martins finally persuaded her friend to let her go back to her own house with Garbage.

'Ah have to pick up de pieces of my life,' she told Jeanette Cromantine, 'and ah know dat you are here, and remember, Gustavius Martins is alive in me, and ah have a growing son to care for.'

She went back to the now dusty house, accompanied by her son; throughout the period in the Cromantine house, Garbage had never once mentioned his father. He went for walks, sat on rocks and fired little pellets with his catapult, but was in general grave and silent. While some of the women in the neighbourhood wondered at his growing up without a father, or prayed that after a decent period a good man might come who his mother would love and marry, while they tried to tell him how his father had been too good for that town with its tragedies, Garbage did not once show any sign that the death of his father had a tragic effect on him. Rather, he seemed to regard the fat hands that touched his woolly head, the large gowns of the expansive matrons who wrapped him up in whirls of tenderness, the cocoa-buttered faces that looked at him with pity, as intrusions in his life. For if his father's death was his rite of passage into a hastened manhood, Garbage Martins had been ready for it since the day he had opened his eyes, when he had seen the dwarfs dancing with him and they had whispered his name into his ears, stamped with the freedom of birds, to find his own destiny.

Isatu Martins went to the Chinese shop a week later and bought a dozen mirrors; she hung them on the parlour walls, festooned with bright violets. Every night, after she had seen her son off to bed, she sat in the darkness of the room, and with the moon's light serving as pilot she paraded naked in front of the mirrors. Then she would call her husband's name, look for his hands and be carried away by the music in her heart which shook the mirrors on the wall. Sometimes she saw him, coming to her clad in a white gown, yet, when she wanted to touch him, Gustavius Martins pulled back from her, as if he was returning to the sea, from where he had come, looking for the resonance of a new name.

Then Isatu Martins understood that her husband had not rejected her but was waiting for his wounds to heal before surrendering his sanguine spirit to the beatitude of her love. If she doubted his presence among them, it was enough for her to look at the flowers in the garden and the smooth faces of the furniture that he had made with his hands, radiant in the lightness of body that she felt in the morning, to face the day. So she removed the mirrors and sent Garbage to the school where Richard Farmer welcomed him as if he were a sage. Because of the magic that his name conjured, the other children treated Garbage with a curiosity of interest. While they enjoyed the prerogatives of childhood, fought and laughed at the presumptive airs of the teachers to mould them into images of their parents, they never invited Garbage to join them.

'That Garbage boy is not like us,' said one of his classmates after he had been with them for almost three months. 'He is too strange for a child.'

Isatu Martins did not think that her child was strange, but even she could not enter into his mind with the brazenness of motherhood; when he came home from school and threw his slate and chalk on the dining table he was warm but distant as if he needed her, yet would resist any attempt to smother him with love. He enjoyed going to school, he replied with a solemnity that amazed her. 'School is all right, but I am waiting for the moment when I can decipher the meaning of the instruction I am getting from a voice at night.' Isatu Martins felt the same tightness in her thought that she had experienced the moment Garbage had been born.

'What voices?' she asked her son.

'Don't know, but I think they are trying to tell me that some strange things are going to happen in this town.'

That evening, Isatu Martins did not know that she had been exposed to the clairvoyance of her son. But soon after, the locusts came, and on a lazy morning the green ships full of the surveyors and then, smelling of the garlic of the Shouf mountains, the Arab traders hawking coral beads, just as Sulaiman the Nubian, otherwise known as Alusine Dunbar, had seen them in the magical mirror many years earlier.

11 The Money-Lender

It took Captain Hammerstone and his men less than two weeks to repair most of the damage done to the garrison by the fire of the women's attack. Long after the women had left, in the charred smoke of his dream, the captain stood on the balcony, his sailor's revolver in his hand, a lone figure dripping in the heat of the evening. Unlike the previous attack, when the fury of the funeral procession had come with an unexpected wind, Captain Hammerstone had not been unprepared for an attempt by the women to release their men. But with Thomas Bookerman in exile the captain had not felt seriously threatened. Now, in what he felt was the illusion of victory that the women and their men had gone away with, he could think of a world that was complex. Malagueta was not a tidal wave or a tamed beast but a difficult mistress. So he would have to be patient in the courtship, win her with acts of generosity and understanding. He prayed that the time would come when the people of the town would get to see that his motives were good, that his men were not the murderous butchers they appeared to be. The river that was between them was not one of blood brewing with hate, but a case of misunderstanding. He was bringing the benefits of civilisation, the justness of English laws, the virtues of a system that had been in the world for many centuries and had served his own people and others well.

So when his men went to the forest to cut wood to repair the damaged garrison he ordered them to treat the area with reverence; earth was generous to men who respected her, and he would not be guilty of destroying what could be useful for other purposes. He saw the day when after Malagueta had become a town stamped with the permanence of English laws, when the blacks were themselves the messengers of the metaphysical transition – darkness to light, neo-paganism to classicism – the encyclopedic mind of the English would be admired by the best sons and daughters of the town.

During the period of mourning for those who died in the inferno, Captain Hammerstone had avoided going into town. His men would sometimes go in large numbers to buy supplies for the garrison, repair some of the shops that had been damaged in the previous fighting and look for women who, in spite of the antagonism that most people felt for the soldiers, sometimes took them in. But they were careful to stay together, to have their weapons near them and go back to the security of the garrison before it was too dark, as the curfew they had imposed had become a dead letter. Things went on like that for several months until some of them began to show signs of restlessness. The promised advantage that Malagueta was supposed to provide had not come to pass; the feeling of security that they had shared even during the siege had now given way to despair. They were impatient for a chance to work in the mills which Captain Hammerstone had told them about but which had not materialised. If they asked when the ships that he was waiting for would arrive from England, the captain would give them a reply that only added to their confusion:

'When the Whigs stop drinking port and provide money for the expedition.'

Although he seldom mentioned it, Captain Hammerstone was

himself beginning to have some doubts about the fate of the expedition that he had been told was coming. Matters were not helped by the fact that since the last letter he had received from London, the captain had received no further news from his superiors. The feeling that he might have been abandoned, and that he was destined for a most unpleasant end in that part of the world, would sometimes push him to doubt his own men. Their trust was not endless, it was not in keeping with the laws of soldiers away from the discipline implied in the motto: to serve king and country.

Forced to wait for a change in his fortunes, Captain Hammerstone had also begun to miss the life he had become accustomed to; he was not a man given to monasticism and the idea of being for so long without a woman was beginning to tell on his nerves. At night, unable to sleep, he sometimes thought of the women he had left in the byways of adventures, of even the pale sexless virgins he had rejected in Devon, but he had set his heart and soul on the day when he would be able to set up a house with a woman in Malagueta and, if providence was kind, have a son.

Nevertheless, when news of the death of Gustavius Martins reached him, Captain Hammersone was moved to remember the man who, next to Thomas Bookerman, had had the exemplary courage to fight for and defend the dignity of man. All his life Captain Hammerstone had known men who were fascinated by lores of brigandage, by the assumption of bravery in the plundering of island relics. Their scope for greatness was limited, their reasoning trivial, so that in the end they were despised by even their own kind. Gustavius Martins was above those men, thought Captain Hammerstone, and he wished their fates had been impaled on the same cross, on the same road to mortality.

'What a terrible thing it is that honest men are always in opposite camps,' he remarked when he heard of the death.

But he quickly regained his élan and, with the garrison almost completely rebuilt, drew up plans for the expansion of the town. He sent his men out every day to dig gutters from the hills leading down into the ocean so that they wouldn't be inundated by water when the rains came. On those missions, the soldiers tried to win the affection of the people by telling them how they were only waiting for the right time to mutiny against their commander and join them. They had suffered neglect, clearing out the weeds and planting new flowers; they were seeking to define a new place for themselves in that treasure hunt which was the heart of man, where hate, greed, forgiveness, compassion, forgetfulness and love sometimes clash for a meaning of destiny.

As the captain waited for a letter to make his now moribund life rebound like a hammer on an anvil, as he sought to understand the earth which had so far resisted his ploughing in Malagueta, his men needed no excuse to show that they were not all the pigs that the people of Malagueta thought them to be. Some were part of that world, had nestled at its breasts, but they were tormented by what they had been made to do: draw blood from the body that was their body. That was why, when they looked at the earth, they saw their faces as if they had been desecrated; they lived once again the terror of being condemned to die without a name in that earth. That was why, without being asked, they went about in groups to repair the roofs of the houses whose owners were too poor to do so; they fetched water for old ladies whose limbs had given up serving them, they chopped wood, pounded rice, laundered, always making sure they had left their weapons behind to show that their intentions were good.

'Dey only waiting for us to invite dem in so dat dey can replace our men,' said Jeanette Cromantine one afternoon, when she had seen a young soldier delivering venison to a young woman whose husband had fled with Thomas Bookerman.

Louisa Turner was waiting for news from Emmanuel Cromantine; since having her child, she had prayed that he would come to her so that he would see what a beautiful daughter they had. As she plaited Fatmatta-Emilia's hair, brought up her wind and fed her, she thought what it would be like if Emmanuel returned. They would set up a house together, where she would bake pumpkin pie as Jeanette Cromantin had taught her; she ached for what she believed would be the pleasure of waiting on him, darning his socks and feeling him inside her once again. She had never desired him so much as she did now, because when Fatmatta-Emilia nursed at her pendulous breasts, Louisa had such a terrible hunger for love that she would lie in bed and cradle her pillow. One morning, after she had put her laundry out to dry, she came and sat in the kitchen with a mug of coffee and started to cry. Jeanette Cromantine came silently into the kitchen and stood beside her. She put her arms round the younger woman, rocked her like a child and wiped away her tears with the back of her hand.

'Don't worry, my child,' she said, 'he missing you as much as you missing him, but ah knows he is safe and gon come back, because dis belly in which he slept, dese breasts dat gave him life, gon bring him back to us.'

'What if he doesn't come, Mother?'

'Den you don't believe in de power of dis land to call a man? Remember how it called Gustavius Martins back, how my own Sebastian was called back by his fader? Things have a way of happening, all in God's time.'

Jeanette Cromantine did not always worry about the soldiers in the streets; she felt that the time would come when the rebelliousness of the land to all things foreign would make their presence unwanted there. 'I may not live to see it,' she told herself, 'but one day de spirits of Rodrigo the Brazilian and of Gustavius Martins will see dat only de sons of those who came here to find peace gon be allowed to stay.' In time, the grief brought about by the absence of her son gave way to the plenitude of being a grandmother; light began to shine on her horizon once more with that child who was the beautiful note in the trombone of God so that what she had lost was given back to her, to feel once again how life renews itself through an unregulated rhythm over which she had no control.

She would have been content to wait for any sign from God that Emmanuel Cromantine was coming, but the peace that she had found in being a grandmother was marred by the realisation that Sebastian Cromantine had gone back to being a recluse.

Ever since coming home from the garrison, the recovery that Jeanette had prayed for in him had not materialised. Twice she had been to the grave of Fatmatta the Bird-Woman to talk to her, bringing her granddaughter with her.

'Life has not been too easy, Fatmatta, but who don't complain? We only here for a time, give names to dem things, have children and see dat we serve God's purpose. Bring Emmanuel back to me, but before dat, give to his fader, my husband, de joy he once had for living; there he is, Fatmatta, sitting on dat porch. Sometimes he talks to me, sometimes he is wrapped up in himself and ah feels as if he not there, if you know what ah mean; and God knows it a heavy burden to bear, what wid things de way dey are, but ah don't complain 'cause we don't know de workings of de master.'

Faith had always served Jeanette Cromantine, even at the bleakest of times, so she went back to believing that the spiders that had entrapped Sebastian Cromantine in their pernicious web of inertia would soon let him go. For his part, Sebastian Cromantine seemed not to be too worried about whether time was passing away, whether the women in the house were engaged in some kind of ritual over what to do about him, now that he seemed to them to have retreated into a pavilion where he had drawn all the curtains down and refused to come out.

The truth was that he was not really as caught up in a web of intrigues as his wife believed, now that he was reconciled to the events of the past months. Things were happening too fast for him; the death of his beloved friend, the birth of his first grandchild, and the trauma brought about by the realisation that following the period of being locked up in the garrison, he would never again be able to think of that place without seeing the face of Gustavius Martins.

When he thought of the dead man, he was reminded of all the things they had planned to do together; how they were going to send their children away so that they would come back one day and check the spread of the disease brought about by the behaviour of the small aristocratic class.

If anything hurt Sebastian more than the loss of his friend, of the feeling that he might never see his son again, it was the way the new class of aristocrats was beginning to influence the social life of Malagueta. With a confidence new since the time they had prevented their sons from fighting on the side of Thomas Bookerman, some of the wealthy citizens came out onto the street to shake the hands of the soldiers as if they were freeing them from a long occupation. Ignoring the anger of Jeanette Cromantine and Isatu Martins who, in the first flush of the defeat of their husbands, were looking for the children whose fathers had fled, some of the men who had hitherto shown a pronounced cowardice for the horror of war came out and threw their arms around the ragged soldiers. Their wives kissed the cheeks of the surprised soldiers, drew them to their breasts and wept. Whereas in the past they had insisted that all who entered their homes wiped their feet on the doormats, they took some of the soldiers home, who, in their mud-spattered boots, walked over their parquet floors and expensive rugs.

With the wild cries of animals of the forest, of men whose only instruments for measuring the good things in life had previously been the bounties that they had plundered, they ate for the first time in their lives the meals cooked by the wives of their admirers, drank port and smoked Portuguese cigars and did their host the honour of spilling some of the port on the rugs when the effect of the alcohol began to dance in their heads.

Captain Hammerstone soon found himself the object of unsolicited gifts; large baskets of the most succulent fruits were delivered at the gates of the garrison every Saturday by men who did not wait to be paid for their labours but went back to the kitchens of the senders of the gifts where they were allowed to scrape the bottom of the pots which contained the most delicious portion of the day's meal. Sometimes, a keg of the finest rum distilled in the brewery owned by Alphonso Garrison, then one of the richest men in town, was delivered to the captain with a note written in purple ink asking the captain to sample the best rum ever produced in Malagueta.

Alphonso Garrison had arrived ten years earlier with his wife Olivia and two daughters aged nine and eight, named Arabella and Matilda. No one knew where they had come from, but because they spoke some Portuguese and were obviously of mixed blood, it was rumoured that the family had escaped from Cape Verde Island where, as a result of bad speculation, Alphonso Garrison had lost the best part of a large plantation producing bananas, citrus fruits and coffee.

When he arrived with his family on a warm November day, they did not bear the signs of economic ravages, nor did they have a place in which to stay. With his wife Regina leaning on his arm, Alphonso Garrison walked down the gangway with the haughtiness of one who, if not born to riches, had nevertheless had some money all his life. He was forty-five, five feet eleven inches tall and, in the stupefying heat, wore a suit of worsted wool with a grey bowler hat on his head to protect his bald patch from the sun.

The first thing he did when they touched ground was to remove his fifty-pound gold watch from his pocket and look at the time. It was one o'clock in the afternoon and a large boom rang in the hill above the harbour, as it had done every day for six months to remind the workers that lunch was over. But Alphonso Garrison, who in spite of his family felt lonely at that time, concluded that the shot was a sign of welcome to all the passengers who had disembarked from the schooner that was bringing them to their new life in Malagueta. Such presumption was to serve him well. In a few years' time he was able to predict the best time to invest in a printing machine, the first one in town and with which, as the proprietor of the only newspaper in town, he printed all the news and gossip worth reading and thus made a fortune.

$$\diamond$$

Alphonso Garrison had always been fascinated with the idea that the only good thing in life was the ability to be able to laugh at oneself.

When he was a boy in school, he shocked his teacher when in answer to the question of what goes on in the minds of worshippers when they knelt at the altar to receive the sacraments, he had answered without hesitation:

'The fact that wine helps to loosen the tongues of men to understand God more, than all the words of the Holy Scriptures.'

For such sacrilege, he was expelled from the school run by the Nuns of the Order of Our Lady of Fatima from Portugal, and his father, an asthmatic horse trainer who had been widowed when the boy's mother had succumbed to malaria, had pulled a few strings and got his son apprenticed to the printer Francisco Gomez.

The first time that Alphonso Garrison went to the room of the compositors he was horrified at how dark the place was, permeated by the smell of a medieval cave. The men who worked there seemed to Alphonso like animals who never came out of their cages, because their clothes were stained with ink. They had the look of men for whom time did not matter; some were arranging cold type in compositing plates, while Alphonso saw that the two machinists working the old German typesetting machines had a certain air of being men of the world about them.

While much of what was printed had to do with social trivia like party invitations, the *Planters' Gazette*, the pamphlet that they printed at the machine told them much about what really went on in the town. Bent over their types, they were sworn to secrecy about what they printed, and because Francisco Gomez paid them only half of their salaries in cash and gave them supplies for the other, he knew he could rely on their confidence. However, this did not prevent them letting Alphonso Garrison into what was going on in the closed circle of the planters. Once they had taught him how the magical words were created, after they had shown him that it was possible to distort a daguerreotype by adding the wrong amount of ink to the film, they considered him one of them, a member of a secret cabal.

'Things are happening in those houses where you and we don't go, but we may as well be there, because we know that those bastards piss on themselves once they get drunk,' the oldest printer told him one evening.

Alphonso heard of other scandals on the island: white planters who looted aboriginal graves for gold necklaces, coins or propitiatory relics that had calmed the wrath of ancestors of a bygone age. They stole all that and more; while, in the sealed-off quarters of the rich, where the eucalyptus dwarfed the quintas, the servants reported on the disintegration of abandoned wives who hated the island as much as they hated their husbands, and were unable to sleep without the wine of atonement, plentifully available.

Alphonso Garrison soon realised that rather than being a banishment, the printing job was a blessing in disguise. Nights of sweating at the machine getting the right Roman letter in place, the scandalous details of the confessional adulteries of the planters as related by their wives, the jealousies in the letters that were printed in the *Planters' Gazette* all told Alphonso that life was a great farce, and that man was immune to the melancholy of his fellow man; greed was a potent drug which could only be flushed out by a violent period of drying-out. It had taken him a long time to come to this conclusion and more. Once he was settled in his job, he had time to reflect on the lapses in his education. A childhood spent with an itinerant father who went from plantation to plantation training horses had not prepared him for anything better than the rudimentary understanding of history. To remedy the situation, he persuaded his father to order, through the shipping company, books on astrology, ancient Chinese mysticism, the writings of Copernicus and others.

And he determinedly explored the history of his island. This was not the place of hurricanes that made men afraid of sharks in the tidal onslaught of the sea; nor the refuge of bloodsucking bats that were the legends created by bandits, of man-eating cannibals who wore human teeth in their noses; men cunning as cobra, who could not be trusted, who were as unclean as the devil; that is if the devil had not vanished on the day God created the island. Cape Verde was a treasure hunt; a woman whose legend lighted up the ships on the high seas when men had set out to plunder her; poets wrote about her in former times; languages had been born. Those poems, in hendecasyllabic verse, had kept her sons at home, made her daughters proud. Her earth had a prodigiousness of gifts, ripe for the picking. As was to be expected, when men not gifted with the reverence of poets, men with the arms of an octopus, heard about her they surrounded Cape Verde, set about her like a bunch of arachnids until they had woven a tight web around her.

Alphonso Garrison was born two hundred and seventy-five years after a mad landscape gardener had transformd the island into a gloss of neatly tonsured coffee and cocoa plantations, heavily guarded quintas, adobe houses prey to the rain and wind, horse-riding farmers and diseases, churches and a cemetery – all reminders of the incestuous relationship between man and earth. Through men like Pedro Samora,

266

the old crippled binder, he came to understand how the islanders had put up with the infractions by the invading planters. Suffering had come in various shades to the native islanders: men who watched helpless while their daughters became the playthings of the rich; men, old enough to be their grandfathers, who worked as peons for boys. There was a distinct quality about their suffering. They bore part of it by losing themselves in the orgiastic worship of a native religion that promised redemption from all damnations in this and other worlds. Music was a narcotic with which they tried to forget the pleurisy brought about by the loss of their manhood. When they could not withstand the needles of their pain, they sometimes took it out on their wives; violence to loved ones was the ultimate release of grief.

Alphonso Garrison observed it all. Caught in the web of conflicting emotions, he sank into the delusion of believing he could care for one, while hating the other whose lifestyle he secretly emulated. When he was not busy at the printing shop, he continued to read and to dream of better times ahead. But deep inside, he was incapable of such duplicity, and one day when he could no longer reconcile the social demons that made it impossible for him to decide whether God was on the side of the planters or was only waiting for time to liberate the peasants, he stood in front of his bedroom mirror, took one look at himself and spoke the lacerating words:

'Coward!' he said. 'That is what you are, like all those bastards in the quintas breeding in their own shit.'

But months later, when he thought he had completely exorcised the demons from his sleep and had persuaded himself to throw in his lot with the peasants by writing a play to satirise the lives of the aristocracy, an unexpected development took place that was to change his life for ever. Much later, when he was a prosperous man, buying up property in Malagueta, watching his money grow, he would remark that 'fate took me by the hand that day, turned my face around and I never looked back'.

On that fateful day, he walked from the first flickering fires of the inferno that was to engulf the island rising behind him. If they tormented him, Alphonso Garrison did not give any signs of being alarmed. Personal disasters took a long time coming to him. He was an eel who knew how to slide through the mud of change, a cat licking his body clean of the slime of upheaval until his good luck ran out.

He had not been to the printing shop for days, the victim of a cold he had tried unsuccessfully to cure by inhaling the vapour from boiled eucalyptus leaves. But a sense of duty had forced him out of bed that morning. He had just pushed the black heavy iron-wrought gates with the two brass lionheads and walked into the compound, when he saw a young woman with a warm smile coming out of the shop. Confused, taken by surprise and irritated by his inability to return her direct look, Alphonso Garrison murmured a hasty good morning, walked past her and hurried inside the shop.

She was Regina, the only child of Francisco Gomez. In keeping with social conventions, she seldom went to the shop. 'The crudity of those men is not fit for the ears of a young woman,' the Reverend Mother of her convent had warned, but Francisco Gomez was sick, and, at the risk of annoying the Reverend Mother, had sent the young woman to his shop to oversee the day's work. Shy, friendly and good-natured, Regina Gomez was receiving instructions in etiquette and the 'proper role of women in an alien society' from the sister of the bishop who had turned down many offers of marriage in Portugal to come and keep house for her brother, because 'what would the poor man do with all those savages here and the drunken lot from my own country who do not even know their catechism?'

When she was twelve, Regina Gomez lost her mother, a mulatress who had drowned herself because, so the story went, she wanted to punish her husband for not protecting her from the ridicule of white women who throughout her marriage had taunted her for 'enticing the good man with her disgraceful sensuality'. 'These half-castes are more pernicious than the dark ones, God help us. If we don't watch our sons they will soon have mongrels running around.' Francisco Gomez had loved his wife and had married her because after they first met she had transformed him from being a man obsessed with the idea of going round the world 'as my forebears had done' into a man prepared to look for 'my worth as a human being here'. Race had not mattered; she was the finest woman he had known, had made him laugh and weaned him away from inebriety during his early days on the island, when he had been a milquetoast afraid of rich landowners. Once she had restored his confidence, Francisco Gomez had earned enough money shipping animal hides to Portugal, bought the printing press and a beautiful house where, to the shock of his fellow Portuguese, he had installed his 'brown whore'.

If she had been unhappy in the last years of their marriage, Francisco Gomez had not been aware of it. He had ceased to regard her as his deity, his good luck charm, and if he turned a deaf ear to her female

268

tormentors it was because Francisco Gomez had considered them stupid dinosaurs, brainless harridans who would one day bite their own tongues. After her death, Francisco Gomez became a broken man. He lost all interest in the printing shop, shut himself up in the house and sent his daughter to be cared for by the nuns. Whereas in the past Francisco Gomez had always been careful about his appearance and had his suits made by the finest tailor in the island, the death of his wife turned the printer into a dour, sad man who would appear only in black and stand by his window. Things would have gone on like that for ever if the maid, fearing that he was going to die because he seldom touched the food that she served him, had not gone to the bishop's sister for assistance.

'You have got to come over, Donna Isabella,' she told the old virgin. 'Don Francisco wants to die for the glory of death.'

Three men accompanied Donna Isabella to the house of Francisco Gomez. When all entreaties to get him to open his door failed, the old spinster ordered them to break it down.

'If I have to go to prison for this,' she said, 'I might as well go to prison for saving a soul for the Virgin Mary.'

They found Francisco Gomez sitting in bed, holding a daguerreotype of his wife. His hair that had always been parted in the middle had not been combed for days, and he had about him the smell of death. Not even her frequent attendance at the extreme unction of the poorest peasants on the island had prepared Donna Isabella for the suffocating air in the room.

'Deo gratias, you are alive, Francisco,' she said, 'because you are turning death into an absurdity.'

Then, without waiting for Francisco Gomez to reply, she ordered the men to open the windows so that 'the angel of the Lord would come and touch this sinful man with her goodness'.

'Look at what you have done to yourself, Francisco. So your wife died and you want to die with her, because you have no faith, like a primitive, like those people out there in the fields, until we brought the word of God to them. To live without faith is bad, but to die without faith is a sin, Francisco!'

It took the spinster two weeks to get Francisco Gomez to look at the sky again. When he did, he saw that the clouds were still there, that the egrets were eating the ticks off the backs of the cows; he smelled the fresh aroma of coffee from the mills and heard the moaning copulations of the cats on the branch of a tree. The harmattan from the big country across

269

the ocean had turned the island into a dusty plateau, mushroomed its gardens with the voracity of crickets. Yet there were people out there struggling to live, getting married, having children and fighting death. As he was mulling over these points, he saw a peasant riding a horse in a field. The horse took the man on a gallop, threw him down and he was killed instantly. Francisco Gomez saw the face of death and from the crucible of despair he leapt onto a new horse, to start living once again.

When Donna Isabella brought his daughter back to him, Francisco Gomez had only to look at the young woman standing in front of him to realise that he was the luckiest man alive. The result of the good deportment that the nuns had rigorously instilled in her was there. Unlike the other children of the planters and other businessmen in the island, she had developed a reserve which made her shyness a charming endowment. So she did not rush into the waiting arms of her father but stood there smiling, waiting for him to walk up to her and embrace her.

'My child, my child. May your mother's soul rest in peace, because as God is my witness I shall be the best father in the world.'

He was as good as his word. He saw to it that no expense was spared to fill his house with *objets d'art* so that when her friends came they would be seduced by the beauty of the bibelots. Worried that he would have to pay later for his past neglect he ordered an astrological chart from Portugal and had a gypsy read her fortune.

'Don't worry too much, Don Francisco,' he told him. 'That child is going to have a house in a country with enough gold to make an empress jealous.'

He was never more proud as when he came home from the printing shop to find her receiving her pianoforte lesson from the German music teacher, while one of the nuns of the convent sat and kept a discreet eye on them. On a trip to Portugal to buy some machinery, he brought the girl along so that, as he told her, she would see the castles that Queen Arabella had built with the gold that Pedro da Cinta had plundered during his fifteenth-century voyage to the primitive parts of the world. He showed her the murals in the cathedrals, the Gothic arches, the fountains in the plaza named after Henry the Navigator and the square where heretics had been condemned to death.

Before they boarded the steamer back for Cape Verde, Francisco Gomez insisted on filling two trunks with the gowns that the seamstresses in Lisbon copied from the fashion then in vogue at the court. The two turbanned Moroccan eunuchs who carried the trunks on their heads to the port did not know that they were taking part in a father's preparation begun several years earlier, when Francisco Gomez decided he was going to make his daughter fit for a king.

They came back to an island in uproar. A long simmering discontent among the black coffee growers had erupted into open revolt, with the workers insisting that they were human beings. With an almost unheard-of audacity, they demanded that they be allowed to spend more time with their wives and tend their own little plots. While the revolt was on, a mysterious letter, which the bishop insisted must have been written by a sympathetic Portuguese, appeared in his office, warning that if he did not preach a sermon telling the planters to stop the deflowering of the peasants' daughters there would be trouble in the island.

It was this threat which had been carried out on the day Francisco Gomez and his daughter returned to the island. Going home late one evening, a group of black workers had been attracted by the rustling noise among the sugarcane. Coming closer to them, they saw the son of the leading coffee farmer raping a local girl who was frantically trying to resist. The rage that had built up in the hearts of the men found expression that evening. They pulled the now frightened boy off the girl, allowed her to go and then set upon the boy. With one brutal blow from his machete, one of the men made him useless for any woman and his body was not discovered until a few days later when some killer-dogs chased off the descending vultures in a swamp.

Francisco Gomez was revolted by the orgy of killings that followed the discovery of the body. Although he shared some of the same notions of superiority held by the planters, his life had been too deeply marked by sorrow for him to engage in any organised act of revenge. As the planters went from house to house at night and dragged the blacks out to murder them, as the black women were raped and their daughters raped in turn, Francisco Gomez stayed in his house, convinced that no one was ever going to be safe on the island after these events. One evening, when the killings had abated, he tried to walk from his house to mass at the cathedral. He barely escaped with his life as a dark hooded figure with a machete tried to cut him down.

'Look at what we have got ourselves into,' he told his daughter, 'all because some men have no control over their desires.'

He became afraid to go out at night and banned Regina from going to the door to let anyone into the house. When Easter came, the procession of saints, the fruit carnival, the triumphant march of the flagellants into the city were banned by the bishop that year. The blacks in their own part of town remained a silent, deadly and unpredictable lot to the planters. Their unpredictability was like a silent god ruling the island at night. No one knew when he would strike, what his arsenals were, but his name was feared enough so that even the most bold of planters began to think of how to appease him, without daring to. They had always taken the absence of such a god for granted, ridiculed his priestesses, but now that blood was running in the lagoons of their memories, now that each coffee plantation harboured a nest of potential killers, they believed there might be such a black god living among the peasants who would one day demand retribution for a crime that could be absolved only by the blood of men.

Gradually, life resumed its normal pace on the island; but the normality was conditioned by an awareness on the part of the white and mulatto planters that things would never be the same again. The easy-going attitude of the house cooks, the docility of the gardeners who had worked for many years in the houses of even the most well-meaning planters, faded away. Henceforth, the cooks came only when they felt like it. They served meals as if it was an act of revenge, sometimes spilling the soup on the fine lace tablecloths. Time had plastered them with a new courage that was magical to behold; in their eyes when they spoke to the sexually starved wives of the planters was a defiance and a probing into secrets which not only frightened the women but dilated their eyes – so that, once they had shut themselves up in their bedrooms, away from their servants, they had to dust with powder the provocative mote of lust in them.

Alphonso Garrison did not have to concern himself about a provocatively lustful wife. He lived in dreams about other people's wives, crisscrossed in his heart with the secretive desire to have one of the peasant girls, whose languorous laugh sometimes rang through the shop floor. But being an honest man, he came to the conclusion that the only reason he wanted a peasant woman was because he lacked the courage to do what he really dreamed of most of all: seduce one of the daughters of Pedro Samora. He could live with the seed of his lust which did not publicly show, but the spider of his cowardice caught him in a web of self-doubt. 'What manner of man am I,' he asked himself, 'if I cannot get my genitals in the right place?'

Lately, he had not given much thought to the play that had laid eggs in his imagination. He became less concerned with the aristocratic pretensions that had so offended his past sensitivity and they were relegated to the dunghill of memory. Now, he saw himself as a witness to a new drama, more real than the puppets that had masqueraded in his dreams. Lacerated by the wounded pride of his own self-doubt, he willed his body to resist all desire, his night to be made of the fiery incantations of dreams alive in the shabbiness of quarters fuelled with the oil of cowdung.

That way, he was able to effect a reversal of what was real, what was permissive, before the floodgates of revolt were open and some people – himself? – were drowned in the torrential rewriting of history. The more Alphonso Garrison looked at the landscape the more he saw how a wayward insistence on giving out charity to those from whom all had been taken was fermenting a seismic unheaving in the depths of the ocean powerful enough to wipe clean the slate.

Francisco Gomez had his own slate-cleaning to do. Around this time, he began to come less and less to the printing shop. Sometimes he came only for a few hours, did his books and drank cup after cup of black coffee from a flask encased in a goatskin bag. Much to the surprise of his friend the bishop, who had more than a passing interest in scurrilous details, he lost his appetite for the gossip of his rich parishioners and stopped publishing the *Planters' Gazette* weekly.

'Fornication is all right,' he told the amazed typesetters, 'but if you cannot let your readers know who the parties are, you might as well draw a picture of two dogs and sell it.'

At the same time that he turned his back on 'all that bedroom garbage', Francisco Gomez began to take a keen interest in the lives of his workers and their families 'as if he is going to put us in his will', said Pedro Samora. He asked questions about things that had never interested him in the past: bilharzia, teething problems, malaria and whooping cough; vigorously, for an old man, he personally supervised the draining of the gutters and stagnant pools in front of the workers' quarters and made generous donations of medical supplies from his chest.

'We cannot have larvae breeding among children,' he told his amused workers. For Christmas that year he had one of his pigs killed, got his cook to stuff it with sliced pineapples and sent it over to the head binder with instructions for 'you all to be with Christ at this time of the year'.

Those were days of the most unexpected changes on the island. Word leaked out from the quarrelsome dining rooms of the rich that mothers were urging their sons to own up to the paternity of children they had fathered on peasant girls.

'Behave like men,' they told their wayward sons, 'and save us from

273

their wrath, although of course you don't have to marry their mothers, God forbid.'

After many years of hard work, Alphonso Garrison had been rewarded with the job of supervisor of the printing press. His natural ability for leadership, the photographic details about faraway places gained from reading the books that his father had ordered, the refinement of his language in spite of his plebeian background, had been noted over the years by Francisco Gomez. Long before his employer launched his programme to give his workers a better deal for their work, Alphonso Garrison had been able to contain the hydra of jealousy over his mercurial rise by his generosity and by his insistence on being called by his first name by the old workers who were now his subordinates.

'We are all God's children,' he told the men. His father had died soon after Alphonso was promoted, satisfied that the blasphemous episode of his son's childhood had been erased from the bishop's ledger.

'God has a way of retrieving lost sheep,' said the bishop when he was administering extreme unction to Henrico Garrison. So the old man died in peace.

Alphonso Garrison was thinking about the changes taking place on the island as he walked to the printing shop that morning, when he saw the beautiful daughter of Francisco Gomez coming towards him. It was four o'clock in the afternoon, and removing his straw hat from his head, he made his mumbled greetings and walked into the plant. He went straight to Pedro Samora who always kept a demijohn of rum under a pile of paper. Without waiting for permission, he took a swig of the drink and went out for a walk. As the fire of the alcohol began to rise in his blood, he sat under the shade of a baobab tree to rest. There, while two monkeys cracked nuts overhead, he fell asleep with a great tension between his legs.

Ten years later, as Alphonso Garrison and his family were about to board the schooner for Malagueta, he fixed his eyes on the evergreen mountains with their volcanic legends; he saw the smoke of vanished illusions, the enfant terrible of nature that had questioned the rights of men like himself to endow that island with their progeny and theirs too. As a flock of seagulls flew overhead, Alphonso Garrison knew he would never come back. From the smouldering lava of sadness, he saw the house where they had lived, with the now ethereal aroma of its coffee trees. He paused one more time to remember the last dog-cries of the animals in the pits where their blood had washed the accumulated diktat of the despised oligarchy. An enigma as confusing as the origins of dreams had been answered that night when the peasants revolted, and coming towards his house again, he saw the hundred torches of the rioters, illumined like the eyes of enraged leopards, as they were hurled at the houses. His inherent good luck saved the family. He was a lucky man, and the island had not been too bad after all, he concluded.

Paradise had been that island for a while. As the big, bald-headed dockers loaded the bananas bound for Portugal in the chaotic afternoon of the other passengers, who, unlike him, were weeping for their lost idyll, Alphonso Garrison brought back from the cameo of happier times the navarin of contentment. Much to his surprise, he had not been thrown out by Francisco Gomez when he had the temerity to ask for the hand of his daughter. The vertigo of events on the island had erased the father's dream of a king as a suitor. The pishogue of the peasants had vanquished him in the sands of oblivion, so Francisco Gomez had been happy to give Regina away to Alphonso, and to add the printing shop as part of his benevolence.

'My child,' he said to the young man after giving them his blessing, 'you have the face of a poet, but I hope you are going to make me a grandfather before all this garbage buries us alive.'

On the night of his wedding, Alphonso Garrison sat waiting for his wife to come to the four-poster in the large bedroom that Francisco had vacated for them. He watched as she removed the pins and carnation flowers from her hair; the black-gold hair, let loose on the nightgown with the fine jabot lace, the memory of his lonely bachelorhood, helped to increase his fervour. He was not a man lacking in experience as he had once found pleasure in the bed of a buxom woman whose sailor-husband had been away for three years. 'You don't know how hungry I am,' the woman had confessed.

Alphonso Garrison raised the mosquito net to let his wife in. She kissed him as if she had been instructed by women other than the veritable matrons in the art of pleasing men; she touched him and felt his hardness, making him groan. When she finally guided him into her, Alphonso Garrison was surprised that she surrendered herself to him without the modesty he had imagined in a woman raised by the bishop's sister, but with a passion that was intense; without coquetry, as if she had also been waiting for this moment all her life.

The memory of the sailor's wife was forgotten in the ornate language that the woman he had married was beginning to create under him. In spite of its being her first rite of spring, she buckled under him like a cow, intent on draining him, and Alphonso for a moment began to wonder whether he was the first for his wife. He was still wrapped up in his thoughts when a firecracker lit by one of the late revellers at his own wedding exploded with a large bang that so jolted him that he lost his erection.

'It's all right, Alphonso,' said his understanding wife. 'The matrons told me such things happen to husbands on their wedding nights, because although they are offered virgins, men can only let go when they are making love to whores.'

Things went more smoothly the next night. Once again, he waited patiently for his wife to come to bed. Convinced by the evidence of the red spot on the sheet that he had been the first, Alphonso Garrison tried to erase the shame of the first night with a fury that surprised even himself. He made love to her as if her long bridal body had been transformed into all the women he had desired but had never had. He turned her into the maiden of the sea who should have come when he had first been apprenticed at the printing shop: an odalisque in the desert harem of his dreams. He made her kiss the hands that before their wedding she would not have looked at with their grease; the lips that had longed for a woman of her class as he had desired the wives in the cotillions. But the more he was brutal, the more passionate she became. She came repeatedly with her wild cries of an alley cat. They were so exhausted the next morning that, to the consternation of the bishop who had hoped to pray for the newly wedded couple at mass, they were fast alseep while the bells chimed away.

When their first daughter Arabella was born, Alphonso Garrison remembered the grandfatherly tenderness that his father-in-law had shown to the child. While his wife busied herself with being a mother, Alphonso Garrison plunged himself into running the printing shop. Trying to convince the workers that things were going to be different under his leadership, he increased their wages and doubled their monthly ration of sugar and milk. As he became a prosperous man, they prospered too, and Alphonso Garrison's social standing in the community increased. Whereas in the past he had merely looked on from the outside at the close circles of the landed gentry, his marriage to Regina brought him into close contact with associates of his father-in-law. In the succeeding years, he found himself openly courted by leaders of the community, invited to give donations to charity, made his first trips to Portugal and became the father of a second daughter.

But the prevailing atmosphere on the island, far from being the peace that Alphonso Garrison had hoped for, was one of infrequent confrontation between the peasants and the landlords. Once in a while, workers on coffee plantations in isolated parts of the island would walk off the job or demand more money for their labour. The unpredictable world of the peasants sometimes exploded when they stayed up all night, beating their drums and reciting ancient verses which, to those landowners who understood their language, sounded like a call to spirits prowling the land to bring down a plague.

One night, as she lay next to her husband, Regina was so worried by the incessant sound of the drumming that she confided her fear to her husband.

'I am afraid they are going to kill all of us, Alphonso,' she said.

'Don't worry,' he said. 'This place is finished, but I have been making other plans for us.'

He had indeed. Unknown to his wife, Alphonso Garrison had been lending money to less prosperous members of the artistocracy. Long before marrying Regina, he had become disillusioned with the idea of living for ever on the island. Brought into the confidence of his father-in-law, he knew which family was being ravaged by alcoholism; the hysteria that had taken hold of some, so that they had abandoned all talk of establishing dynasties on the island and were selling their properties in order that they would be out. The shipping of bananas to Portugal was being sabotaged by the workers who burned the plantations at night, and although the monarchy in Lisbon had promised to send soldiers to guard their properties, he wanted a much calmer place in which to raise his daughters.

The two daughters had each taken after one parent. Arabella had the dark, Mediterranean look of her father and the long legs of a racehorse; she showed an aptitude for the mandolin, and was quiet like her mother, while Matilda, the younger girl, had inherited the fair skin of her mother, had the haughty countenance of a Persian cat and regarded the world with a pair of green eyes that made her seem cruel. She seemed headed for a difficult chubbiness, was cruel to the family dog and servants, and kept her chamberpot unemptied under her bed for days. Asked by her mother why she did not empty her own chamberpot, she replied that no man would respect a girl who sank so low as to smell her own urine. The only object on which she was seen to devote her love was the family parrot which could whistle Italian arias.

Over the course of several years, Alphonso Garrison continued to lend money on a twenty-five per cent commission to men who had not wanted to get out of the island. Sometimes he got his money back, but, offered payment in silverware, porcelain pieces and precious minerals, Alphonso Garrison soon accumulated a large collection of treasures hidden in the basement of his office. Not only was he a rich man, but his position gave him control over the transfer of money from one impoverished grower to another. While he was amassing money, he tried to appease his conscience and to buy time from the oubliette of the revolt that he felt was coming, by keeping in his service a servant whom he paid for information about the goings-on in the peasants' quarters.

However, a reference by Francisco Gomez in the delirium of old age to a place not too far away from the island, where his uncle had gone to live 'like a native', was what convinced Alphonso Garrison that it was time to leave the island for ever. Ever since turning over the printing shop to the young people, Francisco Gomez had begun to think of his dead wife; he blamed himself for her death and took to visiting her grave once every week to put fresh flowers there.

The feeling that he was about to die brought about a terrible lucidity in him. One evening, after the family had eaten dinner, he brought out his wife's jewellery box and called his two granddaughters.

'Come, my grandchildren,' he said. 'Your grandmother was a saint, and I did not know it when she was alive, because men are fools. I hope where she has gone she has forgiven me for keeping her all her life on this island, when all she ever wanted was to go to the country where my uncle had died.'

He spoke of a man who had turned his back on the 'rigid cloth of religion in Portugal', and gone out to that country where he had lived with a native woman.

'He never went back, because life had no meaning for him in a world where only the old, the muledrivers and the dead remain.'

Like the last night of a long love affair he remembered the insolence of his own youth, when he came out to the island, intent on making a fortune and going back to buy a vineyard.

'But providence was too good to us. Labour was cheap; we had the gun which the bandit, Pedro da Cinta, had introduced here, and for a while, we could keep the natives at bay. But things change; life renews itself on the debt that we owe it, and we are never prepared for the atonement of our misdeeds. But you, Alphonso, you are not really like us; you do not condone exploitation, just like my wife. If I had listened to her, maybe we would have been saved; our souls would be less constricted by greed, more confident of salvation.'

He had never been to the land where the uncle had been but 'once, through the kindness of a schooner captain, we had word about him from that place whose name is Malagueta'.

'Forget about this place, Alphonso. Take your family and your money and go and make a life there. I ask only that you let me die here and lie next to my wife.'

Francisco Gomez died planting a new tree in the garden; he had exhausted himself lately going back to the printing shop to say goodbye to the men who had helped him prosper. But when his heart gave way, he had the presence of mind not to fall flat on his face, but to lie on his side facing his house as if, in death, he wanted to have a last look at it. Two months later, when the peasants revolted, Alphonso Garrison had been prepared; he hid with his family, their trunks, one thousand pieces of gold and the Italian aria parrot inside a cave for two days until some loyal servants told him it was safe to leave. Under the protection of armed sailors who arrived on the schooner the next day, he sailed for Malagueta on a violently rainy day.

12   Eyes of the Testicles

Captain Hammerstone's long-awaited ships arrived suddenly one afternoon when the people of Malagueta had begun to adjust themselves to the troops being there, as long as the captain did not try to interfere with their lives. Before that afternoon, he was always accompanied by a dozen of his well-armed men when he went out, and, while visiting the houses of Alphonso Garrison and other recent arrivals who welcomed him, he stayed away from the homes of the oldest members of the town. Once, he tried to enter the Yellow House. He had been attracted to it by the arrival of a group of women from the surrounding country, who restored it to its former charm but who, instead of the dedication to the aesthetic reproduction of passeriformes on paper that had so obsessed the previous girls, had other ideas. They turned the house into a coffee shop during the day, and at night you had only to catch a glimpse of the figures behind the drawn curtains and listen to the enchanting music of a boy who played the flute to know that the house was a ship of pleasure in the untranquil seas of Malagueta. Sailors suffering from beri-beri and seasickness came there to recuperate, and to be assured that they were still men. The steps on which Emmanuel Cromantine had lingered on his way to the first tryst with Louisa creaked under the feet of more resolute men, who were never allowed to stay the night, but who came back with grateful gifts for the women.

On the evening that Captain Hammerstone decided to visit the Yellow House, he made a decision not to wear his sailor's uniform and he was accompanied by only four of his guards. The last thing he wanted was to antagonise the women of the town, after the last rebellion. But when he tried to enter the house, he found his way blocked by a young dark woman with angry, flaming eyes.

'Go away, Captain,' she told him, 'we are only waiting for Phyllis and Thomas Bookerman to come before we kill you.'

Gently but firmly he pushed the woman aside and, beckoning to his men, went up the steps of the house. After he had gone through the door that opened into the parlour, Captain Hammerstone came face to face with eleven women of varying ages and colours. Together with the one who tried to block his entrance, they were the twelve women whom the sailors had named the twelve whores long after the last Virgin had died. But they were neither whores nor bound to any man on earth, because something greater than pleasing men had brought them to that house. And in their lives was a deeper religiosity than those of the Virgins, because they expected neither reward nor gratification. The men who came and went would have been shocked to know that money had not driven those women to offer their bodies, because the most beautiful among them would have made some men lucky husbands and, individually, their intelligence was of a brilliance that shone like a rare diamond.

After the departure of the previous tenants of the Yellow House with the ragtime army of Thomas Bookerman, the twelve young women had come together, intent on a sole purpose. They painted the house a deeper yellow, cleared the struggling bushes around the building and refurbished the mattresses with cotton. Once they had achieved a measure of comfort in the simplicity of their surroundings, they made a secret pact: they swore they would sleep with the men who came with news of Thomas Bookerman and who, in turn, would take messages back to him. While Alphonso Garrison and other prominent citizens wined and dined the captain in their homes, the twelve women gave joy on a promissory note that they hoped to collect when Phyllis returned to make her kites. They never allowed the men of Malagueta to enter the house, and so, when the Captain entered their parlour, he was violating the most selfless resolve that would have impressed the Virgins, if only they had known about it.

As if they were one body, the women walked out of the parlour and went out of the house, leaving the captain and his men standing there. One of his troops tried to stop the women from leaving, but the captain restrained him.

'Let them go,' he said. 'As they say around here, you cannot frighten a pregnant woman with a dead prick. Those women are pregnant with an idea you won't understand.'

He respected them. For that reason, although he searched the rooms of the women after they had gone, Captain Hammerstone felt like an intruder who was being watched by myriad eyes. The cheap silk, the counterfeit Turkish jewellery, the dead roses of the sailors who had been the only men to enter the room before him, were not objects collected to enchant but to make their solitude bearable. Captain Hammerstone felt that the solitude in those rooms, which gave so much satisfaction to men who came from the solitude of the sea into the arms of those women, was something very precious to those women. Nothing was perverse about what those women did, because there was love in that house. Being an intelligent man, he was quick to see that the Yellow House had been transformed into something other than what he had thought. This was no whorehouse, but a Parthenon where he saw the delicate hands that had gone into refurbishing it, and he felt awed and small in the knowledge that if he came again, the women would laugh in his face because he was not the lettuce they wanted for their salad.

He went home that evening feeling lethargic; for the first time in years, Captain Hammerstone experienced the first signs of a neuralgia which he feared more than a defeat at sea or on land. He had been a man of an iron constitution, both in the boundless zest with which he pursued the war and in the past indulgence of the rites of his karma. He felt his head swirling, like a great turkey, and he dreamed: he was dancing alone in a large ballroom whose wall had been lined with pictures of the heroes of his country; the conflagrations wrought by the piratical ambitions that had silenced natives who inveighed against the destruction of their islands. Captain Hammerstone was dancing as he had never danced before; his partner was a tall, graceful woman who resisted coming into his arms. He tried to trick her, promising he would go to the bottom of any ocean to retrieve sunken treasures if only she would stop avoiding him. When eventually she came into his arms she touched him at the back of his neck and Captain Hammerstone felt a lacerating, scorching heat run down his spine; he removed her hand and saw that it was spattered with his blood. He woke up violently, and, for the first time in his life, he saw the face of death.

The next morning, shivering like a wet dog in spite of the burning coalpot in front of him, he thought he heard the sirens of death; but it was the music that he had been waiting for throughout his mad attempt to subdue Malagueta. Turning towards the sea, he saw, dotting that mighty expanse like the floating corpses of baby whales, the ships with the familiar ensign of the British that he had never given up on.

$$\diamond$$

Isatu Martins brought the large mirrors back into the living room, but she had become less obsessed with the idea of looking at them every morning to see how she had changed, what her body was saying to her, alone as she had been since Gustavius had been buried. She had not been prepared for life alone, among so much that was stamped with his memory, his passion an icon she kept close to her heart. She had not been prepared for this widowhood, this quittance which had discharged her from the duty to embroider the picots of an everlasting marriage.

But after the first shock of being alone had passed, Isatu Martins turned her attention to Garbage; she became terribly possessive of him, talked to Richard Farmer about his progress in school, and worried when he came home late from catching crabs on the beach. One thing she did not do: she did not enrol him in the Sunday school started by the Virgins.

'God I can give him at home, but they will turn him against his own mother if I let him go there, because I don't go to church,' she said in answer to Jeanette Cromantine who had wondered why Garbage was not receiving religious instruction.

She did not have to worry. Garbage had been going to the beach alone, among the scavenger birds which came there to dry their wings and to feed on the minnows that sometimes slipped through the nets of the fishermen. Born with a solitary countenance, toughened by the handicap of growing without a father, he viewed the world with the solemn countenance of being a man without passing through the joys of childhood. The father whom he had not really known had seen to it that this son would lack for nothing as far as material things were concerned, but it was the lack of fear in Garbage that worried his mother as she watched him come and go. No grass would have grown where he walked, because his steps were planted with the thud of a giant. His trips to the sea, his unexplained visits to the cemetery where he read sitting under a large frangipani tree, shocked his mother, but she refrained from questioning him. Once, before Jeanette talked her out of it, Isatu insisted on Garbage going with her every time she had to attend a wedding, a wake or the baptism of a new child in the neighbourhood.

'Stop treating him like the man who went away, and think of him as the one who is growing up,' the older woman told her friend.

He developed the stealth of a mongoose to avoid danger. While the mosaic of childhood of the other children of his age showed the scars of broken tissues, the boots that were worn out before their feet had grown to full length, he never had anything as serious as a fall. Once, he almost stepped on a puff-adder, but some sixth sense guided his foot away and the snake remained immobile. The tales of leprechauns that had delighted the children before him and that kept his classmates awake did not arouse any interest in him. Rather, he seemed to prefer the risk involved in exploring some sections of the town where the soldiers paraded every day. He avoided coming up any street when the soldiers were relaxing in the lazy afternoons of the occupation. To divert attention from what was on his mind, he would stop and watch younger children play hopscotch, hop, skip and jump; but no sooner were the sailors engrossed in whistling at the women who went by than Garbage would continue his solitary walk throughout the streets.

In time, he discovered some of the landmarks that he had heard his mother and Jeanette Cromantine talking about. After weeks of dodging the soldiers, and jumping over fences to avoid detection, he came to the charred remains of the large building where the Arcadian mulattos from Louisiana had been the first to introduce the cakewalk, the tap dance, the jive and the maringa. He located the house, much talked about, with the overgrown garden, with the large banyan tree in the back, where hundreds of dipsomaniacal blood-sucking bats made their home. No one had lived in that house in living memory because many years before the first war between Thomas Bookerman and the captain, someone had seen a horse-faced albino dragging a beautiful young woman there, from where she never came back.

For a boy his age, his passion for seeking out what had gone on before his time became an obsession. He tried to get his mother to talk about the one-eyed man whom one of his teachers had mentioned in school, who was said to have gone to live on an island but sent back messages about how he was planning a final assault against Captain Hammerstone and his men. Isatu Martins filled in the details of the history of the town in the yearning mornings when her son sat having breakfast with her. But just as in the first days of her widowhood she had worried about him, when the first signs of introspection had begun to show, she found it hard to hide her concern over the voraciousness of his probing.

'Why have you been going around, sneaking into places, looking for trouble?' she asked him one morning.

'Because something is going to happen soon and I want to see the old town before it disappears for ever,' he replied.

One listless afternoon, when he had been wandering through the crowded streets, he stopped at a bazaar to listen to calypso music and drink some ginger beer. For the first time in his life, he saw an animal show: there were dogs, whose owners had dressed them up to look like dolls, dancing, while six soldiers sang English madrigals; two enormous and very docile gorillas that had resisted all teasing suddenly came alive, started throwing missiles at each other, then suddenly embraced and went back to sleep. When he had grown tired of seeing real animals, Garbage was attracted by the puppets at one end of the fairground, that had attracted a large crowd. Arriving there, he saw two women manipulating the wires that worked two figures made up to look like fighters in different uniforms. One was a puppet of a big, black man, with a patch over one eye, a knife stuck in his sailor's belt and with a red headgear tied round his head. The other was of a white sea captain, with a sailor's cap and tunic, holding a gun. When the women started to work the simple mechanism of the puppets, the crowd went wild as the bald-headed soldier started kicking the sailor. They tossed coins on the stage, and yelled: kill him, kill him, kill him, as if the carnival was real. Suddenly, a group of soldiers from the garrison arrived and ordered the women to stop the show. They had barely given out their orders when the crowd fell upon them. The hot sultry heat of their anger exploded in the most violent confrontation that Malagueta had seen since that evening when Isatu Martins had led the women in an attack against the garrison.

Caught off balance, surrounded by the battering rams of pent-up emotions, the soldiers barely had time to reach for their guns before they were set upon by an enraged crowd. Only the timely arrival of more soldiers saved them from being lynched. One of the soldiers fired his rifle into the air and told the crowd to go home, because the carnival was over. Hurling curses at the soldiers, the crowd broke up and started making for their homes, but not before someone had released a leopard from his cage, which made straight for one of the soldiers and attacked him before it was brought down by another soldier.

Garbage came out of the field with the crowd. But instead of going home where Isatu Martins was waiting for him, so that she could begin the evening meal, he walked past the church where, because of the confusion brought about by the invasion, many of the old families had lost their right to the front pews, and had been replaced by the new arrivals like Alphonso Garrison and his family. The simplicity of the service in the church had been replaced by the high drama of exaggerated communion so that instead of the worshippers coming in as they liked, to receive the body and the blood of Christ, they now had to write letters to the vicar, bring their special communion wines, and appear in their best Sunday suits and frocks to demonstrate their importance. The old Virgins had died, and the memory of their devotion to ecclesiastical if somewhat rigid discipline went with them to their graves. Now, the going to church was a social occasion, and for that reason, Garbage had never been inside the church because Isatu Martins would have nothing to do with such a hideous mockery that worshipping had become.

He stopped in front of the church, sat down and looked at the sea. The dry, dusty winds of the harmattan whistled in the air; rain had not come to Malagueta much that year; lacerating winds scorched the earth where the fowls and the dogs scratched, dug and pecked for worms and bones; flocks of hawks flew overhead, spotted the straggly hens which they carried away into the trees where they feasted and fed their young. The winds bore into his bones and he suddenly remembered how warm it was in the house where Isatu would have a fire going, the warm ginger tea ready with his meals.

He was just about to go back to the house when he saw the most startling sight that he had ever seen in his life. There, travelling like an outstretched python with a thousand search lights on their heads, was the longest column of black ants that he had ever seen. They were little soldiers of war, with a deadly sting which made insects prey to their voracious appetite. Garbage was so fascinated by their orderliness, by the way the outside troopers kept the others in line, and their habit of leaving nothing untouched as they went along, that he did not see the unruly soldier that had got out of line. Only when he felt the terrible sting between his toes was he brought back to reality from the planet of fascination where the disciplined march of the ants had taken him.

He bit his lips, suppressed the pain and then decided to follow the trail of the ants. He inched his way through a vast area of wooded land that had not been purchased when the town had been planned, for the ants preferred the cool provided by the branches of the trees to being in the open space. He watched them dig tunnels under the fences that separated the neat row of houses along January Street and saw them make nonsense of those barricades which the houseowners had put up to give meaning to their ownership of the land, and he watched the column as it avoided the large stones that dotted here and there out of the ground.

Occasionally, the entire column would disappear under the ground, but would reappear through the labyrinth of its own genius, break up, regroup and continue its march. Garbage was so taken up by the parade that he forgot about the dry heat, and he did not even see the large dust storm coming towards him. It was a long march, but just when he thought they were taking him to the end of the land, he saw the column making its way towards a dilapidated shop on the corner of Thomas and January Street.

It was the shop of Theophilus the apothecary, long abandoned after his death. The heavy wooden door beneath the bas-relief of a sick woman lying on a divan, the pioneering inscription: 'Roots: the Medicine for the Bones', the windowsills on which he had displayed the jars of haematic remedies were lost in a dense forest of plants. Garbage pushed his way through the lycopods, the spikes of the bougainvillæa, avoided the bees and the scorpions and came to the door.

Then, as if he were returning to some fairyland where he had played before, he pushed the door open and came into the shop with its smell of combustible peat and the musk of dead animals. He saw, as if someone had arranged them on a table, the jars filled with acaudal lizards, whose skins had dried up in the harmattan. He saw the alembic lamp that Theophilus had used for distilling and heating his potions, the Florence flask in which he had fermented the entrails of lizards, the dried bark of the quassia tree and the urine of goats which he had prescribed to dispel the intestinal worms of death.

If he was afraid of being in that sorcerer's den, Garbage did not let it show, because he had ceased to be a boy of ten and had passed, in one swift moment, into the crypt of manhood. When his father had died, he had not been afraid to go to the cemetery alone, to read under the frangipani tree, to be one with the dead whom he had been told by Jeanette Cromantine watched over young people. So in that room, removed from the prism transparency of childhood, Garbage did not feel menaced by the darkness encircling the place. Animated by the discoveries, he was about to start touching them when his hawk eyes saw a small light through a panel in the wall. He walked over to discover the source of the illumination, when he saw a door move and heard a voice which sounded foreign call his name:

'Come inside, Garbage,' said the voice. 'I have waited one hundred and fifty years for you to come, my son.'

Garbage walked into the room, and saw an old man gnarled by age sitting on the floor, his face wrinkled by the ravages of the sun of the desert. He saw his long spidery hands with their monkey-like hairs, his porcupine-quill nails on his toes of an ostrich and his ears of a Cape hunting dog. Yet, when Garbage looked at his eyes, he saw that the old creature from another time had the kindest pair of eyes that he had seen on anyone. For that reason, Garbage felt relaxed in his presence, and the initial horror at discovering such an ancient animal gave way to one of unrelieved curiosity. Seeing that Garbage was not afraid of him, the old man spoke again in a kind voice.

'How times have changed, Garbage. When I was first here, this place was slightly bigger than a village, and if you rode on a horse everyone noticed you. But look, now the place is so crowded that in order for me to find my way around I had to go through the town seven times until, because the baobab tree is still alive, I discovered this site where a gold merchant once had a splendid house. But that was long before your time.'

'Who are you?' Garbage asked.

'My name is Sulaiman the Nubian, but the sands of the desert erased that from the memory of this town a long time ago. Like the town itself the meaning of that name belonged to a past harmattan which will not be repeated, so I changed it a long time ago to Alusine Dunbar, a name with which I hope to see the future of this town.'

'But you are so old, you are going to die soon,' said Garbage.

'Death is a privilege, my son, because it is neither final nor the treacherous villain that some men have made it to be. If there is any villainy about it, it is that some of us try to see in death an ally for appeasing the remorseless demons we create in our lives. We wish death for others, but we cannot pay it off with the things we have accumulated through greed, because, in reality, everything we have is loaned to us.'

'How do you know all this?' Garbage wanted to know.

The old man was patient because he knew he had struck a chord in the mind of the ten-year-old boy who had the intelligence of a twenty-year-old. He felt elated, shifted his bag of bones and hunched forward to relax his back.

'I know, for instance, that you were given a name which in other times, to other people, would have been an embarrassment; but to you, it was an act of love, when your parents looked at you. They had also given your grandfather the most treasured gift he ever had, because you both passed through the same tunnel on your opposite voyages. I saw him on the morning you were born, he was happy because your birth freed him from the torment of treating death like an enemy.'

Alusine Dunbar let that sink into the head of the young man, but he did not wish to enlarge the map of confusion that he was already beginning to create in Garbage's mind. He saw in the harrier-hawk intelligence of his eyes, his ears of a wizened antelope and the furrows in his young-old man's face, that Garbage had taken everything in; much better, Alusine thought, than even that gold merchant he had mesmerised like a rabbit.

In the high plateau of the dead from where he had a vantage point to see how the living were messing up their lives, Alusine Dunbar had been shocked by what was going on in Malagueta since the predictable omen at the bottom of the calabash, when his hands had trembled as he saw Jeanette Cromantine getting ready to plant her potatoes which would bring the plague. Time, patience and the plenitude of wisdom had raised the level of his power so that he could see beyond the frontiers of imagination. And, in spite of the opium of old age which had weakened his bones, he was a tough camel of the desert who could still drag those bones around; an aged tortoise who had escaped the rapacious mouths of exploitation in other parts of the world. Now, he was returning to Malagueta because, as he told Garbage, 'I had seen the leopards going for the goats and I had to come before they ate all of them.'

He came through the idyllic gardens of the savannah and saw the pageant of the migratory birds going back to Europe with their impertinent looks and their fanciful plumages. Not having been in that part of the world for a while, he strayed into the sandy desolation of the desert, to see what changes the discovery of the compass had made since the days of the camel. His patience was rewarded: on the vast plateau in the awesome silence of the sand, Alusine Dunbar saw the majestic castles and caves of Tassili n' Ajir, the fantastic drawings of the nomadic painters; he rested on the stones in the rock garden of antiquity and read the epigram, 'Gold is the king of jewels but do not love it more than the sands of the desert', that a witty poet had scrawled on the tomb of the gold king over whom N'jai the gold merchant had forsaken the pleasures of enjoying the weasel-like body of Mariamu.

A herd of oryx brought him out of the desert and, keeping to the clouds of the locusts which have no respect for the borders between wet and dry regions, he arrived, invincible, in Malagueta, because Alusine Dunbar had conquered the last mystery of how to be alive in the same place where he had died over a hundred years before. Nothing in his occult weaponry had prepared him for the vandalism that greeted him. Gone were the enchanting bazaars that the sedentary Tuaregs had built when they had given up hawking the condiments of the Moors; he looked in vain for the chapman corner where the female beggars had peddled the imitation jewellery from Tangiers and read the palms of fortune seekers. The courtyard where he had brought back the armadillo from extinction was lost in the revolting expanse of shops, and, in the swamps where he had hoped to find the world unchanged, he was aghast to see that the pigmy hippos were being reduced to curiosity jokes, while the peaceful siestas of the crocodiles had been disturbed by the cunning skinhunters.

'The destruction has started,' the old man lamented.

Looking for more familiar landmarks, Alusine Dunbar walked through the noisy marketplace on January Street and stopped at the stalls of the Yoruba women where the spices and minerals from Lagos were sold. He sniffed the oriental delicacies in the Chinese carts and watched the sharks being butchered in the fish section. Malagueta was having a wedding on the other side of the street, and Alusine Dunbar heard the harsh tones of the Christian bells for the first time in his life. Like some masquerade from a bygone age, he saw the men entering the church in their morning coats and the women in their Victorian gowns. He was aghast. A great crowd stood on the opposite side of the church to watch the bridal procession come in. The bride was a young woman, not more than nineteen, who, as she entered the church, had a string of abuses hurled at her by a much older woman in the crowd.

'Bitch,' the woman in the crowd said. 'After I have cooked and scrubbed for Josiah, he had to marry someone like you, just because you tricked him about being pregnant and your father has a brick house. But you and I have a lot to settle, you will see.'

The violence of the deserted woman's anger led to a fight between the supporters of both women. Having once had his own troubles with women, Alusine Dunbar concluded that a man was better off staying away from getting married, because it would put an end to the happiness of enjoying a woman without anyone interfering. He went down to the wharf and warehouses near the river where he had cured the entire populace of Kasila at the time of the plague; to the monument to a man named Rodrigo who had saved 'our potatoes, God bless him' and the Fulani porters carrying all kinds of loads on their heads behind the market women going home for the day. A house on January Street with an old man sitting on the porch talking to himself caught his attention, and Alusine Dunbar went there to see what it was like to be among these people who were already making him puke.

It was the house of Sebastian and Jeanette Cromantine, and Alusine had only to look at the man on the porch, at the monk-like serenity of his face, listen to the red bishops serenade him on the trellis, to see the hands of the arch-angel upon the man.

'He looks so happy,' said Alusine, 'that he is going to die!'

'Good morning,' the leathery man said in a friendly voice to the gnarled man who was passing through the last stages of life in that place.

Sebastian Crormantine did not move or open his eyes, but answered in a griffon vulture's voice:

'Let me give you de gold watch so I can fly off to join ma fader.'

Jeanette Cromantine, coming to the veranda with a bowl of soup for her husband, did not see Alusine and was shocked to hear her husband talking to himself. Lately, she had begun to wonder whether he would last long enough to see his son, if and when he returned from the ends of the world. She had already ordered a 'laying out' suit for her husband from the tailors, and made a deposit for a coffin and prepared herself for the moment when he would no longer be there. One thing she begged God was that she would not suffer the indignity of having to bury her husband on a Saturday when the mercenaries hired by Captain Hammerstone usually came to town, and would be glad to carry the coffin.

Alusine Dunbar stood for a while to watch the old woman give her husband his meal. He saw her pick the bones from the fish so that he would not choke on them, wipe the slime of the okra off his beard, and rub his chest when Sebastian started to sneeze and to complain that there was too much pepper in the soup. When the man had eaten and had brought his face to a spectre of contentment, in the presence of his wife, Alusine Dunbar left them sitting on the porch. Three blocks later, he came across the school where Gabriel Farmer had been immortalised, and where Richard Farmer sat humped over a map of West Africa drawn by Cresques of Majorca; he stood in awe as Richard Farmer pointed to the great city of Djenne, and spoke of the advances that the doctors of science had made there, of the treaty signed between the King of Mali and the King of Portugal in the sixteenth century so that the European monarch could help the African wipe out the French bandits who were beginning to harass his people. Alusine was elated.

'Knowledge at least will survive in this wasteland,' he decided.

Just when he thought he had lost all traces of the old caravan routes that he had taken, and was resigned to going back to the pathways of the dead, having given up the prismatic habit of seeing the world through a glass, he saw the house near the baobab with the two hundred vultures on its branches, ringed by the lycopods.

When Garbage had come to terms with the reality that the old vagabond sitting on the goatskin mat was not a fraud, but was the owner of the voice that had been talking to him during the nights when he had slept in the room next to his mother's, he discovered that, rather than being surprised at meeting the old man in that deserted house, he had been waiting for him to come to lead him through the labyrinth of the past, now that many of the old people in Malagueta had been overcome by the persistence of death or had succumbed to the senile voracity of old age. He was still thinking about the way the ants had brought him to the old man when he heard the bells of the church on George Street summoning the penitent to the Lent service that evening.

He remembered his mother, said goodbye to the old man and asked whether he could come again. 'You are always welcome, my son,' Alusine answered: 'But before you go, help this old man to his feet.'

Garbage went to the aid of the old man and felt the leathery parchment of skin. He had never touched anyone so old, but the sound of the dislocations of the bones of the old man as he tried to stand on his feet added only a small thread to the ligature that Garbage was tying up in his mind. Unexpectedly, as if to add one more element of mystery to the discoveries that he had made that evening, he saw two small rays flickering on the floor, beaming from the old man's crotch. There, almost touching the floor, like a bloated udder, Garbage saw the herniated testicles of the old man, the cylindrical notches in the drooping pants and the light from the optic lens behind the corneas shaped like a map of the world.

A great dizziness clouded him. He lost his grip of the old man and was about to stumble when the hand that had guided many a novice into the kingdom where all knowledge was transmuted through the reordering of the world steadied him on his feet, as he felt his strength returned, while the voice of the old man calmed him down.

'Don't be afraid, my son: I have been carrying this globe around so as not to waste time moving from place to place. Right now, there is a new moon rising, and that, my child, is disastrous for Malagueta.' Garbage went home hungry late at night. Asked by his worried mother where he had been, he answered with a matured terseness:

'Where the ground has eyes.'

◇

The sight of the two ships in the harbour was enough to check the inertia in Captain Hammerstone. The fever that had been racing through his blood throughout the night, the look of a drowning man trying to remember what land looked like, were checked by this most dramatic event. He called up enough reserve of strength to order his troops to get ready to go down to the harbour; in the first flush of his elation, he almost choked himself to death drinking the bitter herbal remedy that one of his men had prepared for him and ordered his ensign to press his captain's uniform and polish his ceremonial high boots.

After not having thought for a while of such epicurean delights as dining in the ballroom of a ship or going hunting for wild boar in the jungles of Java, he saw in the coming of the ships not only his chance to impose the institutions of English rule in Malagueta, but also the unlimited possibilities of enjoying himself in the future.

'Men,' he said, when he was ready to lead his troops out of the garrison, 'the time has come for you to show your mettle.'

They marched through the anxiety-ridden streets of Malagueta to the music of a brass band, passed the fairground where a pygmy was exhibiting a chimpanzee that could write with its toes and heard the young Arabella Garrison singing the part of Esther from Handel's oratorio, accompanied on the organ by her new teacher. Being a sailor with an ear for music, Captain Hammerstone was moved by the feat of the young girl, and, in an attempt to encourage the handful of Englishmen marching with him, he started to sing a song from his past.

> The Bull by force in field doth raigne:
> But Bull by skill good will doth gayne.

It was the first time that his men had heard him sing. Something different happened that moment. The long wait had impaired the confidence of most of the captain's men; if they had been waiting to test their mettle, they had grown less manly in their balls, which had suffered ostracism at the hands of most of the women in Malagueta. The stores that they had plundered, the animals that they had corralled, had not been recompense enough for the various lives that they had left behind to be mercenaries of the captain. Thus, in their idle moments, boredom had made them think of the tortured whirlpools of their past, and at times they had considered murdering the captain because he had seemed to them not a man of song, but a creature driven by the steely wheel of ambition.

Captain Hammerstone's black soldiers were ignorant of the lyrics of his song, but they were men who had risen in the fires of past music, and, as they marched behind the man who had been transformed in their eyes, they felt their own manhood reborn in the captain's song.

Louisa Turner was having a discussion with Jeanette Cromantine over whether to allow Fatmatta-Emilia to eat and write with her left hand when the troops turned into their street. Old age had not dampened the capacity for work or her distrust of narrowmindedness in Jeanette, but in what she considered practical matters such as how to bring up a child, the belief in the supernatural and its effect on people, the presence of good and evil spirits, she had a Manichaean view, quite the opposite of her daughter-in-law. While Louisa insisted that the use of the left hand by her daughter was a sign that she was going to grow up into a free thinker, without prejudice, and hoped that she would not make the same mistake that she had made as a young woman when she had got mixed up with those 'old maids' and 'their church business', Jeanette Cromantine, propelled by a wave of lucidity, had never been more poetic, now that she was enjoying being a grandmother. Consequently, she insisted that the use of the left hand was the sign of lecherousness, thievery and cunning which were the traits of a cat. Furthermore, as this was a matter involving her own granddaughter – which did not dispute the fact that Louisa was the child's mother – she wanted to be sure that Fatmatta-Emilia would grow up to be a proper lady using her right hand, because society was changing. Also, it was unhygienic for a person to use the same hand to eat and wipe your you-know-what after coming from the latrine. The only ones who did that were those heathens marching like slaves behind that white man who does not know his left hand from his right. Not her granddaughter.

They forgot about the unscripted almanac of the child's future for a while to watch the troops go by. Louisa was the first to respond to the presence of such a large force on the streets of Malagueta for the first time since the war. Holding Fatmatta-Emilia by the hand, she came out into the yard, unlatched the gate and gave the men a most contemptuous look. She asked a young soldier who had once delivered coal at the Cromantines why they were making all that noise, disturbing 'decent people first thing in the morning'.

'It's not us, ma'am,' he replied. 'The countrymen of the captain have arrived and he wants to welcome them in style.'

Three hundred and seventy-five men arrived on the two ships to be greeted by Captain Hammerstone. They were pale creatures who had been carefully selected in Liverpool and London, more for their voracity for adventure than for their skills in any of the objectives that the captain had underlined in his numerous letters to his superiors in England during the lugubrious period of waiting for them to respond. Coming down the gangways they looked sheepish and were uncomfortable in their clothes, but were glad that the captain had turned up to welcome them in the abyss of the unknown.

Garbage acknowledged the arrival of the foreigners in Malagueta by carving the date on the trunk of a tree so that he would remember it for ever. Bits of evidence fallen from the lips of his mother had told him of the other time when the captain had come to the town, with his book open, convinced he could begin to write his own history. When the commotion of their arrival had died down and they were comfortably ensconced in the houses that the captain and his troops had commandered because their owners had fled with that 'treacherous Booker-man' as the captain informed his guests, Garbage went to see Alusine Dunbar.

He found the old man moving about, weighed down by his herniated testicles, with the glowing light of his knowledge flickering between his legs. He saw that the old sage had not bothered to leave his room since the last time he was there, except to go to the latrine behind his house, because he had so arranged his life, drawn so many circles of convenience, that it was not necessary for him to go too far to get anything. He was wearing the same sandpaper clothes, with his small spidery arms encased in them, but they had an airiness about them, smelled like the fresh clothes of a laundrywoman, and he looked the picture of good health, much to the surprise of the young Garbage who did not know that it was possible to make peace with the decrepitude of the body and overcome the disintegration of the mind.

'You have come about the newcomers,' said Alusine Dunbar, before Garbage could say anything.

'How do you know what I am thinking?' asked Garbage.

'Because it had to be something terrible to bother you; but don't worry, it was foreseen a long time ago that they were coming.'

Garbage put that into some corner of his mind where he could retrieve it later for a clarity of meaning. He was still fascinated by the particulars of revelations, not to be seduced by the fantasia of a single declaration. The florescence of his mind, now that it was exposed to the sun of Alusine Dunbar, needed pages of illumination for it to spread its petals in the turbulent journey towards knowledge. While his father remained an ideal for him, Garbage saw in the old man the chance to leap over the conflagration that had consumed his father, to grow into adulthood. Consequently, he came often to the house. He would arrive in the mornings when Alusine Dunbar was starting a fire in front of which he sat crossed-legged in a trance; he heard the old man as he was exposed, through the awesome power of his illuminating testicles, into the future where Malagueta was a wounded doe and the voracious birds of prey, the treacherous hyenas in the town and the incendiary bombs of the new foreigners would bring her down.

'I am afraid for your generation,' said the old man, 'because you are going to see such changes here that nothing would be left of the memory of Fatmatta the Bird-Woman.'

'Who was she?' asked Garbage.

'That was before your time, my son, when the world was a thousand times saner than it is now, and a man could teach his children about the simple things in life.'

'You have any children?'

Alusine Dunbar avoided the question but promised Garbage that one day he would tell him about the Philosopher's Stone, the heedlessness through which all that was good in life would be lost, the unpredictable nature of man and the false acquisition of wealth. 'You who have lost a father must be careful you don't become a victim of avarice, so that the need to be a man without love does not possess you.' When he was sure he had the attention of Garbage, he told him how much better it was to be interested in the happiness of other people and not in one's own selfish personal opinions. He teased him about leaving his mother for long periods, all on her own, while he went out in search of 'the fascinations of youth'. But it was all right, Alusine Dunbar told him, because Garbage had been stamped with a glorious mark that made him free of the conformities of filiation which had drawn them together. So the boy was free to wander, as he himself had crossed the meridian of life and death, to be present at the turning of the wheel which was about to begin in Malagueta. Telling Garbage that he hoped he would come back when he felt like it, Alusine Dunbar touched the boy on his shoulder, with the effect that Garbage was enveloped in an atmosphere of gnosis and thought of the voice that had sometimes troubled his sleep. That night he slept peacefully; a man with the celestial face of an angel hovered above him in his dream, told him how sorry he was that he had not been around to see him grow; but in spite of the antipodean journeys on which they were travelling, the angel told him that he was happy, the fire that had burst a blood vessel in his body had not damaged his hands, and he was free to come and go.

It was the first time that Garbage had ever dreamed. Later in the morning, while he was having a breakfast of pancakes sweetened with molasses, he told Isatu Martins about it.

'It's him,' she said. 'It's your father, and he is going to be roaming around the world until he is seventy, before we stop hearing about him.' Gustavius Martins had died at fifty, she remembered.

Unknown to Garbage, someone had told his mother of seeing her husband standing in front of an estuary, not too far from Malagueta, where the water was peaceful; how he was smoking a pipe. Then, to add to the mysterious air that his death had brought about, ever since the day of his funeral when Isatu Martins noticed that the grandfather clock in the living room had chimed twent-four times instead of twelve, which was the hour at which they were getting ready to close his coffin, and that she alone had seen him as he opened and closed his eyes as if he was taking one final look at the people in the house, Gustavius Martins appeared to his wife one night when she was putting on the stiff widow's gown that she had worn for years since he died. In a voice that was gentle, when she had drifted into the dream world of their past, he told her how much he appreciated the way she had kept his memory alive, the tenderness with which she had handled the growing pains of manhood in Garbage, the consistency of her rejections of all the entreaties made by members of the captain's forces to paint her house for her and the encyclopedic details that she had assembled of all the things that he had created in Malagueta. But, much to her surprise, he told her that widowhood was not an encumbrance to happiness, a stifling embroidery of the mind; he pointed to the fact that she was still a handsome woman, a good woman who should be free of the pernicious embrace of martyrdom. 'Take off the cloth of the widow and begin to live again,' he told her. Because to let the crust of death settle in the fresh dough of life was against nature. Having concluded that only he could convince his wife that the burden of living only for him was not a sanction that she should carry to her grave, Gustavius Martins told her to stop wearing the iron garment of her widowhood, to put on some make-up, and to open her heart to the possibility of living for herself and for someone other than himself.

It was the first and only time that Isatu Martins dreamed about her husband. When she had overcome the shock brought about by not only his visit but by the ambrosia of his speech, she stayed in bed longer than she was used to. Then she started to cry for the pleasure of having known that man, and for the judiciousness of his spirit. While she was crying, she did not hear Garbage walk into her room, but she felt the chrysanthemum of his love which sprang about her in a brilliant flabellum of colours.

'Why are you crying?' he wanted to know.

'It's all right, ma son. It is just dat your mother is happy, and ah know you gon to be all right, too; but let us pray for Malagueta.'

◇

Rapidly, Malagueta underwent a transformation. The plans for the development of the town that Captain Hammerstone had drawn up were eagerly accepted by his associates. But after declaring himself governor, he allowed contrary views to be expressed by his men. In them, they appealed to him for understanding, trying to convince him that the difficult task of modernising that part of the world required a combination of skills and the experience derived from previous endeavours of a similar kind. They spoke of the urgency of acquiring more *Lebensraum*. 'We have to think ahead, Captain, to the time when trade would be good.' They jolted him with the dazzling prospect of expanding Malagueta from the Guinea coast right to the very reaches of the desert; the merchants in Liverpool, the stockbrokers in London, and even the church would each contribute a hundred pounds for the realisation of the project. Eventually, they won the captain over and the English surveyors went to work.

Jeanette Cromantine, out shopping for some spices, had to restrain herself from slapping the young guard who told her not to walk in front of where one of the surveyors was beginning to mount his magnetic compass. So she cursed the black man, told him that his children and those not yet born would curse him for being there on the day Malagueta was being measured for the profit of those who had not laboured to build it. But everywhere she turned it was as if the world was turning round again, because the Englishmen were the largest number of their race that she had seen since that distant, amortised morning when she and Sebastian had extinguished the last fires of exile in the wetlands of England.

For the next two years, the streets of Malagueta shook with the obsessive digging and shovelling of the surveyors and their labourers. They measured the volume of the earth to see whether it was hard enough to hold the mortar for the building of an administrative block; protected by Captain Hammerstone's mercenaries, they disturbed the two o'clock siestas of the dead by marching through the cemetery at that time and turned the street of the peaceful sanctuary of the Virgins into a pool, trying to determine the depth for a reservoir. In order that they might have an accurate reading of the four corners of the land, they mounted a vernier on the roof of the church on George Street, over the vigorous protest of the sexton who had begun to drowse in the cubicle below the belfry. Ever since the war, Malagueta had seen a tide of madness. It came slowly at first, into the homes of those whose sons had been bitten by the scorpion of regret for not having fought alongside Thomas Bookerman, so that not even the repeated assurance by their parents that Bookerman was a bandit best forgotten could stop them from running into the streets, pulling off their clothes and pissing in front of everyone. It struck in the middle of a dinner party in some woman who could not hold back the confession that had pricked her conscience, like a needle, because she had made a huge profit selling contraband goods, which she had obtained from the troops, to her fellow Malaguetans. Sometimes, the madness was swift and shameless in its victims. One evening, there was a commotion on the corner of February and George streets because a mad couple were copulating on the ground in view of everyone, just as the surveyors were coming to that part of the town to test the accuracy of their spirit level for the construction of a theatre. Angry that their lovemaking was interrupted, the paradisaical couple tried to attack the four soldiers it took to break them up. After they were marched away in chains, the surveyors cancelled their plans for the theatre. Saying that the people of Malagueta derived instant gratification from open air performances, and thus did not need to bother going out of their way to enjoy their Sundays, they put down stakes for an asylum on the spot where they had witnessed the coupling, so that they could minimise the chances of seeing a repetition of that act.

Soon, the weariness suffered from the relentless heat, the loneliness of their day in the unfathomable illusion of civilisation, began to take their toll on the seamen. Some grew beards to protect their newt-like skins and rewrote letters which were never dispatched to the mothers, wives and girlfriends who waited in the fearful gales for word of their men. Once those men were settled into the routine of work, all the unforeseen consequences of being in that 'dark place' began to unfold, to torment them and make some of them less resolute in their determination to conquer Malagueta for the Queen of England. They lost weight thinking of the falling rhythm of their lives and became victims of the vertigos of insomnia, especially in the unguarded moments when they knew they could be murdered. It was natural, they believed, for the Malaguetans to hate their guts, and to be able to produce the excalibur with which to murder them in their beds.

To prevent sabotage, Captain Hammerstone ordered some of his troops to guard the buildings as they went up. While the surveyors and builders vorked hard to have their stones and bricks in place before the now delayed rains; while three hundred labourers who had been rounded up by the captain demolished some of the old houses so that new ones could be erected, and even some of the tombstones in the cemetery that were the symbols of family neglect were moved out of the way (which made the dead grumble that no sooner were they settled in one comfortable resting place than some spurious town planner was smashing up their parlour), the other, equally ambitious men put their ideas into action, with an esurience, as if motivated by some idea of martyrdom.

Out of such determination, and inspired by a sense of vocation that even some of the most intransigent Malaguetans would have admired, a large dispensary was set up which was stocked with enough medical remedies to cure many of the diseases then breaking out in the town. Once they had convinced the citizens that the price of being treated in the dispensary was within the reach of most of them, two white doctors who ran the place soon found themselves busy with the throng of sick people who came every morning before the doors were opened. One of the two doctors was a young Londoner, Dr Patrick Smith, who in the first six months of treating patients had not taken time to see what the town offered in the area of social recreation. By nature and temperament he was a quiet man. His coming to Malagueta had been decided upon after a prolonged analysis of the condition of the human race glimpsed from the wretched conditions of many people in the London tenements where he had had to fight his way through armies of large rats, child prostitutes and beggars. Unable to do much about the tyranny of landlords and money speculators who profited from the misery of working-class people, he had originally thought of joining the colonial army and shipping out to Bombay, but stories about the prospect for the discovery of new diseases and ways of curing them in Malagueta had swayed him towards the idea of coming there. He, unlike many others, did not have someone waiting for him back in London. Thus, he was freed of the burdens of history, and the bellicose rhythm of jingoism. Malagueta was not a battleground for Dr Smith where he could test his superiority over lesser races, but a place where he could discover the quotidian fever that made every man and woman tremble at the very idea of death. Others set up more schools; a few joined the school of Richard Farmer, which was raised to the status of a teaching college for clerics and teachers.

But it was one act on the part of the Englishmen that turned a sizeable number of the Malaguetans against them. In the vacant lot where the people had turned out in the first years of the settlement to watch the acrobatic wizardry of Orlando and Septimus Blackstone who had earned a lot of money before disappearing one night, the Englishmen built a large clubhouse, enclosed by a one-foot-thick stone wall with a heavy iron gate at the entrance. With diligence and love, they coaxed a beautiful garden out of the ground, which was in a rocky part of town, and soon had a sanctuary with a touch of the country that they were beginning to miss, to go to and be away from the Malaguetans. One morning, they hung a large sign on the gate, just as the Virgins had done, in former times, but with the ill-considered inscription: 'Africans and dogs not allowed'. The insult was not permitted to go on for long. A week later, someone threw the head of a large white dog dripping with blood inside the compound, to which was attached the inscription: 'We skins Englishmen and dogs, so you be careful'. The sign on the gate was quickly removed though the prohibition on Africans and dogs was quietly enforced until much later when the clubhouse was burnt down in a violent riot.

If the people of Malagueta had hoped for rain that year in the belief that the invaders and their endeavours would be wiped off, then their dreams were the withered ears of corns, the parched tongues of leaves which made them inedible even to goats. Streams and rivers dried up in the merciless onslaught of the sun; crocodiles came inland to hide in the shades of the mangroves and the mornings were clouded in the windy dust of the harmattan, which in the night was cold and bore into the bones of not only the Malaguetans but into the already cold joints of the Englishmen who were surprised that they could shiver in that expanse of underdevelopment, and made them desire the fireplaces they had not thought of building in their new mountain homes and in the club.

Told of what was happening in the town, Sebastian Cromantine, who had not been out of his house for almost two years, did not even change his position in the chair on the veranda to make a pronouncement on the future of Malagueta.

'Those English goats can eat all dey like now,' he said, 'but, mark my word, dey gon come down wid a bad case of diarrhoea later, even if ah ain't here to see it.'

It was the last time that he let himself be bothered by the vargaries of the future of the town. He was a drooling man now, prone to the lapses of dotage. As he sat on the geranium porch the world went by, without bothering him. Lizards would crawl up his trousers thinking that his legs were vines, and only when he felt their cold-blooded tongues licking his fingers was he bothered. He asked Jeanette Cromantine the same questions every day, got the same answers every day, and repeated the same questions because he was no longer aware of the disconsolation in the hearts of other people. Except for the brilliance of a single thought about that wayward son who had gone away, he closed the shutters of his mind and drifted into a gratifying sleep every day.

Suddenly, after more than three years without rain, the dry, dusty spell of the harmattan gave way to a terrible thunder in the middle of the night in March. Jeanette Cromantine was sitting in the parlour with Louisa, knitting some cashmere stockings, when they heard the first sound of the impending fury.

'It's coming again,' the old woman said to her daughter-in-law.

'What is coming?' asked the younger woman.

'It's de sister of de hurricane dat destroyed de first settlement we built before you came here. Ah knows it.'

She relived once again the terrifying moment when the wind of their misfortune had blown through their cabin and made nonsense of the delusion of glory that the founding fathers and mothers had tormented the earth with, when the earth had not been readied for their coming, because they had not then learnt the limerick with which to hold back the rain. Working like two mad women, Jeanette Cromantine and Louisa brought the will of their bodies to the heavy sideboard which they moved into a defensive position behind the main door of the house.

Later, they found Emmanuel Cromantine's carpentry tools and boarded up the windows while the decibel of the wind rose to an ominous roar.

In a room within the garrison, Captain Hammerstone had just started to make love to a woman he knew, who had come to the garrison to ask for his help in getting her son to England, when the evidence of the wind disturbed his concentration. It was the first time since coming to Malagueta that he had found a woman to make him forget the duodenal ulcers that he had developed as a result of the frenzied pace of the attempt to transform that land. After such a long time without a woman, he had lost the formalised language with which he had seduced other women; the embroidered details of his voyages which had fascinated them, as they went to bed with him, when he had conquered their hearts with the tales of the islands that he had seen; the Pasiphaes of the sun writhing their golden bodies under him. Now his lovemaking was a methodical formula, like the mapping out of a territory which required interest but very little love. He was almost about to relieve himself of the torment that he had carried around between his legs for so long when the thud of a bird against his window distracted him,. But, being a man who did not believe in doing things in half measures, he finished making love to the woman before turning his attention to the disorder that was raging outside. When he opened the window to let in some fresh air, Captain Hammerstone barely had time to move back from the velocity of the wind and the avalanche of dying birds, that landed in his room.

Five hundred flycatchers died that night, blown out of the trees by the raging storm of the rain; the streets and the gutters of Malagueta were turned into busy straits bearing the corpses of even more dead animals than the luckless birds. Sebastian Cromantine, who had just begun to drift into the world of unknowing, was roused from the decrepitude of old age and brought back into the fountain of his youth by the fractious lamentation of the rain. He trained his now useless eyes to see if there were coffee trees falling on the ground, and he went from room to room, looking into every nook and cranny to see whether a snake had crept into the house in search of shelter from the rain. Trying to show that he was not entirely useless, he offered to go out into the yard to check on the fowls, and to see whether the goats and sheep were secured in the cellar under the house. Jeanette Cromantine was aghast.

'You old fool,' she screamed. 'You not young any more and you gon be blown apart by de wind.'

The rain pounded the houses with the relentless force of its accumulated delay. While the Cromantines watched from their parlour, they saw the bedraggled vultures being blown off the trees as if they were leaves, while a nascent spring raged under the foundation of their house. The roofs of some of the houses that were in the direction of the wind were blown off with the whimsical protestation of their rich owners who had stayed up in various stages of fright, with the legs of their pyjamas caught in thick folds of fat around their legs.

Garbage was waiting for a respite from the rain to go to the dilapidated house to see whether Alusine Dunbar was there. One week had passed since the downpour first started and he would have gone out on the first morning, but Isatu Martins would hear nothing of it. She had secured the locks of the doors, burned incense in an urn every night to drive away the evil spirits she believed would seize the occasion of the rain to invade her house, and even prayed, something she seldom did, that the sharp knives of the rain would not attack the almond tree under which she had taken to sitting in the hot afternoons, reading with a pair of newly acquired spectacles the first volume of the history of Malagueta by Thomas Bookerman which Richard Farmer had had printed for use in the school.

But she was unable to restrain her son from leaving the house. He was tormented not only by the gloom of the silent house but by the worms of rebellion which had made his young man's body uncomfortable in that house during the rain. Moreover, the raging fires lit in his body by the discovery of the old vagabond had made him fearless of storms and the whirlpool of water. Added to that, there were some children on the streets, foolish and carefree, who, mindless of the pleas of their parents, came out to play in the grey mornings of rain.

When he escaped from the house, Garbage came face to face with the floating cemetery of dead animals on their way to a sea grave; he waded through the now dangerous streets, held firmly to a large tree trunk, and let himself be carried downstream, until he was hurled against a coach immersed in the mud. With a strength unusual in someone so young, he held tightly to the coach while the water flowed by, and it was not until an hour later that he was able to make his way out of that treacherous onslaught and get to the house, which, miraculously, had survived the battering of the past week.

'I knew you would come,' said Alusine Dunbar, when Garbage came into the room where the old man sat in front of a fire, as if his bones needed the nourishing in the dampness. Sitting Buddha-like, he was working the bellows that regulated the flame of the fire, which sprang from the live charcoals burning in a forge. Garbage had never seen anything like that before and stood speechless.

'You have come just in time to see me making a ring for a prince who is coming here as soon as this rain stops falling,' said Alusine Dunbar.

Enthralled by the magic of the dancing flames, Garbage forgot about the rain falling outside; he stood riveted in one spot while the gold ingot came alive in hues of yellow and red, and the dancing snakes of the smoke rose above the head of the magician who worked the goatskin bellows which themselves were sometimes as large as his testicles that were pressed under him.

'What are you doing?' asked the mesmerised boy.

'Ah, so you want to know, just like the gold merchant almost one hundred and fifty years ago – except that in his case he was a robber of gold, not a maker. Age transforms everything, Garbage, so we do those things that the passage of time demands. One age is about to end in Malagueta, a new reign without honour but with the embellishment of falsehood, such as to make the dead tremble in their grave, is about to begin, so we must say goodbye to the old ways by giving this ring to the old power.'

Pleased that his old friend was safe, Garbage stayed for a while in that new kingdom where the language of the gold was being formed. Whoever the prince was, it did not matter; but he thought he had to be important for Alusine Dunbar to make him worthy of that accolade, of which, he was sure, the ring was merely the outward symbol. If he could have trusted his young mind to wander into the territory of discovery, he would have asked the old man for details of the prince: how old he was, where he was coming from. But he was convinced that questions bored the old man, though he had been appreciative of the youth's desire to learn. So Garbage contented himself with being in the goldsmith's aura, to watch the smoke as it crowned him in aureoles of yellow light, and to dream of his father, Gustavius Martins, as if the dead man ruled in the princedom.

When he left the mysterious house, Garbage was thrown into a riotous avalanche of personal effects which had come from those bereaved houses whose owners had not had the gift of foresight to make them strong or to move the now useless objects out of the way of the rain. Some would drift right into the sea, carry the tales of damaged labour with them, break dreams about sons who would return from studies in England to take over from their fathers, who had begun to warm up to the newly arrived English for favourable positions in their administration when those newly minted black English men should apply to join their service. The rain had tired a bit of its own fury and seemed headed southwards towards the sea, and the monotonous drumming of water in the streets seemed less terrifying now than when he reached the house of his distraught mother. He found her sweeping away hundreds of rainflies that the wind had blown onto the porch. The fowls were making quite a feast of the ants and the goats had found their feet to come out of their shelter to eat the young tendrils which had fallen off the trellis on the porch. Isatu Martins cleared her worried throat and admonished her son for going out into the rain.

'What a caring son you be,' she said, 'leaving your mother all alone in de house, not to talk of risking your life, when you know you can't swim. What if de water carried you off?'

He was drenched from the rain, and went in and dried himself with a large towel; but he felt strong and warm because he was immune to colds and fever, that combination of ailments which was always held in check by the banana-grove grandfather. He ate a small supper, crawled into his bed and was quickly taken up by a peaceful sleep.

In the dilapidated house, Alusine Dunbar had just finished making the ring for the prince and, after examining it with the scrutiny of a master craftsman, was beginning to drift into a deep state of oneiromancy, when he felt the heat of his herniated testicles rising. Noisy jingles sounded in the alarm of the balls and the flicker of light that was transmitted shone with a brilliance that stunned even the sage himself. Suddenly, he knew that the level of the deep waters of his own knowledge was rising, and that the revelation of things to come demanded more than the mere idea of concentration. A herd of wild buffaloes charged across a field against a hunter that had tormented them for a long time and a plague of locusts emerged out of the clouds in the wake of that bovine fury. When the rays of the light of the illuminating testicles rose in the dark room, Alusine Dunbar saw in the distant edges of the surrounding forest a large one-eyed man, flanked by a beautiful woman and a young man with the lean face of a poet, leading a large group of well-armed men, and he saw in the harmattan of another time the dust raised by those people as they had begun the journey to Malagueta. It was four o'clock in the morning, an hour good for divination in the prism of his art. As the column advanced, he trained his balls so that the men would be guarded by their light and be led over the terrible rabbit traps, then plentiful in the countryside. A large thunderbolt rocked Malagueta, jolting Sebastian Cromantine out of his old man's solipsism. Throughout his life, he had not found God and now that his life was coming to an end, the absence of his son convinced him even more that religion was a farce and that those who hoped for redemption in another life ought to have their heads examined, although he could conceive of stubborn ghosts, like his father's, who refused to settle into a permanent life. So that when he heard the awesome cannon in the clouds, he came to the only tangible conclusion that he could think of at that time.

'It's de minnow season, and time to ketch 'em before de big fish get to 'em.'

Alusine Dunbar did not have any difficulty in recognising the prefiguration of a major event in the planetary movements in the clouds. So many times in the past, he had been forewarned about changes in various parts of the world, about the demise of an idea, just by letting himself be carried away by the rhythm of his own seance. Thus, he saw the well-calculated steps of the marchers as they approached Mala-gueta; he heard the beautiful woman who walked beside the one-eyed man singing an enchanting song to encourage the young men in the group. Now and then, the one-eyed man had to be carried in a hammock by some young men, because he was himself an old warrior now and couldn't keep up with the pace of the young men. Alusine Dunbar reflected on how lucky the old man was, unlike Sebastian Cromantine, that he could still march for days in the terrible drought-land of exile.

The people of Malagueta were just waking up to another day when the town was shaken by the sound of gunfire. Garbage was one of the first to realise that fighting had broken out between the troops of the captain and an invading force. Hurriedly finishing his breakfast, he went out into the streets, followed the sound of the conflict and was soon lost in the large crowd of people making their way to the scene of the battle on January Street.

'It's de general and Emmanuel,' someone shouted. Garbage had to move out of the way of the people to avoid being crushed, as they were elated by the lightning of that revelation.

It had been almost ten years since Thomas Bookerman, Phyllis Dundas and Emmanuel Cromantine had gone into exile, following their defeat by the captain's ragtime black soldiers, so that for many of the people milling about in the streets their names were little more than a page in the history of the town. But, for the oldest men and women, for Jeanette Cromantine and Isatu Martins, an implacably stubborn conviction that those exiles would come back never left them. Accordingly, when they had recovered from the first flush of their happiness, they went with the others into the streets to watch the battle raging.

When she had cut her way through the crowd, Jeanette Cromantine saw her son leading the attack on the madhouse that Captain Hammerstone's construction brigade had built on the waterfront. Volumes of pride and gratitude blazed in the maternal tenderness of her heart: she was proud that he had become more than the man that she had wished for her in a son, and grateful to God that he had spared her life and that of Sebastian Cromantine to see this day.

Although he was not leading his men in the fighting against the captain's troops, Thomas Bookerman was there, the undisputed leader of the homecoming. Some welcomed him in the last flickers of recognition, because their own light was about to go out; old men and women with bald pates and flattened breasts, leaning on their canes and content to die in the last fires of defiance. Young men and women weaned on the milk of his legend pushed each other to get a glimpse of him, and even a few Englishmen not taking part in the fighting but who had heard of his name in the seafront rum cafés surged forward to have a close look at Bookerman.

He too had aged, but still had the brilliant fires of rebellion in his eyes that had inspired many of the Malaguetans to attack the garrison many years earlier. As the fighting raged on for control of the port area, the returning exiles seemed emboldened by his courage to press on with their attack. They met stiff resistance from the captain's now greatly increased numbers. Emmanuel Cromantine, toughened by the years of exile, had arrived on Malaguetan soil determined to drive out the captain for good and to wipe out all vestiges of the influence of the English. While he had been in exile, news would sometimes reach him about the changes that had been introduced in Malagueta; the compromising attitudes of some of the leading citizens to the occupation; the introduction of discriminatory laws against his people; the hermatic soliloquies of his father and the destruction of many of the historical landmarks as the new administrators tried to stamp their rule on the town.

After three days of fighting, during which time the port area changed hands, the exiles managed to seize a sizeable part of the district that had undergone the most radical changes in the years that they had been away. Thomas Bookerman and Phyllis regained control of their former home which had not been inhabited in all the years of occupation. As soon as she had swept out the cobwebs, repaired the broken windows and burned onion peels to keep the snakes out, Phyllis restored the house to a measure of its former tranquillity. Emmanuel Cromantine stationed two dozen of his best men to guard the house, and once he was sure that his men were in control of the area, he walked the few blocks to the house on January Street to see his family.

Although they had prepared for this day, over and over in the lacerating years, Jeanette and Louisa were not prepared for the transformation that had taken place in Emmanuel Cromantine. Where there had been a young man marked with the solemn dignity of a poet, they found a man with the even deeper solemnity of a warrior. He looked sad and was turning the first corners of greying; his eyes told of the pain of being away from the town where he had nursed a young man's dream; of the endless solitude that exile had been, and of the tormented wish to be back with them. Jeanette Cromantine was the first to respond to his presence. Crying 'My son, my son,' she threw herself into his arms, drying her tears with her headgear. 'How ah prayed to God dat he would bring you back to me,' she cried. 'Ah never stopped believing in his mercy, 'specially as you is de only one and he knows a moder's heart won't rest until she sees her son; and what a man you is now, though am afraid for you, my son, wid all dis fighting business, 'specially as Malagueta not de same place dat you left before. All de new people who have come, de white and de black, dey different from us; all dey concerned about is demselves, and their children; not de town, and worse, dey have no respect for old people, no fear of God, but come, you have a beautiful daughter dat Louisa born after you left, though you did not tell your moder dat she was your intended, as if ah would have opposed such a serious daughter-in-law. Ah will let you two have some time togeder before ah take you to your fader who is asleep, and bin waiting for you to come before he dies.'

When they found themselves alone, Emmanuel and Louisa did not rush to embrace. Over the years, each had dreamed of what they would say to each other when they met; how they would give themselves over to the tempestuous fires of their renewed love, especially as that love had produced a child. But the long separation and the reality of being in the old people's house brought an awkwardness into their limbs. So that rather than the mad rush of a passion that had characterised her former response to him, Louisa was overcome by an awkward shyness. She stood glued to one spot, holding young Fatmatta-Emilia by the hand, while a large kori bustard fluttered its wings of desire in her heart. With an almost gentle reserve, Emmanuel Cromantine touched the cheek of the flushed woman, kissed her and then embraced her. Suddenly, the dam in her broke, and she forgot the house, the child and the bright light in the parlour. The lost years were lost in the molten fires of her hunger as she kissed him all over his face, told him how terribly lonely she had been without him, and how she would have died if he had not come back. 'There would have been nothing for me to live for, not even for Fatmatta-Emilia.'

It was then that she picked up the shy child, who had been confused by all the drama occasioned by the arrival of the tall, grave man.

'Say hello to your daddy,' Louisa said to the silent child, as she handed her over to Emmanuel Cromantine. Fatmatta-Emilia was nine at that time, and had been told over and over again of the man who was her father, but who had gone away with other 'good daddies' because the bad ones hated them, but how he would come back. Now that she was in his arms, she scrutinised him with the clinical honesty of a child, made a face when he ran his strong hand over her head and brought the first real sign of a relaxed look to his face with the piercing lance of her comment: 'You smell strange,' she said.

It was the smell of the long journey back to Malagueta that she was inhaling, when he and his men had gone without a bath for a week, had slept on the damp blanket of trampled leaves, and had eaten wild huckleberries which had left a lingering odour on them.

'Better go take a bath,' he said, 'before my daughter decides I am some kind of wild animal. But, first, let us go and see the old man.'

He found Sebastian Cromantine on the last train of his life, more aged than Malagueta itself, with his mind and body ossified beyond the dullest look of recognition. For the past three days, he had been grasping the solid gold watch that Rodrigo the Brazilian had given to him in that unforgettable season before the potato plague; holding it as if time was essential to him in the unforeseen hourglass where the last sands of his mortality were falling. Emmanuel Cromantine and Louisa had to prop him up with a couple of pillows before the glint of recognition lit up his eyes. When he realised who the tall man was, Sebastian Cromantine's old man's face lit up with the fresh petals of happiness. After he had brought his lips to a formation of speech, he said the first words he had uttered in days: 'De king has come, and now dis old tree kin fall on de ground.' He pulled Emmanuel down by the neck, so that the young man's head rested on the leather of the old man's chest. Then, with the steady movement with which he had fashioned the tombstones that had made his fortune, he hung the chain of the gold watch round the neck of his son, blessed him for coming back, told him to have more children because 'your mama and me sure are going soon', and then fell into a deep sleep.

Later that night, Louisa and Emmanuel Cromantine were making love in bed in the midst of a strange howling of the dogs in the neighbourhood. Overcome with the happiness of having Emmanuel in his own bed, her passion knew no bounds. This time it was she who rode on the strong animal of his manhood, moaning and crying for the pleasure of having him back with her; not in the tumultuous seas of former times, but in the slow, calm lagoon of a mature woman who had had a child and knew how to make a man feel loved and wanted. When she had exhausted herself, she made him come on top of her so that she could engulf him in the sunny cotyledons of her love. From the deep reservoir where he had kept her face floating in the transparent waters of his love, he made love to her with the intense rhythm of a man who had come through hell to the threshold of maturity where he could not only be responsible for the men who served under him, but could come to the woman with the certainty that he would love her for ever in the quiet ways that he had always loved her.

It was while they were resting from rediscovering the sensual lines of their bodies that they became aware of the strange howling of the dogs. Louisa who had known many dog-nights when they had howled and kept the people in the area awake, did not think much of the night's concert. But, after it had gone on for an hour, Louisa, who was also more inclined to believe in premonition, decided that something was amiss.

'That howling is not normal, Emmanuel,' she said. 'Someone important is either coming to the town or is about to die.'

Sebastian Cromantine was shaking his cornstalk legs in his bed when his thoughts started to drift from the happy reunion with his son, to the last time he had thought of his father. He saw the old runaway as he had appeared to him, over seventy-five years ago, shaking the waterjugs and demijohns in that other country, and he remembered the livid fear in his belly when he had not understood that the presence of the old man in his cabin was the prelude to the great changes that would occur in his own life. Great, bald griffon vultures appeared in the sky and Sebastian Cromantine was shocked that even in his delirium he could make out the different shapes of their faces. He saw that one of the vultures was small and had the face of a woman from a remote past, whom he had buried on the shores of a town when he and the other mourners had had the perspicacity and gravity of a language formed in the plantations, with

310

which they had sung her home. He discerned in the look of another vulture that it had come a long way and that it was holding a potato pod in its beak. A great joy swept through his heart when he recognised the friendly eyes of the last vulture, with its look of a man whose heart had once been eaten by love for a timid local woman named Isatu, and who had said, 'I may be crazy, but that is what loves is all about, a little craziness.' Suddenly, the smallest vulture with the face of a woman flapped her wings and Sebastian Cromantine felt the lids of his eyes shut for ever. The last thing he remembered was the feeling of the vultures picking him up with their beaks so that he flew skyward in their midst, freed of all worries in that world which he had helped to give a name. Next morning, Emmanuel Cromantine found him stiff and cold as a dog's nose in bed. He drew a sheet over the dead man's face and went to the next room to tell Louisa.

◇

Emmanuel Cromantine consolidated his position, established head-quarters in a house on February Street because his mother was afraid of all 'dis soja business wid gun, gun, my son', and preferred to look after her granddaughter now that Sebastian had been buried at the foot of the large jarcaranda tree in the yard. Nine months later, both sides of the conflict had still not moved against each other. Captain Hammerstone and his men stayed in the garrison, except for the troops that protected the homes of the English. Work stopped on some of the buildings that they were putting up because they were afraid of sabotage, and the club with the offending sign became deserted. Much as he hated the superior airs of the newcomers and was determined to keep them cloistered in their mountain retreat, Emmanuel Cromantine was a man with a profound respect for the values of education, the importance of science and the preservation of culture. So that although he ordered the destruction of the madhouse where those who had opposed the occupying army had been sent, he was secretly pleased with the discovery of the new college, the music school where he was told two bright young women named Arabella and Matilda Garrison were inflaming the hearts of young men with their expertise on the piano and the enchanting warmth of Arabella's voice.

One evening, he received a visit from Richard Farmer. He was glad to see the brother of his late friend and venerated teacher, and the two men had a lot to talk about. From Richard Farmer, Emmanuel heard of the brilliance and precociousness of the young son of Gustavius Martins, who had taken to coming to the bookshop to read all day long, and had a very serious countenance and insisted on being called Garbage despite the teasing of many young women, who wondered how on earth he had got that name that was so laughable.

'He is very much like you, Emmanuel: brooding and meditative, and he writes poetry, just like your old friend, my brother.'

The new situation in Malagueta did not leave Emmanuel Cromantine much time to think about the things he wanted most in life: the pleasure and satisfaction he thought he would derive from the life of a savant. He spent what time he had with his family, helped Fatmatta-Emilia with her homework, though when he visited the house his mother would not let him bring the soldiers inside because 'all dis war business is bad for de soul'. When he could get away from the routine of signing papers, he played chess with Richard Farmer or visited Isatu Martins. He never met Garbage because the young man was as undecided about meeting him, just as much as Emmanuel was looking forward to meeting him.

Thomas Bookerman, protected in his seaside house, had resumed the writing of the final volume of the *History of Malagueta* which he had postponed several times during the uncertainties of exile. When a delegation of civic leaders headed by Alphonso Garrison sought to meet him to see if a lasting truce could be arranged between the old settlers and the newcomers with the captain in charge, he removed the monocle he had taken to wearing and spoke to Alphonso Garrison in a voice that made Alphonso tremble:

'Never thought ah would see de day when de men of dis town gon talk 'bout going to share dere freedom wid some Englishfolk who ain't worth nuthin.'

After Alphonso Garrison had left, Thomas Bookerman sent one of the men guarding the headquarters of Emmanuel Cromantine with a long letter. In it, he told the young commander not to waste his time fighting for the glory of Malagueta because war was a cancer, and in any case, there were very few decent men left who remembered what it was like to be honourable. 'Look at all the shuffling and bowing they doing to the whitefolks; and the grandchildren of them that came from cabins in Canada ain't want to be mixing with them whose granddaddy done come off the slaveship from Calabar,' he protested. He reminded Emmanuel that he was a savant and stated that future generations would be grateful to him, not for prolonging a useless war, but for having expanded the college, encouraged the musical evenings in town as Gabriel Farmer, bless his soul, had done, and for building new roads.

Yet he urged him never to surrender. 'Malaguetans don't surrender!' he wrote. 'At least, not the true born ones who ain't afraid to stand up and be counted, so that their children and wives going be mighty proud of them.' Instead, he urged him to accept a truce if the captain declared one; to let the English stay, but never as masters, because 'that ain't what we found this town for before your time'.

It was ten o'clock at night when Emmanuel Cromantine finished reading the letter. Except for the six men in the next room who constantly guarded him, he was alone in the small room which served both as an office and sleeping quarters. He had not slept for days and he looked lean and tired, but his mind had never been clearer. Satisfied that Thomas Bookerman had written the letter from the loftiest ideal, he was nevertheless perplexed by the contradictory appeal in it. When he had assumed command of the men whose loyalty had now been tested by the rigours of stone, mud and the slimy feel of water, he had not imagined this loneliness, this exactness of his spirits, the draining of his elements, because he was lonely; lonelier than the naked words in the letter, which had served only to confirm his aloneness from the mishmash of the war, the pitfalls of arrogance, fame and the cummerbund of leadership. Darkness hung heavy like a sentence in the air, mysterious, absolute and unchanging. He tried to come to terms with the aloneness as if he had been cast off, yet was needed to save others from the neatly wedged cuneiforms of their lives. When he allowed his mind to wander over all that had happened in his life, he saw the cars of the roller coaster where the dreams that he and Gabriel Farmer had nursed had fallen off a cliff; the wall of death where the names of Gustavius Martins, his father and, soon, that of his mother would be written, because their suns had been drenched by the rains of the clouds that had gathered over Malagueta like a great bird. In the distance, he saw the constellation of stars and wondered what names would be written there in another twenty, fifty years; where the dam would burst, because there was a huge dam in Malagueta, of men, women, stones, on an uncharted course, where a new reality would be born, because Emmanuel Cromantine realised he had no more control over the future of Malagueta, just as Thomas Bookerman had been unable to determine the course of the last war.

While his mind was still engaged in the unresolved details of the war, he was brought into the glaring light of the present one by a brilliant translucence of images. Large camp fires rose in the territory surrounding his headquarters, where his men were brewing coffee and roasting generous helpings of beef, as the first signs of morning stirred in a black and white drapery of crows against a mosaic of stony hills, green valleys and a blue, glassy sky. Lately, he had been suffering from a bout of malaria which he had fought off with a strong dose of herbal remedy prepared by his mother, but the effect had left him listless in body though not in spirit, and Emmanuel Cromantine decided to sleep for a while.

He found it hard to sleep and was just starting to think of the appropriateness of language that he would use for his reply to Thomas Bookerman when the shattering impact of gunfire shook the ground under the building. Captain Hammerstone's men had regrouped and were attacking the seafront in a determined effort to capture the headquarters of Emmanuel Cromantine. Once again, the streets of Malagueta were in commotion. The new shopkeepers who had arrived during the interval between the two wars and had prayed for peace were the first to react to the renewal of fighting. They bolted their shops, went to the schools to pick up their children and went home to their houses where they tried to live with the discomfort by drinking brandy and ginger.

'This war is between the forces of progress and those of backwardness,' Alphonso Garrison said to his wife and daughters, after he had come home from his newspaper office, 'and I hope that rebel Cromantine is captured so we can have some peace here.' His wife who did not share his views about Emmanuel Cromantine, offered a blunt reply.

'But the captain is less justified in waging war here than those who built the town,' she said.

That night, while the fighting raged on, Alphonso Garrison wrote a sharp editorial which he hoped to publish in the next edition of his paper when it came out. In it, he denounced the obstinacy of Emmanuel Cromantine, his recklessness for prolonging the war, his refusal to come to some form of accommodation with the English. He pointed to the progress that had taken place since he had come from Cape Verde – the business connections that the leading merchants had made with suppliers in Liverpool and Birmingham so that the shops were full, while the number of young people who had gone to England to become lawyers and doctors had tripled in ten years.

'This turkey Malagueta,' he raged, 'is not for roasting by upstarts; it should be allowed to grow so that we shall all reap some benefit.'

After almost a week of fighting, Emmanuel Cromantine and his men were still holding out against the much better armed forces of the captain. In a bid to bring the fighting to an end, Captain Hammerstone sent a note to Thomas Bookerman. In it, he asked him to advise the young commander to think of the unforeseen consequences of holding out too long. 'Don't let pride and the vanity of youth lead him to destroy all that you have built,' he pleaded. A solution was possible. The English should be allowed to have a dominant say in the running of the country, keep all the land on the hilltop that they had expropriated, and, most importantly, the port area should be declared a free zone to which all would have access. If Emmanuel Cromantine did not agreee to his terms, Captain Hammerstone threatened to bombard his headquarters and to send all prisoners taken in the fighting to the island of Fernando Po where they would work as peons on cocoa plantations 'for a pittance'.

The new emissaries had no more luck than the delegation headed by Alphonso Garrison which had made an earlier visit to Thomas Bookerman. The two Englishmen and two Africans who set out in the silver morning dripped with sweat as they roasted in their woollen suits. They mopped their brows with the white handkerchiefs that they had brought with them as tokens of peace, but when they had been allowed safe passage through the ranks of enemy troops they found their way blocked by those who were guarding the house of Thomas Bookerman, who tore up the letter and told them to go back to their homes.

'Tell de captain dat if dere is any talking to do de general be de one to do de talking,' one of the guards said.

Captain Hammerstone flew into a rage when he received news of the failed mission. Searching for a way to make Thomas Bookerman pay for the insults of his guard, he searched his mind for remnants of past insults done to him. He brought back from the graves of the past campaign, the bones of the unappeased ghosts who had tormented him throughout his long undertaking to bring Malagueta down to its knees. There was a laudanum of thwarted glory numbing his senses as he thought of the long period he had had to wait for the surveyors and others to come to put into effect the ideas that had fired his imagination, that evening, very, very long ago, when he had been drinking in the London pub. For ensconced in Captain Hammerstone's head lately was a feeling such as he had never felt before, and the thought that he might die – because he too was old – without leaving Malagueta in the hands of capable men and women, filled him with dread. Accordingly, he planned one final attack against Emmanuel Cromantine's forces, when he hoped he would remove for ever all resistance to the new order that he and his men had introducd into Malagueta.

'So be it, men,' he said to his commanders, when they were assembled in the garrison. 'Cromantine and Bookerman have decided to dig their own graves, and we are going to bury them there.'

The fierceness with which he attacked the seafront that night surprised even Emmanuel Cromantine who had been expecting it. He touched the metal reassurance of the revolver which was lying on his desk, but he had never needed that confirmation of his preparedness to defend the cause for which he had been willing to lay down his life. Thus, even after he had put the gun in its holster, he did not immediately set out to confront his adversary. He thought of the two o'clock 'washing' of his body that he had promised his mother he would undergo to get rid of the malaria, once and for all: of the old house of Theophilus the apothecary, which he had been planning to repair as soon as he had the time, before he finally walked into the room where his guards had been waiting for him. They came to attention as Emmanuel Cromantin entered the room. Then, in a voice that trembled with rage, such as his men had never known he possessed, he gave the command to move.

'Let's get this snake out of Malagueta, once and for all,' he said.

He led his men into what had degenerated into hand-to-hand fighting for the control of the narrow streets in the area. With a recklessness unusual for him, Emmanuel Cromantine fought his way through a heavily cordoned-off street to get to the rest of his troops who were defending the large Saturday market opposite the church; shells fired by Captain Hammerstone's troops fell into the grounds of the college where the theological and musical students were trapped. In later life, after she had abandoned her considerable skills at the pianoforte, Arabella Garrison would remember that moment as the time when she saw Garbage leaping over the walls of the college with a large roll of paper in his hands, as he tried to get to a dilapidated house much covered by the thick armoury of lycopods. When he was almost there, Garbage was just about to enter the house when he saw the trail of black ants once again. Whereas at the time of his first discovery they had marched to the house, he saw several hundred wingless soldiers marching towards the battle-ground; he saw them as they demolished the citadels of lesser soldiers in their path, gathered up the leaves and tossed them out of the way.

When the trail turned into the corner of January Street, Garbage stopped in his track, held by the dazzling force of his discovery. Alusine Dunbar stood in the middle of the street encircled by an iridescent glow, with the telescopic eyes of his testicles projected at a great distance.

Guided by the iridescence, Garbage saw Alusine Dunbar bring Emmanuel Cromantine into view; he saw Emmanuel Cromantine as he was about to fire a shot at Captain Hammerstone who was charging at him. A great shattering bullet lodged in the cranium of the captain, where he had confused the dolphins of adventure bred in the cold seas of his life with the quicksands of glory, which had produced the fatalism of martyrdom in him. As he fell off his horse, Captain Hammerstone remembered, in one quick moment, the pleas of the Tamil woman as she had held his sailor's collar, begging him to give up the sea for the tranquil beauty of her island; she promised she would cook crabfish for him and wait on him for the rest of her life so that his white body would become brown with the cocoa butter of her love, which had begun with the gift of the son that she had given him. He suffered an instant of torment, remembering how he had left the other one, the woman in Calabar, who had told him that Africa was a difficult breast: drink a little of her milk but don't bleed the source dry. Then, in that last moment when everything ended for him, David Hammerstone recalled the inverterate virgins in Devon, one or two of whom had been prepared to give up the rhythm of English poetry for him, if only he would teach them to release the rhythm of their depraved bodies. Alas, he had not heeded any, driven by the spurious assertion of glory, now brutally abnegated in the tricky governorship of Malagueta.

The light of the testicles glowed, and, for the first time, Emmanuel Cromantine saw Garbage in the town, with the grave look that had so troubled his mother.

'So you are the poet,' Emmanuel Cromantine said to him. 'Let's hope you write about this when it is all over.'

He raised the arm that had silenced the life of Captain Hammerstone, as if in accolade to Garbage, but Emmanuel Cromantine did not have a chance to bring it down again. Out of the turmoil of the day, three shots rang out hitting him in his chest, paralysing for ever the reflexes of his arm in the airless morning, where the arm was raised as if in beatitude. The shots sent his horse into a gallop, but Emmanuel Cromantine was not thrown off its back. A blazing light, like a giant constellation, shot out from the testicles of revelation, and Garbage saw the celestial face of a beautiful woman appear, borne by the wings of an angel. Swooping down like a bird, she caught Emmanuel Cromantine before he hit the ground, kissed him on the forehead, leaving everyone confused, except for Alusine Dunbar, who knew through what crypt a great scorpion had passed to light up the eyes of the woman so that she could come through the looking-glass of all eternity, with the golden amulets round her arms, to stop Emmanuel Cromantine falling into the slough of degradation.

In the compound of the Cromantines, Jeanette had just started driving away a dog that was digging a hole under a large mango tree when a voice whispered in her head, calling her name. She shook her head, thought she was dizzy, but dismissed the possibility that she was going senile, because, although she was almost eighty-five, she still had her faculties right, read her Bible without spectacles and slept very lightly at night, so that 'if ma pikin comes, he won't have to make all dat noise wid dem soja boots, to disturb de dead'.

'Get away from here,' she said to the frantic dog. 'Who you want to bury?'

No sooner had she said that than she saw the angel descending from the clouds into her compound.

'Lawd have mercy! It's Fatmatta the Bird-Woman and ma boy,' she cried.

With a gentle movement of her arms, the angel laid the dead man at the feet of the old woman; she called the old woman 'my sister' just as she had done many, many years ago, when Jeanette Cromantine had been in a terrible middle passage, between life and death, on the threshold of motherhood, bringing her boy into the world, but who had now been returned to her for ever from the whirlwind of the harmattan blowing over Malagueta.

Louisa was trying a new dress on Fatmatta-Emilia when she was attracted by the screaming of her mother-in-law. She rushed out of the house to see the old woman crying over the body of her son.

'Fire! Fire! The cotton tree has fallen,' the younger woman cried, moving the old woman away from the man as the angel disappeared into the seablue clouds, surrounded by a great school of larks.

Garbage saw the clouds as the angel ascended. He had woken up from the daze that Alusine Dunbar had thrown over him, and started to run in the direction of the house with the lycopods. When he got there, all traces of it had been wiped out, as if a great hurricane had blown it off the face of the earth, carted it away into the depths of the sea, like a fabled ship full of the wonders of that magician, beyond the vertigoes of rediscovery.

◇

Two weeks later, the combined forces of the English and the mercenaries who had served the captain so well had taken over the town completely. They buried the captain in the grounds of the garrison with full military honours. With the dignity befitting him, Jeanette Cromantine and Louisa buried Emmanuel Cromantine in the old cemetery. Malagueta had never seen such a large crowd. While the troops stayed away from the route, four mules pulled the coffin in a fruit cart away to its resting place. As the funeral was taking place, one last thread of the old Malagueta was being severed. Thomas Bookerman and Phyllis, who had been captured on the night of Emmanuel's death, were put on a ship for the Gold Coast where they were allowed to pass their last days in relative peace, shut up in a fort that the Portuguese had built to hold the slaves on their way to the wasteland of America. The English had captured it, and there they could intern men and women like Bookerman and Phyllis, so that never again would they resist the designs of invaders.

BOOK FOUR

13   Marriage of Convenience

No one could have predicted the changes that would take place in Malagueta over the next fifty years. The wheels of change rolled on with their unstoppable force; history, as it had been before the time of the last war, was confined to the faded flowers of Jeanette Cromantine's memory. She, when they had brought her son to rest for ever, had found the strength to go on living by taking in a young girl as ward, so that 'Ah don't become a burden on Louisa and ma grandpikin!' To everyone's surprise, she insisted there would be no mourning for Emmanuel Cromantine; she even forbade Louisa to wear the black clothes of mourning, told her it was a sin to blame what had happened on the evil designs of the foreigners and their local supporters. It was, she said, finding comfort in the mysterious exegeses of life that had guided her since the time of the potato plague, the will of God that he had seen fit to take her husband and her son, and leave her to bear her tribulation in old age.

'It's de workin of de master, ma daughter,' she comforted Louisa in the bitter lacuna of the younger woman's happiness.

Working with a relentless vigour, Jeanette Cromantine went through the papers that Emmanuel had accumulated over the years on such subjects as botany, biology and poetry. These, she sent over to the college with instructions that if the teachers there did not want them, they should return them, so that she could keep them tied in a trunk, where she had kept her golden trinkets and other valuables over the years. Once, every month, she went to the cemetery with her daughter-in-law and granddaughter to put fresh flowers on Emmanuel's grave, but when she received two bottles of brandy with a note from Alphonso Garrison expressing his sympathy for the loss of her son and promising

321

to do whatever he could to make her last days on earth 'painless', she rejected the gesture, returned the brandy back with a note scribbled in her delicate old woman's handwriting, saying that but for the death, the likes of Alphonso Garrison would not have dared write to her, because if her son had been alive, he would have thrown the newcomer out of the town and others like him too.

Alphonso Garrison had in fact been waiting for a chance to mediate between the old members of the community and the new arrivals. Being one of the wealthiest men at the time of the last conflict, he had secretly supported the English forces and their Malaguetan allies with supplies and with a series of clandestine articles that would appear in the homes of leading merchants and civic leaders. The letters all had the sweet smell of camellia leaves, written in the exasperated language of a man for whom the last war had been a disaster because his supply of printing paper and other materials had rotted at the docks, his workers had refused to cross the lines of the warring parties and even his houseboys sometimes stayed away. Yet he was careful to keep his lines open to the enemies of the captain, gave generously to the various charities looking after the widows of men who had died during the storming of the garrison by Isatu Martins and the other women, helped with the restoration of a wing of the church and sent his daughters to a mixed school, rather than to the parochial anachronism of the English school in the hills above Malagueta.

Therefore, when order had been restored by the new administration, his importance as a businessman was recognised when he was named mayor of Malagueta with the responsibility for civic and social order. It was the chance that Alphonso Garrison had been waiting for. On the morning he put on his ceremonial robe of ermine, scarlet hat and white gloves and the heavy chain with the pendant of the Queen dangling from his neck, it was obvious that he had been preparing for such a role since that afternoon when he had landed in Malagueta, a refugee from what, in the years since leaving Cape Verde, he had come to view as the harum-scarum of barbarians who did not know what was good for them. How could they have revolted against people who only wanted to do the right things for them, feed them, clothe them, and insure that they did not die from excessive drinking, harlotry and witchcraft to which they were so prone? he had wondered. But such concerns had been forgotten on the byways of adventure where much of the early disappointment in his life had been incurred. What remained was the feeling that he was embarking upon a new experience which could last until the end of his life.

'Let them see what this son of a horse trainer can do,' he told his wife, while they waited for the guests to arrive at the party that he was throwing to celebrate his appointment.

No expense was spared to see that things went according to the plan Alphonso Garrison had for the evening. His pride was his family and his assets were his daughters, rather than the vast amount of gold that he had earned over the years. So when the guests arrived they were enchanted by the inordinately charming women who met them at the door, by the fine speech of the daughters into which a lot of money had been poured, and by their expensive coiffures. It was difficult for many of the guests to distinguish between the daughters and the mother because the bedrock of wealth, the tranquillity of their Elysian life in Malagueta, had all contributed to a feeling of robust health and elegance in them. While the barefooted servants dressed in white hurried from guest to guest serving the food that the Morrocan cook had prepared, Arabella Garrison sat at the pianoforte to entertain the governor. She made the keyboard sing with the tender melodies of Mozart which brought a large spectre of contentment to the face of the governor. Even the Italian aria parrot, which had been moved from its favourite place on the veranda, joined in the hyperborean delight as the young pianist transformed that tropical room into a Viennese salon. The bird flapped its wings and was heard to say: 'Play the two o'clock waltz and lull me to sleep,' which made the guests laugh.

Alphonso Garrison went to bed a happy man that night. As a parting gift to him before he left, the governor took him aside, and whispered in what may have been taken to be a conspiratorial voice, 'If I had such lovely daughters like yours, I would not be running this hell-hole, but would be content to see them married off to princes.'

They had indeed been raised to be married to princes, and there was no shortage of suitors, but what troubled Alphonso Garrison was the blunt refusal of his daughters to consider any of the offers of marriage that they had received from the sons of the leading doctors and lawyers in Malagueta. Rather, they seemed more concerned with defusing the friction that had arisen over the report that the governor was preparing to hang some of the captured rebels as a deterrent to others. Knowing how much their father valued their opinion, how he would never refuse them anything when they were young, even the expense of ordering Portuguese dolls that could move their eyelids, or hiring personal servants to wash their clothes, cut their nails and dress them until their mother had protested that their father was spoiling them, the girls worked on him and got him to appeal to the governor for a repeal of the sentences.

'Hang them, and you will have a dozen rebellions on your hands,' Arabella argued.

He was quietly pleased with their reasoning, their devotion to their studies, and when at the end of his first year as mayor nothing happened to disturb his happiness, he began to think of sending them away to England where they would complete their studies. But there was a loose thread in the tapestry that Alphonso Garrison had been trying to sew since he became mayor: all his entreaties to Jeanette Cromantine, and the two other widows who were the talk of the town because of their family names, had been rejected. They never once opened the invitations he sent to them, and once Jeanette Cromantine even turned her dog on the official messenger who had brought an invitation to a party to mark the birthday of the Queen. Raising her voice high enough for the neighbours to hear, she stood in the middle of her compound, pushed her chest forward, and sent a stiff message to the mayor.

'You tell dat man not to trouble dis old lady 'cause ah prefer to eat ma salt and pepper wid a little fish dan all dat steak he got in dat mansion.'

Salt and pepper were more than what Jeanette Cromantine had on her mind at that time. The young girl that she had taken in as a ward kept the old woman from going mad when she had amassed an accumulation of grief over her son. Death had touched her so many times that she was familiar with its many brushes: its blue brush of youth which had painted Rodrigo, the grey ashes of burnt wood where Gustavius had perished. So she was fortified by a perseverance experienced in the vortex of her knowledge that everything that grows eventually dies. Wealth and prosperity had come to her and Sebastian; joy had radiated in her garden where Emmanuel had played, and even to the roof of the house where she had thrown his milk teeth when he had begun to grow the permanent ones of manhood. Therefore it was under the roof of the old house where she had known so much happiness, where she had fought off so many trials that she collected the human treasures of her life, whom she hoped would survive her.

Forty days after the death of her son, she had the house painted a bright white, changed the flowers on the veranda and took down the white curtains that had hung on the windows. Binta the dutiful maid who had been with them for years had gone back to her 'country' when

Emmanuel Cromantine came back from exile, but when the news of his death reached her, she had sent a young girl to the Cromantines. On the first night in the house she almost burnt it down when she forgot to put the candle out before going to sleep.

Louisa went back to teaching after the death of Emmanuel Cromantine. Jeanette Cromantine had urged her to do so.

'Go back to de classroom, ma child; dat is where you two met, and ah sure he will be dere smiling, if ah knows dat son of mine.'

Isatu Martins also helped to get her to face the world again.

'Now, we are three women without men, but not without their love,' she said. 'So let us remember them by being alive in their memory.'

◇

Soon after Louisa went back to teaching, broughams appeared on the streets of Malagueta for the first time. The children of the noveau riche mixed with the few sons of the colonial administration in the grammar schools. Their expensive jackets and ties marked them out as belonging to a specail breed; they stood out like precious bulls: proud, stubborn and opinionated. They had a brazenness and arrogance which came from a claim to the world that was the preserve of those who wielded power and meted out justice. If life had been an enigma for the children of the old families, the new ones regarded it as a large dinner to be eaten at one go.

Louisa would sometimes complain to her mother-in-law about how difficult it was to teach the new children. Jeanette Cromantine had a ready answer:

'Don't worry your head over dat,' she said. 'It's like a marriage of convenience so let's see how long it gon last.'

Some of the grandchildren of the original founders of the town were indeed drawn into all kinds of marriages with the new rulers. They were so fascinated with the prospect of being accepted into the houses of the English that they went to the Notary Public and changed their names from African to 'Christian' ones so that the pronunciation would not break the jaws of the English when they met at parties. Alphonso Garrison would sometimes take his daughters to those parties. To the strings of music played by a black band that had been trained to play 'classical music' they forced their unclassical bodies to respond to the torturous strains of the baptism from 'native' to 'civilised', while the oestrogen in their immature bodies multiplied with a vigorous sexuality.

For their part, the young black men endured the summer prisons of their dinner jackets and the traps of their patent shoes. They learned how not to drop their aitches, how to bow in front of ladies, which foot to put forward when dancing the foxtrot, how to eat properly with a knife and fork and never to refer to themselves as 'natives'.

'That is for others,' said a young lawyer who had been courting Matilda Garrison for three years with no evident success.

Regina Garrison did not always go along with what she considered the pretensions of the new ruling class. She balked at the idea of seeing her daughters at those soirées just so that they could parade 'like peacocks'. 'What kind of father are you,' she would berate her husband, 'allowing those ill-bred English boys and the sons of haberdashers to examine your daughters as if they were inferior china?'

'It's all right, Regina,' Alphonso Garrison would reply. 'Even precious china has to be brought out of the cupboard now and then.'

Then she would resign herself to being a long-suffering wife who had allowed her husband to ride the vainglorious waves of the mayoral sea over the years, to forget their early independence in Cape Verde, and turn his newspaper into a tabloid for the publication of high falutin 'rubbish' by all kinds of 'high-muck-a-muck' who, in her view, would be nobodies 'where they come from, if you ask me'.

Gradually, Malagueta began to attract a new breed of settlers. They came from the surrounding towns: colourful men with bright glassy bead necklaces, gaps in their teeth and women distinguished by a terracotta beauty. With large bundles on their heads, they settled into the outskirts of Malagueta, went to work as houseboys, labourers and dock workers and allowed themselves to be conscripted into the new army that the administration was assembling to serve the Queen. One such conscript was a man named Sheku Masimiara, whose grandson was to stage an unsuccessful coup against a corrupt president seventy-five years later.

Suddenly, like a creature from a forgotten era, the old bookstore owner Richard Farmer died. He was seventy-five years old and, since the death of his brother Gabriel, had holed up in the bookstore where cobwebs, lizard droppings and cockroaches had done untold harm to the books over the years. The letters of ardent love that had flourished in that lovers' nest in the early days of the town had continued to bring many young people there, in spite of the bookseller's reputation as a cantankerous old man who swore under his breath every time one of the children of the 'hoi polloi' came to his store, spent his time swinging a broom at the spiders and lizards that made his place look like a sorcerer's den, and wore a black cap all the time.

'Teach us how to write a love letter, Grandpa,' they would say to him to get him to talk. Then he would give them endless lectures on the many species of beetles in Malagueta, on why they should never cook turtle eggs because snakes had a habit of laying their own eggs in the same place as turtles; the trustworthiness of dogs as opposed to the treachery of some types of human beings and the 'good woman' Louisa, who was wasting her time trying to 'break the heads' of children who were too spoiled to learn anything.

'Pound for pound, if you ask me,' he would say, 'I would rather have a mule to teach than some of those children.'

When his will was read, it was discovered that he had left his house and bookstore to Garbage. In a fine italic document, he thanked Garbage for keeping the memory of his brother alive by coming to their house to read all the books on medieval poetry, Shakespeare and such rarities as the astronomical discoveries of Copernicus and the haiku of the Japanese. Literature, he wrote, may yet save this place from 'the barbarians', though I am not convinced they 'prefer literary refinement to the hackneyed pleasures of religious dogma'.

'Do what you like with our common properties, but keep the beauty of literature alive,' he wrote.

Against the objections of Isatu Martins, Garbage moved into the house three months later. After convincing his mother that she was better off with a young maid than with a young man who needed to 'stand on his own two feet', he soon settled into a routine whereby he went to his mother's house every day for his meals, but returned home in the evening, to read the books in the house.

No one had any idea about how he spent his time in that house; he guarded his privacy like a hermit crab and, except for his mother, no one was seen to visit him. Sometimes, he would come out and go to the grocer's for a leg of lamb, a pound of potatoes or kippers, which he would take to his mother's, stay for a while and talk a little. He was never sick, had never been to the dentist's and ate very little. His neighbours would have sworn he did everything inside his house, except that when he went to the latrine in the outhouse he would stay there for almost an hour, only to emerge sweating profusely later.

'Must be dem books he is reading in dere wid all dat smell; but dat man sure is crazy, if you ask me,' said one of his neighbours, trying to understand the long stays in the outhouse.

While he had been going through the papers of Gabriel Farmer, Garbage had discovered the poems that the lovesick man had written over forty years ago for Phyllis, but which had remained intact, in spite of the humidity, inside a brown envelope. There were twenty-five poems written on ten pages, with the last whiff of the camphor balls that the unhappy poet had put inside the envelope to preserve his plaintive couplets against the voracity of the termites.

Garbage read them slowly, as if to explore the soul of the man who could write such fine, albeit unrequited, lines. Nightingales sang in the soul of Gabriel Farmer, orchids bloomed and withered in the poems, without the woman knowing, while the nights of the poet had been filled with the deepest longings for her, though he knew she would never come to his house, because he never once invited her.

When he had read twelve of the poems, Garbage put the rest away and began to play on an ocarina a slow, sad tune that he had learned from his mother's maid. The instrument had been made for him by the man who came round to clean his house, who had told him: 'You look too serious; have something to take your mind off the world.' He continued playing it late into the night, at first with an exquisite solemnity, then giving himself over to a flight of joy which, however, did not last, because the instrument was of a kind that did not sustain the mortality of joy, whose language Garbage had not mastered. Much later, when he had exhausted the possibilities of music, he put the instrument away and went to sleep. It was a peaceful sleep, unlike many troubled ones in the past, and when he woke seven hours later, his mind had been unburdened of the alkali of Emmanuel's death, the elusive mysticism of Alusine Dunbar and even the disquiet felt over the decision of his mother to go on living in the big house, when she could have moved in with Jeanette and Louisa. He cooked himself a big breakfast of beans and cornbread, drank two cups of tea imported from the country where Emmanuel had been in exile, and, after he had put the plate away, began to pace up and down the parlour.

Suddenly, as if buoyed by an effulgent light, he sat down at the writing desk, took out a sheet of paper from one of the drawers and began to write a poem. At first it was a slow river, blocked by a foliage of trees with chattering monkeys and rhapsodic barbets whose songs drowned the one that the poet was struggling to write. A dam slowed the river, further impeding its course, but Garbage fought with the force of words to leap over the hardness of stones and the flanges of steel. Then the turbulence began and, after he had gathered the fresh ferns of songs, he began to sail with a flourish of words. He searched for Malagueta in the tempestuous seas of former times where the conches of its birth stones had been trapped by the planktons of oblivion since the time of the first war. He brought back from the unfathomable bottom of the sea the coelacanth that had guided Sebastian and Jeanette Cromantine, clumsily navigating the route to the promised land. When he had put their trembling feet on that land, and welcomed them with garlands of sea lilies, he made them drink from a gourd of aged wine, so that their parched lips would be healed for ever. He wrote more poems; poems about his mother in the vista of his own childhood, when the two of them had been drawn together by the blues of his dead father's soul; poems for even the Virgins, because, in the drabness of their gowns and the rigidity of their comportment, they had meant well for Malagueta. In the stormy petrel of his poet's soul, he made Thomas Bookerman and Phyllis Dundas escape from their banishment in the Gold Coast to the New World, just so that they could tell the grandchildren of those who had been left behind that Malagueta was a dream come true, in spite of the banditry of David Hammerstone and the treachery of the quislings who had fought for him.

As soon as he was satisfied with his poems, Garbage walked into the offices of the *Malaguetan Star* and demanded to see the publisher who was also the mayor of the town. Shown into his office, the young poet was welcomed by Alphonso Garrison like a long-lost friend. He enquired after his mother and asked whether she had received the invitation to the ceremony honouring her dead husband and others who had contributed so much to the founding of the town. After which he turned to the papers that Garbage was holding.

'What have you got there?' Alphonso Garrison wanted to know.

'My poems,' replied the poet.

He stood on the quicksand of anxiety while the mayor read two of the poems. If Alphonso Garrison understood the dance of the winged serpent that Garbage had created on the pages, he did not let it show on his face. Rather, he promised to get back to the poet as soon as possible with a word about publication.

Later that evening, the mayor took the poems home and showed them to his wife and elder daughter Arabella.

'They are by that young man with the incredible name of dustbin,' he said.

Regina Garrison read one of the poems and was so shaken by its disquieting power that she did not even attempt to read another one, before handing them over to her daughter.

'He is a poet, all right,' the mayor's wife said, 'but what a tormented man he is!'

Arabella went to her room with the poems after dinner, opened her windows in the warm night and, after lighting the desk lamp, started to read. The extravagance of Garbage's passion, the deep reservoir of his brooding and the zoological garden of his images that had frightened Regina Garrison created such a glandular disturbance in Arabella after she had read the first five poems that she felt hot in spite of the rush of a breeze, and had to remove the pins of her bodice in order that she might be able to breathe in the fire of Garbage's verse. Throughout her days at school, in the wood-panelled library of the Victorian house where Alphonso Garrison had raised his daughters so that they would receive the entreaties of illustrious men, Arabella had been introduced to the beauty of English poetry, the paradisaical gardens of Spain and the arabesque fountains of Rome. And she had dreamed of the other enchanting wonders of those lands so often that she already knew some of their names intimately, and was only waiting for her father to give up what she considered that thankless business of running a crazy town where no one appreciated his efforts, and take them on a holiday. But nothing that she had read in those Arabian Nights tales had so shaken her that she had felt the need to be freed of that garment that was a sign of her proper upbringing.

Consequently, when she had put the poems away and tried to sleep, she felt the pointed quill of the poet pricking her heart; she tried to remember what it was like when the priest had touched her head on the day she had received her first communion; whether she had felt anything, a transmission of the Holy Spirit. Lying in her warm bed, she realised that she was losing her body heat, that she was shivering, but told herself that she was being foolish, letting herself be disturbed by the tormented scribbling of a man who was not really of her class, and who was probably not interested in her class either.

At six o'clock in the morning, the first flickers of light found Arabella Garrison in bed, still tossing her restless body on the rumpled sheets. Throughout the night, she had not been able to resolve the contradictory feelings she had for the poet; she felt drawn to him because of his agony, yet was repelled by the naked fires of his passion which rose in brutal flames of desires, such that she felt the spidery hands of the man crawling all over her body, which until then had not been aroused by the

330

provocative passions of other poets. She was still lying in bed when at seven o'clock, the male servant rang the bell for breakfast. When she had washed and dressed her tired body, Arabella Garrison came down to the large ornate room where her parents were waiting. Her sister with whom she might have shared her feelings was away at the college, spending the weekend with the female English teacher in order that they might rehearse Matilda's part in *A Midsummer Night's Dream* in time for the New Year's party.

The protean sun of morning shone into the warm room with the morning smell of fresh fruits as Arabella sat down to breakfast with her brown parents who were robust in the golden light, as was to be expected of people who had often been out in the infra-light of the sun.

'Well, have you made up your mind about our poet?' enquired the publisher of his daughter, when he had put the last spoonful of oats inside his mouth.

'I like some of them, though I can't say for certain that I understand them,' she replied modestly.

'They are not subversive?' the mayoral voice asked.

'Not that I can tell, except that in some he seems to find our kind repugnant to a fault, because of our insistent obsession with status and what have you,' she replied.

Regina Garrison attempted to insert herself into the conversation.

'If you ask me,' she said, 'there is a lot of sense in what the young man is saying, for we seem to have lost all notion of self-esteem, what with the inordinate lengths to which we have gone to ensure our daughters are rightly connected.'

Alphonso Garrison dismissed the criticism of his wife with a tightening of his brow. Their marriage, which had known such delicious pleasures in the beginning, had foundered on the rocks of Malagueta in recent years, as the publisher had expanded his business, built a lot of houses and continued to lend money to people who used their houses as collateral, which they were sometimes unable to retrieve. He decided he would publish the poems of Garbage as proof to his wife that his heart was still in the right place.

A great public shock broke throughout the town when the poems were published. Isatu Martins was inundated with enquiries about the poet's childhood so that articles could be written about him by the leading men of letters who were versifiers of the old school of Romantic poetry. Other representatives of the establishment considered some of the poems injudicious and decided to keep an eye on the young man. Much to his surprise, Garbage found himself invited to visit the homes of many of the leading citizens of Malagueta. He went to a few where he was treated like a rare specimen by the husbands, while their bejewelled wives fed their lustful eyes on him. He treated the men with scorn while humouring their wives, though he never let himself be talked into making a speech. He would arrive at their homes dressed in the most outrageous bohemianism, which did a lot to his fame as a maverick. He gave public readings of his poems in the Farmer bookstore and at the college where Arabella and Matilda Garrison sat in the front row to listen to his passionate voice.

A few months later, Arabella confessed to her sister that she had a liking for the poet. The two sisters had evolved into very different creatures. While the elder had grown up with the dark skin that was so evident in her childhood, had long wavy hair and high cheekbones, was of a pleasant disposition and passionate about music, Matilda had not been able to shed all the fat that had plagued her childhood. But she was attractive in a supercilious way, was of a very light complexion and insisted on the servants addressing her as 'miss', unlike her sister who was content with being addressed by her first name. She still kept her chamberpot unemptied under her bed every morning, until her servant would arrive to open her windows and empty the receptacle. In keeping with the high opinion she had of herself, she regarded some of the grandchildren of the original founders of Malagueta as uncouth barbarians – though terrified of Garbage because of his brilliance and the contemptuous fire of his words she would not reduce herself to the indignity of considering him as worthy of her attention. She was therefore aghast when she heard the confession of her sister.

'He may be a poet,' she said, 'but you mustn't forget that he is the son of a stonemason.'

Arabella was not given to such scurrilous prejudice. Her innate good nature, her love of mankind, which was universal, and her appreciation of creative genius were enough to overcome whatever reservations she might have felt about Garbage when she first read his poems. She decided she would write to him.

Two weeks later, a maid who had been sworn to secrecy delivered a fine envelope to Garbage on which his name was written by the delicate and refined hand of Arabella Garrison. In her letter, she began by criticising his excessive show of emotions, which she found terrifying; his tendency to be disdainful of 'Christian values', and his contempt for the authorities. 'They are not all that bad,' she pleaded, 'if only you would give them a chance.' Then she admitted how much she had enjoyed reading his poems, though she confessed she had not understood some of them. 'But you as a man of letters, must be careful not to judge us lesser mortals from your high pedestal, if we find you lacking in those values that we hold dear.' She hoped that as two artists, they could share notes together on the beauty of music and poetry. 'Consider me a kindred spirit and may God bless you,' she concluded.

Garbage did not know what to make of the letter, because he was wrapped up in a world where the desires of women did not exist, especially those he believed might want to trap him into marriage. When he felt the need for one, he would go to the Yellow House where the women took him in and served him wine and food before going to bed with him, because in their eyes he was the most moody man God had ever made and needed someone to make him laugh. But such pleasures as he derived from those transient loves were not allowed to compete with his work. He never allowed any of the women to visit him, and the only woman ever seen around the house was his mother.

'Find yourself a woman,' Isatu Martins would advise her son, looking at the disorder in his room. Yet she knew that her son was stamped with the sign of a free spirit from the moment he had been given to her a long time ago. But she prayed that he might make her a grandmother soon so that she would not suffer the same anguish that her own father, the banana-grove man, had suffered during the long wait for her to give him a grandchild.

The letter remained unanswered for over three months. During that time, to the shock of everyone who knew her, Matilda Garrison married the wealthy but not too bright son of a merchant who was a functionary in the administrative service. They had an expensive wedding at the cathedral on George Street, followed by a reception in the town hall, where the guests drank the six dozen cases of wine that Alphonso Garrison had ordered from a cellar in Portugal. Arabella felt a tightness in her throat on the night of her sister's wedding; although the bonds of sisterhood had never really been strong between them, she felt a mixture of joy and unhappiness when the servants came down from the house with the two trunks containing Matilda's trousseau, while the bride kissed her goodbye before hurrying to join her husband in the brougham, holding the cage of the Italian aria parrot in her left hand.

Arabella found some solace in her music. The house would awaken at seven o'clock in the morning to the brilliant fires of a Hungarian rhapsody by Liszt, be serenaded at two in the afternoon by the gentle melody of a Chopin polonaise, and, when the mayor came home from his office, he had his after-dinner cigar and brandy to the brooding air of a Beethoven sonata.

Being an observant mother, Regina Garrison had been noticing the changes in her daughter's attitude, but was discreet enough not to let her concern show. She worried when Arabella stayed up late at night writing letters which were never posted, because Arabella would tear them up and burn them in an urn the next day. For someone who had never been guilty of the excesses of vanity, such as could be said of her sister, Arabella had begun to spend a long time in front of the rococo mirror in the bathroom, looking at her face. Regina knew this from the maid who had been spying on her daughter. She became convinced that something was deeply wrong when Arabella began to eat 'like a wolf' when hitherto she had eaten 'like a chicken'. Thinking that a trip abroad might cheer her up, she suggested to her husband that the young woman be sent away, although she did not divulge the reasons for her worries to him, reasoning that it was a woman's affair.

Arabella thanked her mother for the idea but turned down the trip, leaving Regina Garrison more confused in the involucrum of the young woman's unhappiness. As a last resort, she consulted the family doctor with the 'symptoms' of her daughter's 'illness', adding that while Arabella had been punctilious about using her bath salts in the past, she was now getting inside the bathtub filled with hard water as if she wanted to punish her body.

The doctor, whose eyes had been made gentle by the years of wearing spectacles and whose patience had been improved by the hours spent listening to fretful mothers, considered Regina's concern for a while, before offering what sounded like a non-medical reply.

'It's all right, Mrs Garrison,' the doctor said. 'Some people need to punish their bodies for sins imagined, just as in Catholic regions the flagellants scourge themselves to achieve religious discipline. Arabella is subjecting hers to the kind of rigour that only a young woman in danger of losing her caution would do, though I can't say over what.'

Matters were not helped when, while Arabella was walking around the Garrison house looking forlorn, the gossip telegraph in Malagueta would buzz with the news that Garbage had been seen in the Botanical Gardens with the daughter of a leading churchman, or that the wife of one of the lecturers at the college was leaving her husband for the poet. Arabella started looking even more woebegone, and ate with a gluttony that frightened her mother, and, for once, Regina Garrison spoke to her.

'If you want to kill yourself, then do so like a lady and not like a pig.'

Weeks went by and Arabella continued to walk around in a state of perpetual dream. Sometimes she would begin to practise a new piece on the piano only to abandon it in the middle. She broke out in a rash of pimples but mercilessly squeezed them dry, leaving her face ugly for a while. Suddenly, she could bear it no longer. She shut herself up in her room for days, became even more despondent and gave herself over to a frightening look of dishevelment. In the midst of such despair, she abandoned all ideas of her social status and wrote an angry letter to Garbage.

In it, she called him a cad, 'like the rest of you local men', and angrily blamed herself for writing to him in the first place. She told him how she had been the one who had persuaded her father to publish his poems, even though it was quite clear from them that there was a crudity in his manners and he lacked a complete understanding of the basic rules of grammar. 'But, rest assured that although I have now written to you twice, I am not in any way under your spell, and for all I care you can go on seeing those women who are more or less your type, because they satisfy your basest needs. Goodbye and don't even bother to reply because our ideals in the pursuit of artistic values do not meet at the same altar of refinement,' she concluded, and sent her trusted maid to deliver the letter.

Shortly after, on Christmas Eve, the governor gave a party to which all the leading families in Malagueta had been invited. Arabella had refused to go, saying that she had a headache, and did not even go to the door to bid her parents goodbye. She had a bath and went to her room, where, unable to sleep, she started making a sweater to keep her warm in the harmattan. She had kept her window open so as to enjoy the breeze coming from the sea, and, except for the flannel nightgown, was naked. She had just pricked her finger with a needle when a stone with a white piece of paper wrapped round it landed inside her room. She dropped her knitting, picked the stone up and read the note. There, in the familiar handwriting that she had seen on that first night when her father had brought the poems home, was the reply of Garbage, the tersest note she had ever read: I am down here.

Arabella went to her window and saw the silhouette of a man standing against the faint light of the moon. A hand shot out in the dark, and then the man started to climb the wall of the house. A great horror gripped Arabella Garrison, but although she opened her mouth in readiness to scream, she was unable to do so, because her heart would not let her.

Rather, she moved away from the window and stood in awe as Garbage came through the window.

A dog barked in the garden outside, and Arabella saw a beautiful owl fly from the branch of a guava tree to land on the roof of the house. Then, in two short steps, Garbage stood in front of her, and touched her face. But when he attempted to kiss her, he felt Arabella's back stiffen and the piano keys of her teeth jam. She tried to move away, but gently, he picked her up like a waxed doll and dumped her on her bed.

'If you don't go away, I shall scream,' she threatened, but she knew that Garbage had been to the governor's party because he held the crumpled invitation in one hand, and must have seen her parents there. She locked her knees together, as he came on top of her, bit his hands and cried No, No, No. But it was a weak cry which made Arabella look more beautiful than at any time since she had been bitten by the moths of desire, and which released her from the hurt and humiliation suffered during the long months of waiting for a reply from him.

A cruel look appeared on her face, and Arabella Garrison raised her right hand in a well-aimed slap at Garbage's face. It never landed. He caught it with the same skill with which he had trapped the elusive sunbirds of the muse and, with a deftness that caught Arabella off guard, unlocked the gates to her maidenhood and paralysed her legs. Unguarded, a tumultuously delirious piece of music possessed her body, numbed her senses with its raptures of wine, transporting her to a fabled land that she had sometimes dreamed of as she played the pianoforte in the past. She struggled to resist the source of the music, but when Garbage relaxed the tempo, he saw the look of a frightened animal on Arabella's face, terrified that the music would stop. She threw her arms into a powerful pinion round the back of the man, awed by the spasmodic force of the tidal wave that he could release in her as he increased the tempo. It was the most beautiful piece of music that Arabella Garrison had ever heard, and she wept with joy, grateful that God had given her the dexterity of body and the nimbleness of fingers to respond to the unbearable pleasures of its passion.

14 Matilda and her Seven Houses

Jeanette Cromantine had so recovered from the loss of her son that she never allowed herself to dwell on her fate or sink into the mire of self pity.

With only a few years to go before she reached a century, she had turned over the running of the house to Louisa and the ward. But not even the weakening of her prodigious strength or the onslaught of death could put her off from the one task that had kept her alive after Emmanuel's death: the raising of Fatmatta-Emilia. Tall, graceful and shy, she had grown into a lovely woman under the watchful eyes of her grandmother. While Louisa killed the pain of losing Emmanuel by teaching and by serving on several charity bodies that collected old clothes and medicines to be sent to the town surrounding Malagueta, while Isatu Martins remembered Gustavius by being generous to the young men who wanted to learn the trade of builder, Jeanette Cromantine slaved and laboured over her granddaughter with a single-minded dedication. She fought agues with all kinds of remedies, walked with her to school every day until Fatmatta-Emilia was twelve, and taught her the catechism in time for confirmation, against the wishes of Louisa. When Fatmatta-Emilia turned thirteen, her grandmother delved into her considerable savings and threw a large party for her to which she invited fifty guests.

'She is ma source of strength, the reason ah am living,' she would say to people who felt she was spoiling her granddaughter. She argued with a teacher in school who made an unguarded comment about 'a rebel's daughter', telling her that if it wasn't for the likes of her son, the likes of the teacher would not be alive. She changed the furniture in her room every two years, ordered shoes for her from a catalogue that was printed in Manchester, and a complete set of encyclopedias so 'dat ma grandpikin kin know de worl' de way ah never knowed it'. She derived great pleasure listening to her granddaughter telling her about the world: about Eskimos who lived all their lives buried under snow, about the Zulu king who had sacrificed love for the sake of his country, which Jeanette Cromantine found 'too much'.

But in spite of the lavished love of her grandmother, Fatmatta–Emilia was not spoiled and was something of a bookworm, which brought back memories of her father to the twilight years of her grandmother. In fact, she was so dutiful to her grandmother that she never went out on dates, even on chaperoned ones, but preferred to stay at home with her grandmother, learning how to crochet from the old woman. When Jeanette Cromantine teased her about whether she had 'an intended', Fatmatta-Emilia always dodged the question.

'I am happy being with you, Grandma,' she would say.

So that when the gossip tongues started wagging about Fatmatta-

Emilia having an affair with Septimus Doherty, the husband of Matilda Garrison, Jeanette Cromantine had to summon all her restraint not to unleash a string of insults against her granddaughter as she imagined the devotion and love of her last twenty-one years going up in flames. For days, she went around with a long stick, talking to herself, saying snake, snake, snake. Asked where it was by Louisa so that she might kill it, the old woman pointed outside, but went on groaning for days. She avoided looking at Fatmatta-Emilia, unless the two of them came face to face first thing in the morning, and her attitude was so unusual that her daughter-in-law thought that senility was finally catching up with her. Then, out of the blue, a golden idea struck her. Saying that it had been a long time since she went out of the house, she hired a brougham and had the ward come with her for a ride round the town.

'Let me go see what dey done to dis town before dey send me to ma grave,' she told Louisa, although her real intention was to have a look at the man who was 'dat snake'.

Wrapped up against the cold, she drove round a town that had grown beyond her recognition since the time of the last war. On the site of the first settlement that they had built almost eighty years ago, she saw the fort built as a new home for the white governor, next to the splendid courthouse where they administered the laws of their Queen. The streets had been widened to make room for the coaches of the new merchant class; the harbour was crowded with the ships of the trading nations with which Malagueta was doing business. But it was the new administrative building of the colonial regime that held her spellbound: huge, imposing and occupying much of the land where some of the fiercest battles had taken place. Jeanette Cromantine watched the young white officials going in; some black clerks were eating their lunch on the grounds of the building and the old woman came down from the car and walked over to them.

'Son,' she said to one of them, 'which one of you is Septimus Doherty?'

He pointed to a room in the basement of the building, saying that 'Mr Doherty is one of the black big shots with his own office.' Jeanette Cromantine walked in and came face to face with a small man, brown in complexion, already balding in his youth, and with the timid eyes of an unloved dog. He got up from his chair when the old woman walked in, and offered her a seat.

When she had made herself comfortable in the large chair, Jeanette Cromantine removed the silk headgear from her head, and fixed a steady, wicked look at Septimus Doherty.

'Mister,' she said, 'dis white head done know a lotta trouble before you wus born, before dis building done come up, and de Lawd knows ah done ma share to make dis town fit for living in ma days. De train done leave us behind, but dat don't mean you newcomers can mess wid us; so ah swear to de memory of ma dead boy, Emmanuel Cromantine, dat if you don't stop molesting ma granddaughter, ah gon run you outta dis town.'

Septimus Doherty had removed his spectacles from his unloved puppy face while the old woman was speaking. Tears ran down the face which at one time had been a handsome one, but had been made pudgy by a combination of sleeplessness and unhappiness. Jeanette Cromantine had not been privy to the crying of a man since that evening, almost seventy-five years ago, when Sebastian had collapsed on the marital bed, unsure of his manhood. So by the time Septimus had found his voice to speak, some of the anger had left the old woman.

'Mama,' Septimus said in the gentlest voice the old woman had ever heard, 'I would rather die than hurt you; or shame the memory of your famous son. On my word as a Christian, I have never touched your granddaughter. All I did was to mention to my wife that if I had any sense I should have told my father to go to hell with his money, and married a fine woman like your Fatmatta-Emilia, whom I have only seen in church, rather than the shrew I was forced to marry. It's she who has been spreading the rumour that I have been seeing your grand-daughter, and that is the whole truth.'

Septimus Doherty was the only son of a widower who had made a good deal of money planting coffee trees and cacao when the country around Malagueta had been joined to the original town. Strong, aggressive and bullying, Robert Doherty had considered it a natural match when he had contracted a 'business marriage' between his son and the wilful daughter of the mayor.

'If that boy is going to inherit my money,' he told Alphonso Garrison over lunch one afternoon, 'then he needs someone like your daughter to see that it is well spent.'

The marriage was a disaster from the very beginning. Although she had originally been charmed by the idea of marrying someone who was a 'rising star' in the colonial administration, with the prospect of going overseas for further training, followed by a possible attachment to the governor of Barbados, Matilda Doherty discovered on the night of their wedding that Septimus Doherty was not the man she had imagined for a husband. Not having been advised by her mother about what to do or expect on her wedding night, Matilda had spent half an hour in the bathroom trying on the half-dozen nightgowns of her trousseau to see which one would hide her chubby body, of which she was ashamed; she applied a mentholated balm to her nostrils, as she had done for weeks, to fight the effects of a prolonged cold, massed her hair into a bishop's mitre, and drank a glass of water containing Epsom salts to ward off any bowel movement during the night. Then, kneeling down in front of the large mirror, she assumed the form of a praying mantis, and asked the Virgin Mary for guidance, before going into the bedroom to meet her husband.

She had a shock. Septimus Doherty had stripped himself naked and stood in a state of erect preparedness waiting for his wife. When Matilda saw his portentous animal, her legs turned jelly and she thought she was going to faint. She had imagined a man who would turn his back on her, while she undressed in the dark, and who would himself undress likewise; because in some twisted corner of her mind, Matilda Garrison had connected the coming together of man and woman with the prudish sanction of the church, under a double-layered sheet, and strictly for the propagation of the species. For that last reason, she had been prepared to suffer the act of deflowering, but the animal terror induced in her by the vertical summons of her husband was more than she had prepared herself for. She ran back to the bathroom, bolted the door and after making the sign of the cross, was violently sick. The marriage was never consummated. Matilda went to Friday mass the next day, but refused to enter the confessional booth, and when her mother arrived in the afternoon with fresh fruits, Matilda had never looked more radiant. She behaved as if nothing had happened, gave orders to the cook to keep the soup warm for Septimus, and arranged and rearranged the flowers on the dining table.

Yet, when she was preparing for bed that night, she put on a complicated array of armour consisting of tightly knitted drawers firmly secured round her waist by a cord, which she interlaced into a granny knot, completed with a flannel nightgown buttoned from her neck to midriff.

When he saw her come into the bedroom, Septimus Doherty, who unlike the previous night, had put on his pyjamas, did not even bother to claim his marital right. He took his pillow and walked out of the room, but not before he had paused at the door to deliver a verbal blow to his wife.

340

'Don't worry,' he said, 'you can light your own fire with a candle and I hope it burns right down to your twisted heart.'

They kept up the pretence of being a happy couple for quite a while. Matilda was a gracious hostess when her husband entertained his father or his superiors in the administrative staff. Being well read, she impressed them with her knowledge of such subjects as horseback riding which had recently been introduced into the town, the pleasure of cultivating rhododendrons and the difficulty of playing Lady Macbeth in a town 'where most women do not identify with that role'. On Sundays they went to church fairly regularly, although when she felt the need for greater spiritual rectitude Matilda, who was a Catholic, went to mass alone.

Things would have gone on like this for a long time if Regina Garrison had not noticed that contrary to her manifest happiness, Matilda Doherty was losing the ability to communicate with people, and that she had entered into a state of unnatural paleness, which was obvious even in someone so white. Large crow's feet, when she woke up in the morning, told of Matilda's sleepless nights. According to her maid, she talked to herself during the day and spent a good deal of time teaching the Italian aria parrot to whistle a tune from Puccini's *The Virtuous Maid*. 'Make this miserable woman happy today, my pet,' she would cue to the bird on the evanescent evening, while the rhododendrons shielded her from view.

Regina Garrison decided to confront her daughter after she was convinced that the roots of her excessive pride, the insufferable prudishness of her mind, and a reluctance to admit that she was ever wrong, meant that Matilda would never open up to her. She chose the right time, waiting for Matilda's husband to be away at the office before confronting her daughter.

'I may not be as bright as you are, young lady,' she said to her, 'but I can see beyond my nose, and I know that you and your husband are not sleeping in the same bed.'

Matilda was aghast. She had thought her problem was a well-guarded secret, but had not reckoned with the vigilance of her maid, who would go in to make the bed in the marital bedroom and, not finding a strand of her master's hair on the pillows, had gossiped to the other maids during the day off, that Matilda was a 'frigid woman who done drove dat poor man to liquor'.

Which was not true, because Septimus had overcome the indignity of being a henpecked husband by confining his wife to the fraudulence of his father and the mischance of a bad dream. If he drank at all, it was more out of boredom and lassitude than from any damage to his manhood suffered as a result of his wife's puritanical stricture. For while she was engaged in other matters than the one for which Robert Doherty had contracted the marriage – 'the prolongation of my seed' – he found time to give chess lessons to the boys in the youth club at the college, play cricket for the 'colonials' and serve as a church official. It was in this last capacity that he had met Fatmatta-Emilia and, after inviting her out to tea, had walked her halfway home, to preserve her honour. So that when his wife heard about it, she circulated the rumour about the 'affair' as proof that she had married a lecher who was responsible for her unhappiness.

On the other hand, while Matilda Doherty continued to apply the mentholated balm to her nostrils and put on her chastity belt before going to bed, Arabella was enjoying a radiant tropical bloom of happiness. Freed from the shackles of her sheltered childhood by the daring seduction by Garbage, she displayed such an unsuspecting and gifted aptitude for love that she soon had the poet enthralled in the romantic fires of her passion. Secretive, cautious and a little afraid at first, she would devise elaborate plans for leaving the house, taking her musical books with her, as if she was going to the Conservatory at the college, while her parents snoozed away during the enchanting summer months.

To the extent that it was she who had been appalled by the brutal conjectures of his mind, by the purient metaphors of his heart, she was the one who turned her newly discovered ardour for lovemaking into an aesthetic vocation. Once she had overcome her initial shyness, she revealed a much more moving eurythmic understanding of the un-bridled possibilities and positions of lovemaking than the poet with all his experience in manipulating words. On his narrow monk's bed, in the clutter of his room, she would make him lie in a position of dutiful surrender, before going to work on him. She fell on him with the voluptuous hunger of her sensual mouth, so that never again would she be hungry for love, and the worms that had tormented her during the long months of waiting for him to respond would be silenced for ever in the marshes of her belly. While he lay there, the ripples of her exploding wine, the radiant light of her joy and the flexible cords of her legs would transport him into a celestial sphere. In the torrent of such scandalous pleasures, she taught him how it was possible for a woman to make love without being afraid; not in the darkness of Hades, but in the brilliant light of the Magi, protected by the sword of Diana, because the avenging angels were fictions of the imaginations of depraved spinsters who were better off locked up in convents.

'I am shameless with you,' she would laugh during their intervals, 'while with another man I might have been ashamed, because you found me before I was corrupted by the church.'

Garbage forgot about the torturous sentences that he had always struggled to write in the everglades of poetry; he became a man dazed by the sensuality of Arabella's heat, the plethora of her skills, the mesmerism of her eyes and the languid movements of her body. While she treated love as if it were an endangered species which had to be brought back from the brink of extinction by her arousing hands, her cooing-bird voice and the enchantment of her music, he developed the look of a serene monk, the air of an intoxicated man and the contentment of a well-fed cat. She freed him from the past anguish of waiting for his muse to come in the treacherous waters of inspiration; she erased from his mind the belief that all women preferred men to take the lead in lovemaking and were raised to satisfy the gratification of men. Once, when he found it hard to work at his desk, Arabella crept up stark naked behind him, took him by the hand and led him to the austere bed. One hour later, after he had swam in the delta of her passionate lovemaking, he went back to his desk and wrote until two in the morning, long after she had gone.

Such goings-on in the poet's house could not have gone on for ever without arousing the suspicions of Arabella's mother. She began to notice the rainbow of the butterflies in her eyes, the growth of her breasts, and the fact that Arabella was paying less and less attention to her music. She wondered what was taking Arabella to such flights of happiness when the joys of life had been amortised in the heart of her other daughter. Then, unexpectedly, as if the foundation of the house had been shaken by a hurricane in that society of propriety and gossip, Regina Garrison's world was shattered by the explosion of the discovery that she made. Arabella began to spend a lot of time in the bathroom at all hours of the day where she would wind folds and folds of cotton round her belly before putting on her dress. She became listless in the morning, slept in the heat of the afternoon and, when her feet started to swell, she exchanged her formal shoes for the comfort of a pair of tropical sandals, explaining to her mother that the heat was responsible for the excretion of water between her toes. But when she started sending the maid out to buy green mangoes, which she would hide from her parents, Regina

343

found out about it and decided to investigate. One evening, while they were entertaining guests, Arabella asked to be excused. Saying that she wasn't feeling well, she went to her room, and started to eat the green mangoes. Thinking that her parents were engaged in the business of making their guests feel welcomed, she had not bothered to lock the door.

Regina Garrison crept up the steps with the silence of a cat; she pushed Arabella's door open and caught her in the act of eating the forbidden fruit. With a violence unusual in her, Regina Garrison grabbed her daughter by the scruff of her neck and dragged her to the bathroom.

'Vomit it out,' she commanded the now visibly sick woman.

Then Regina saw the black nipples of her daughter's breasts, she felt the heat of her warm body, saw the pallor of her cheeks, and knew what she had suspected all along, but had not dared to hint at, because theirs was not a family that laid themselves open to the possibility that a young woman's passion would overtake her, and find fruition in the embryonic stirrings of a child.

$$\diamond$$

While Malagueta was carried away on the crest of modernisation, peace had reigned in the Cromantine house after Jeanette Cromantine's mind had been laid to rest about the chastity of her granddaughter. Yet, after she had passed one hundred years she began to tidy up her affairs so that, as she put it to her friend Isatu Martins, 'ma work gon be done'. She made a long, binding will in which she left seventy-five per cent of her assets to her granddaughter, twenty per cent to her ward and the rest to the church, so 'dat dem tiffing lawyers don't tiff all dat ma Sebastian and me done wuk for in dis worl'. Admitting that mortality was an immeasurable gift, that the convolutions of the recent events could force her granddaughter to leave that part of the world, she arranged with a shipping company for Fatmatta-Emilia to leave any time she felt like it, ''cause dat place where her granddaddy and me done come from, got dem college where dey train young womens now, and she kin come back to Malagueta when she done finish learning de book'. Next, she would have such flights of fantasy that she began to see her dead husband in the faraway paradise of their early days in Malagueta, when the world had been young, and Captain Hammerstone had not been tempted by the lure of the sea to sail to that part of the world. She became obsessed with the notion that in spite of everything, in spite of the porcupine needles that had pricked them now and then, theirs had been a beautiful life; that 'de Lawd' had been good to them. Consequently, now that Fatmatta-Emilia was a 'big girl', and could look after herself, she was ready to meet her maker. One last thing she prayed for was that her granddaughter would find a strong man, such as 'ma boy or de grandfader' who would make her happy. She begged God that if that did not happen, Fatmatta-Emilia would serve him, but swore that if she became 'de mistress of one of dem new peoples done come to dis town, ah gone harass her from ma grave'.

Thus, when she had come to an accommodation with the fading lights of her mortality, she began to talk about death with a pleasure that in any other person, at any other time, would have been taken as the first sign of senility.

'Ah knows de good Lawd don't forget me down here,' she would complain to her friend, Isatu Martins, when she had prepared her for the possibility of her going. 'Look at all de young people dying; dem dat should bury me, while ah been waiting in de qucuc all dis time for him to call me home.'

So saying, she began to compose a petition in her mind, which she hoped would get to God. She would take it to the grave of her son, who was in 'Abraham's bosom', and ask him to appeal to 'de Master' to call her home. In it, she thanked God for having given her a long life, which, in spite of all 'de ups and downs', she had enjoyed. But her old bones were tired, her eyes were losing their brilliance, and she did not want to get to the point where they would have to put her out to dry in the sun like beans. 'Imagine me, Lawd,' she appealed, 'not able to use ma faculties; not able to move about; just sitting in one place, while dem lizards run all over de floor, the fowls gon mess up de flower pots. But ah knows you are a good Master, and you won't let dis lady wait too long for de angel to come.'

She had been ready for him for a long time, and had selected the spot, next to her husband, where she wanted to be buried. The dampness that was the scourge of good clothes had been chased by the three dozen mothballs that she had spread in the trunk where the dress she wanted to be laid out in had been folded in the shape of a large fish, because she had seen herself swimming in the 'Jordan River', washing her body clean, as she was convinced one had to appear clean before God. During the lachrymose years of her long life, while she fought to help her husband plant his feet on the land, while she moulded her son, faced life again after their deaths, Jeanette Cromantine had composed the songs

345

she wanted sung at her funeral. Not for her the lamentations of regrets, the dirges about 'dis sinful worl' and temporal gratitude. The petunia of sunlight would brighten up the church on the day they were singing for her; larks would fly over her coffin in the open carriage that would take her to the church, and the trombones and trumpets of a life richly lived would shake the very foundations of the church, where four ministers would officiate at the service. She was ready to meet her maker, if only the angel would come to whisper in her ear that God was ready to receive her.

$$\diamond$$

It goes without saying that Regina Garrison was shattered by the discovery that Arabella was pregnant. For although she did not share her husband's wish that Arabella would marry the son of a prosperous man, as Matilda had done, or would at least settle for an up-and-coming young graduate teacher or doctor, the discovery of an unwanted pregnancy in her household had never, in her wildest dreams, figured in her plans. But once she had overcome her shock, she turned her mind to what her husband would say, fearing the worst; she was also deeply worried about the scandal that would accompany the disclosure of the news in the community, and wondered how she would explain to the Head of the Conservatory that this daughter with a great deal of promise, this daughter who could have gone on to become a concert pianist, had thrown everything overboard for the fickleness of passion. Momentarily, a disappointed mother's anger gripped her, and she lashed out at her daughter:

'And who is the dog you have disgraced yourself for and for which you ought to have your head shaven?'

'He is not a dog, Mother. He is someone I respect.'

'Respect? What do you know of respect? Something that leads to a cheap passion, scandal, disgrace, and the risk that your father will throw you out? You could at least have had the decency to run away and save me the shame of having to explain that my own daughter is a tart. But come on, who is this man?'

'You could shave off my hair, mother, lock me up, beat me or send me away, but I won't talk.'

'Then he is a married man; someone who can't marry you; which makes your disgrace even more scandalous.'

'He is not married, Mother, and I love him.'

'Very well then; I shall assume that he is a gentleman and will do the right thing by marrying you.'

Arabella conceded that her lover was a gentleman, though not of the kind that her mother probably had in mind. Beyond that, she stubbornly refused to divulge his name. Regina threatened, she cajoled, she yelled at her daughter and cursed her, but nothing would get Arabella to disclose the name of the man who had given her so much pleasure and for whom she was prepared to suffer the scorn and damnation not only of her parents but even of her class. Paradoxically, it was this willingness in her to give up everything for love that impressed her mother. For when her anger had abated, Regina Garrison realised that she loved this daughter who was the opposite of Matilda, though she wondered about the cruel twist of fate that had made it possible for Arabella to be the one to become pregnant out of wedlock, when Matilda was not even sleeping in the same bed as her husband. She recalled her own childhood in the paradisaical island, before her mother had killed herself, in the unmistaken belief that her husband did not love her enough to protect her from the insults and envy of other women. That fate, she vowed, would not happen to Arabella. Regina Garrison decided she would stand by her daaughter in the hope of discovering who her lover was, so that as a mother she could persuade the young man to marry Arabella.

Alphonso Garrison reacted violently to the news that his daughter was pregnant; he felt his pride wounded, his life ruined by this one act of 'sinful lust' by his daughter. Brutally, he cut her off, erased her name from his will and threw her out of his house. Regina dared to intervene.

'If she goes, I go too,' she found the voice to stand up to her husband.

Alphonso Garrison was stunned. Although he blamed his wife for not having raised Arabella 'to have some shame', he had never doubted the loyalty of his wife, her duty to him, but, above all, her respect for his decisions over matters concerning the future of their children. He gave vent to his anger.

'This is none of your business,' he raged at his wife.

'My business, as much as it is yours, and I repeat that if she goes, I shall also leave your house.'

'Then, so be it, for I shall not have a loose daughter in my house.'

Regina Garrison and Arabella went to live in one of the many houses that the Garrisons owned jointly. Regina had not forgotten that it was the head start given to her husband by her father that had provided the basis of their prosperity, so that she was not afraid that he would cut them off. Now that they were living in another part of the city, away from the hub of activities and the vicious knives of the tonguewaggers, Garbage found out from the maid about Arabella's condition. He was greatly elated by the prospect of becoming a father, and, on the next day, he put on his poet's cape, bought a ring from the jeweller's, and after dusting up the old Bible of the Farmer brothers, turned up at the new house and offered to marry Arabella.

'So it is to you that I owe the credit for the dishonour of my daughter,' Regina Garrison said to Garbage, when the rivet of admission had sunk into her head.

In the intransigence of her daughter's disgrace, Regina Garrison had not drawn the name of the poet out of the lottery of suspected seducers responsible for lighting the charcoals in Arabella's heart. Yet, when she had got over the revelation, she felt a wicked tinge of delight, more to spite her husband than anything else, that it was the poet with the imponderable name who was responsible for disturbing the peace of their house. She liked Garbage, respected his work and admired his stubborn dignity and pride in refusing to change his name. Although she had not been there when Garbage was born, she knew about the long wait of Isatu Martins to have that son, about the respectable way in which Gustavius Martins had worked to make their lives comfortable. Honour and nobility were part of the tradition that she had grown up with in Cape Verde, not the vulgarity and impertinence of the nouveau riche, the drunkenness and chicanery of some of the officials whom she did not care for in the first place, and most definitely did not fancy as the sort of people from among whom a potential son-in-law of hers should come.

Garbage had done the honourable thing, she reasoned, by owning up to his paternity, an act of love if ever there was one. As a mother with her own fortune, as someone who remembered the way she herself had trembled in the hands of the man she had married, before the vanity of hobnobbing with the politicians had destroyed their marriage, she would see to it that the young people were happy, after they had been married in church.

So that when Arabella flatly refused to marry Garbage, her mother felt betrayed.

'Young woman,' she lectured her daughter in a severe voice, 'I have given up my home for you, have possibly lost some friends because of you – not that I cared for them. Like all mothers I had dreamed of you going up the aisle, a maiden in white, but I am prepared to settle for a small wedding, in a small church. Yet you have the effrontery to reject this man who it seems has more honour than you do.'

But, in what may have been taken to be ingratitude to her mother, Arabella stubbornly refused to consider the offer of marriage. She looked at the man who had made her happy, drenched him with the unmistakable tears of her love, yet was unable to walk away with him into the sanctuary of marriage.

'Can't you see,' she pleaded with her eyes, 'that I am doing this for you, can't you see that if I let you do what you think is right, you will come to hate me in the end? You are a poet, Garbage, and you belong to the world, to all eternity, and not in the prison of marriage.'

Such reasoning, such clarity of argument in her daughter did not however change Regina's mind, because there was the overriding concern for the fate of an unmarried mother that she had to contend with. Although Malagueta was changing and one or two girls had children for men they did not marry, they were women from a section of society for whom the notion of propriety did not matter. She was adamant that Arabella should marry Garbage, but nothing that she said or threatened her daughter with could get her to change her mind; not even when Regina threatened to send her away to the only relative they still had on the island of Cape Verde.

'Do that, and I shall kill myself,' Arabella replied.

Regina Garrison resigned herself to being a grandmother. For a while, she worried about what she would say to the priest when Arabella's condition became obvious, but telling herself that it was God who had put the child in her daughter, she steeled herself for a confrontation with the cleric, and decided that if the church did not baptise her grandchild, she would stop going there.

Garbage and Arabella entered into a period of unending bliss. He would come to the house to spend evenings there, would sit on the veranda and read his latest poems to Arabella while Regina served them tea in the evanescent sunlight. Now that Regina Garrison had cut herself off from the circles of her husband, it was the poet who brought her up to date on the latest development in the town, the weekly details about how the condescending lawyers and civil servants were knifing each other to rise up in society. It was a peaceful idyll, with interludes of music when Arabella would sit at the piano, already visibly pregnant, and play her mother and lover the compositions of her favourite master, now that the difficulty of lying on her back prevented her from getting into bed with the poet at his place. Then, one Sunday, when they were holding hands in the veranda, drinking the colours of sunlight in the brilliant butterflies, riot broke out on the streets of Malagueta when the colonial police tried to arrest three men who had refused to salute the carriage of the governor as it tore through the veins of the narrow streets to a remembrance service for the dead overseas monarch. When the explosions of temper had died down, ten men were discovered to have been shot and killed; many others were arrested and held in the local jail, while their angry families collected money in order that they might bail them out or bring them bundles of food the next day.

When Garbage heard about the killings and the arrests, he gave a reading in the Public Square at which the authorities were denounced. In a trembling, raging voice, he blamed the coming of the authorities for the riots, and tore up a copy of the colonial flag. Some troops present at the reading tried to arrest the poet, but in the ensuing confusion he escaped, helped by willing hands and the folds of cotton that the women draped over the heads of soldiers which blindfolded them. He hid in the houses of friends and admirers, careful not to stay in the same house for more than two days. One of the houses in which he hid was the home of Septimus Doherty, who greatly admired the poet, and dared his wife to report his presence to the authorities. It was the first time that Matilda Garrison had come so close to Garbage. At breakfast the next morning she eyed him behind her teacup, saw the brutal determination of his lips, the fierce intelligence of his eyes and felt a glacial rumbling in her stomach.

Four soldiers scented his trail and, lying in wait for him near Regina's house, arrested him when he tried to visit Arabella. Half of the troops in the town had to be deployed when he was tried as the 'intellectual instigator' of the riots, for the fiery furnace of his poetry, and sentenced to six months in jail. Fearing an even bigger riot, and an attack on the jail, they whisked the poet off to an island jail, the same one in which, not too long after, a black president would incarcerate General Tamba Masimiara. Here Garbage served three months of the sentence before being released without any explanation. Jail had toughened him, everyone could see, when he came out. Whereas he had been accommodating of some of the actions of the colonial regime before the riot, he was now a relentless foe in the storm that was blowing over Malagueta. In the months that followed, he wrote even more incendiary verses; he denounced not only the authorities but even the new monarch; the policy of sending young inexperienced doctors to Malagueta to replace experienced Malaguetans who had qualified overseas and had been doing a fine job. He raged against the injustices that kept Malaguetans of a certain class confined to the poor areas of the town, while the colonial class and their black lackeys could move about as they liked. When his friends worried about him, he dismissed their fears outright.

'As long as God gives me the spirit, I shall go on defending the cause in which I believe because it is just.'

He found time to visit Arabella now and then, to play with their son, Faramah, who had been born while Garbage was in jail. At first, the joys of fatherhood brought a measure of peace to him; his nights at the house were made peaceful by the gentle flicker of candle light, by the aroma of Regina's cooking, because Arabella was not a cook, and by the decanter of Portuguese wine that rounded off the meals. During those peaceful interludes, he would try out his new poems on the woman who had originally been captivated by the intensity of his imagination. Inevitably, their souls would respond to each other and they would find each other like two fish, breaking through the impregnable coral reefs of his public domain, to swim to each other, plaster their bodies together, after she had healed, and sit up naked in bed, drinking ginger tea, while Faramah giggled in his crib.

But, slowly, inexorably, the pull of the public chariot which had been dragging him away from Arabella since he came back from jail became more pronounced. He became the rallying point for many of the opposition figures in the anti-colonial campaign. As the son of one of the original founders of the town, many of the young men asked him to organise a new revolt to wage one last war, bigger than anything Malagueta had ever known, so that they could push the English into the sea. Others asked him to lead a delegation to London in order that they might denounce the injustices of the colonial administrators.

'Any time you are ready, we are ready to supply the money,' promised a few who could afford it.

Much to their surprise, he stayed his ground and tried to reassure them that poetry was a much more dangerous weapon than a whole army.

'Look at the way they have been trying to ban my poems!' he exclaimed at one meeting in his house. But the more the authorities tried to ban his poems the more they were circulated quite openly. He found himself more in demand than at any time since he first burst into prominence. And the more he was called upon by angry workers and students to lead them, the less the poet was able to see Arabella.

Yet, because she had known from the very beginning that the laurels of his poethood would crown him beyond his hopes, because she had seen him as he would lead others, be fearless in the ephemeral flames of repression; the way the muse would take him, yielding, into the unknown straits of creation, Arabella had been prepared to share him with Malagueta, with the world, and even with other women. Happily, she waited for him in the animated twilight, looking for his legs, as he would sometimes emerge like a bird from the circinated leaves and branches to spend a night in the aura of her love, from which she would release him into the whirlpools of other loves.

He had another child: by a woman who followed him from reading to reading, tormenting him with the vermilion redness of her adoration and the persistent onslaught of her gifts. She sent him fruits, scented handkerchiefs, legs of Morrocan lamb, Ivory Coast coffee and Jamaican rum, promising never to bother him if only she could have his child.

He had more children: a set of twins by the strong-willed daughter of a rich Fulani cattle herder; a girl who did not understand a word of his poetry but was captivated by the magic of his readings to risk having her throat slit for sleeping with that 'infidel'.

He had another child: by the granddaughter of the Chinese who had come there with his Fukien delicacies, hoping that the curling stone of his magic would make him prosperous in the days of Thomas Booker-man, but who had now degenerated into Confucian senility as he sat every morning, in front of his house, waiting for the young boys to come and piss into his soup bowl, glad that he could drink their urine to flush out his kidney stones.

He had one last child: by a Scottish lass drawn to Malagueta by her missionary heart, who believed he was the reincarnation of Ossian, the legendary Gaelic poet. For her 'indiscretion' she was shipped home by her order, an Irish one, bless her Scottish heart, to a home for unmarried mothers in Belfast, where she poisoned herself, heartbroken over being made to give up her child.

He never married any of the women because, as Arabella Garrison had known, he was married to the world.

Isatu Martins, who had passed the age of eighty-five, deprived of her longed-for wish to die in bed with her husband, was at that time the happiest woman in Malagueta. She derived a wicked pleasure thinking that although fate had robbed her of that passionate wish, her son was making some young women happy, while making the mothers of those women miserable in their old age. To those who complained to her that her famous, but very virile, son had 'ruined' their daughters, Isatu

Martins would adjust herself into a comfortable condescension in her wicker chair, before delivering the arrows of her reply.

'He must have what it takes as a man,' she said, 'for de girls to flock to him like dat; after all, what good is a son for, if he won't make his poor mother happy in her old age by giving her many grandchildren.'

Sometimes, she lectured them on the laudanum of grief, the spider-web of death and the power of recovering after sorrow. She told them about her long, painful wait to have Garbage; how she had wanted to kill herself when he had not been born, because she had been able to convince herself that she was bewitched.

'So consider yourselves lucky that your daughters are also making you grandmothers, though of course I can understand that some of you had hoped to marry them off to some aristocrats,' she would dismiss them cynically.

Unexpectedly, while Isatu Martins sated herself on the grand-motherly wine proffered by her son, Jeanette Cromantine died peace-fully in her bed, on a Sunday evening. Ten hours before, she had woken up at seven o'clock as usual, complaining about how late Fatmatta-Emilia slept, the high cost of kippers imported from England, now that 'dem newcomers done take over de shopkeeping business', and the problem of remembering the days of the week. Lately, she had begun to forget the names of some people, the dates of events, such as when she told Fatmatta-Emilia that Thomas Bookerman had gone fishing with her husband the day before but that they had not come back. 'Am still waiting for dem to come back wid some fish, so dat ah kin cook some potatoes,' she said only the week before. But on this Sunday morning, her mind had never been more lucid. After eating her breakfast of pancakes and syrup, washed down with a cup of tea, she sat down in the parlour to dictate to her ward a list of things she wanted done: the carpenter had to come and take care of a leak in the roof of the house; the trees needed to be trimmed so that more light could enter the house, and she had to get the ward to plant more lemon grass in front of the house, so that she could go on sitting on the porch without being bothered by mosquitoes.

But at four o'clock she complained to Fatmatta-Emilia that she was tired. 'Help dis old lady get to her bed,' she asked her granddaughter. Then, as if she knew that it was the end, she told Fatmatta-Emilia to get her mirror from the chest of drawers.

'Let me see what dis old lady looks like,' she joked. It was a request so unlike her that her granddaughter was touched by its note of vanity, because not only was Jeanette Cromantine unable to see, but the lines of her face had been blurred in the parchment of old age. Whatever she might have hoped to see would remain a riddle to her granddaughter, but after running her leathery fingers over her face while holding the silent mirror, Jeanette Cromantine lay down on her bed, and soon drifted into a trance.

In some dimly remembered past, she saw the face of a young woman in the illuminated dawn, as she waited for her man to come on board the ship that was sailing to a part of the world which was only a name that they were beginning to learn. The details of knowledge were fast fading in her memory, but she saw the same woman struggling to get out of the quagmire of mud that was pulling her down; the face of the man who had lifted her out of that first place of death, as if he had been an angel. Now, it was the face of a woman, neither young nor old, it was difficult to tell, who was coming to her; to tell her not to be afraid, because this was the journey that they had both planned, when they would be together in a paradisaical garden, sitting on a bench, where they would talk about the glass beads that both had worn, at one time or the other; about how it had helped them to understand that in the beginning, God had made women to give life and joy to men; to bear children, raise them, and, hopefully, derive some pleasure from this life, which was eternal, and that once they understood its endlessness, its transcendence over such impertinent humbugs like a slavebreeder named Andrew McKinley and the pirate David Hammerstone, they could go on living for ever, supporting each other with that fearlessness that God had given them, to bear testimony to the birth and growth of Malagueta: their child.

A peaceful smile appeared on Jeanette Cromantine's face, and she had never looked more serene and happy as she did to her grand-daughter who covered the old woman's face.

Jeanette Cromantine's funeral brought together the descendants of the old families and even some of the newcomers. On a bright, sunny day, they gave her the kind of send-off that she had requested: joyous, colourful and rowdy with a brass band playing the calypsos that had made Malagueta such an enchanting place in the beginning. When the cortège was half-way between the church and the grave in her compound, where she was to be buried alongside her husband as she had requested, ten strong men took the coffin out of the hearse and began to dance with it, winding here and there, through the decorated streets, while coins, flowers and grains of rice rained down on the mahogany wood. In what was the best tribute to the dead that

Malagueta had ever seen, many shopkeepers opened their businesses, which was against the sabbath, and invited everyone to come in and eat, have a glass of rum before rejoining the carnival, whirling to not only the music of the brass band but to the crescendoes of drums, castanets and triangles, which the influence of the rum greatly inspired in the musicians. At the graveside, Isatu Martins, who was now the oldest person in Malagueta, came out of the house surrounded by her grandchildren and Fatmatta-Emilia. Saying that she didn't need anyone to support her, she stood on her feet for ten minutes and sang for her lifelong friend in a great contralto voice, extolling the dead woman's generosity, her kindness and loyalty, such that Isatu Martins said she was prepared to jump into the grave and go with her friend, but 'Ah knows Ah cannot jump before God's time, and dat Ah will have to wait for my turn in de queue of de dead.' But it was all said in good spirit, and after they had covered the coffin, with a lot of soil, to the noisy drumming of the musicians, the closest families, their friends and some gatecrashers stayed up all night in a revelry to honour Jeanette Cromantine which was enough to make anyone who was alive envious that the dead could have so much happiness, while life was hard for some of the living.

Matilda Doherty's life had assumed a comic-tragedy air lately. Tired of presiding over a house where she had herself become part of the furniture, whose position was changed every month, according to her mood, so that when her visitors came she could impress them with her flair for housekeeping, which she would say had been copied from one of the catalogues from Manchester, she developed the habit of picking up stray cats and, to the consternation of her maids, gave them the run of the kitchen, where they played regular concerts with their hungry miaows at seven o'clock in the morning and their mating howls at seven o'clock in the evening. They drove the maids crazy by bringing in birds and lizards and by their habit of leaving half-eaten prey on the floor. More than five years after their wedding, Matilda was still wearing her chastity belt as if it were a badge of honour, before going to bed in her lonely bedroom. Out of a fear that Septimus Doherty might one day decide to enter the room to claim his marital rights, she had a carpenter put a new lock in the door and hung a schoolbell behind it, which she hoped would alert her in case of danger. The Italian aria parrot developed a case of genuine hysteria when he saw his mistress bringing in all those noisy cats, and devoting to them all the love that she had not been able to give to her husband. The bird, which had hitherto been

Matilda's only companion, which had always responded to her 'come along, my pet, sing this lonely lady, a nice song', would sit in a corner of its cage all day, refuse to eat and, to the amazement of his mistress, would fluster and develop hiccups every time she came near him.

Matilda did not know what to make of her predicament; like most people who had expected much out of life but had been made miserable by the vagaries of fate, she had not been prepared for the response of her husband to her bouts of bad temper and her endless talk about what fate had done to her. While she preserved her ageing virginity, played her whimsical game of parrot and cats, trimmed the rhododendrons, and, when she felt like it, would dress like a queen and acted the role of Cleopatra in her fairy kingdom, Septimus Doherty had embarked upon a kind of goodtempered tolerance of the idiosyncrasies of his wife. He flattered her about her chances of getting old without the ravages of childbirth, so that her beauty would be eternal, and she could die without any lines on her body; of going to heaven for her piety and for having preserved her virginity against all men.

'Think of what pleasure it would give the undertakers preparing you to meet God when they look at you with all your jewels because there would be no child to inherit them,' he would remark without any hint of bitterness in his voice.

Six months into their non-consummated marriage, Septimus Doherty had come to the conclusion that his wife was a fairy and that she was living in a make-believe world. Luckily for him, the fever that was eating away at Matilda's heart had not been allowed to spread all over the house. For this reason, despite the look of an unhappy dog that had touched Jeanette Cromantine's heart, Septimus Doherty had found a way to deal with the explosions of temper, her receding into self-pity and the outburst of pride in her father's name that served as a tonic for Matilda's fanciful slights. He grew accustomed to hearing her lament her 'confinement' in a house where 'there was no sunshine', because Matilda Doherty's mind did not work according to the belief that happiness was a gift to be shared or that it came from within oneself. She never stopped reminding her husband that she was the daughter of one of the richest men in Malagueta; that their house had been one of the first where the servants wore white tunics, that they served meals with wine, and the guests wiped their mouths with linen table napkins. Overcome by the toxin of bitterness in her heart over the lack of interest her husband was showing in her, she would taunt him about how she had been destined to be married to a cultured man, a man who would have known how to behave on his wedding night, a man who would have been gallant enough to go down on his knees and beg forgiveness of his wife for being so shameless as to expose himself to a lady who had never seen a man naked before, as God was her witness. At other times, she railed against her mother who, in Matilda's view, was devoting too much time to helping Arabella raise her 'bastard' son, while blaming Matilda for the uncomfortable position in which she lived with her husband. The happiness of Arabella, in spite of what Matilda considered to be her sister's wayward behaviour, was one of the sources of her unremitting grievances against life. On the occasions when she visited her mother and sister, Matilda would let her unhappiness show by complaining about imagined illnesses, blowing her nose into a silk handkerchief and indulging in a drink or two, which she did not do in her own house, where she kept up an image of sobriety. Regina who, contrary to her own initial doubts, was enjoying living with her unmarried daughter, tried to resolve Matilda's problem by suggesting a separation between the Dohertys. Matilda was quick to reject the idea.

'Being with that man is like lying on a bed of thorns, but at least he comes home every night to sleep in his own bed.' The causticness of the remark was meant to wound Arabella who was never sure where Garbage was when he was not with her, but Arabella was so incapable of malice that she felt a deep pity for her sister, and tried to soothe her with expressions of concern.

'Matilda,' she said, 'don't let the disease of envy destroy your heart when Septimus could be keeping his alive for someone else.'

He was indeed keeping his heart alive, not for someone else as Arabella Garrison had said, but in the study of the many species of trees and plants in the Botanical Gardens. With a single-minded dedication that Emmanuel Cromantine would have appreciated, Septimus Doherty would go to the ponds in the gardens at three o'clock in the afternoon, every day of the week, to feed the ducks and fish, or simply to sit on one of the many benches there. The enchantment of the place, the wild aroma of the smell of the flowers of the trees, the feel of the lilies and lotuses in the pond were enough to make Septimus Doherty forget his wife during those afternoons of euphoria, so that by the time he went home in the evening, Matilda had been lost in the shades of other trees, which had not questioned his manhood, or the naked body of his love. For Septimus Doherty was a man who, in spite of his shyness, could only love someone or something in the natural state of being, with the purity of his heart and soul. He had wanted Matilda not in the lustful bestiality

357

of possessing her body alone but in something higher, such that he could have loved her as he was learning to love the trees; because Septimus Doherty had not loved the haughty woman his father had chosen for him, but had been prepared to live with her in the tranquillity of the present, in the hope that their lives would mature into a stable pattern, giving each of them the chance to dream their separate dreams, and, with the money to be inherited, they would have cut a decent pair to the beholden eyes of those Malaguetans who paid so much attention to social graces and manners. If she had not seen the purity of his intentions, then she was as blind as a bat.

That Matilda's mind had been too warped in the torturous fires of her upbringing which had made her not merely prudish, but dry to the possibilities of so much rain of affection, was for Septimus Doherty a case of an illness beyond care. When he had sufficiently learned the names of the trees and had been taken up by the strength of the trees, by their response to his care, he relegated Matilda Doherty to a pile of manure so that she could learn to like the feel of dung and, hopefully, be warmed by its pastoral heat.

Matilda Doherty increased the number of cats in her house. Surprisingly, for someone who had been meticulous with her housekeeping, who would spend hours arranging and rearranging her flowers in porcelain vases, who straightened the antimacassars on the backs of the chairs, so that the embroidered cocks, the ornamental horses and the green landscape blended well with the rest of the furniture, she let the cats have the run of the entire house, while she was hallucinated by the thought of death. In no time, the cats had destroyed the sofas, made holes in the Morrocan carpets and, when they started to have litters, hid their kittens in the most remote corners of the house, which drove the maids crazy. The smell of cat's mess, the craftiness of their habits, the laxity with which they deposited half-eaten lizards in the living room proved too much for the maids. One morning, telling Matilda that she came from a people who ate cats and that the feline delicacy tasted like young chicken when garnished with red pepper, the younger of the two maids left without notice. She was so agitated that she did not bother to collect her wages, but did not leave without giving her ex-mistress a parting lecture.

'I leave you with your animals. Maybe their catcalls will bring you back from the dead, that is if you can see your way clear through all that mess they have been putting on the floor,' she concluded.

Matilda Doherty's hallucination so deepened over the succeeding months that she became afraid of mirrors; she was haunted by the fear that her beauty was fading, that she was becoming obese, when in fact she had never looked more alluring, now that she had succumbed to the habit of walking about the house in a loose frock and without slippers, though when her husband was around, she went back to the prison of her formal dresses, superimposed over her chastity belt. She had the mirrors removed from the walls, except for the one in her husband's bedroom, which he used for shaving his face. Dissipated by the fever that was eating away at her heart, she spent most mornings reading the latest journals of the Homoeopathic Society of Great Britain, paid for by her father. Now that she was left with only one maid, she did not even bother with such trivialities as going into the kitchen, or selecting the menus as she had done in the past. Yet every evening she waited at the head of the large mahogany table, while the maid served her dinner. Septimus Doherty who, when the cats had taken over the house, had cordoned off a part of the large bedroom where he could sleep in peace, stopped eating at home soon after, so that Matilda was left presiding over the mass at the high table, proud like an actress waiting for the curtains to open on her great performance.

She kept up the role for over a year, never varying the script or showing boredom for the role; she sat at the table at the same hour every day, waited for her maid to serve her at the same angle every day. She never complained about the menu and ate whatever was put in front of her. She would eat a simple fish stew with the same unconcern with which she approached a bowl of beef bouillion or a plate of groundnut stew served with rice. Unexpectedly, one evening, when the maid went into the dining room to serve her mistress her dinner, Matilda Doherty was not at her table. Thinking that her mistress was sick, the maid went to Matilda's room, but there was no sign of her, so the young woman put her mistress's absence down to a case of a wandering mind who had for once forgotten about her dinner, and was probably at the house of her mother and sister.

Matilda Doherty had in fact not forgotten about her dinner hour, but had gone out of the house precisely at the time the maid was beginning to cook the evening's meal. Earlier, as she was getting ready to dress for her role, Matilda had been struck by the feeling that she was going to die that evening. But being a woman who did not fancy herself dying on a Sunday with the problem of the pressure cabin of her heart still unresolved, she thought she would go out for a last look at Malagueta, before going to her priest to confess her bitterness against fate, her envy of Arabella and the despair into which her husband's lack of concern had thrown her.

In what may have been taken to be an act of inspiration for her final role on earth, Matilda Doherty did not wear the formal black dress that evening that she had worn for so many lonely nights at the altar of her dinner. Instead, she unwrapped the finely embroidered muslin gown of her ill-fated wedding, quivering at the touch of that garment that had hinted at so much happiness on that memorable day. When she had recovered from the slight tremor in her heart, she felt her body easing into a lassitude that made the wearing of the dress feel like a thing she had done every day. Shorn, for once, of her fear of mirrors, as she went into her husband's room to look at herself.

Taking care that she was not seen, she slipped out of her house and, with her wedding dress hidden under her light raincoat, she came out into a brilliant evening, like the colour of an opal, with the light of the sun radiant above the trees, as if the light had conspired with the spirits to make her chosen day, her death-wish day, the brightest in the universe. This was not the colour of death that Matilda had been prepared for, yet she was powerless to overcome the inertia that had gripped her, to pull back from the lane where the sirens of the angels were whispering. For Matilda Doherty was enchanted by death just as her heart had been mortified for years by the rancour of pride and the self-abnegation of her womanhood. Borne by her own wind, she drifted to the shoreline of the city, intent on drowning herself, hoping that her body would not be recovered. But when she came face to face with the corpse of a manatee that had been washed ashore, Matilda Doherty recoiled from that image of death. She walked around for about an hour, in the now fading light, temporised by its soft rays, past the Drama School at the college where the students were rehearsing *Othello*, and where she had been destined to find glory if she had not been married off to the man with a future. But in her state of mind, she was past caring about the pinnacle of acting or the tragedy of the Moor. Nothing existed for her, except that she was carried away by a feeling of denouement, out of the labyrinth of her complicated life, which was now not subject to her control. That was how, without meaning to, she came into the peaceful world of the Botanical Gardens, caught the whiff of the jacaranda and heard the evensong of the nestling birds.

A desire to have one last look at the fish in the pond brought her to the centre of the park, but as she neared the water, the sight of two people sitting on a bench stopped her in her track. She saw her husband and

Fatmatta-Emilia engrossed in a conversation, with a discreet distance between them. If they were aware of her presence they did not let it show because the face of the man was so peaceful that Matilda Doherty realised that her husband had finally found someone who was prepared to listen to him, and that he had never really been bothered by the dissipation of a wife petrified by the fear of his hounds.

An even greater lassitude possessed her body and Matilda Doherty felt the weight of her upbringing crashing down on her, like a ton of bricks. The glittering chandeliers, the booklined study, the expensive soirées at which her father had paraded them were little recompense for the unhappiness that she had experienced in her life; if anything, she felt cheated by her strictures, and wished that her mother had told her that life offered no planned route, that the mirrors she had been afraid of were no more tormenting than the face of death, or that while she was letting her body rot, she could not hope for a pristine state of mind. Suddenly, she realised that her repression was a far greater sin than if she had eaten the wild strawberries that her husband had proffered her on their wedding night.

Hurriedly, she came out of the park, buoyed by a new wind blowing against her face. Two drunken labourers had stopped to pee in front of the house of an old woman, who told them to go somewhere else, but Matilda did not even seem bothered by such an indecency. She turned into a dark street where the light of the moon was blanketed by a cluster of mango trees. Not caring whether she was seen, she came to the door of a house that had been the home of two dreamers who had come to Malagueta long before her time, which to her surprise was opened.

Garbage was dreaming about a woman who was drowning herself in the stream of his contemplation, polluting the ferns of his poetry with the mud of her shoes, when Matilda Doherty walked silently into his room. As usual, he was sleeping naked, because he liked the feel of the breeze on his body, now that it was the dry season and there were no mosquitoes to bother him.

It took Matilda Doherty one minute to rid herself of the gown that she had worn as a sign of her chastity on the day she had been cast on her uncertain fate, and when the sleeping Garbage rolled over on his back, Matilda Doherty saw a man endowed with a portentous weapon, more prepared and terrifying than the one that had frightened her on her husband. As she lowered herself into the bed, Garbage opened his eyes and saw a woman with a body like alabaster clay, more white than any he had seen before.

'Get away,' he said, thinking that it was the woman who was drowning who had changed her mind and was now in his room.

Matilda did not give him a chance to move; she pressed her depraved body to him, and felt herself being opened up by a lance which freed her from not only her hunger, but rid her mind of her fear of the unknown, for at that moment Matilda Doherty did not want to know what the face of death looked like, because her heart was pounding with an explosion of relief as she collapsed onto the broad chest of her liberator, sinking her nails into his shoulders to steady her fits.

◇

One month later, Alphonso Garrison was found dead in what the Society Page Editor of his own paper referred to as 'mysterious circumstances'. On the other hand, the gossip columnist of a new, rival paper wrote that the 'shame' of having a daughter who had a child 'out of wedlock' for that 'renegade poet' and the distress brought about by the 'unforgivable' behaviour of the mayor's wife in 'abandoning such a decent man', was too heavy a cross for Mr Garrison to carry. There were dark hints at a suicide; yet when his body was found there was no bullet wound on it, no slashed wrists, and an autopsy did not turn up any evidence to suggest that Alphonso Garrison had poisoned himself as a result of the tribulation he had suffered because of his women. His death remained an unsolved mystery, a dinner party conversation when it was not unusual to hear some of his old friends making a bitter comment on his fate:

'With women like those,' his former deputy once said, 'you might as well kill yourself, because, as sure as hell, they will drive you to your grave.'

A reading of his will revealed that Alphonso Garrison had restored Arabella's name, and left the bulk of his estate which included nine houses, a printing press, a distillery and a small farm to his two daughters, with the stipulation that 'neither my wife nor the poet should have a hand in administering that portion of my estate over which my wife has no control'. Regina, who had been deeply shaken by his death and who, in spite of the fact that they had been living apart had gone back to the house to take charge of the funeral and had stoutly borne her grief at the ceremony with a sincerity that convinced everyone, offered only one comment after the reading.

'Poor man,' she said; 'he was so busy piling up riches that his heart must have died a long time before his body succumbed to death.'

Matilda Doherty wasted no time in trying to get the intricacies of her father's will sorted out. She wore out the patience of a dozen lawyers, kept two judges sitting during the holiday of the court, harassed the lives of the court clerks, and wrote three dozen petitions to the governor, all guaranteed to win them over to her side so that the best part of the properties would go to her. She wrote an article in the *Malaguetan Gazette* about how her father had intended that she should take over the running of the business because Arabella had her head in the clouds, and was in any case not interested in the day-to-day running of a newspaper; that because she was married she would be more respected by the clients the family would have to deal with. With a manipulative mind that no one had suspected she possessed, she schemed, argued and bullied her way into all strata of Malagueta, portraying herself as the wounded daughter, yet at the same time, the loved one; the one who had been obedient, who had allowed herself to be married off to a man she did not love, simply because she wanted to please her father; what more could they ask of a loving daughter, a dutiful daughter who deserved to inherit the best part of her father's estate so that she could live the rest of her unhappy life in comfort?

But, as if to wound her pride, as if she did not even figure in their day-to-day life, which had been an outpouring of endless joy, Regina and Arabella Garrison went to Alphonso Garrison's lawyer. To the consternation of the old man, they asked him to draw up a deed of gift which they would sign, giving everything to Matilda.

'She wants everything,' Arabella said, 'so she can have everything and leave us in peace in our little house, which is all we want.'

The lawyer would not even consider such a proposition at the point of death, he informed the two women.

Sounding more like a cleric, he voiced his objection.

'In the eyes of God,' he said, 'greed is worse than murder, than even infidelity; and since we do not take anything with us when we leave this world, Matilda cannot have everything.'

Eventually, it was agreed that Matilda Garrison would be given seven of the nine houses, and the distillery. Conspiratorially, the lawyer suggested to Arabella that she should hold on to the newspaper so 'that splendid friend of yours could go on publishing his fine poems and articles and you and your mother can always go away and relax on the farm'.

After such unexpected, undignified behaviour by Matilda over what Regina called 'the properties that the dead did not enjoy', she forbade

Matilda to set foot in her house ever again. She cut her daughter out as if she were some embarrassing growth, and from that moment Regina Garrison did not refer to her daughter again, or permit anyone to mention Matilda's name in her presence.

'To me, she is as good as dead, and she will remain dead,' she said.

But if Matilda Doherty was dead in her mother's consideration, she was very much alive in the new world she had discovered. The large inheritance coming on top of her freedom from the pernicious worship of her virginity transformed her into a woman beyond recognition, even to herself. She granted her husband a divorce so that Septimus could marry Fatmatta-Emilia and go and live in England. Next, she threw out those garments in her wardrobe, many of them expensive, which reminded her of her failed glory in the cloister of her marriage; and once she was ensconced with her two dozen cats in one of her seven houses, Matilda Doherty was ready for a new role. Only one thing disappointed her at first: the reluctance of Garbage to engage in a secret relationship with her. For although she had gone back to the poet's house after the night of her unexpected descent into his bed, Garbage flatly refused to sleep with her again. Telling her that he wanted to forget about that night, because it was like a bad toothache in his mouth, Matilda Doherty was not even hurt but spoke like a woman who knew she had something other men would want.

'Other women may have given you children, Garbage,' she said, 'but think of the seven days of pleasure I could give you in my seven houses.'

With the same dedication with which she had hounded the lawyers, with the same steadfastness that she had used to defend her role as an unloved wife, Matilda Doherty began to poach on other people's men: husbands, bachelors, fathers and lovers. She tempted them with the comfort of lying on a bed with silk linen, with the ten dozen cases of Portuguese wine that her father had stored away, with relishing the prospect of sleeping with the daughter of the famous newspaper proprietor and mayor, and with the dazzling choice of seducing her in any of her seven houses. While Arabella was content with loving Garbage and raising their son, Matilda was unveiling a voracity for men that shocked Malagueta. At three o'clock in the afternoon, when the offices closed, she would sit in her new car waiting for her preys to come out; she hounded them like a ghost, appearing at the back of their heads, when they sat in front of the barber's mirror; to those who were a little afraid of being discovered by their wives, she made it appear as if she was considering them for positions in the distillery, that she needed their advice on how to run the houses.

'I am just a lonely woman, love, who needs help,' she told a young wife, after she had kept her husband overnight in one of the faraway houses from which he couldn't walk back to town.

She never varied the colour of her men, their ages or build. She chose the darkest men, as if to compensate for the fact that she was herself so light that not even a regular exposure to the sun had been able to give her a touch of brown hue. With the vanity of an ageing woman, she preferred young men on whom she lavished generous gifts, wine and time; some were ten years younger, at first intimidated by her wealth, but who, once she had demonstrated that she was a woman in her prime who knew a good deal more about pleasing men than the petrified girls they sent Sunday school letters to, feasted on her, while Matilda Doherty sank into the delusion that because she was sleeping with younger men she was prolonging the period of her desire for sex, while teaching her young lovers the pleasure of enjoying an older woman.

But after years of prowling around for the men who dressed daintily for the office, the ones with the choirboy innocence on their way to church, and the self-centred lawyers who wore their wigs while making love, Matilda Doherty got tired of them, and started looking for a new type of man. She had arrived at a point in her life – ageing, vain but still alluring – where she divided men into two categories: the choirboy ones whom she dismissed as too sentimental, too full of themselves but also the most easily corruptible, whereas the other type, the ones who looked like henpecked husbands, or the 'green snakes' as she preferred to call them, were very unpredictable.

Sonny McKrae was one such man. He was a housebuilder and carpenter, who wore the khaki suit of his profession with dignity, drank cheap rum and cursed in public. Matilda had picked him out at a wake because she was fascinated by the rough cadences of his voice and also because of the beauty of his work which she could see in the coffin that he had made for the dead. Thinking that he would be grateful to have such an upper-class woman look at him, she invited him to her house, the one near the Lieutenant Governor's mansion, where, because of his workman's suit, she felt his presence would not arouse the suspicion of the guards. She showed him the bright, beautifully decorated rooms, the white-walled kitchen, complaining about how difficult it was to keep the cockroaches out of her cupboards; about the stream of black ants that would cruise through her back door once the rains began. She asked where she should hang a hammock on the veranda so that she could take her three o'clock siesta without being bothered by the sun. It was all a desultory talk designed to muddle the head of the carpenter while Matilda was waiting for the brandy that she had been drinking to start having its effect on her. Eventually, she asked him to have a look at the bathroom ceiling where there was a leak, and when a gust of wind blew from the sea, and made her languorous, she had to hold on to the cistern to steady her legs, while her back was arched at a provocative angle towards the door.

Sonny McKrae did not need any further prompting. Like an enraged ram that had escaped the sacrificial knife after a battering charge, he impaled her on the cistern, gored her with his ringed horns and drove into her womb with a relentless power that left Matilda Doherty gasping at his workman's audacity. Whereas others had been intimidated by her wealth, her high-bred look, and had made love to her as if she were some kind of Chinese porcelain, Sonny McKrae had no such hang-ups about his own worth as a man. Following that evening, he made Matilda search for him in the most rundown bars in the town, in the backstreet gambling houses where he played chequers and at every wake, where the sound of his wakekeeper's voice was powerful enough to wake up the dead. He turned her into a stray dog panting for him at six o'clock in the evening, and kept her in a perpetual state of heat. During a week of untiring lovemaking, she took him to each of her seven houses so that he could see the vastness of her wealth. Sonny McKrae did not even bother to admire the beauty of the other six houses, but fell upon her in each one. He rocked inside her to the rumbling of the coaches that went by near her coastal house, transformed her into a plucked bird on the terrazzo floor of her mountain retreat and carved her up on the desk in the library of the house, next to the museum, where Alphonso Garrison had written some of his best editorials.

Once, she dared to chide him for being too rough with her; but, without raising his voice or losing his workman's dignity, he put her in her place.

'Don't flatter yourself, sweetheart,' he said. 'Dem aristo boys don't have de mind to fix you up good and proper de way ah been doing, and you are getting on in years anyway.'

She became a slave to his every wish, lost her sense of time, prayed that her biological rhythm would get mixed up so that she might become pregnant, and even started cooking again, after she had given that up in the first months of her disastrous marriage. Breaking a strict code of hers, she lavished large sums of money on Sonny McKrae and once, when her lover was convalescing from a short illness in a private hospital room that she had paid for, Matilda bribed a nurse and checked into an adjoining room so that she could feel the animal power of the man in a place different from hers.

In the midst of such unbridled debauchery, she tried to rent three of her houses out, but they had fallen into such a state of ruinous abandonment that she had a difficult time getting the right sort of tenants. A foreign doctor who served as an unofficial consul for his country showed an interest in the large house where Alphonso Garrison had held court when he was mayor of the town. Built in the pleasant style of the upper class, with its French windows, its venetian blinds and large verandas designed for musical evenings in the summer, it was an ideal house for a consulate and should have fetched a good rent.

Matilda agreed to lease it for a ten-year period, but no sooner was the house occupied than she started to hound the consul with her ideas about how the house should be maintained. She insisted on inspecting the types of carpets that were laid out on the floor, ordering that they matched the partitioned walls; she told them what types of furniture they could bring inside the house so as not to damage the tiles on the floor. She argued with the painters when she saw them painting the house blue, saying that her father had always preferred white, and she went to great lengths trying to prevent the consul, an amateur astrologer, installing a large telescope in the study so that he could read the stars at night. Eventually, his patience was worn out and he obtained a court order banning Matilda Doherty from interfering with the running of the house, and allowing some peace for the rest of the ten years.

But the damage had been done. She had no more luck trying to rent her other houses out because her name became synonymous with a plague, and the thought of being in one of her houses sent shivers down the spine of would-be renters. Waking from the delirium of middle-aged depravity into which Sonny McKrae had thrown her, she had the other houses restored and posted For Rent signs in front of them, but there were no takers.

Regina Garrison enjoyed a delicious revenge when she heard about her daughter's problems. Without exactly breaking her own sanction against mentioning Matilda's name in her presence, she forced herself to comment at a charity meeting, where they were sorting out hand-me-down clothes for the poor among the people in the surrounding towns, that 'children who want to wear their mother's frock, which is too large for them, should not be surprised to discover that they need a large belt to hold it up'.

Then, after what seemed like an endless affair, Sonny McKrae dropped his aristocratic lover like a dead duck, and went back to the women at the wakes whose uninhibited laughter and dull coffee smell he had missed during his involvement with Matilda. For her part, the break could not have come at a worse time for Matilda. The mood of the public towards people of her class was changing. A rising tide of resentment against the colonial regime and its local supporters was finding expressions in a boycott of stores, pressures on local workers to go on strike and an occasional spate of unexplained fires in various parts of Malagueta. In one night, two of Matilda's houses were looted, the distillery lost half its storage of corn and someone scrolled an obscenity on the body of her car. Because of her high-handed behaviour with workers she had a difficult time getting anyone to do the repairs, and even when she could persuade anyone to come, she couldn't help interfering to the point that they would walk out in the middle of the job.

Abandoned to her own devices, some of her early dissipation returned to Matilda in her middle age; she who had led such a wild life suddenly retreated into a prudish petulance, cutting people down over the 'desecration of her father's name', the insult to her when people refused to rent her ruined properties, and giving out lozenges to young girls at bazaars, where she warned them about the treachery of men and the unreliability of relatives. While her homes succumbed to the vandalism of hooligans who had moved into Malagueta from the surrounding towns, and to the inexorable destruction by termites, she retreated into a lonely twilight in the only house left in good condition where, in the emptiness of its rooms, she discovered the emptiness of her soul and the tormenting shadows of her greed. Eventually, she ended up living alone with her cats as the last of her maids had walked out on her, and when she went shopping she was the object of derision. One evening, when she was going back to her car with a large bag of laundry, a young girl who had rejected her lozenges made a wry comment on Matilda's condition.

'Poor woman,' she said, 'she would be lucky to die on the street so that her body would be discovered before it rots.'

She died six months later in her house, and the scent of the decomposing was not caught until a week later, when the guards in front of the Lieutenant Governor's residence realised that her cats had been howling inside the house for days, and went to investigate.

15 Ali Baba and the Forty Thieves

Isatu Martins finally came down from her throne almost one hundred and two years after Gustavius Martins had crowned her there with his castaway jewels and acrobatic monkeys. On the day Garbage was doing a son's duty to his mother – by interning her as she had requested: standing up in her coffin with a dozen peacock fans, a cowbell to 'announce mesself over dere', and by slaughtering a bull for her – some of the people of Malagueta were being deprived of one of their rights which would remain unresolved until the day General Tamba Masimiara staged his unsuccessful coup against President Sanka Maru, some years later. Using the last uprising as an excuse, the colonial regime invited the leaders of the people from the surrounding towns, which were now part of Malagueta, to sign a treaty which barred the great-grandchildren of the founders of Malagueta from ever owning land outside the area that Thomas Bookerman had painstakingly laid out.

Garbage was outraged when he heard about it the next day and sent the governor a strong protest, calling the treaty a disgrace and a fraud.

'It's an insult to the memory of Sebastian Cromantine and the other founders of this town that the descendants of those who worked to open up the area around Malagueta cannot even plant a tree there, while the people from that area can come to this town to ruin it.'

Septimus Doherty and Fatmatta-Emilia, who were then living the life of exiles in England, tried to have the treaty revoked by petitioning Parliament. But after months of waiting for the politicians to emerge from their committees, braving the insufferable English weather to chase them to their clubs and demonstrating outside newspaper offices for months, the couple gave up their mad attempt and, one afternoon, went to Trafalgar Square where, after they had fed the grateful pigeons, they scattered the two hundred and thirty-seven copies of the petition.

'Maybe one of them will find its way to the home of one of those politicians,' said Fatmatta-Emilia, whose respect for that breed of mankind had never really been high.

Malagueta entered into a period of internal turmoil; the marriage of convenience, or what was left of such a union, began to break at the seams of society. With an arrogance mitigated only by their fear of the terrifying power of darkness, the darkness of space and of man, the members of the colonial regime worked their lips into a stiff upper position and refused to admit the injustices of their act. Of questionable backgrounds, they were mostly rejects from the churning machine of the

English class madness: men, and sometimes women, who would have preferred to go to India where they would have sat in the outlandish clubs, pygmy sahibs dwarfed by their beautifully turbaned servants, while they drank gin and tonic; or would have gone hunting for Bengali tigers; or if the desert was in their souls, would have preferred falconry in Arabia to what they regarded as the hellhole of Malagueta.

They hated the equally arrogant great-grandchildren of the founders of the town who came back from England, proud of their learning and contemptuous of the members of the colonial class and some of the people in the surrounding towns. At the now dwindling parties where the two sides met, they treated each other with admirable intolerance, drank their rum in a hurry and hurried home with or to their wives who wilted in the heat, weighed down by their jewellery.

In the heat of such social discomfort, the incredible tale of Matilda Garrison and her seven houses found its way into the repertoire of Man-Friday, the jiving calypso king of the day. For a fee of one penny, he claimed he could compose a song for any occasion, console anyone or calm the souls of the dead. Thus it was that Matilda travelled from bar to bar, was toasted here, remembered there, loved by some and pitied by others. The street urchins who had taken over three of her houses swore that in the middle of the torrential storms that were the gifts of August in Malagueta, they would see Matilda still searching for Sonny McKrae, leaving a whiff of her French perfume behind, which not even the rains could wash away. Sailors who arrived in Malagueta bringing the calypso of Trinidad and Aruba would report seeing a woman dressed in white, standing in a large veranda of a house lighted like a ballroom at the top of the hill, waving a flag like an abandoned queen.

Garbage continued to visit the women who had children for him while his fame spread beyond the boundaries of Malagueta. But it was in the house of Arabella that he seemed to find the peace that had eluded him for most of his life, and which, more than anything else, he desired with the advent of middle age. Now that Faramah had gone away to study archaeology in an English university, the test of their love was that they had each given up something for the other. Garbage was grateful to Arabella that although they had never married, she had made her house a home for him where he could come to be happy, relax and drink the teacups of her refreshing love. After Regina had retired to the country estate so that, as she put it to her daughter, she could enjoy her remaining years on earth without being bothered by 'you two lovebirds', Arabella had learned to cook and had even 'domesticated' Garbage. In the mellowing fires of their passion, they had arrived at a stage where they did not always have to be naked to find themselves, because they were certain that their love would last, as it was built on such acts of tenderness as the way they looked after each other when they were sick, the sweaters that she would knit him for the harmattan, and the trouble to which he would go to search for the conches and shells washed up by the sea, with which she liked to decorate her house. She was grateful to him that he had been kind to her with his public words about her, and had loved her above everyone else, despite the demands of other women and the chariot of his public life.

'I always knew that if I freed you to love me in your own way, you would always come back to me, and we would grow old together,' she told him one evening when they had settled down to cakes and tea, the ducks in the pond that he had built for her swimming leisurely in the soft light of November.

One day, he received a large carton of books without any postal stamp or note, delivered anonymously to his house. He took the carton to his study and once he had opened it, had only to look at the contents to know who had sent it. Over the span of thirty-five years, he recognised the telluric preoccupations of the man who had introduced him to the magic properties of gold and the incantatory powers of his strange eyes. Like the tales from a world he had never imagined, he discovered the poetry of the Lamp of the Seers, the Drum Poem of the Ashanti, the Admonition to the Disciples by Hasan of Basra and the Song for the Sun That Disappeared Behind the Rainclouds by the Hottentots, all arranged in that gift of knowledge by the unmistakable hands of Alusine Dunbar. For days, Garbage did not leave his house and did not receive anyone; not even Arabella. Steadfastly, he delved into the mysteries of those worlds, the lamentations of the songs and the hopeful fires at the end of man's life, which no one could extinguish. He saw in the Admonition to the Disciples how he was not exempt from the quagmires of life, but how as a seeker of truth he had to pull himself out of all pits where lesser men, especially politicians, would try to throw him. Thus he understood that Malagueta was like a sun which would disappear for a while but would reappear after the rain. That was why he felt Alusine Dunbar would come back to Malagueta, and knew he would be ready and waiting for the vagabond seer with the excitement of a disciple when the old man reappeared.

Louisa Turner had not been a seer, but in the last twenty-five years had spent her time turning out girls at the college who would themselves become great women in Malagueta. They were teachers, with the optimism of young lambs, who were prepared to sacrifice their lives so that women in Malagueta and beyond would have a better life than some of their mothers had dreamed of; nurses who, fired by the example of Florence Nightingale, went everywhere, tending the wounded men, because at that time Malagueta had sent the first of her sons to die in the first slaughterhouse of the two European wars of the century; women who were not dry to the passions of men, for Louisa Turner had told them that they held the keys to not only the kingdom of happiness, but of prolonging that happiness beyond conceivable time. She told them never to be eaten up by bitterness against men, because it was unworthy of the best women on earth; that love could conquer all injustices and that the only thing greater than having a child, second only to creation which was in the hands of God, was the love that a woman had for a man, and that they should not use their learning as combative arrows against men, but as complimentary songs which would be endless, because they would renew themselves with new lyrics every time they fell in love.

Thus, when she died, two thousand roses and gardenias were strewn all over her grave; six men who had been about to board a ship for Fernando Po with their wives on that day were forced to postpone the trip so that the women could attend the funeral. The governor sent his condolences, and a detachment of women drawn from the Women's Auxiliary and Teachers' Association marched behind the cortège. Due to some delay in the arrival of the ship's message from the harbour in Malagueta, telling them that Louisa was 'fading', Fatmatta-Emilia and Septimus Doherty arrived too late for the funeral, but stayed behind for a week to hear a Girls' Choir at the college sing 'When de saints go marchin' home', which would have pleased Louisa because she had loved the songs of her people very much.

Garbage continued to write his poems and to be fascinated by the mysticism of Alusine Dunbar; convinced that it was only a matter of time before the elusive saint reappeared in Malagueta, the poet began to read the stars: to imagine horses striding across Venus, on one of which might be the old man; he searched for a formation of clouds, looked at the face of the moon and would stand for hours on the shoreline of Malagueta, looking for propitious movements in the tidal waves. At other times, he would go into a bar, where because of the excitement that his name created, the oldtimers would force glasses of rum on him, pat him on his back, laughing and saying gladtomakeyouracquaintance, and talk about what the town was like before the time of the poet. While old age sated on the rum of nostalgia, he would listen to their talk of seceding from the 'unholy' union that the colonial agents had forced 'our town into with those places where they were still waiting for the light'. Each of them, Garbage and those men, were waiting for their own light because Malagueta was a grey town in those days, only lighted up by the occasional fires of his poetry.

Suddenly, one evening, as if the whole town had been captivated by the delirium of the past, the streets of Malagueta shook to the boisterous music of the Arabs from the Shouf mountains and the markets of Damascus. Garbage and Arabella were strolling in the Botanical Garden when they heard the boom-boom of the drums in the streets near by, and came out to investigate. On the street where Modibo the Diviner had shown the acrobatic skills of his dog in the days of Gustavius and Isatu Martins, they saw a spectacle more enchanting than anything Malagueta had seen before: colourful creatures in their outlandish costumes with their bandit's knives stuck in the red bands wrapped around their waists, their pervasive smell of garlic that would permeate the town even after they had gone into other regions outside Malagueta; and their necklaces of coral beads dangling from their necks. They had appeared from nowhere, spoke a barbarous language and, once they had brought out the crowd into the street, would leap into the air, swirl like flying dervish, then land on their heads where they would remain motionless for five minutes, before walking with their hands, which the crowd swore was the most unbelievable sight in Malagueta since the afternoon when, some people insist, they had seen a naked woman riding on a horse, with two overgrown children suckling at her splendid breasts: a fate, they claimed, she had brought upon herself by giving her twins the last name of a rich man who was not their father, but who had given the woman a large sum of money so that she could spread the story that the twins' father was a eunuch.

But on that mysterious day of the arrival of the Arabs, they had more wonders for the people of Malagueta. Coming up in the rear was the largest caravan that had ever passed through the town, being pulled by four splendid horses; a small Arab, not quite three feet, with a grotesque nose but with lively eyes and a well-trimmed beard, emerged from under the caravan to make a sign language to the crowd, indicating that its door was about to be opened, and that something or someone large was about to emerge from inside. When the door was opened by four men, panic broke out among the crowd, with some people running away, while those who remained stood mesmerised by the sight of the creature coming down the steps of the caravan.

She had the face of a child's doll but a body the size of a baby elephant and her arms were so hairy that six combs would have been lost in them. Around her waist she had a skirt that had been stitched together with twenty different brands of cotton.

Walking with the steps of a lazy giantess, she leaned against a large mango tree and, once she had been commanded by the dwarf, lifted her colourful skirt to reveal ten little girls who looked alike, who had the same smile and wore the same dress, much to the amazement of the crowd. Her name was Hediza Farouka, a breeding cow who was once the most beautiful female in Damascus, but who had also driven men to their death because she would appear in public without a veil, causing the men to tear their eyes out over her. Instead of stoning her to death, the guardians of morality had offered her mother the other choice of selling her to a caravan chieftain famed for his vagabondage, and who promised to take her to a place where she would no longer torment men. On the first night he tried to sleep with her, he discovered that she had grown to the size of an elephant, driving him out of the tent, but she reverted to her original size the next morning. Six days later, he came unnoticed upon her as a small brown snake was licking her all over. Convinced that it was the serpent that was responsible for her miraculous transformation at night, he killed the snake and made love to her for one night, after which she regained her giant size for ever. He kept her in his retinue, planning to show her off as a freak of nature, but when nine months later she produced the ten girls who once they reached the age of ten had stopped growing, he remarked with the joy of a man who had discovered the answer to a life-long problem:

'Allah may have given the sultan the most beautiful wives in the world who cannot go anywhere,' he said, 'but he has given me the most enchanting daughters in the world who will line my chests with gold.'

He went round the world showing off his fairies, passing them off as the most perfect creatures in the history of creation: nymphs who could stand and sit at the same time without a command, who went to sleep at the same time, woke up at the same time and had the power to keep a man in a state of perpetual erection for days until he had agreed to give all his gold to lift their spell on him. Once, they drove a desert prince mad after they had turned him down as a 'desert fool slightly better than a camel'.

Their father, Farouk Baba, had considered himself a lucky man until a Basran sheik versed in the art of studying sylphidine creatures had consulted a Book of Gnomes and concluded that the ten sylphs were the reincarnations of ten witches who had been chased out of the gardens of Constantinople in the Byzantine year of 1420. Since the ten sylphs had been born exactly five hundred years later, during the inglorious feuding between the Corsican and Sardinian bandits, and to all intent and purpose had picked up the pork-eating habits of the descendants of the Avars and Magyars who were Christians and therefore infidels, and, furthermore, because the ten girls had conspired against all the known laws of gravity and had refused to grow beyond a certain height, but preferred to hide inside their mother's skirt of motley colours, sucking their fingers, as reported by the giantess herself, everything considered made these girls witches and he recommended to the ruler that they should be put to death immediately.

Farouk Baba fled in his caravan that night, but not before a kindhearted Maulana had consoled him with the thought that a misfortune in one part of the world was a blessing in another. The learned man told the merchant that unlike that foolish African merchant in the Tale of the Distant Projection who spent a fortune on a wasted journey to a Middle Eastern country in search of salvation when he already had spiritual enlightenment and other riches in Africa, Farouk Baba should go to that place, which should not cost him anything because his daughters were his assets.

'Go to the land of the blacks where they are waiting for the wizardry of your daughters; I see it in the Book of Revelation.'

At first, Malagueta found the enchantment of the caravan a relief from the boredom brought about by the arrival of the rains. On the days when there was a glimmer of sunlight, the Arabs turned the streets of the veritable Virgins into a boisterous carnival with the men beating their drums, while the nymphs danced over flaming gourds and swallowed gold coins which the enthralled Malaguetans threw at them.

Garbage was not amused. As an intelligent man, he began to think of a reason why such a strange group of travellers would have come to town at the other side of the globe and finally came up with the suspicion that they were fakes; marauding bandits out to trick the unsuspecting people of the town. He sent letters to the governor protesting their invasion, calling for their expulsion, but his appeal fell on deaf ears, and the Arabs were allowed to stay in those areas where Jeanette Cromantine and others had first made their fortune.

After they had made enough money showing off their antics, they went from door to door peddling their coral beads, cheap bracelets and amulets which they tried to pass off as the charms of a certain magician in Beirut, more potent than those that the Tuaregs had sold in bygone years. Next, they began to open little shops where they sold cheap prints from the bazaars of Damascus and the factories of Istanbul. In this, they were helped by the colonial regime which, because of its antagonism to the rebellious Malaguetans, offered favourable concessions to the Arabs so that they could spread their influence. Spread they did, on the day when after eating a giant pumpkin, the ten girls all grew to the size of full women and went on to produce one hundred women who themselves in a short time produced one thousand women, so that the rumour of the prowess and parasitic breeding of the Arabs, their pugnacious competitiveness and the smell of their garlic breath reached an alarming proportion in a few years.

Farouk Baba did not know what to make of his unexpected good luck, but if he thought he had been given enough by Divine Providence, he had not counted on the gifts that nature had given to that part of the world, which were more than enough for half the people of the world. While Europe was preparing for the second slaughterhouse of the century, one of his granddaughters who had married a man from a town one hundred and fifty miles away from Malagueta, and had gone there to live with him, was playing with her son Ali Baba near a swamp when the boy picked up a shiny pebble, the size of a duck's egg but with the dazzling colours of a rainbow.

The colonial official who inspected the pebble did not at first realise what had had happened to that part of the world on that day, but when they had sent the pebble to London, it took a geologist only one minute to look at the stone, before jumping out of his chair in excitement:

'It's a rare diamond!' he exclaimed.

Malagueta was invaded from all parts of the world that day. In the excitement of the discovery, the colonial regime drew up contingency plans to bring in the railway and machinery so that they could exploit the land and ship the gem to the jewellery houses of Europe. Grateful for the pugnacity of the Arabs, they bent the rules for them, arranging loans from foreign and local banks to speed up the operations, while barring Malaguetans from the region, when, naturally, the breakup of many of the established homes started. The once respectable businessmen who had dined with the governor and had given out cigars when their daughters got married or their sons came home from England with their brand-new degrees signed by the monarch himself, who was the almighty chancellor of all the universities that accepted overseas students, suddenly found themselves selling their homes, not knowing that they were selling themselves into a new kind of slavery more pernicious than the one Sebastian and Jeanette Cromantine had escaped from. Because they had nowhere to go now, and as these ungrateful great-grandchildren of those tough pioneers had come back to Malagueta with a new philosophy called Individualism, they did not band together to fight the spread of the Arabs but went to court where they tore themselves up over the wills of their fathers, who turned over in their graves, mortified that they could have produced such fratricidal worms for children.

When she heard about the selling of the old Malaguetan homes Fatmatta-Emilia, who had not been too happy in England, woke her husband up at six o'clock one morning to tell him that she was packing up and going back to Malagueta, because no one on earth was going to live in the house of a Cromantine but a Cromantine, for which reason she had given her husband three healthy children who would ensure the continuation of that family. Septimus, who had found happiness with Fatmatta-Emilia after his disastrous union with Matilda, agreed with his wife that England was a miserable place good only for turkeys and puddings, which no full-blooded Malaguetan could stand for long. So that on a cold, windy day, opening her parasol as her grandmother had done over one hundred and fifty years ago, Fatmatta-Emilia Cromantine stood on the deck of an English ship with her husband and three children: a girl, Sadatu, and the boys Henry and Christopher, sailing back to Malagueta.

Yet Malagueta was slowly being bought up by the Arabs who, resorting to their Byzantine cunning for buying up ruined relics, rescued some of Matilda Garrison's houses from the insatiable destruction of termites and the lovemaking howling of stray cats. Restoring them to their former charm, they painted the walls white, hung the framed portraits of desert ancestors with their fierce peasant look, sat in the patios on sybaritic Sundays, enjoying the effects of opium in their water pipes, while feeding steak to their dogs.

Garbage was not the only one who wondered at the turn of events in Malagueta brought about by the rising influence of the Arabs, who, once they had started buying up the old properties facing the sea, wrote home to their peasant mothers who sent them brides dressed like mummies because they could not stand the glare of the sun. In what was one last attempt to check their influence, he teamed with some nationalists who used Arabella's newspaper to vent out their frustrations:

'What an incredible mess we now have in this country,' they fumed. 'A colonial regime that behaves like a bandit, building a one-track railway to take out the best diamonds, and a barbarian race from the desert that smuggles out the rest.'

Renewed riots broke out on the streets, which the colonial regime sent the army and police to quell, but they were unable to stop thousands of men moving to the mining area with dreams of getting rich quick. Ali Baba was one of them. Being of mixed Arab and African ancestry, he naturally had his feet in both camps and was able to play one off against the other: he recruited large numbers of African labourers who damaged their lungs in the new mines or succumbed to the deadly opium of alcohol, while he took their diamonds back to his Arab ancestors. When he had become very rich, he started a chain of businesses, corrupted colonial officials and village chieftains. Arabs flocked to his house to sleep with nubile African girls, because they couldn't bear to look at their wives who, once they had had two children, would grow to the elephantine size of their great original grandmother, Hediza Farouka. His African grandmother tried to reproach him once for 'prostituting your own kind'.

'Don't worry, Granny,' he told her. 'These girls are so happy to have mulutto children that you don't even have to take precautions with them.'

It was while he was building his empire that Ali Baba met the hairy giant Sanka Maru who had once been a dogcatcher in the Colonial Police before drifting to the mines where he began to organise the men, demanding better pay for them, sometimes going to jail with them, but never really being one of them because he was a man who had his mind on greater things. Raised by a respectable Malaguetan family, he was nevertheless a man from the north of that town, though when he spoke the language of the Malaguetans he gave no indications about his origins. Years later, when he was at the pinnacle of power, he would revert to a jingoism so vile and cheap, belittling all the good that his foster parents had done for him and, worse, he presided over the destruction of some of the great institutions in Malagueta.

Drawn together by an avarice and cunning, Sanka Maru and Ali Baba were to become lifelong friends. It was the giant who, using his wonderful gift for languages and flattery, would pacify rebellious miners when they demanded more money from Ali Baba. Handsome, witty and always well dressed when he was not in the mines, Sanka Maru enjoyed retelling the bawdy jokes of the swamps, the vulgar ballads of the sailor, and had been in the beds of some of the most respectable women and meanest loud-mouthed whores in that part of the country. He drank more than anyone else, ate with the relish of a village tyrant, and, when the fancy took him, could show off his stud prowess by laying half a dozen girls in the same bed during those three o'clock revelries that were part of the miners' life on the Saturdays they received their pay. As he rose up in life, he never lost his common man's touch, his gab for sophistry, or his bandit's instinct for seizing a golden opportunity. So he was well placed to become their leader, when the miners and other workers banded together to form a trade union which rose up against the colonial regime, on the day that American soldiers were dying for a spurious democracy in Korea while the lucky ones were being assured of their manhood in the cheap Chinese brothels on the island of Singapore, a prelude to going back and marrying their high school sweethearts in Omaha, Nebraska and other such Christian towns.

Railway tracks were uprooted in one week, preventing the transporting of the diamonds, while the streets of Malagueta were thrown into an eerie darkness when the streetlamps were smashed. A white lieutenant leading African troops tried to stop an enraged mob entering the grounds of the police headquarters. When the mob did not heed his call to keep back, he panicked, opened fire and killed one worker. A great pandemonium broke out throughout the town that evening, ending with the unfortunate lieutenant having his throat slashed.

Watching from the window of his house, a boy named Lookdown Akongo, saw the men as they fled from the menacing bullets of the police; he saw their petrified look, the speed of their legs as they picked up their dead and wounded in what one report called 'crowd control'. Two thousand workers died that night and were buried in common graves, while the leaders of the rebellion were shipped to the crocodile-infested island of Fernando Po to work on the cocoa plantations. Sanka Maru escaped arrest and fled to the neighbouring country where he brooded, cultivated manioc and waited for the call to come for him to return home.

Convinced that Malagueta was now ungovernable, the colonial regime embarked upon radical measures to save face. Withdrawing the English troops from the streets, they tried to stave off the bad omen, terrified that their days were numbered in Malagueta, by promoting their African soldiers to senior ranks, recruiting others, and by appointing a 'Transitional Government' to run the place. The man they chose to head the army was a bright, bespectacled brigadier named Tamba Masimiara. When he was hurriedly promoted to major-general, his men let off firecrackers in their barracks, smuggled in liquor and engaged in a week-long celebration which was eventually broken up by the general himself.

After many years of disenchantment, the people of Malagueta returned to the unforgettable pleasure avenues of former times. The damaged lamps were replaced, the park was reopened and, once again, the children rode on the merry-go-round, made faces at the monkeys and see-sawed on the bronze lions. Money was available and the cinemas and bars stayed open late so that cinemagoers could forget about the present by being lost in the fantasy conjured by the cameras in Hollywood and by that Ape-man Tarzan, who had never been to Africa. No one left a bar until the last drink was sold, because it was considered bad luck for a proprietor to send a man home to a nagging woman or to an empty room when there was still a good pint of liquor sitting on the shelf. Trying to bring back the delirium of past bacchanals, the authorities reopened the Yellow House, which had been closed for years. That house, made famous by the many 'men of their days' who went there, by its exotic women and in the saturated calypsos of Man-Friday, eventually regained its past glory and brightened up the district with its colourful neons and plentiful sex. On those evenings when the 'aristocracy' dined at their clubs, young men from respectable homes, workers and American sailors who paid ten shillings for the pleasure of sleeping with a sixteen-year-old girl and half that for one older, went there to be reminded how Adam and Eve did it. Wearing their exotic skirts, their tight-fitting blouses that showed off their ample figures, complete with the cheap Indian jewellery and gaudy bandeaux that the few poor Arabs peddled to them, the women would sit in front of the house, in the languorous poses of odaliques, being enchanted by the drunken lyricism of their new idol, Calendar the Left-Handed, while waiting for their customers. Once inside those rooms filled with the nostalgia of restored virility, the ghost of transient loves, and decorated with the posters of glamorous Hollywood stars and cheap African art, the nymphs made the American sailors forget about the beri-beri that had troubled them when they had been stranded on those islands where they couldn't get their vitamins. They put them back on the road to recovery, gave them their cheap photographs and bade them goodbye, singing Rum 'n' Coca Cola and Yankee Dollar. Arousing the grammar school boys with their hands, they asked them how they liked it: whether lying down or if the women should touch their toes, which would have cost the students five shillings more. At those beginners' rites, they gave the boys their first cigarettes, cleaned them up with a towel afterwards, and sent them happily home to their mothers, who sometimes detected a sprightliness in their sons but chose not to ask them where they had been.

Ali Baba was one of the members of the 'Transitional Government' inspired by the vision of moustachioed expatriates who were suddenly tired of the mosquitoes, the unfriendly 'natives', the unbearable weather and the lack of cigars. One unforgettable morning, he found himself summoned to a meeting at the governor's mansion where there were forty Africans waiting, besides the aides.

'Men,' the governor said in a voice used to issuing commands, 'I suppose you could say your hour has come. After a period of relative peace, good government and civility, not to speak of the benefits of English laws, we are handing back this country to you. We trust that after we have gone you will improve on those cherished things that we gave to you. God Save the Queen.'

The encyclopedic pillaging and theft that would grip Malagueta until General Masimiara staged his coup began on the day that Ali Baba and the forty African ministers took over the reins of Malagueta. Finding themselves in charge of the entire region where the nomadic Tuaregs had once brought the spices of the desert through the camel route, down to the area where Sebastian Cromantine had buried Fatmatta the Bird-Woman, they lost no time in unleashing the unbelievable avalanche of their greed. They swooped down on Malagueta as if they were hawks, searching here, digging there, turning over its soil, falsifying books to make it appear as if Malagueta had not been much of a place until they had been put in charge.

Saying that education was irrelevant in the new Malagueta, they put men in charge of institutions whose only qualification for the job was that they shared a common dislike of the old values for which the Virgins had crossed the ocean, while Louisa Turner had gone to heaven. Those were miserable times for many old Malaguetans. They sat in their parlours, behind drawn curtains, and worried about how they were going to survive in the new scheme of things. They saw their buying power being eroded by the new moneyed class who spent cash as if there were no tomorrow, and who threatened to bring their masquerades into the churches of the Malaguetans, where they would dance, to show the old buggers they were not worth a cent.

'That would be the day,' said a sexton as he rang the bell in his church. 'I shall be waiting to kill them with my bare hands when they come.'

The rot was spreading: an old, distinguished Malaguetan civil servant went to see Ali Baba to complain about the incompetence of some of the new administrators, who were 'messing up the system'.

Ali Baba became red in the neck and removed his Cuban cigar from his fat lips. 'You can go to hell with your system, because we have ours,' he raged. 'And just in case you have forgotten, the people who gave this land to your ancestors have taken it back.'

In a few years, they not only squandered much of the goodwill that some of the descendants of the original founders had been prepared to grant them, but made the terrible days of David Hammerstone pale in comparison. Whereas David Hammerstone and his men had been respectful of the history of the original town before he had linked it with the surrounding areas, the ministers had neither the knowledge nor the inclination to preserve that part of the heritage of Malagueta that was rich. They let the enchanting forest fall to the saws of the concessionary companies, allowed the peasants to come to the heart of Malagueta, to piss into the fountains, spit all over the place and poach the fish in the pond of the Botanical Gardens where Septimus Doherty had banished the tormented ghost of Matilda Garrison.

Nothing that David Hammerstone had conceived of in the name of his king could match the vanity of the new rulers. They sent long cablegrams to Germany for the automobile manufacturers there to ship out the largest, most expensive automobiles in the world, built houses that would have rivalled the castles of antiquity yet ended up blackening the walls, cooking on charcoal braziers in their living rooms.

Stupefied by their voracity and crudity, Garbage and Arabella had retreated into the sanity of their love to watch the inevitable destruction of all that the founders of Malagueta had died for; old age had not dampened the indomitable courage of his spirit, but Garbage had not been able to write lately because the rheumatic joints of his fingers would not respond to the fierce protest in his heart. As a consequence, while Arabella watered her flowers, gave charming dinners to their friends and listened to some of the students of the Conservatory play the piano in her living room for her, she would let herself be carried away by the feeling that in spite of the arrogance and obstinacy of some of the original Malaguetans, and notwithstanding the fact that some of them had been contemptuous of the people around them, they had been fired by an idealism that was lofty: to make their lives better, to help others become decent people, and to live a lasting legacy which would spread not only throughout the enlarged community that was now a country, but even beyond. Garbage continued to be haunted by the thoughts of Alusine Dunbar. In the quiet of his room, the poet would muse on the ways of Divine Providence to reveal all things to come, and how he could prepare himself. Time was running short, he knew; old age was not to be feared, but he wanted a deeper clarity, less confusing than the elliptical pronouncements of that vagabond saint, wherever he was at the moment. Thinking of the destruction wrought by the new class of rulers, he concluded that the decision to hand over Malagueta to Ali Baba and the forty ministers, whom he called 'Forty Thieves', was an act of treachery designed to return Malagueta into a bondage more terrible than the Babylonian captivity.

'We were betrayed!' he raged one evening, sitting on his veranda. This was not why Emmanuel Cromantine had fought the last war against Captain Hammerstone, he decided; nor the reason why Alusine Dunbar had been shaken by the involuntary movements of the beads at the bottom of the calabash, telling him that Jeanette Cromantine would come to plant the potatoes of Rodrigo the Brazilian, before the first Malaguetans would be chased off their land by the ferocious attack of their Kasilan neighbours in that terrible baptism of fire. Such insidiousness and inhumanity could have come only from a people who were either very insecure or were themselves outside the brotherhood of man.

Mournfully, he remembered his father, Gustavius Martins, who had been a man of two worlds, happy in his homecoming to Malagueta. He thought of his mother, Isatu Martins, the 'native woman' who had taken Gustavius Martins to her heart, in spite of his 'strange talk'. Lastly, he recalled the heroic kindness of Jeanette Cromantine, who had stood by his mother in the painful season of her martyrdom, and who had introduced 'dem American dresses to de women of Kasila'.

Once his lucidity had reached a stage where he could feel a sadness rather than anger for what was happening, he prayed that his own children would never be eaten up by the voracious passions of greed and the narrow visions of race. They were out there, somewhere in the world; but he knew they would come back, because they belonged to a race that had Malagueta in its blood.

A large, beautiful eagle swooped down to eat the ants at the foot of a large avocado tree. Garbage got up from his wicker chair to go and admire its beautiful plumage. He never made it. A small tremor in his heart clouded his senses, drained the flow of his old man's blood, and threw him down; but not before he had seen and been heartened by the face of another old man: more aged than time, trailing the column of ants.

Arabella followed soon after. They buried them near each other, and because of the violent protest of some of the former colonials who had served in Malagueta, the poet was declared a national hero and his tomb a shrine.

16   A Fatal Mistake

At three o'clock in the morning one wintry day, General Tamba Masimiara received a call in Soviet Central Asia asking him to come home because some rebellious army officers had overthrown the corrupt government of Ali Baba and the forty thieves. They named him Head of a Military Government in a follow-up cable, and asked him to respond immediately.

His reply was brief: 'Keep the bastards locked up, arriving tomorrow at six.'

He came to a city jubilant over the turn of events, with young university girls offering roses to the troops who made clenched fists, riding in the open trucks. For one unforgettable week, Malaguetans who had never really liked to have soldiers in town forgot about their prejudices, threw liberation parties and sent letters to their friends in distant lands, assuring them that they could come home to visit; the nightmare of the forty thieves was over.

Finding himself in charge of the nation, General Tamba Masimiara assembled his senior army colleagues in his office the next day, to map out a strategy for running the play. Sitting next to Colonel Lookdown Akongo, his second-in-command, the general outlined his plan.

'Men,' he said, 'we can either screw up everything or try to save some of the good that this country was famous for.' His men accepted that line of reasoning and, beginning that afternoon, Malagueta experienced a brief respite from the mad plundering of the previous regime. One week into his administration, General Tamba Masimiara signed a decree firing forty per cent of the incompetent civil servants appointed by Ali Baba. He flew into a rage, confronted with the scandalous contracts that Ali Baba had signed and had them revoked. He issued a warrant for the arrest of the former diamond boss who had escaped capture and was reported to be living in Lebanon. Being a soldier who did not relish the absoluteness of power, his style was to involve his second-in-command in all decisions affecting the country. That was how, one morning, General Tamba Masimiara put the colonel in charge of the Rice Distribution Board to get rid of the mess that Ali Baba and the forty thieves had created there.

'Colonel,' the general said to his second-in-command, 'the last man who occupied that post and who is now at large said the rats ate all the rice, and the bags too; so try to keep the creatures out.'

Nothing had prepared General Masimiara for the role of Head of State. Throughout his long period as a soldier, he had been convinced that a soldier's life was one of the most honourable in the world. He had fought in Burma, where he had been captivated by the beauty of the country, the charm of its women and the monkish slowness of life. Returning home to Malagueta, he had risen quickly up the ranks, married a beautiful Malaguetan and had not had to worry about putting down too many rebellions, a duty that had been left to the police. If there was one moment that he had felt troubled, it was at the military reception for a visiting ruler where he had met the estimable Miss Sadatu Agnes Cromantine-Doherty, great-granddaughter of Sebastian and Jeanette Cromantine, the founders of Malagueta.

He fell under her spell: the lure of her charm and the legend of her name. He bought books about her famous grandparents which he tried to read, but gave up the effort because he was not a great reader. Before meeting her, General Tamba Masimiara had been happily married to his wife for fifteen years and, except for the soldier's indiscretion in the loneliness of Burma, no woman had troubled his soul that much.

At her insistence, he met leaders of the university and agreed to name Thomas Bookerman a national hero. She introduced him to the joys of folk and classical music, the pleasure of driving to the countryside and the refinement of good wine. Once she had begun to warm up to his soldier's dedication to her, she gave some of herself, but held back the rest of her person. She never gave him her soul, for that was reserved for the task that Sadatu Doherty had chosen as her life's work: the writing of a full-length biography of her legendary grandfather, Emmanuel Cromantine.

One evening when they had been seeing each other for six months, she teased him about his job. 'How can you stand all that rubbish – the military bands, the sirens and the hypocrisy of ambassadors who before they came here couldn't even find Malagueta on the map of Africa?'

He had been attracted to her because of her haughtiness, the brilliant shape of her lips, and when he replied he was always patient with her.

'Not all of us have legendary grandfathers, Sadatu, and besides, I am doing it for the country.'

Two months later, though, the tormenting words of his mistress began to have some effect on the general. Removing the involucrum of power, he began to see how very little he cared for the trappings of office. He found the long cablegrams informing him about the activities of smugglers too tedious; he became bored with the demands made upon him to come and open this factory, to speak at this dinner, to honour our 'august occasion by your distinguished presence'. Something deep inside him wanted peace; the peace that he missed, now that he was spending too much time away from his family, and which was only discreetly available with Sadatu.

Colonel Lookdown Akongo, on the other hand, had been enjoying being second-in-command to the general. With a soldier's toughness that his chief admired, but found awesome, it was the colonel who got civil servants to report for duty on time, who confronted the international bankers and told them they would have to wait until Malagueta could get back its money from Ali Baba and the forty thieves before they would be paid.

He found those vestiges of power which had so riled his boss rather to his liking, and had a flagpost mounted up in his yard where the flag was raised in the morning as he left for his office, and lowered when he came home in the evening. If the general had come to the stage where there was no glory in the governorship of Malagueta, Colonel Lookdown Akongo had never really doubted that fate had been preparing him all along for his present military position, and, that when the general retired, he could have the number one position in the army. The bitter drags that he had been forced to drink when they had denied him a place in the school named after the womanising prince had never really been forgotten; and not even the women who cooed under him for their rice, the ones who sullied their husbands' names, could get him to forget how his youth had been one long nightmare when he had not had enough to eat, and how he had to wait until he was in the last year of secondary school before his mother, bless her soul, had been able to afford the cost of his first decent pair of shoes.

Nine months after the military government had been in power, General Tamba Masimiara threw a bombshell during a regular staff meeting in his office.

'Fellow officers,' he said, 'I am a military man and not a politician and this job is one terrible mistake. I wish to resign now, and let a new man take over.'

They urged him to reconsider his decision, told him Malagueta needed him, and that if he resigned, the country would fall into the hands of the bandits once more. He was adamant.

'Then stay in office for at least six months, until the colonel can come to grips with understudying the job,' they argued.

Colonel Lookdown Akongo had not been prepared for the shock of the general's resignation. If it had come two years later he would have been ready for it, especially if the general had told him about his intentions beforehand. He felt angry at being made to seem too eager, and flatly turned down the offer with an affected show of loyalty.

'No one in this room can do the job as well as you are doing it, General,' he said.

'In that case,' said General Masimiara, 'let us invite the trade union leader Sanku Maru to take over.'

Sanka Maru had passed his time in exile running a chicken farm and listening to the radio bulletins from Malagueta, which he could pick up on his cheap Japanese radio. Throughout the period that he had counted the eggs of his birds and fed them their own droppings so that they would multiply faster, while he could use the money to buy subversive literature which found their way to Malagueta, he had never doubted that his hour would come. What had only been a dream in the swampy region of his heart, when he had led the miners, had now become a gem of the finest carat, which he would use to erase the shameful memories of his dog-catcher days.

The excitement generated by his arrival lasted a whole month, which would have gone on for ever had not the rains fallen to wipe out the floats, the regattas that choked the harbour so that ships couldn't even dock, and the pledges of loyalty that came from all the regions of Malagueta. For weeks, he refused the protection offered him by the army, had General Tamba Masimiara remove the guards from his house, saying the people themselves would protect him.

'I have nothing to be afraid of, General, because I am a man of the people,' he said after he had been sworn in as premier of a new civilian government.

He cultivated the best minds in the university, listened to them with an eternal patience, asked their advice, admitting that although he himself had been given some 'book learning' as a trade unionist, that was nothing to match the time spent learning in a university. Quickly, he restored the many civil servants who had been dismissed in the infamous purges of the previous regime, and always had a minute for even the most troublesome problems, because he was, after all, the one who had been in the swamp, who knew what it was like leading other men, soothing their wounds and appearing to care.

His style was never to be seen to be in a hurry, for Sanka Maru had not spent years in the mines, in the bitter valleys of exiles, only to give a false sign at the beginning of what promised to be a long reign.

Once, he asked his Chief of Protocol what he thought the people were saying about their new leader.

'That you are the best thing to happen in this country since they got rid of that colonial regime, Excellency,' the aide replied.

From the French windows of his office, Sanka Maru could see the sea, the span of the city, and the unbroken stretch of beach, for which Malagueta was famous. In a quiet corner of his heart, he thought of the potential wealth of his country, the species of fish in the sea, the virgin forest of the regions which had never been tapped, because in their desire to plunder the gems of Malagueta the colonial regime had not had time to look at the other sources of wealth. Time was on his side, so that after he had been in power for two years, Sanka Maru had still not given any signs for General Tamba Masimiara to regret inviting him home.

The general had in fact not thought much about the problems of running Malagueta lately. Now that he was out of what he considered the 'hot seat', he had time to indulge in his two passions: foreign travel and football. Like some migratory bird sick of the rains in Malagueta, he would fly off to dry his wings in the warmth of other lands, sample the confectionery delights in the shops and come back laden with gifts for his family. During those absences, Colonel Lookdown Akongo would keep him informed about the premier, the innocuous gambling in the barracks, the two football matches a week and the obligatory Sunday services.

'Life is so peaceful here, General, that you can prolong your holiday,' he said in one cable.

Colonel Lookdown Akongo gave contradictory advice to the premier on the next day. Asked by Sanka Maru how the 'boys were behaving in the barracks', to told the premier that they missed their bush camps, the three months extra rations during that exercise, and the need to keep them busy.

'There are soldiers, Premier, untamed animals who should not be left idle so that they do not have ideas in their heads.'

'What do you suggest I do, Colonel?' asked Sanka Maru.

'That you make yourself President of the Republic, and do away with this "people's style of leadership" which the men cannot understand.'

Three months later, Sanka Maru had one of the brightest lawyers in Malagueta write him a new constitution, which the compliant Congress packed with his friends and favour-hopefuls, readily passed. They named him President of the Republic, Commander-in-Chief of the Armed Forces, granting him more powers than he had hoped for. Once the investiture was over, he issued a decree creating a Presidential Guard, so that his arrival would be announced by the playing of the National Anthem, for his powers were now eternal and unstoppable, witnessed by the fact that as soon as he had put on his presidential sash, Sanka Maru had created a Palace Guard which would protect him from conspirators.

Frightened by the monster that was revealing himself, the students came down to town from their Olympian tower, where they had not really taken him seriously, because he had been able to convince them that he was harmless, could not harm a fly, what with his lack of a 'proper education' that made him terribly dependent on their kind. Now that the octopoid menace of his power was unfolding, they tried to stop him; they paralysed the flow of traffic, frog-marched their Vice-Chancellor to his office so that he could tell him that although he was president, he couldn't flout the law.

He quartered them in their rooms with the brutality of his special security unit, whom he had made more powerful than the army, because he couldn't rely on that colonial creation to protect him.

Watching from his position as Army Commander, General Tamba Masimiara took a long time convincing himself that the president was creating a tyranny more despicable than the one the soldiers had overthrown. As usual, his mistress had been the one to point out the outrages of the president: 'Look at the way he has been trying to muzzle the press; sending his thugs to smash up the printing machines,' she said to her lover, after the last of the free press had been forced to close after criticising the president. Angry, blaming himself for letting the president come back, General Tamba Masimiara watched while the president sold off the railway as 'useless scrap'; he argued with him about the damage to the economy, the loss of confidence in the national currency due to the country's image abroad.

Urged on by Sadatu, General Tamba Masimiara went to see the president in his heavily defended office one evening. 'Be reasonable,' he said to the giant. 'This is not what we brought you back for, because a storm is gathering out there which the army may not be able to contain.'

In the stupor of his drunken man's power, President Sanka Maru did not even bother to justify his acts. He dismissed the general's protest with a wave of his hairy hand.

'Don't worry too much, General,' he said. 'What was begun by me must be completed.'

His critics underestimated him. While they argued about the arbitrariness of his laws, the profligacy of his mistresses and the shameless nepotism of his government, he outsmarted them like a long-distance runner, and left them gasping for breath in the glaring light of their impotence. He compromised the lawyers, whetted their appetites for the ephermeral glory of power by making them judges. When he couldn't corrupt them, he tricked them. He had foreign universities offer scholarships to their children, which he had really paid for, and, when his own university lecturers protested, he made them powerless in the nebulous theatre of politics by sending them as ambassadors to his friends, who could be relied on to keep an eye on his critics.

Not everyone fell for his charm or was afraid of him. One courageous man who stood up to him was the journalist Tarik Alkali. Deprived of a local paper, he wrote a blistering attack on the president which he sent to a foreign organ, calling on the people to vote him out of office at the next elections. Sanka Maru had him executed as a plotter, and had the dead man displayed in front of the prison to serve as an example to others.

Asked by his wife how he could kill and sleep at night, Sanka Maru did not even turn to face her to reply:

'It's easy,' he said, 'it is like killing a chicken. You slit its throat and leave it to dance to its own death.'

A worldwide outrage followed the execution of the journalist, but once he had instructed his ambassadors to deal with the international press, he dismissed that small matter. Secure in his office, he had never been bothered by the insomnia of remorse. Lately, however, he began to complain about a skin disease to his doctor.

'It's your diet,' the doctor replied.

Dr Hamidou Jarim was a direct descendant of the rich Fulani cattle herder whose only daughter had 'disgraced' herself for that renegade poet, Garbage, and for which she had been 'exiled' from her people. Proud of the 'purity' of his lineage, Dr Hamidou Jarim had met the president during a regular reception at the palace. Sanka Maru,who at that time had begun to doubt the loyalty of his old Malaguetan doctor, found in Dr Hamidou Jarim a man who was arrogant, pretentious and ruthless. The doctor had never forgotten his difficult days at the medical school, the taunts of his fellow students, who couldn't get over the incredible tenacity of a former herdboy who wanted to become a doctor.

Hired immediately by the president, he had proved such a reliable doctor that he was his most trusted confidante. They shared information on not only health matters but about the private lives of the president's enemies. So on this day, it was to him that he turned for an explanation about why, suddenly, the students were against him.

'Goddammit, Doctor,' he said to Hamidou Jarim, 'what is the world coming to, that these *pissers*, these children on whose breath you could still smell their mother's milk, should tell me how to run this country? Where were they when we killed the English police officer, the one who was shooting pointblank at our men, at the railway workers? I could have smashed his balls myself, titillate his lily-white cock with a little alligator pepper, just to let him know who was going to be calling the shots here; that this is not Kenya, but a black man's country, where the mosquitoes had driven the white man out. Yes, tell me, Doctor, where were these boys and girls at that time? They were still in their shirt-tails playing hopscotch while we were in the swamps fighting for the rights of workers. But now that they have somehow gone to the university, they want to tell me how to run this place. The bastards, I spit on their education: I keep telling them that politics is not for them, but for commonsense people, like you and me. Look at the mess we now have on our hands, Doctor; so-called 'educated people' who do not want to dirty their hands doing an honest day's work but want to be in an office.'

'Don't let them excite you, and, in any case what you need is a lot of rest,' the doctor said.

'Not rest, my friend, but someone with enough guts to take on some of this elephant's load.'

Three months later, in one calculated act that left even his stoutest defenders protesting, he brought back from the involuntary brooding of his exile the half-caste Ali Baba, his partner in the diamond-exporting and whore-importing business. Resuming their friendship, they carved up the country so that nothing would be left for others; they brought the trawler boats of the Spaniards, the sea captains of the Koreans to sail the coast for shrimps, because the sea was theirs, and their power was unfathomable, like the bottom of the ocean.

Ali Baba repaid the kindness. On the president's birthday, he came hurrying into the official office, puffing on his cigar.

'Have a drink on my birthday,' Sanka Maru said to his friend.

'Not before you have seen what I have for you, Excellency,' the half-caste replied.

Sanku Maru went to the window with the beautiful view of the ocean. Two blocks away, he saw a float coming up the street towards his office, with a dozen Arab women riding in it. Once his massive bulk had been recognised by the women, they blew him kisses and started chanting Happy Birthday, Mr President.

'Your birthday present, Excellency,' said Ali Baba. 'They are the best whores in Beirut that not even a sheikh can afford.'

News of the extravagance of the president's birthday reached General Tamba Masimiara in California where he had been looking over some military hardware. Lately, he had been troubled by the symbolism of a dream his wife had had and by the persistent disregard his advice had been getting from the president. Nothing strange had happened to his wife since she had the dream about lizards swimming in her cooking pot; yet the sign of bad omen implied by the nature of the dream had followed the general to America, where he had been able to relax and think about his own position in the madhouse of Sanka Maru's government. Like most honest men, he had considered resigning, but had been prevailed upon to stay by those of his troops on whose loyalty he could still count. But twelve hours before he was due to return home, someone showed him an article about how President Sanka Maru had agreed to have toxic waste dumped in Malagueta. An indescribable rage gripped the general, and once he had got over the horror of the publication he decided he had to act. Two weeks later, he summoned his second-in-command, Colonel Lookdown Akongo, to his office.

'Colonel,' the grim-faced general said. 'We have to stop the president before he destroys the country.'

It was a fatal mistake.

EPILOGUE

General Tamba Masimiara went to the gallows at six o'clock in the morning, one year after he was arrested. On the last night in his cell he had not been able to to sleep, not because he was terrified of the noose but due to the intriguing signs of the premonition that he had experienced the day before. No one had told him when they would come for him yet, for the first time since his wife had had her dream the lizards in the swirling torment of her nightmare had crossed through his mind, like the fate of a dead man. So that he saw himself already shaven, smooth like a lizard, marching blindfolded to the hangman; intrepid as he had been in the rain-drenched solitude of his ordeal.

If they had hoped to break him down by confining him in that dungeon for a year they had not succeeded, for General Tamba Masimiara had been kept alive by the transparent spectre of his thinking and the redoubtable strength of his convictions. Throughout the year he had never once questioned the rightness of his action, because something greater than altruism had inspired his coup in the first place; the feeling that his action, whether it had failed or succeeded, was only the prelude to the inevitable storm in Malagueta; something more terrible, he believed, than the one that had erupted when the colonial regime had opened fire on the striking workers who were uprooting the railway tracks. Denied his freedom to talk to anyone, he had only to look at the vastness of the sea, the flight of an osprey, to feel how without words he had been able to understand the thinking of other men and the courage and endurance on past voyages. In that way, he had resolved something that had troubled him lately: he saw with the clarity of hindsight that Thomas Bookerman had not come all the way from Canada, with the invincible marks of his chains, in search of Sebastian and Jeanette Cromantine, simply to get away from the bitter despair of broken promises; that if the one-eyed man had attacked the garrison built by David Hammerstone he had done so not to have Malagueta fall into the hands of a black president more despicable than the English pirate, but to add a few pages to the remarkable history of its people.

Once in a while, the general had been lonely. Then he would remember the endearing moments: the rhapsody of his childhood, happy, carefree in the frivolous mornings, playing barefoot with the other children in the neighbourhood; until he had been bitten by a dog, which had to be shot, while he had been injected against rabies. Exposed to the cold of the island, General Tamba Masimiara would recall the fires of his boy scout's outings, the charcoal brazier that his mother had put in his room when he had been sick with malaria. Somewhere in that memorable tapestry, he saw the face of his mother when he had come home to tell her he had joined the army; how she had held him to her breasts, crying:

'My son, my son; don't let them take you away from me, you are all I have.'

He came back to her, toughened by his experiences in the downs of England, where his exemplary acts of courage had impressed his instructors. Much later, he had met the other women who would make him happy: his wife who had given him sons, and his bookish mistress who had introduced him to the fantastic poetry of Garbage, revealing that a land which had engendered so much artistic beauty and love in the soul of a poet could not be destroyed by the treachery of Colonel Lookdown Akongo or the vanity of Sanka Maru. So that seeing the lizards mirrored in the labyrinth of his own premonition, General Tamba Masimiara was overcome by the thought that the dancing motion of their heads was his own head dangling on a rope, and that the motley colours of their bodies were the conspiracies hatched by Sanka Maru which, notwithstanding the cunning of the president, woud not succeed.

'Everything is clear in the eyes of God!' the general exclaimed, as he was marched to the gallows.

A terrifying bolt of lightning ripped through the sky on the morning of the execution, bringing the electric pylons down and scattering the crowd that had gathered in front of the prison to have a glimpse of the dead man. Rain had not come to Malagueta for months, a brown dust draped the capital, and the chorus of the dead could be heard as they came out at night, searching for water. Yet, when the shattering note of the lightning repeated itself, the evil omen of its arrival did not readily register in the minds of the people. In the anticipatory wait for the rain, they heard the agitated fowls banging their wings against their coops, they saw the dog-faced bats crashing into the trees, more solemn than the face of death itself, and they felt the ground under their feet raging like the beginnings of an earthquake. An eerie silence gripped Malagueta, and coming from the solitary peak of the mountain where Sebastian and Jeanette Cromantine had holed up in the aftermath of their banishment, the people of the town heard the wind gathering its prehistoric force, they saw it stretching its two thousand hands, navigating here, whirling there, breaking through the sound barrier of the unspeakable dryness with its dog-cry whistle and its woodcutter saw.

When it had covered the streets with a vegetation of brown dust, it slowed down a little; but, as if inspired by the enraged ghosts of the founders of the town, it found its strength again, ripping through the eaves of the houses and shattering the windows, which left His Excellency wondering what the hell was going on, General Tamba Masimiara should be dead by now.

President Sanka Maru walked to a window, pushed the curtains aside and saw a magic carpet flying in the air, not knowing that it had come a long way and that its arrival had been predicted by an albino afraid of light. Mesmerised by the occurrence, Sanka Maru thought he was seeing things when an old man lowered himself from the carpet, waved to him, and disappeared under a tree.

'It is a miracle,' said the giant, as he remained near the window.

Sadatu Cromantine-Doherty had also been standing by a window, watching the course of the wind; praying that the spirit of her great-grandmother would divert its direction away from her house. She had just finished her prayers when she saw an old man standing under a tree, who waved to her.

She opened a small space in the window and shouted at the old man.

'Get out of the wind, you fool!' she said. 'You will be blown to pieces.'

Once again, he waved to her, and moved away. Suddenly, she realised that the spell of the evil omen of the wind had been lifted by the hand of the old man, and that the hands of the clock on her mantelpiece had stopped at six o'clock that morning, while a column of black ants had entered her house.

'He is dead!' she cried, picking up a framed photograph of General Tamba Masimiara lying on the mantelpiece.

That evening, the streets of Malagueta looked like they did in the early days of Jeanette Cromantine: dead leaves were strewn everywhere, trees clogged the gutters, and the dogs kept a howling vigil. Free to roam as he pleased, an old man walked through the streets, unseen by the dogs, weighed down by the incongruous shape of a large gourd between his legs. He had not been in Malagueta for a long time, yet he knew the arteries of that world better than anyone on earth, because he had been destined to follow its progress since that morning, over three hundred years ago, when Sulaiman the Nubian had been moved by the words of a gold merchant who had spoken of a place beyond the enchanting forest, whose streets were paved with gold, and to which the old man had come, bringing the legends of Nasrudin and the invention of the looking-glass.

Everything had been mirrored: first, the daughter with the eyes of a scorpion who would torment a dozen slave masters and make them impotent for ever, because children descended from Sulaiman the Nubian were immune to the impertinence of lesser beings. Next, he had known when the people from America would come; how Isatu Martins would give one of them a son named Garbage; to whom, once Sulaiman the Nubian had changed his name to Alusine Dunbar, he would reveal himself. Nothing had escaped the glare of the looking-glass or the eyes of the testicles, because it had been predicted that Malagueta would be invaded by the Arabs from the Shouf mountains and that they would spread, thanks to that elephant great-grandmother Hediza Farouka, but that their expansion would not have been easy if they had not been helped by the docility and greed of the indiginous people.

Consequently, enlightened by the remarkable powers of his clair-voyance, Alusine Dunbar had known at what hour General Masimiara would die: proud that as a soldier he had not sought fame or glory, but had been prepared to die so that Malagueta could go on shining like a star in that part of the world where the veritable Virgins had prayed for peace, and where, despite the outrages of the most despicable govern-ment that the world had ever known, men would go on looking for happiness in the Yellow House, where the women and Calendar the Left-Handed had said that life was not worth living if it were not for love.

The sound of the evil omen of the harmattan rang through Malagueta one more time. Sanka Maru was just about to sign a decree declaring a national disaster so that once the ranging storm was over they could clear the dead dogs and birds off the streets. Concentrating on the stylistic movement of his pen that had condemned General Tamba Masimiara to death, he suddenly had a shock when he saw an old man come in, walking past the guards who did not bother him. The old creature came straight to him, with the blazing light of his power growing from his testicles. Sanka Maru lowered his hand to get his revolver, not knowing that that movement had been imagined in all the decrees that he would sign, since time immemorial, when he had not even been born. It was the last thing that he did. The light of the testicles glowed with a fierce brilliance, and he felt himself lifted out of the grandiloquent illusion of power, borne into space as if he were a dwarf, by a force too terrible to contemplate but which left him awed by the realisation that in the history of creation no one had told him that what had been ordained by Divine Providence could not be altered by man; not even by a presidential decree, as he came crashing down in the middle of a street so that when the dust had been cleared, his countrymen and women would see not the eyes of a dead general, but the paralysed wreck of Sanku Maru.

Colonel Lookdown Akongo had been expecting a call from the president to confirm that General Tamba Masimiara was dead. Throughout the bellowing of the wind, the colonel had been with a woman who, with a promissory note for a thousand bags of rice safely put away, had been trying to mitigate the effect of a bad conscience that the colonel had been experiencing lately. Snuggling up to him, she had just began to arouse him with her hand when the colonel felt a chill down his back.

'I don't feel up to it,' he said. 'I feel as if a dead man is watching us.'

Moments later though, after she had succeeded in calming him down, Colonel Lookdown Akongo banished the ghost of his former boss. Entwined between the legs of his svelte mistress, he was just thinking about his promotion to general, when he felt the fingers of a powerful creature picking him up. He tried to come away from the woman, but felt the two of them being lifted together in an insoluble tryst, where they had been star-crossed to go on making love intact like a pair of dogs. Hungry for power he had not realised that relationships conceived on the margin of treachery and greed were doomed for ever, and that the telephone call he had been expecting was a delusion lodged in his traitor's brain, and as he had never bothered to think about the bittersweet history of Malagueta, he couldn't understand that whereas Emmanuel Cromantine and Louisa Turner had loved each other like two crabs that could come unstuck any time they wanted, he and his concubine could not hope for deliverance from their lust, because they had been condemned to an eternal public disgrace in *The Last Harmattan of Alusine Dunbar*.

MAIDUGURI–IOWA CITY–FREETOWN
1984–1989